DANCE OF THE BUTTERFLY

Scott Carruba

DANCE OF THE BUTTERFLY
©2016 Scott Carruba
First Edition
All rights reserved
Edited by Christina Hargis Smith
Cover art by Jeffrey Kosh Graphics
Published by Optimus Maximus Publishing, LLC

This book is a work of fiction. Names, characters, businesses, organizations, places, events, and incidents either are the product of the author's imagination or are used fictitiously. Any resemblance to actual persons living, dead, or otherwise, events, or locales is entirely coincidental.

This book is protected under the copyright laws of the United States of America. Any reproduction or unauthorized use of the material or artwork contained herein is prohibited without the express written permission of the author.

ISBN-10: 1-944732-09-8
ISBN-13: 978-1-944732-09-7

Acknowledgment and Dedication

Dance of the Butterfly is a tale that very nearly did not happen. It took time to take hold and even more time to truly blossom. Were it not for the ceaseless help of a very dear, close friend, it would not have been done. In a very real way, it parallels that relationship, taking from that story to add to its own. For this, I deeply thank you, Jane.

I also wish to thank my publisher, beta readers, and you, dear reader. I hope you enjoy the book.

Not even one of them can fall to the ground without your Father's knowing it

DANCE OF THE BUTTERFLY

A Novel by
Scott Carruba

SCOTT CARRUBA

DANCE OF THE BUTTERFLY

CHAPTER ONE

He glances down at the tracks, peering over them for a moment, the collection of depressions heavy in this copse, depicting a recent scurry due to some excitement. He stays there, crouched, thick legs bent at the knee, then he inhales. He catches the scent of their spore nearby. The air is crisp, cool, eager to carry smell and sound. He raises his rifle, a custom modified FN FAL, but he does not bring it up to aim, still peering out into the distance over the land. Trees block his view in many directions, growing thicker further out.

His eyes move quickly, narrowing. It is apparent, sudden, and he easily identifies it as the sound of many feet running toward him. He hears the panting not long after, but he does not yet smell the beasts. They are approaching downwind of his own position.

He turns, booted feet shifting in place, then raises the weapon, his knee dropping to the ground as he tucks the butt of the rifle into his right shoulder, left elbow resting on his other leg. His movements display a smooth, practiced ease. He peers through the small scope, waiting, breath flowing calmly.

The pack of wolves comes into view about fifty meters away, healthy beasts running tightly together, the alpha in the lead. They lope easily up the gentle incline toward his position. These are the ones he has been tracking, and they have found him.

He continues looking through the scope, the green shade to its lenses helping to bring greater focus. Both eyes remain open, increasing his field of view, indicating his lack of focus on a specific target. The barrel of the firearm moves, sweeping, seeking prey. The wolf pack continues its approach, quickly covering the ground.

Just before they reach him, he lowers the weapon, and they move in, their posture not one of aggression, and they move up close, seeking attention.

"Nothing out there, hmm?" he speaks, his voice a mid-range bass.

He pats the alpha on his left side as the animal presses into him a moment. They display excitement. He finally looks down, a light smile taking his lips.

"Alright then. Work's done. Go … *hunt*," he emphasizes the command, and the pack emits a few eager sounds and heads out.

He stands, moving his bulk to this upright posture with an ease that suggests a good deal of muscle. He lets his eyes follow the direction of the beasts as they disappear into the trees. He glances about again, exhaling slowly, scanning the area before he finally turns to head back to the house.

The Victorian mansion holds place like a sentinel in the clearing. The expanse of property on which it stands covers many acres, most of which gives way to trees, the forest becoming denser as one moves further from the estate. Hints of gothic and baroque show themselves in the detailing and columns. The front entrance beckons, but he does not approach that way, coming in from the west side and heading for the rear entrance. The ground slopes downward, giving a suggestion of the hidden, though the secrets within the home are much better occluded than this door. He passes through easily enough, the sophisticated security systems having already identified him.

He removes the dark watchman's cap, then adds his gloves to the small pile he creates on the countertop space in the workroom. Casting and reloading mechanisms tell of the gunsmithing that occurs here, but they are ignored as he unslings his rifle, setting it in a cabinet amidst others.

He walks through, heading into other areas of the manor, the rooms taking on a more artistic, polished flair. He passes near a small team of people going about their own business. They barely take notice of him, the senior woman giving direction to the others as they work at cataloging various items. He moves up the large, curving staircase, each step broad, the impressive structure composed of dark, rich wood.

DANCE OF THE BUTTERFLY

He finally finds him, Skothiam, the Head of the House, busy at work amidst old books that lie open, baring their contents in stark contrast to the small bank of slim monitors and other electronic equipment. As though to add to the potentially confusing ambience, candles and incense leak their leavings into the air.

"Everything alright out there, Jericho?" the man speaks, not looking up from peering over a thick tome, studying the page with a magnifying lens.

"Yes."

"What about the wolves?"

"I told them to go hunt."

A moment passes, and it might seem that this last has gone unheard, but these two have known each other for decades, and they need not always communicate in obvious words. The other finally looks up from the book's page, setting the glass aside.

"Good, good," he says, nodding, then exhales. "Seems neither of us found anything, though that's not a positive result for me."

The taller one merely observes, for just as the outside, the hunt, are his elements, this sanctum is somewhat alien to him in its role to the other.

"Doesn't matter, really," Skothiam speaks after a short pause, then he picks up what appears to be a small, thin, plastic window of sorts, its right side showing advanced gadgetry of electronic equipment and indicator lights.

He presses on some of the icons in the graphical interface then sets the device over the page of the book. A rendering of that same page quickly resolves, a duplicate suspended above itself, given life from the translucent window.

"Maybe the analysis program will find something that I- ahh, Sharon," Skot pauses, smiling warmly as the woman enters the room.

She wears a uniform that bespeaks of her role as a maid or attendant, her garments pressed and professional, mingling modern utilitarian with an antiquated aesthetic. She holds up a tray on which are balanced two tall glasses bearing blue-grayish, thick contents.

"Gentlemen?" she offers.

"Thanks, Sharon," Jericho says, taking a glass, and then she moves to the other who does the same, offering his thanks with a dip of his head.

"Anything else?" she asks, stepping back.

"Nothing else, Sharon. Thank you," Skothiam says, continuing to offer the same warm expression, lips curved within the thinly trimmed goatee, blue eyes crinkled a bit at their sides. "You seem capable of sensing our needs prior to our even asking, anyway."

She smiles, taking the compliment, then gives a tiny bow before exiting. Both men then sip of their blended drinks, swallowing, then looking at each other, nodding. A short chuckle is shared between them.

"It's good," Jericho comments.

"It is."

"So, what are you working on?" the guardsman peers at the advanced contraption at work over the open book, then glides his eyes to the monitors, the depictions on their screens also obvious signs of work going on within the powerful computer.

"More of the same."

Jericho gives a nod, vague hints of dissatisfaction taking his expression as he does. He glances about, giving cursory observance to the various analyses taking place.

"It's a never-ending battle," he offers.

"I suppose they calls those 'wars', hmm?" comes the retort, tempered with a light smile and perk of eyebrows.

He is greeted with a serious stare. His friend is not bereft of humor, his boisterous laugh well known, but he may just as easily, if not more so, resolve into this quiet intensity. The sudden, rising tension is interrupted by a beep from the electronic device analyzing the open book, and Skothiam blinks, turning thankfully to it, but his expression changes dramatically once he sees what is there.

A figure resolves, rising from the device or the book just as easily as it appears to be emerging from nothing. It suggests one of the three dimensional images which may be rendered by the advanced tool, but some of it is hazy, indistinct, and it continues to increase in size. It has a definite anthropomorphic shape, looking like a person rising from some depths.

DANCE OF THE BUTTERFLY

The two observers do not move. They merely watch, held in awesome silence. Jericho is not as familiar with this device, but even he knows this is very much out of the ordinary for its function. He is aware that the gadget is connected to the house's elaborate and powerful network, just as with most every other electronic appliance on the grounds, but he can also tell from the other man's reaction that this is very unexpected.

"What in the Nine Hells?" Skothiam breathes, looking upon the form as it takes on a finer definition, his expression morphing from bewilderment to a more focused study. "Father?" he finally dares to ask.

The apparition smiles, moving its head in affirmation. The man's father was not known for being overly exuberant in his expression of emotions, but this is most definitely the very image of the well-respected man, dead now these past four years.

"Dad?" he tries again, hope painting his voice like daring whispers, "Is that really you? What … what's going on? How did you get here?" he asks, looking down again at the experimental device still in place over the book as it dutifully, if not blindly, continues its work.

The apparition nods again, still giving that characteristic light, pleasant grin. It rises further, taking on more distinction, even as it shows no more coloring than might a sepia-toned photograph.

"Can you not speak?" he asks of it, for the illness that claimed his father took his ability to speak before taking him.

The ghostly image shakes its head, and he nods in understanding fashion.

"Why are you here?" he finally asks.

The color-starved specter gives a piercing look, though it is still pleasant, like the smile, closing toward him. He dares not move. Then the apparition turns and heads away, passing through the unopened door in slow, hovering locomotion, the two corporeal beings in quick pursuit.

"Is that really your father?" Jericho asks, speaking in an urgent whisper as the two head down the large staircase.

"I don't know," is the honest response, "But it *feels* like him. I don't know how else to explain it, but … regardless, I am left wondering how this is happening at all, much less who or why."

Jericho takes this in with no outward response, merely following, ever-watchful. They tail the moving apparition into the impressive library. They see as the entity stops, then turns to them. Is it waiting? Has it come to its intended place? No answer seems forthcoming as it moves no further, just looking at what may be its son, a kind, calm expression to its appearance.

The man looks at the books, noting them well. He moves his eyes back, but gets nothing more from the apparition. He again looks over the books nearby, scanning over them with rapid, greedy movements of his eyes.

"I don't understand," he finally admits, looking back at the ghost, "Is this ... I know of these books, but ... what is it you are trying to tell me?"

And then he experiences a dawning, as though a chemical recomposition caused by the slow spread of heat from a focal point, and that point is the apparition, staring at him, *into* him. His eyes widen, his form stiffening, and then a hand is placed on his left arm, close to his shoulder.

"Are you alright, Skot?" comes the voice of his friend and companion.

Skothiam pulls in a breath through his nose, turning to look at the larger man.

"I just ... *felt* something. As if he spoke to me."

Jericho tilts his head, brow furrowing, "What?"

"It's one of the Three Books!" he exclaims. "He says he found it and hid it here in the library." And then Skothiam moves quickly, going to nearby shelves, searching, running fingers rapidly over spines, pushing books aside, seeking for some hidden treasure.

"What!" the other tries again.

"One of the Three," Skothiam speaks from the other side of the shelf, "I don't know how I know. I don't know how he is even here, but I feel certain. He found it before he became ill, then he hid it in here in the library. We must find it!"

The other man shakes his head, a mute commentary contained in the economic gesture. He then proceeds to try to help, going about in search amongst the crammed, tall, numerous shelves.

DANCE OF THE BUTTERFLY

"How will I even know if I find it?" he calls out.

"You'll know," comes the reply from some ways away in the expansive room.

"That's not my specialty, Skot. You know that. Hell, if anything, I may be resistant to any-"

"Resistant does not mean deaf. Let's just keep looking. Even if you just see something that seems out of the ordinary …"

He gives forth a huff accompanied by a roll of the eyes but continues the search.

The sudden, sharp intrusion of the alarm interrupts their activity. Both stand up straight, startled by the noise. They consult small, electronic devices – Skot pulling forth a slim cell phone, the larger man looking at an item buckled about his wrist. They move to each other.

"Fire," they say in near unison.

"We have to get out of here," Jericho declares.

"Dammit!" Skothiam curses, a pleading look given to his friend, "But the book."

"Don't make me carry you."

"This can't be a coincidence."

"Don't … make me … carry you," and this time it is delivered with more insistent tinges of threat.

Skot's eyes snap back up to the tall guardsman. "The fire's on the first floor, front east side. It may even be contained before it gets here."

"Good, then it won't damage the books, and you can continue the search after we know everything is safe, now … don't make me ca-," and the words are cut off by the sound of a loud explosion.

*****

He sits outside, a safe distance from the burning house. It will take some time for the fire department to arrive, even though they have been alerted and are on their way. He can even hear the sirens, but the estate is located on the outskirts of town, tucked away within the large expanse of privately-held land.

He does not know when he finally allowed himself to sit, just plopped here on the grass, watching as his home burns. His eyes are glassy, the moist sheen reflecting the chaotic dance of the flames, but he does not cry. His thoughts move from the many valuables inside to the good fortune that so few people were here at all. Sometimes, the mansion is filled, but his mother has been spending time with his sister, and his son is off with friends.

He glances over as Mary nears him, the elder woman acting as Chief of Staff. He sees the comforting, careful expression. He offers a meager smile.

"They'll be here soon. It won't be a total loss," she tries.

He nods, then glances back at the house. Her assessment is correct, but the fire is already licking and lapping hungrily through the library. Despite the immense value of the possessions in the house, they are insured or backed-up, but the main thing that is irreplaceable haunts him.

One of the Three Books ...

With the life he has led, he rarely gives credence to coincidence, and he does not now. The trigger for the fire and explosion relates to the appearance of the apparition and realization of that immensely important book having been hid away in the library for no telling how long. The book that is now ash.

He hears a question off a ways, and it taps at his awareness like an annoying nibble. He blinks back into focus, turning to where most of the others are gathered. Not everyone is here. He moves closer to them, eyes searching about, then he turns, peering in the distance at various angles, then back at the house.

"Jericho? he calls out, his practiced voice evincing a sudden, controlled boom of volume and power, but despite this, there is no reply, so after a time, he tries again, calling the name of his old friend, "Jericho!"

"There!" someone else calls out, and he jerks his head over to see them point.

He follows the angle of that indication, and he sees the unmistakable, hulking figure of Jericho lumbering toward them, moving quite quickly, the form enshrouded by flame and smoke. It appears the guardsman is coming from behind the house, perhaps being forced to evacuate from the rear once he had made sure everyone inside was safe, an invaluable friend.

DANCE OF THE BUTTERFLY

Skothiam smiles more openly, relieved, "Good to see you-."

"Here's your book," comes the flat interruption, and an object having been carefully cradled by the large man is extended toward him.

His eyes gape, disbelief held there even as he reaches to take the proffered item. He holds the rare and valuable tome now in his own hands, looking it over. He gently brushes his right hand over its cover, then turns it, looking at the spine, before exhaling in evident relief.

It is true. It is the book – one of the Three.

*****

She doesn't often reshelf books, but she doesn't mind helping. There is an entire staff here, and though she is not Head Librarian, she is high enough up the chain that she does not need to engage in such mundane activities. Still, she sometimes craves the common, and there is something calming, perhaps even oddly meditative in putting the books back in their place.

It is quiet at least, and even though this is a library, not all areas of it prove so peaceful.

The continued, exponential growth of the information age has given rise to a much greater presence of computers and electronics and digital options here, perhaps more seeming than hard copies of traditional books. Archaic, some may say, even outdated or obsolete. Still, she appreciates the physical look and feel of a book, and though the demands on putting them back on the shelves may be much lesser than what some of the more senior employees here recall, there is still this occasional need.

Four books left on the dolly, and she takes her time.

Thus Spoke Zarathustra, Nietzsche. She casually wonders why someone had this one checked out and what they may have thought of it, even as she moves upon her lithe legs in the direction of where the book shall repose until called again. She is passingly familiar with the work, and she recalls a portion speaking of joy wanting eternity. What a lovely, romantic thought. Still, practicality, if not cynicism, may tend otherwise.

She has worked here for a few years, having moved up in the ranks quite quickly, demonstrating an acumen that landed her the coveted spot she now holds. It demands its own degree of responsibility that some would never wish to embrace, but she thrives on it. And really, once all the ducks are in a row, being a curator to rarities is not that terribly demanding.

She finds the place for the book, moving her glasses down to double check the numbers, though she knows she is in the correct locale, then slipping the tome into its place by its brethren. Three books left, and she wanders away toward where the others call home, the heels of her sensible, yet attractive shoes clicking on the tiled floor.

Some might even find the footwear a bit much for her position, but she possesses an athleticism and poise that does not allow her to be hindered by these four inch heels. If one were inclined to pay attention, one may note the flex of her developed calves as she walks, her smart skirt stopping just at her knees.

She does catch the eye of the occasional student, more than occasional really, and also the sometime member of faculty. These go unnoticed by her, and her appearance and attitude may give others to think of her as aloof, arrogant, cold. She is none of these, but she does not feel compelled to correct misconceptions, even if she were aware of them.

She finally finishes the chore, setting the cart back in its proper place. There are few people at this late hour, the library's accessibility running through most of the day in order to give the students the convenience of visitation. She glances at her watch, the slim black leather band giving over to the steel face.

"Marcel, I'm going to head out," she says to the student who is one of the sparse staff at this final shift of the night.

"Okay, Lilja." He casually raises a hand, bending it up from the wrist, as most of his focus is on a small tablet, studying its contents.

She is the senior person here on the actual paid roster, but it is quite normal to leave the student volunteers to finish up the last shift. She trusts Marcel, anyway, and he is not the only one here. He is a fifth year senior student, working toward three degrees, and he has proven very responsible. Lilja shrugs into her light, red coat, heading out.

DANCE OF THE BUTTERFLY

She sees the janitors getting out of their white van, preparing to go in and begin cleaning in advance of the closing hour. They trade a friendly wave and greeting, and she begins the short walk home, one that generally takes her less than a half hour. This one will take much longer.

Lilja would not recognize him even if he were not hiding in the narrow alleyway here on the campus grounds. He is a student of the prestigious university, but even with their exclusivity, they do not psychologically evaluate when deciding to admit students. He has been spending a lot of time of late in the library, watching her, germinating fantasies in his mind, developing an emotional attachment that he feels should be reciprocated. He has even watched her go home a few times, not following her, just observing, and he has noticed she does not usually drive a car, and when on foot, this is her normal route. He has waited long enough, simmering in his need and desire for her. She will walk by here soon. He hears the telltale click of her steady approach. He waits just inside the shadows, the darkness helping to hide his bulk. Tonight is the night.

As she moves by the mouth of the passageway, he lunges, ambushing her in an instant, his thick arms spread out, his coat giving him the semblance of a bird of prey. It may be quite alarming how fast a human being may move, and before Lilja has time to register it, he has her in a strong bear hug, pulling her petite frame back into the alleyway, away from prying eyes.

His left arm is about her chest, working to pin her arms, the right hand is up and over her mouth, hoping to thwart screams. He does not even register the lack of protests or screams. His large legs move rapidly, muscle residing there beneath the layers of fat, pulling her further into that throat of darkness betwixt the two buildings.

And in a blinking instance, Lilja stomps down with her right foot, the heel of her shoe digging in, and he cries out with the sudden pain. She does not stop there, moving with a fluid ease, dropping down into a quick squat to loosen the hold, lowering her central gravity and raising her arms out, getting free of him. She shoots back with her right arm, using her hips to add to the force, elbowing, and he feels a sharp pain. What he does not know is that Lilja has delivered a liver strike to him, and he reels momentarily from the sudden, shocking report. That is all the time needed, and moving with the quick speed of regular practice, she uses his own energy against him, gripping his right hand and wrist with both of her hands, twisting and pulling, using her entire body as leverage to bring him down in a bungling crash, both legs going over him in a much different manner than he may have fantasized. Her left leg presses over his neck, and as he reaches desperately with his left arm, Lilja catches it, locking her ankles, holding him, his right arm hyperextended within the cross armlock.

He yelps out in pain, frustration, and as he struggles, his violent need trying to regain the surface, she exerts pressure. He cries out again.

"Let me ... go ... Aaaahh!" His efforts are again greeted with a pull that lets him feel the full pain of the possibility of a dislocation or break in several areas.

She waits a moment, then uses her left hand to reach for her phone, which she keeps on her, not in her purse, and quickly gets a hold of the campus security service, calmly explaining the situation. It does not take them long to get there, but Lilja has to apply the extra force once more to compel her attacker. By the time they do arrive, the student has completely given up, tears leaking from his eyes as he hitches and sobs.

After a time, the situation has turned to one of which the assailant likely did not fantasize.

"Wow, Miss Perhonen, you ought to join security, though you'd make us all look bad," the young security guard says, grinning somewhat awkwardly, eyes moving from where the perpetrator is being led, handcuffed, into the back of a squad car, to return to the short, petite redhead.

Lilja smiles good-naturedly, not responding to the comment. They offered her a blanket and a coffee, both of which she declined, merely offering what limited information seems needed for Officer Shermont to fill out his report as they wait for the police to arrive. She knows him, though she has not interacted with him very often, and she answers his few remaining questions. He takes the information, interfacing somewhat inelegantly with the electronic tablet.

After she is done giving similar information to the local authorities, she has to decline Shermont's offer for a ride home several times, reiterating that she'll be fine, as if the very scenario that brought them out here were not proof enough. The young man finally gives in, reminding her to call if she needs help. And again, she smiles, thinking she just sufficiently demonstrated she is prepared to do just that.

She spends the time walking home to ponder, thinking of what this will entail. She wonders if the student has a well-connected or well-off family, and if this situation may turn out to work negatively toward her. She passes these concerns quite quickly, letting other thoughts that she considers more important to take her mind.

She is not very tired when she gets home, so she decides to burn off some steam with some exercises. It doesn't take long for her to settle, and eventually, sleep is found, something that often eludes her.

*****

The three men sit about the table, the remnants of a meal holding place in front of only one of them, though all three have glasses from which they occasionally sip. They show few shades in their individual palettes, wearing mostly black, other tones earthier, reduced. The man finishing the meal also shows intricate tattoos atop his hands, even his fingers, though his dark suit does not show much more of him than that. His eyes are narrow, a deep brown, and he focuses them beneath his thinning, graying hair upon the other two, a forkful of food being reduced to a goop by the steady motion of his jaw.

"Is there some secret program within the police for more covert, special operations type of work against organized crime?"

The other two share a look, one of them in the middle of a drink, which he finishes, setting down the stout glass.

"If it was secret, how would we know?" he throws out.

The other slits his already narrow eyes, staring, then after a moment, he takes up fork and knife, slicing the meat, slipping it in his mouth for more of his determined chewing.

"Then why do I pay you two? Hmm?" eyebrows raised, still masticating the flesh in his mouth, "You are supposed to be my eyes and ears inside, yes?"

"Hey, we've helped you plenty," the one speaks again, the more senior of the two by a small amount, also the larger of the two by much more, judging from his somewhat overweight appearance.

His head shows some lack where his body does not, thinning, dark hair about a bald spot which he doesn't hide, but he shows intent at hanging onto what hair he has left in contrast to the suited man, whose remaining locks are shorn quite short. The drinker never takes his hand away from the glass, holding it now at rest atop the table as he returns the steely gaze of the eater.

"Why are you asking, Gnegon?" speaks the third, a slightly younger, much more fit man of darker coloring.

His clothing might mark him more as one of the 'street', but he cares much more about his appearance than his partner. The man at the meal looks at him, nodding slowly, finally swallowing his food.

"Now *that* is a good question." He dips his head with more emphasis, then turns, indicating with his fork to the other, "You ought to be less defensive and more insightful, like Quain," he indicates back again with a tilt of his head to the right, then proceeds to cutting another piece of meat.

The other furrows his brow but seems to think better of a further response, merely bringing his glass up for more drink, draining the contents. Gnegon leans back in his chair, chewing. His eyes note the empty glass, and he snaps his fingers. A person emerges from the surroundings, the area occupied by many men of various appearances, none directly involved in this discussion, though several are paying attention. There are also women here, but their appearance suggests other intents. The empty glass is refilled from a bottle of bourbon.

"I am being harassed," he begins after wiping his mouth with a cloth napkin.

"Hey, look," the larger one begins quickly, his glass held up.

"I don't mean *you*, Alec" he says, impatience coloring the tone, jaw flexing. "Someone is bothering my operation," he continues, sitting back, resolving to his usual posture. "It took some work to figure it out. I thought it was isolated events. These things happen in the engagement of risky business, no? A shipment lost here, some men attacked there. Sometimes we even let the police get an arrest to appease your masters,"

DANCE OF THE BUTTERFLY

he adds, giving purposeful looks to both men. "But then we picked up on the hacking, and we noticed larger ... intrusions were taking place."

"What are you talking about?" Alec asks, leaning over the table on his elbows.

"Someone's poking at you," Quain assesses, "Testing your defenses, your reactions, and they must be doing a good job. You said you just realized they were related, and you asked if we knew of any covert operation in the force. Well, I don't, for what that's worth. Maybe it's not local. What've you got? What ties it together?"

Gnegon looks at the other detective, eyebrows raised, moving his head as though asking a question. Alec rolls his eyes, deciding to have more of his drink. The host smirks, looking back over.

"We started to suspect we might be under more focus than we realized, so we put some counter-measures in place. We've managed to get a few surveillance images, and it seems there is some similar signature to the electronic infiltrations. Not enough to trace anything, I am told, but enough to know it is the same person," he explains, then nods in a particular direction, and a man steps forward, handing over a small, thick paper stock folder.

He hands it to Quain who opens it immediately, looking at the prints inside, giving a cursory examine before sliding them to his partner. The small pictures show blurry, distorted shots of an obvious human figure, garbed in dark clothing, quite often blending in with the background, sometimes in motion.

"What the hell?" he asks, "You've got a ninja problem?" he chuckles, an action that is not joined by anyone else.

"Looks like spec ops to me," Quain says.

"So, what do you want us to do about it?"

Gnegon just looks at the portly man for a moment, studying him, then he finally speaks, "Maybe you could find out if there is any sort of classified effort like this coming from the local police. If not, then maybe you could find out if it is being done by other police in *your* city, hmm? And maybe, just maybe, you could wipe your own ass from time to time."

Alec shoots up to his feet, the chair sliding back loudly on the floor.

"You better be careful how you talk to me," he threatens, anger evident over his form, clenched fingers, slightly bared teeth.

"Fuck you, Detective," Gnegon replies.

"Now, hold on, fellas," Quain says, raising his hands, placatingly.

Gnegon continues to smirk, leaning back in his chair, looking between the two men.

"Your partner is much smarter than you are, Alec," he says, "You are armed. If you are so angry, draw your weapon. See what happens, hmm? Why do you think I let you remain armed in my presence?"

Alec seethes, bulky torso moving with his increasing breath, his dully colored shirt showing more within his open blazer. He points a thick finger at their host.

"You ...," he draws out through gritted teeth.

"I ... what?" Gnegon again perks the meager eyebrows over his narrow eyes, "We do not have to like each other, and we will both endure some amount of disrespect, but I *will* get something for my money, or you are a waste."

Alec just stands there, his large body moving in the continued respiration of his anger.

"We got you, Gnegon," says the younger one, "We're on it. Mind if I take these pics?"

"Of course not," Gnegon says, motioning with his right hand, graciously, "That is why I had them made," he adds, then throws in a somewhat patronizing smile, chin raised as he does so.

"Thanks," Quain says, snatching up the photographs and their folder, then he grabs his partner's arm, encouraging him to leave, "Let's go."

Alec spares more of a needling look for their patron in corruption, then turns, following the other's exit.

CHAPTER TWO

"Yes, the accommodations are very nice," speaks the voice, and were it not for the small device in his ear with the tiny, blue light, it may seem he talks to no one.

He spares a moment for the screen of his laptop, the machine ensconced in a dark, metal traveling case, open now for his use as he sits in the expansive, very posh hotel room.

"I've thought about that quite a lot, even had some analyses of various kinds run on it," he continues speaking after listening for a moment, "Yes, it appears most likely they were behind the attack. It's just too overt, too lethal to have been the Malkuths," and he pauses, nodding his head a bit, even as he listens and continues interfacing with his computer.

He gives a further moment to the monitor, eyes following the action on the screen. Then he rises, heading to the bar, dropping two ice cubes into a fine glass before adding even finer scotch into it.

"They could not have known it was one of the Three. They'd not risk destroying it. We all want them," he says, swirling the glass, then taking a generous sip of the cooling liquid. A light perk of his eyebrows is all the commentary he gives to the taste.

"The trap is rather eloquent if you think about it." Another pause as he listens, nodding, then, "They had to have known something unusual had been added to the library but not what it was, so they set the trap to lie in wait in case it was ever found, thus destroying the item and whomsoever else may have been unlucky enough to be caught in the fire," then in a musing tone that implies compliment, "Like a very patient fisherman."

"Well, I don't know," he adds after another pause, "If they had just blown up the library, they may not have gotten anyone in the blast. This way, they know at least one person is there. I do not know exactly how they think, Mother, but they do love to kill us if given the chance."

"Yes, it is worrisome that they were able to set the trap at all, but the house is gutted, and it seems a poor idea to rebuild. Charleston is working to find us a suitable replacement. Just stay with Nicole until then. I'm sure you two will love to have more time together," he says in a somewhat teasing tone, and the expression drops after a moment of listening, traded for something very serious, laden with emotion.

"It was him, Mother. I don't know how to explain it, but it was him. Somehow, he was triggered to appear, but it ... felt like Dad," he explains, more emotion trickling into his voice. "He was eager to show me the book. I don't know when or how or where he found it, but it had been in the library all this time. I suppose he was waiting until the right moment to tell me."

"Well, I'm not sure," after further waiting for his mother to talk, "You know him better than I do. You tell me why he did it," and more time passes as she speaks, "I suppose it may well be related to the breakthrough regarding the second book. We'll know more tomorrow after my appointment."

He listens more, going back to the computer, more tastes taken of the liquid in the glass, and he pulls up files, looking at a photograph along with textual information.

"I do not believe in coincidence," he says, "They must know, too, or they highly suspect. Still, this seems too careful, too ... slow for them, so I figure their intelligence lags behind ours. If they knew the book was in the collection, they'd probably just steal it.

"Well, yes, I suppose they know it is there and have discerned the security is too much for them to risk," he speaks, a subtle cast of sarcasm to his voice, but it is easily detected by one who knows him so well. "Yes, Mother," he says, exhaling, a short roll of his blue eyes, "I know the school is very wealthy and prestigious, so they may indeed have rather strong protection in place for their collection of rare books," though his tone suggests he is humoring her.

DANCE OF THE BUTTERFLY

"I'll get as close as I am able tomorrow, and if it turns out it is one of the Three, then I will inquire through the proper channels, make an offer or try to buy or extensively borrow the book or some such," then a pause as he listens, "Of course that is not normal, but if it is one of the Three, then we must do whatever is within our power. I'll offer to give the school an endowment if I have to."

"Hmmm," he ponders after further listening, "That's not a bad idea. Let me examine the book first, then if needed, Nicole can come here, but you know that means you'd have to take care of the grandchildren. I am sure you'd *hate* that," and now the sarcasm is more evident, along with the teasing, and were anyone else in the room, they'd hear the laughter from his mother emerging through the device, only to dissolve into a normal tone of voice, as he gives ear. "Oh, he's fine," then in something of an aside aspect, "I wish he were enrolled at this school, but yes, well, we'll see about motivating him to not wastes his gifts some other time, or you feel free to give him a call."

He chuckles at his mother's response.

"Yes, Mom, you sleep well, alright? Give my greetings to Nicole and everyone else. Yes, you, too. I love you, too. Good night."

He ends the call, going back to studying information on his screen, drinking more deeply of the dwindling contents in the glass. He pulls up a photograph of the Curator of the library's rare book collection, reading the dossier attached. He is surprised at the bright red coloring of her long hair, not having expected something so unconventional. Judging from the information about her, they have someone very serious about such tomes in charge, but he has no clue as to any security measures. Still, he is more curious to keep others out. He does not plan to skirt the law in this, so long as he is able.

*****

The black Kawasaki Ninja ZX-6R follows the semi-trailer truck at a decent distance along the gently curving roads here outside the city. It is night, and no normally discernable lights emit from the motorcycle, for it is in stealth mode. The customized resonator muffler gives forth little more than a minimal purring as the bike pursues in the wake of the large truck. Its driver's goggles allow enhanced modes of vision that dispel the usual impediment of driving in the dark without the benefit of conventional illumination. The twin headlamps at the fore of the vehicle are there, but it is obvious they have also been customized. A small device beneath the trailer emits an electronic signal in case sight of the truck is lost.

The tailing proves easy enough as they finally enter the city. The driver dares to follow closer, though the size of the semi-trailer keeps it from making any sudden turns, even if it were engaged in pro-active efforts of evasion. From what has been discerned prior to this transport trip, little caution has been employed.

The truck eventually makes it way to the warehouse, still here on the outskirts of the metropolis, driving through the entrance. The metal gates slide closed once the carrier is through, rolling and jiggling, ending in a loud report of the locking mechanism activating.

"Do you see anything?" emerges a voice over a comlink.

Two men hold position atop the main building, garbed in dark clothing, looking out over the direction from which the semi-trailer has arrived. One holds a pair of large binoculars, the other peers through a sophisticated scope attached to a suppressed sniper rifle. "Nothing," replies the man with the binoculars after taking a moment to scan and looking at his comrade for verification, "Anything from the cameras?"

"Negative," replies the voice, "We're monitoring. If anything comes up, we'll sound the alarm."

"So will we. Out," answers the spotter, then mumbling to the sniper, "Do they think we're stupid?"

"Shut up."

The motorcycle that had lately been in pursuit of the transport stands now quietly on the other side of a block of buildings across from the warehouse, its theft-deterrent measures engaged. The rider is atop a three story structure, moving low and slow, nearing the edge. Once there, observation is made through quite small binoculars, different modes of view engaged with the touch of a button. Cameras are noticed. They have been seen before, but their increased numbers are evident. The team atop the building is also made, despite being somewhat well hidden. The

DANCE OF THE BUTTERFLY

spotter is too eager, rising up and sweeping with the reflective binoculars too openly. They must be anticipating an arrival.

An alternate plan is quickly devised, along with considering abandoning the mission. There is doubt that this is merely increased security measures for its own sake. They have finally figured out they are being targeted, despite their time of success and the continued bribes to local law enforcement.

A frontal assault had also been considered – take out the sniper team and a few cameras, then scale the gate and engage. There is worry, though, for the safety of those inside who are innocent. The risk is too great.

The motorcycle is left where it is, the rider moving back along the ground, keeping to shadows, though it seems no one is about. The jika-tabi make very little sound on the concrete as the driver sprints across an area of potential exposure, continuing obliquely from the warehouse, moving along the street to gain a different angle of approach.

It appears that the occupants of the warehouse have placed their expectation on an approach from the front. The number of cameras from this angle is fewer, the wall about the rear transitioning from metal to concrete, visually estimated at around four meters high. Some time is spared for surveillance, taking note that the team on top of the building appears content to only observe a limited field from the forward vantage.

The rider moves toward the wall with an even, medium speed stride, having chosen an approach that holds in a generous blind spot of the cameras. The left foot finds high purchase, the other coming up as well from the momentum, propulsion carrying as hands work in tandem until they find the top of the wall. The figure crouches low, holding still and quiet, observing for any sign that presence has been detected.

And there is the semi-trailer, backed into an open bay, its cargo already emptied. Bright lights illuminate that area, even as the large, rolling garage door remains open. A person is spied outside, smoking, a Vz. 61 Skorpion strapped over his right shoulder. The infiltrator atop the wall does not move, merely watching as further drags are taken on the cigarette by the sentry. The man's eyes scan about somewhat, even coming close to peering at the intruder until the smoke break is done, and with a toss of the butt, he turns and heads back inside through the docking bay, ignoring the adjacent door. Voices are heard from within, and then the cacophony of metal erupts onto the night quiet as the garage door is closed.

Time to move.

The figure scurries atop the wall, keeping low, then shifts left with an effortless smoothness, dropping to the inside of the wall, landing upon bent knees, rocking forward a bit to balance with hands, holding place now in an area of shadow. There are other lights here, but they are not as radiant, and a quick scan shows one method of ingress along the warehouse's brick back wall – a single door positioned in the center, above which hangs a lamp and a camera.

The FN P90 submachine gun strapped tight to the figure's torso is taken in both gloved hands, aimed at the camera, the red dot and infrared sight clearly showing the way. A coughing sound is produced by the subsonic ammunition fired through a suppressor, and the camera is rendered ineffective.

The reaction is somewhat quick, though it does belie the level of readiness and training on the part of the defense here. The team atop the building rushes over, making far too much noise, peering down over the rear of the building, both looking near and far for any sign of an intruder. They see nothing, for the shooter has moved back, staying close to the wall, returning to the loading dock area.

Two doors then open in quick unison. The rear spills forth two guards, both armed with Skorpions, and one must assume the team on the roof has given some sort of a clear sign to them from their observation above. The two men swing their barrels about, searching somewhat erratically, seeming little concerned with protecting one another or even themselves and blindly hopeful of spotting an intruder.

The door leading into the garage area gives passage to the one who had just been outside on smoke break, but before he may do much searching, he is surprised from behind by an expert choke hold applied along with full body weight upon his back. He instinctively reaches, hands clasping at the arm about his throat, releasing his hold on the SMG. It dangles there by its shoulder strap. His reactionary struggles are miniscule, ineffective, and within seconds, he is unconscious. Zip-ties

DANCE OF THE BUTTERFLY

are quickly applied to his wrists and ankles just as the other guards begin to realize something is going on.

Tactical lights shine over the supine body of the guard, moving about as the two on the ground rush over to investigate even as the sniper team atop the building adds their own bright spotlight to the scene. No one else is there.

"Yuri's down, tied up," the spotter speaks into his comlink, "Someone's on the premises."

"We're going into lockdown, sounding the alarm," replies the voice on the other end. "Get the intruder, alive if possible."

And then a noise permeates the area, not too loud, but loud enough to effectively do its job. Lights also snap on where most of the building had been held in darkness, but there are still areas where one may remain hidden. The two men on the ground rush inside the open door leading to the bay, while those on the roof claim duty over the outside area. They pause once inside, angling weapons up to the noise of approaching footsteps, though it proves to be another guard coming in on the second floor, looking down from a catwalk. They trade rudimentary acknowledgement and hand signals, then get back to business.

It takes a moment for the one to realize he is alone, and he begins another sort of search here in the large area.

"Clay?" he calls out, looking around, jerking the barrel of his gun about. "Clay!" he tries more insistently, and then he sees something back in the dark distance, behind a long, tall shelf baring of various items and boxes.

The form moves, moaning.

"Clay?"

He flicks on his tactical beam, shining it to see the his colleague, held at the wrists and ankles by zip-ties, obvious signs of having just regained consciousness and experiencing trouble grasping it.

"Shit!" comes the adequate assessment, and he turns just as his ears pick up the sounds of approaching feet.

His finger goes to the trigger of his weapon, and then the gun is knocked from his hands, flying free and scraping across the concrete floor. He barely registers the black-garbed figure, moving so quickly. He tries to strike out, and his attempt is easily dodged. He turns in the direction the blurry intruder has moved only to feel a sharp pain in his side, followed all too quickly by a bloom of pain in his sternum, then his left knee. He crumbles, and the hit to his temple helps him complete his journey to the ground. He is quickly tied and left.

He cries out, a mixture of pain, frustration, and anger, but no one responds.

A couple of guards later, and the intruder creeps slowly down a hallway on the second floor. There are openings to either side, no doors, and within most of the cramped rooms are girls and women of various ages, though none look to be older than their twenties, despite the condition of their appearance, and many seem frighteningly young. Some of them lull in the apparent stupor of drugs, others are alert, eyes open wide, watchful, fearful, but all of them are bound in one way or another.

The infiltrator holds a black-gloved finger over the place where a mouth would be behind the obscuring mask, an easily understood sign. There is no real noise from the women, other than the whimpering cries of some. None of these are probably the recently unloaded "cargo".

The space at the end of the hallway turns out to be some sort of break room, with the worn drip coffee maker, Styrofoam cups, small television, and other such common accoutrements for killing time. The unarmed man in here looks as though he is probably the driver of the truck. Once his threat potential has been assessed, the intruder moves into view, looking about.

The driver cries out, startled, then pushes back against a countertop, trying to increase the distance between himself and the other. He then pulls a knife from a set nearby, brandishing the piece of cutlery. The intruder looks at him briefly, the distance far too great for the man to do any real damage with the impromptu weapon, even had he the training. The man stares, head tilting, brow furrow beneath the cap on his head.

"You …" he speaks, gesturing with the knife, "You … you're … what the-?"

And a black object is suddenly in the intruder's hands, aimed, a button pressed and the prongs shoot out on wires, delivering a debilitating shock. The man is taut, held like a bow string, teeth and jaw clenched as the other walks nearer. The button is released, and he slumps, incapacitated. The zip-ties are quickly applied, prongs removed, and the stunner reset.

A few more minutes pass before it seems all that may be left is the sniper team and those behind the locked door. A door which presumably leads to the command center of the warehouse. Cameras have been disabled along the way, just like the tied up guards.

"Who is it!" a voice from within demands to the gentle rapping on the door.

Yes, someone is indeed inside, and moments later, a loud crack of noise indicates the locking mechanism being breached, the controlled force of which thrusts the door open. Gunfire responds almost immediately, and a small object is slid inside the room, exploding with a loud flash of blinding light. The intruder then rolls on the ground from the perpendicular hallway some three meters distant, firing the suppressed P90, wounding the two men in the legs.

They cry out, falling, still randomly firing their SMG's, but the attacker has rolled back out of view, simply waiting until they have quickly expended their magazines.

"He's here!" a pained voice speaks, "Control room … gaaah," more outbursts of pain, coupled with the cluttering noise of rushed panic as at least one of the men tries to reload.

The steady sound of jika-tabi announces the arrival of the intruder, and the one trying to reload sucks in a breath through parted lips and gritted teeth, reeling back as much as he is able until he is struck with the butt of the gun, lapsing into unconsciousness. The SMG is quickly aimed at the other, who greets this with hands raised.

"I surrender! I surrender!"

"Turn around; hands behind your back," emerges a powerful command from behind the mask, the words clear, strong, and confident, delivered from deep within the chest.

The man nods, feebly, but he displays some confusion. His hands are jerked down sharply, and he grunts in pain as his wrists are tied. A cell phone is retrieved from one of many pockets on the infiltrator's black, non-reflective suit, buttons pressed, then it is set down on the counter near the man.

"The police are on their way," comes the whispered announcement, the man cringing, for the assailant has leaned near, no doubt to also transmit this to the sniper team.

The intruder stays crouched somewhat low, looking out over the impressive windows to the north and east side of the command room. One can view a good portion of the large warehouse from here, but not all of it. Of course, the cameras were meant to make up for that.

Is the sniper team waiting, approaching, or did they flee? Exfiltration must occur before the arrival of law enforcement. They would not treat the intruder kindly, for vigilantism *is* against the law.

Once outside, it seems the sniper team did make their escape. They were not so stupid after all. The finely tuned engine of the motorcycle fires up, and the rider is off. Mission accomplished.

*****

He has deliberately arrived early for the appointment, but he does not announce himself. It may be seen nearly as rude to show up premature as to cause undue delay beyond an expected time, and besides, he wishes to take advantage of this for some reconnaissance. He drew some notice from the young man behind the counter when he entered, a bit of a study of him within a sidelong look cast briefly from whatever reading material took his attention. He takes it that this young man feels somewhat comfortable with his knowledge of people here at this small, acclaimed private school, and the visitor certainly shows age beyond that of a standard student and is not a member of the faculty.

If the attendant feels so inclined to question him or raise any alarm, that moment passes as he confidently walks further into the building. He has learned that appearance and attitude may shirk suspicion, and his finely tailored suit and smooth stride seem to have allayed any doubt that may be kindling in the young man.

He wanders about, eventually moving up the stairs to the second floor. There are four to this building, and what he hopes to see resides on the lower one, below ground. He bides his time, examining the books, glancing over spines for hints of tales to be told. There is a decent-sized bank of computers on the uppermost story available for the use of

DANCE OF THE BUTTERFLY

students. He has heard that the machines are quite top notch, though he suspects most of the members of the learning body here have arrived with their own expensive, sleek laptops. It is not easy to get into this school, and though they do offer scholarships and grants, most of those attending come from money.

He loses his thoughts again to wondering why his own son is not a student here, but he shan't give himself over to too much regret. There are many avenues to excellence, and sometimes a formal education of this caliber may have no place in that journey.

He glances at the dark gray face of his Vacheron Constantin Patrimony Contemporaine watch, noting that the time shows near enough that he may make his presence known without seeming untoward. He returns to the young man at the front, doing just that, heading over to wait in one of the comfortable leather chairs here in the foyer as the attendant uses the phone.

He has picked up a pamphlet in his short explorations, something about the collections of books and art held by the university, and he is perusing its slim contents when he hears the approach of heels.

"Mr. Felcraft?"

He looks up, smiling warmly, and he is greeted with a vision. He had, of course, seen her staff photograph before coming here, and though it had proved rather complimentary, it was still a work picture. She is not wearing the glasses from the image, and her hair is out, natural and long, that vibrant red catching his eye. He notes that her clothes are rather smart and well fitted, even if nowhere in the league of cost of his own. Still, price tags only determine one form of worth, and they may not always be very precise at that. He rises smoothly, extending his hand to meet her own. A firm shake is given, though warm in the greeting, much less guarded. "Ms. Perhonen, is it?" he replies, pronouncing the name with a short, slipped roll of the 'r'.

She gives a slight, surprised, but pleased smile at hearing the enunciation. "I hope you've not been waiting too long," she speaks, her accent rather unexpected and refined. "Marcel mentioned you'd been here a while."

"Marcel?" he asks, brow furrowing, face moving a touch to the right in the inquisitive expression.

"Oh, the volunteer there at the front desk," she informs, turning and indicating with a relaxed gesture of her hand, and she finally smiles, emitting a short, nearly silent chuckle as though a bit embarrassed to have imparted the information this way.

He finds it utterly charming.

"Ahhh, did he now?" he plays along, smiling further, then gives a glance over, dipping his head once when he notices Marcel watching them. "I arrived early for our engagement, so I killed some time. Your library is quite remarkable."

She smiles further, "Thank you, but it's not mine."

Ah, is she teasing, making a joke?

"Of course not," he adds, "But it may seem as much the property of those who care for it as those who pay for it … if not more so. Spending money may be easier than taking the time to embrace real responsibility over something."

He notes the shadow of a smirk on her lips, though the expression does not fully resolve.

"Well, then, follow me, if you please," she invites, and with a smoothly murmured, 'thank you', he does just that.

"I know of you, Mr. Felcraft," she speaks into the short silence as they make their way to the separate staircase that leads to the lower level.

"You do?"

She nods, "Your family's collection is well known amongst those like me."

"And what might that be?" he pitches the question with a touch of playfulness.

She pauses at a locked set of double doors, peering back at him, one hand poised near the keypad, a card held in the embrace of slender digits tipped with a daring red polish.

"Librarians," she answers flatly, then slides her card, punching in a code with the quick ease of familiarity, causing the lock to disengage, and they enter.

He follows her ingress, though his attention is temporarily taken with the environ, glancing about at the bookcases, most of which are fronted with locked, glass doors. A few books lie open on pedestals, which he suspects is not normal and may perhaps have even been done

DANCE OF THE BUTTERFLY

on his account. This room may act as a museum but it is more often controlled, secure storage.

She moves in further, not bothering to give him any sort of introductory spiel about the collection. He is here for a specific reason, and she knows it. He moves in her wake, eyes still casting about, until they reach a rear area. An imposing wood and glass cabinet holds a half dozen books in two rows, each displayed forward, each behind their own glass window. She retrieves an electronic key from a small collection on her person and places the tip against the unobtrusive receptacle at one portal. A light shifts position, a small click is heard, and she opens the window, retrieving the book.

She presents it to him in both hands, and he bends forward a touch from the waist, peering at it. He moves his eyes from the cover to hers, noting the piercing gaze, and he brings his hands forward, fingers extended in a relaxed fashion.

"May I?"

"Yes," she says, a curl just touching the edge of her lips, "I am sure you noticed the tables and chairs in here. Feel free to use them as you wish to examine the book, but it mustn't leave this room."

"Of course," he moves his head forward once in acquiescence, "I presume you'll be remaining in here to chaperone me."

She gives a polite smile, nodding her head. He then takes the tome, but he does not move. He allows himself to experience its heft. It is a decent sized one, roughly six by ten inches, most closely to octavo, adhering to the golden mean ratio, somewhat thick, baring of approximately six hundred pages. He looks at the spine, delicately running his fingers down it, feeling the five ridges. It is bound in dark, Moroccan leather, the gilding silver. He opens it, flipping to the back, examining the colophon, noting the information presented as well as the small sigil. The names and dates match the first book. Everything seems in order. He tries to remain calm, as though he were examining a common rare book of immense value and not one that may hold secrets capable of protecting or destroying this planet's very way of life.

He glances up at her after losing himself to this scrutiny. She is merely watching him, standing quite patiently.

"What do you think?" she asks.

"Exquisite," he replies, then gives her a brief moment of his smile before heading over to the large, circular wooden table near the entrance.

He takes a seat in one of the chairs, the fine upholstery offering comfort as well as aesthetic. He sets the book down with some delicacy, though the fortitude is evident in the robust and pristine appearance at its age. He flips it open to a random page, looking over the words, not really reading, just drifting, moving to another leaf, then another, noting the impressive woodcut images, the sophistication and artistry quite breathtaking.

"I'm surprised you did not bring anything on which to take notes. I could fetch a pad and pen, if you like," she offers.

"Oh," he looks up, smiling, "No, thank you. Frankly, I was not sure if this was the book I am seeking. I had planned to just make a cursory examination."

"Ah," she nods, her hands held before herself, at her lower belly, her right hand lightly grasping the index finger of her left, "I can assure you of its authenticity."

He notices she wears no rings of any kind. "I do not doubt you at all, Ms. Perhonen," he says. "I am seeking a particular book, very rare, and I was not sure this would be the one, but it seems to be."

She tilts her head a bit, pale brow knitting, and she moves a half-step closer. "That is … curious. I cannot say I've ever known of that sort of motivation for visiting our collection."

He glances back at her, offering a short smile, one that could be placating or even awkward, but its intent is not entirely clear. His attention returns to the book, and he holds his hands over the open pages.

"Mr. Felcraft? Are you alright?" she asks, moving closer, concern taking her features.

"Oh, yes," another smile emerges, this one more controlled, "It is just rather monumental for me to have found it."

Some more time passes as he looks at the book, and she spends that time observing him.

"I am sure, in your line of work, you may appreciate rare, important things, and as you have chosen the Library Sciences, I presume you are aware of the power of knowledge. We have so many ways now to share information, but older times were not so fortunate," he slowly flips

DANCE OF THE BUTTERFLY

through a few more pages as he speaks in this musing tone, hands occasionally moving the paper in a delicate stroke, as though he were imbibing the information through his fingertips.

She watches silently, noting the slender length of his digits, the obvious manicure, the nails longer than may be conventionally expected on a man.

"One may posit that due to the cost and limitations on books, especially prior to the sixteenth century, the knowledge placed in them was carefully chosen. This could be political, religious, academic, and that may say something in and of itself. Books may well be the purveyors of secrets." He closes the tome, looking up at her, "How much do you know of this one, Ms. Perhonen?"

She blinks, perhaps having been lost in her observation and his speech. Her eyes widen a bit, eyebrows rising, the blue catching light like shards of ice. "I was not very much involved in its identification and authentication. I am just a curator."

He turns to fully face her, catching her eyes, "Is that so?"

"Yes," she nods.

"You are the Lead Curator and Archivist for a rather special collection, well on your way to becoming Director of the entire library, and at your age," he continues, still wearing that pleasant smile on his lips, "You are obviously accomplished, and I suspect you care for the books here, even as such may be a reflection of your professional performance. We learn in many ways, do we not, Ms. Perhonen?"

She blinks, eyes still on him, but she does not move further or nearer to where he sits. "You seem to have done some checking up on me before coming here," she finally speaks, "Is there a particular reason for this?"

"I care about books," he replies, pushing back a tad from the table, turning his chair toward her as he does, folding his hands in his lap, "And not just about books, but many things which may be considered art or treasure, and I do not just mean in the literal sense, for what is 'treasure' but that upon which we ascribe some subjective value? I suspect you know this, and that you have done some checking up of your own. "This book," he slowly reaches out his right hand, placing it atop the cover of said treatise, "is one of particular importance to me, and if it were possible, I would acquire it for my private collection. In the stead of that, I'd feel more comfortable if I knew it were secure and well cared for."

"With all due respect, Mr. Felcraft, and I do appreciate your status as a collector, but I work for the university, and though we obviously afford some opportunities to those outside the school, my primary duty is to the institution, not to you."

"I'd have thought your primary duty might be to the books," he retorts, the gentle smile on his lips blunting any potential edge to the words.

And there it is again, that shadow of a smirk trying to have its way with her lips.

"What good is a book without someone to read it?" she pitches.

He grins more openly, a quiet chuckle passing through his throat. He then raises the index finger of his right hand. "Exactly," he agrees.

"So," she looks more serious after sharing a brief smile, eyes moving to the valuable folio, "What is so special about this book, then?"

"Ah, yes, well," he replies, eyebrows perking for a moment as his own gaze travels to the item in question, "It ... hmmm ..."

And her eyes glide back to his in that moment of hesitation, and she shifts more toward him in a barely discernable manner.

"This book is under some of our tightest security, and it receives the utmost care. Such is warranted for one of this value. It would be welcome to know more of it. *I* would welcome it," she says.

And he looks up to see a pleasant smile on her lips. He may have more experience, but neither of them are without some skill at diplomacy. "Perhaps it would be better if I completed some study of it first," he offers, turning it into the suggestion of a question at the end, "I should be certain."

She looks at him, obviously evaluating his words, but she dips her head once, "Of course. How much time would you like? I can get you materials you may need, even refreshments?"

"Thank you, you are very kind and accommodating. Is there a way to set up an extended loan of the book?"

Her brow furrows, "I am afraid the book is not allowed to leave this room except for under the most special of circumstances, and that would not include examination and study by a private collector, no matter how reputable or prestigious that person may be."

He smiles at this offering, nodding slowly, "I completely understand," and he slides his chair back, rising, "I was not sure if this would be *the* book, so I fear I did not allot enough time on my schedule. I am still not one hundred percent certain, but this initial check gives me reason to warrant further examination, if you do not mind, of course?"

She smiles politely in return, "Of course not. You will not mind if I am here during that time, will you?"

"I'd prefer no other chaperone," he is quick to say, and they both share a similar twist to their grins and short, quiet chuckle at his words.

"I am not the security, Mr. Felcraft, but perhaps I may aid you in your study, if you need it."

Something in the way she says this gives him a brief pause, and he moves his head ever-so-slightly to the left, peering. The moment passes quickly enough to not intrude on the conversation. He extends his hand, which she takes.

"Thank you, Ms. Perhonen, I do appreciate it. If it is not too much trouble, I'd like to return tomorrow, and I'd also like to bring some of my materials."

"Of course, though I'll need to look over them before they are used."

"I do understand. Thank you again. I can see that this collection is in very capable hands. Good day to you."

"Good day to you, Mr. Felcraft."

This handshake does not last through all of their talking, but it did hold a bit longer than the introductory one.

He turns to leave, walking out calmly, his mind not only preoccupied with the book. He knows it is the second of the Three, but further study is warranted. Still, he'd prefer to have it in his collection. He does not expect that to happen easily, and the more difficult it would prove, the more others may take notice. He thinks more on the curator, Lilja Perhonen, mulling over many options involving her.

*****

"Mind if I join you?"

She looks up from the book held in her lap, taking some time here in the school's Commons for a snack and some coffee before heading back to work. Her initial default mode of polite, yet firm refusal dissolves instantly when she sees who it is.

"Oh, Billy," she offers a little smile, "Sure," she nods toward the open chairs at the table, and the campus security guard sits at the one across from her, setting down his tray which holds a full meal.

"Hi, Miss Perhonen," he grins somewhat bashfully, trying to get comfortable in the metal chair, "How are you doing?"

"I'm fine, thanks, and you can call me Lilja," she offers, her smile becoming warmer.

She'd have preferred to not be interrupted, but at least this is someone she sort of knows. She ought to make efforts to be more sociable, at least according to the indelicate reminders from her mother.

"Uh, right," he shifts his eyes to her then back to his food, "Lilja ... right," then shoves a forkful into his mouth, chewing and talking, "So, you're okay since the attack?"

"Yes," she grins, showing her nice teeth, "I think he fared worse than I did."

He laughs more openly, following with a slurp of his tea, as he resolves into a short cough, swallowing, "You got that right. Poor guy is expelled and facing criminal charges ... what am I saying 'poor guy'?" he glances at her, his expression changed to one of concern, "Sorry about that. He deserves what he gets. No telling what he planned to do to you."

She gives another conciliatory grin, lips pressed together, "It's okay, Billy. I'm glad he is in custody, and that he didn't choose a less prepared target."

"Yeah, how was he supposed to know you are a ninja in training?" he beams a grin at her, chewing more of his food.

She gives a good-natured roll of her eyes, "I study karate and jujutsu. I am not a ninja."

"Heheh," he offers an awkward chuckle, "I know, just teasing. Don't knock me out!"

She shakes her head a bit, having more of her strong coffee.

"So, what're you reading?" he asks, motioning his head up to indicate the material in her lap, slipping another fork-load into his mouth.

"Oh, something riveting," and she holds up the magazine, which appears to be a publication on book collecting.

He narrows his eyes, leaning forward to peer at it, then he smirks, shrugging, "Not my sort of thing." Then he has more of his food, chewing exuberantly, setting back in the chair as he drinks of his tea, eyes on Lilja even as she goes back to the article which before held her attention.

"It's yours, though, yeah," he says, and she glances over at him, looking over the thin metal frames of her somewhat narrow glasses. "Why doesn't a pretty lady like you date?" he bluntly asks, wiping his mouth with his napkin.

She is somewhat aghast at the question, but she says nothing. He even asked her out once some time ago, and he seems to have taken her negative reply in good enough stride.

"I'm married to my work," she offers a shrug, deciding to not take offense and just answer the question as plainly as she will.

"Yeah, I figured," he nods, making this statement with no judgment, going back to his quite rapidly disappearing meal, "You do a good job, though, I know that, and you still have time to learn how to drop a ninety-five kilo guy like he's nothing."

"I can't say as I've had the best luck with relationships, anyway," she says, and she immediately wonders why she has offered this.

"Oh, yeah? Well, if some guy hurt you in the past, then he was an idiot. A lady like you deserves to be treated right."

She gives a genuine smile, "Thanks, Billy."

"You're welcome." He smiles back, scraping up the remnants of his food, following it with the rest of his tea. "I've gotta run. We don't get long for our breaks. I'll see you around."

He gets up, holding his tray, offering a departing smile and little wave. She waves back, watching as he leaves, getting lost in her own thoughts.

It has been a few years since she's been involved, having tried one date with one person after the unpleasant ending of the only serious relationship in which she has ever been. Now it just seems that the idea of a romantic relationship never enters her mind. She certainly garners her share of attention, but it just doesn't seem an option. She doesn't want to be hurt, and she doesn't want others to get hurt.

She glances back at the open magazine, the one she pulled from storage at the library. It is over two years old, and it will need to be digitized and disposed of soon. She wanted it for the article on noted collectors, having a little read-up on Mr. Skothiam Felcraft.

CHAPTER THREE

"Christmas came early for you guys. What's to complain about?" says one of the men in the coffee room, looking over from pouring some of the dark, settling ichor into a plastic cup.

"Yeah, well, don't tell the press, or we'll look like idiots."

A few sips of coffee, some chuckles, but not everyone is so joyous.

"And now we have some self-righteous vigilante to chase. Yeah, Christmas," asserts a grumbler.

"We sure were doing a great job," sarcastically adds another cynical, displeased person, "That warehouse operating right under our noses, and you know they weren't just using it for human trafficking."

Looks are exchanged, one in particular taking close note of the conversation. The most recent speaker continues into the sudden silence.

"We should be glad for the help. How can that place have been there without us knowing it?" and accusatory eyes are angled out at the impromptu gathering.

"Since when did you get a warrant to go into any place you want?"

"You can excuse it anyway you like-"

"You better watch what you're implying," comes the challenge, this cop getting right up to the other, despite her being a woman.

"Hey, calm it down," orders a gruff, forceful voice, "We're all on the same side here, and that vigilante is breaking the law, just like those people using the warehouse. It's a good bust for us, but this goes beyond a 'helpful' citizen."

"Don't expect me to arrest this 'helpful' citizen," says one, and a few laugh.

"Shut that shit up," growls out the forceful one, "You especially don't want the lieutenant hearing that kind of talk."

Silence greets this, but the one who spoke about not arresting merely shrugs.

"What do you think, Alec?" one asks, up-nodding to the officer seated at a table by himself, having a snack of a pastry.

He raises his eyes, wide, noting all attention suddenly on him. Laughter results.

"Alec is busy," says one, and the raucous increases, and Alec scowls, generating more chuckles.

"Come on, Alec, join the conversation."

The big man shrugs, pursing out a lower lip, "Eh, I'll take the help, but I guess if I have no other choice, I'll have to arrest the guy, but if he's as good as he seems, I'd rather just wait until he's gone, right?" he says with a big grin.

And this gets more chuckles in response from most, while some scoff and others look potentially offended.

"A lot of help you are!" calls out one.

"Hey, hey, I know my civic duty. I'll volunteer to help when I'm not busy."

"Oh yeah, right," come various and myriad responses of disbelief.

Alec stands, smirking, squaring his ample shoulders.

"I'm serious. If I can help, I'll help."

"Yeah, yeah, well go talk to Kenneth, then, if you're serious. The lieutenant gave him that Task Squad."

"I will," Alec announces, mostly to teasing disbelief expressed on the part of his coworkers, but he, of course, means it.

*****

He studies the open book, looking over the finely printed text, leaned over and somewhat close as if proximity may aid in plumbing the secrets hidden within the words. His laptop is on the table, near the book, and he occasionally consults it, looking over images, quickly tapping on the keyboard to keep track of his own notes. After a time, he sits back in the chair, evincing fatigue, perhaps even frustration, in his posture.

"Do you speak Latin?" she asks, not too far away, occupied with some of her own work.

DANCE OF THE BUTTERFLY

He looks over, smiling lightly, "Yes, though I don't often seem to find myself in situations requiring it."

She returns the grin, though it drops for a more inquisitive gaze as his own has disappeared as he looks away. "Is everything alright?" she asks.

"Oh, yes, thank you." He returns his eyes to hers, the polite curve returning to his lips, "Just trying to unravel the mystery, but the threads are not being terribly cooperative."

She nods, returning to her own chores, so he gets back to his work after taking a sip of the strong coffee she has so generously made available to him during his visits of the past few days.

"May I confess something to you?" her voice then breaks the shortly resuming silence.

He looks up, naught but open sincerity with a coloring touch of guarded stupefaction on his face, "Of course."

She takes a few tentative steps closer, looking also quite serious. "Your being here to examine the book is really quite curious, especially coming back and spending so much time with it, so I decided to do a little investigating myself."

He merely nods to this, the gesture slow, deliberate-seeming.

"Did you know this book is mentioned in Nicholas Rémy's *Daemonolatreiae libri tres*?"

He blinks, just studying her. She shirks the barest bit under the scrutiny, her head moving a few degrees to the right and down, and her hands, yet held together in that same arrangement they seem so wont to show, display the subtle movement of fingers.

"Are you familiar with it?" she asks in the encroaching quiet.

"I am," he nods once, though he is not inclined to tell her why.

"Ah, then I've not told you anything you do not already know. I'm sorry for interrupting."

"No, no," he says, surprising himself with the tone of urgency, sitting up further in the chair, bringing himself more attentive to her place in the room. "That is not an easy clue to come by."

"Oh, well," she exhales a single, audible breath into a short smile, "I do have … some experience with this sort of thing."

He perks his eyebrows. "A curator is not necessarily a book detective," he says with a warm grin, "I'd not turn away assistance, if you know of anything else regarding this."

"I don't really know much more than the usual information and listings, but it is intriguing that the book is mentioned in one of the most famous treatises on capital witch trials, doesn't it?"

"Well, I suppose it depends on how one views witchcraft and witches," he replies, pushing away from the table, opening more toward her, inviting her to also sit with a very subtle gesture of his head toward the nearby chair, and she sets herself in, facing him.

"How do you mean?"

"Well, I think you'd find that most people do not believe in witchcraft in a literal, supernatural sense, which means that the persecution these people suffered was largely socio-political and religious. If that is the case, then it may not be odd at all to find any number of texts in the possession of these people that purports to convey knowledge prohibited by the Church."

She blinks, brow furrowing, "This book was so restricted?" she asks, her blue eyes looking darker as they cast quickly to the folio then back up to him.

"It did not figure as prominently on any list of banned books, but the information contained in some parts was not looked upon kindly by the Church."

She nods, glancing back down at the text as though ready to spot some heresy on the open page, then again looking back at him.

"I'm not that familiar with its contents."

"I don't expect it's on too many peoples' lists of recommended books, either. It is really quite unknown, and you are aware of its rarity," he offers, smiling gently.

She nods, glancing again from the open book then to him, letting a very light smile trace her lips.

"What is it about?"

He looks at her, that barest of a curl on the edges of his mouth, just gazing. She meets his eyes openly, not shirking in the exchange. He notes that she returns the subtly hinting smile, and then she blinks,

DANCE OF THE BUTTERFLY

adjusting a stray lock of her vibrant hair which has fallen over the left side of her face.

"May I tell you tonight over dinner?" he invites.

Her smile grows in size and warmth, though still coquettish, and only a brief moment passes before she answers, "Yes, that would be nice."

*****

The two men walk into the dingy bar, the afternoon sun pouring in through the door to announce their arrival. A few muted groans and some not so reduced scowls greet the arrival of the contrasting pair. The various people in here, the vast majority of which are male, engage in what one may expect in this sort of establishment – drinking, talking, playing billiards, darts.

The place is mainly composed of a treated wood, disguised as darker and higher quality by the glossy finish which is smudged, worn, and chipped, giving hints to the brittle skeleton beneath. The general lack of décor also indicates the no-nonsense and very masculine nature of the business. The only places that deviate from the dark, earthy palette of chamber and customers being the rolling balls on the green felt and the eye-catching labels of bottles behind the bar.

The two men are greeted with a nod from the bartender, the stubbled head atop the thick neck offering a single dip of some measure of respect.

"What can I get you?" he offers, setting aside an opened bottle of beer and placing both hands atop the bar, palms pressing in the edge near him.

"Vodka," says the larger, paler man.

The barkeep nods once more, curt, then his eyes settle on the other.

"Nothing," the leaner, darker man says, dismissively, then turns to look about the place.

A short glance is spared back to the other, a non-verbal commentary compressed into that one look, then the man turns, fetching a tumbler, into which he pours a generous amount of Russian vodka. The customer raises it, taking in a decent swallow, then nods approvingly. The bartender goes back to whatever occupies his time when not needed, and the drinking man turns to casually look out over the occupants of the bar. He raises the glass to have another sip, eyes shifting to his partner, then in the direction the other man observes. He takes that drink, then follows his comrade as he walks away.

The man stops at a distant table, one somewhat obscured by the varying levels of darkness in the dimly-lit place. The three men sitting there, drinking, look up, none too pleased with the potential interruption.

"We just got out, Quain. What do you want?" one of them asks, his voice carrying a deep undertone, like muddy water gurgling over stubborn rocks.

"You didn't just get out," the man replies, looking the three over, no sign of being intimidated at all showing on him.

The other of the duo steps over, pulling out the unoccupied fourth chair with a loud scrape and sitting his bulk in it. He gives a good look to the three, bringing up his drink for another sip, not leaving much after this most recent taste.

"We need to talk to you guys before too much time passes and you rot your memories with drink or drugs," he unceremoniously declares.

The three look at him, one baring of a somewhat vacant, rheumy gaze, the other two evincing more disgust, even challenge.

"What do you want?" the original speaker demands.

"Haven't you heard?" Quain asks. "Alec and I are assisting the Task Force that's hunting that vigilante."

"Yes," Alec says, "The one that handed you your asses," and he emits a low chuckle, then downs the remnants of his vodka.

"And before you get all bent out of shape," Quain says, leaning onto the table, arms outstretched within his black leather coat, palms on the wood, "Gnegon sent us."

The man lights up a cigarette, the paper giving forth a sickly, yellowed look. He squints his eyes at both, exhaling a thick plume after a lengthy inhale.

"You leashed dogs do good tricks," he observes.

"What the fuck did you say?" Alec sits up in his chair, brow furrowing, jaw flexing from clenched teeth as he brings up his right arm, elbow bent, chunky fingers curled into a tight fist.

DANCE OF THE BUTTERFLY

Quain looks right, placing a hand on his partner's shoulder, encouraging him to calm down. He holds it there for a moment, his mocha skin a contrast to the dingy gray of Alec's blazer, until the large man settles back down. He then turns to the smoker, who wears a self-satisfied smirk, and Quain lashes out with sudden speed, striking the guy in the mouth, crushing the cigarette in the process.

He looks at the other two, only one of whom reacts in any real manner, the rheumy-eyed one looking barely startled for a passing moment. He does not bother with gauging the responses of anyone else in the bar, just sets his eyes back on the smoker, who now holds his bleeding lip with one hand.

"We all have our leashes. You're right," he says, calmly, nodding, contemplatively, "My collar has a badge on it, too. You want to go back into a cell?"

The man just peers at him, eyes slit, anger evident.

"Hey, asshole," Alec chimes in, a huge smirk now on his lips, "My partner asked you a question."

The man just shakes his head.

"Good," Quain assesses. "Now, we're going to ask you some more questions. We know you didn't give much to the officers who interrogated you when you were arrested."

"Nothing at all, really," Alec expands, speaking in an aside manner, and Quain nods.

"But this is different, so you need to answer us. Okay?"

The gangster who has lately stopped smoking just looks at Quain, still seeming incapable of doing much more than squinting, head tilted to the right, almost as though he gains more sight from his left eye.

"Okay?" Quain tries again, leaning toward the man, perking his eyebrows.

"Okay," the man grumbles.

"Great," Quain grins, and he slides a chair over from a nearby table, settling into it, "Let's get started."

*****

They meet at Yami at eight in the evening, perhaps late for some, but her work schedule had dictated the time of their rendezvous. Skothiam had offered, of course, to pick her up, but she had insisted on meeting at the eatery. He understands the caution.

He had arrived earlier, wanting to be there first and have a moment to evaluate the restaurant. The warm illumination and tones please him, the décor a pristine, modern take on traditional Asian styles. The place is somewhat busy, but not overly so, and he manages to procure a corner table in a more romantic section, the walls a mahogany hue, the carpet a more obvious red dispersed with black patterns.

Lilja arrives not long after, and he sees her across the way, her striking hair drawing the eye. He notices that she has changed since work, opting for a somewhat darker arrangement of clothing with her button-down blouse, skirt at mid-thigh, and black pumps. It all even further accentuates the contrast of her vivid red locks tumbling down past her shoulders. He watches as she speaks to the hostess, then looks about. Her sparkling eyes finally find him, and he gives a signaling wave with the gentle raise of his right hand, standing as she walks over to the table, a light smile on her lips.

She notices that he also has opted for something different for this evening out, indeed continuing the similarity in having gone for tones of a darker hue, the thin, barely perceptible, vertical stripes of his shirt serving as the only hindrance to a uniform blackness. The sleeves are French style, folded back and secured with cuff links of what appears silver and black onyx. He does not sport a jacket, though, and the shirt is open at the collar.

"Please," he says, gesturing to the other chair, reaching the short distance and aiding in pulling it out.

"Thank you," she replies, slipping into it, accepting his assistance at settling in.

He gazes upon her for a moment, long enough to take in the sight but not so much a duration as to cause awkwardness. Her lips are very well formed, lush, but not overly so, the top shaped delicately, demure, the bottom fuller. A subtle splash of freckling accents both sides of her face from below each temple to down over her cheeks, the bones beneath giving a high, smooth appearance to them. Her nose is subtly aquiline,

DANCE OF THE BUTTERFLY

the tip soft. Her chin provides a graceful curve, showing some prominence, the width a bit more than that of her bottom lip.

Her pale skin is smooth, soft-looking, alabaster, and her almond eyes look fully upon him, seeming to sparkle, giving forth shades of such a frosty blue as to appear white, darkening toward the edges of the iris, some parts even gray. Her lashes are long, thick, brought forth even more by the touch of her make-up.

"You look very nice," he comments, after he has reseated himself, giving her a pleasant smile.

"Thank you," she smiles in return, "So do you."

He grins further at this, dipping his head once, "Thank you."

He cannot quite figure her out, though that would be expected at this juncture, but she holds an interesting mix of bold and bashful. She notes the strength in his forwardness, even as much as it is carried in culture and gentility, though one could presume a touch of impatience in such things.

A moment of silence passes. He looks upon her, noting that she casts her eyes about. She eventually looks back, noting his observation, and the barest touch of a flush touches her cheeks.

"Are you familiar with this place?" he asks.

"No," she shakes her head very lightly, "Are you?"

He emits a short, soft chuckle, "No. I enjoy Japanese food, but I am not that familiar with the city, so I just looked up a place that might be suitable. I do hope you like it."

"Is it your favorite?" she asks, moving in the chair, making herself more comfortable.

"Japanese food?" he replies, a smile on his lips beneath the blink of his eyes, a touch befuddled by the question.

She nods, then raises her chin at the end of the motion, peering into his eyes, eager for the answer.

"Well, I had not much thought on it," he says, still smiling, indecisive as well as perhaps wilting the barest bit under her scrutiny. "Hmmm, well, I suppose it is, though I much prefer sushi over the other options."

She nods slowly, absorbing this information as carefully as she might do the same in her profession. Her attention shifting as she does, looking more right, outward, as though to again casually study her surroundings. He watches this, even glancing briefly in the direction of her gaze.

Their waiter arrives, but he is quickly dismissed after they place a drink order.

"And yours?" he says, looking at her.

She returns her focus to him, blinking, her face looking open, fresh, somewhat unlike the more generally studied, polite, if not even subtly guarded expression to which he has grown used.

"My ...?" she leads.

"-Favorite food," he elaborates, still showing that pleasant smile, though the right side tries to edge up further.

"Oh," she nods, looking down, her lips coming together.

He notices a movement at the lower edges of her jaw as she ponders. A few minutes pass. Their drinks are delivered amidst quietly murmured thanks, and then she finally speaks.

"I'm not really sure what is my favorite food. It changes. I like many foods, if they are prepared well. I like a good steak, I really enjoy well-made pasta, I like smoked and raw salmon. I like sushi. I like reindeer. I like soups. I like good food, and I really can't name one absolute favorite. I'm also open to try different foods."

His grin has grown throughout her response, and when she stops, she blinks at him, her head tilting to the left. He notices as her own smile changes, lips parting, then she looks down as her cheeks become more prominent from the increasing grin.

"And I thought we had to pick one," he comments, and they share a brief chuckle.

"Sorry," she finally says, shoulders coming up a bit as her eyes shift to him, then away.

"It's fine. Really."

They continue the exchange of light-seeming, though subtly insightful banter throughout the meal, taking their time. He has ordered a bottle of Rikyubai sake, served chilled, which they finish off over the course of the evening. Once they have completed the meal, she asks the waiter to bring them a pot of sencha green tea.

DANCE OF THE BUTTERFLY

It takes but a moment to arrive, but the short time has been spent in quiet, the two looking at each other, occasional glances given to their surroundings, but the main focus still shared betwixt the pair. The ceramic pot is set down on the table, somewhat ornate, but not overly so, accompanied by two matching drinking bowls. She politely dismisses the waiter then raises the small lid of the pot to peer inside, leaning over for an inhale through her nose. He watches her closely, baring of a respectful amusement, and she nods to him, agreeable to what she has discerned.

She then pours a decent amount of the steaming, green liquid into a cup, and he is surprised when she turns the vessel, then dips her head to him and offers him the drink. He blinks in confusion but manages to return the gesture, taking the bowl.

"Thank you."

She smiles at him, pleasantly, then after it is obvious he is waiting, she bids of him, "Drink."

"Aren't you going to join me?"

"Just drink," she invites again.

He then raises the cup, sipping from it under her keenly watchful eye.

"Is it good?"

"Oh, yes," he says.

She smiles at this then holds out her hands, a light motion of the first two fingers of her right hand indicating to him that she wants the bowl. He decides not to question and gives it back to her. She smiles again, giving another dip of her head, which he returns, and then she turns the object, partaking of its contents.

"Mmmm, yes," she says whilst nodding, swallowing, "It is very good."

She then pours some tea into the other bowl, handing this one to him. He looks at her with some confusion but takes this, sipping of it as she continues with the other. A moment passes as they quietly enjoy the beverage.

"Was that a sort of tea ceremony?" he finally asks.

She offers him a gentle smile, "Not quite. They do have a nice enough flower arrangement there," she points behind him, and he turns to see that indeed there is an unobtrusive arrangement of white flowers in a tall, narrow vase, standing atop a pedestal there in the corner, back-lit, "But many of the crucial elements are missing, and you really ought to prepare the tea yourself for the ceremony. I just wanted to do something similar."

"Thank you," he smiles, and she returns it. "That has made it very special," he adds, and this causes a very light flush to take her pale flesh, but she does not look away.

*****

"The research is coming along well," he says, having taken the time to change into a pair of black, silk pajamas and pour a small measure of brandy.

"I hope so," speaks the person on the monitor.

He glances over from his casual wanderings in the room, noting the image of his mother. She had left him a message, wanting to know how things were going, asking him to call tonight, no matter the hour. He knows she is something of a night owl, but he also knows that regardless of how old they get, she will always be the worrying mother.

She also does not look her age, which is just shy of seventy. Her full, straight hair is out, the silver coloring a luster, where it had once been a rich sable. She also appears to have already made herself ready for bed, perhaps reading or some such until he had called.

He prepares to speak again, but she presses on.

"You've been at it for a full week now. Have you learned anything?"

"Yes," he says, sipping from the brandy, letting the warmth have its way with him, "But you know as well as I do that the Three Books comprise a mystery of their own. They do not easily reveal the secret. It is another of the reasons we do not fully understand them. Were they written as a safeguard or as a weapon of annihilation?"

She sighs, and he pauses in his sudden drift into musing, his eyes blinking back to her crisp image. He knows his own is being relayed to her, the small, state-of-the-art camera even set to track his movement.

DANCE OF THE BUTTERFLY

"You and your father are much better at this than I am," she remarks, and he nods. "Though I did have an interesting talk with Nicole."

"Oh?" he leads, eyebrows perking, and he slips into the fine, cushioned leather chair.

"You were out late tonight," she observes, "And you sound a bit anxious. Is everything alright?"

"Yes, everything is fine," he says, giving a very slight curl to his lips.

"Anything on Denman?" she shifts gears again, mentioning the Malkuth who had recently come on staff at the university.

"Nothing out of the ordinary. I am sparing some surveillance to that end, but I'd think that less attention from us would be the better method."

"Yes, well, if we're to assume he does not know you are there. He's very subtle and tricky."

"Yes," he nods slowly, deeply, "I know," exhaling at length through his nose, as he looks away, pondering. "I might risk more general observation."

"Has he been to see the Book?" she asks. "If he is there, they obviously suspect, and the first place he'd look would be the library's collection."

"That is quite an assumption," he replies, eyes back to hers, and he notes the narrowing. "Not of which I am aware," he tries to placate by answering her question, "I have been spending a good portion of the days there, and he has not stopped by when I've been there. I can't exactly ask the librarian if he has been by. That would arouse too much suspicion."

"We just need to get that book out of the collection."

"I am working on that, but it seems the university is not in any mood to part with it. They have money, so offering an endowment may be less attractive than the prestige of having the book itself."

"Then offer them more."

He exhales, pausing in his response to sip of his brandy, "The negotiations are underway. It has only been a week. I cannot appear too eager. I am sure the Malkuths would be watching for something of that sort, just as are we."

"If we're to assume they know the book is in the collection at all," she hurls a barb at him, a self-satisfied smirk to her lips.

He grins, a forced exhalation of breath though his nostrils, "Yes, Mother."

They both share a short chuckle at that.

"Oh, I spoke with Charleston," she brings up, and he raises his chin, eyes widening to a more open, neutral gaze. "He's found a few decent choices. He'll need your input, of course, but I helped to eliminate some more obvious options."

"Thank you," he gives a warm smile, "I'll contact him tomorrow."

She nods, also smiling, "Nicole may also call you tomorrow. She has some ideas on how to assess and protect the situation."

"Alright," he acquiesces, for there is little reason to object, and he senses it would result in an argument.

His sister has quite different methods than his own, her attunement to certain ways far out-stripping anything in recent history. It sometimes worries him, to be honest, as though her mind had evolved beyond typical human expectation. She can be very useful with particular things, but he worries she'd compromise the subtlety required here. She is certainly not that reckless, but the very uniqueness of her presence and methods may be a beacon.

"I'll let you go, then," she offers another warm smile, "Good night, Skot. I love you."

"Good night, Mom. I love you, too," and the call is ended.

He sits for a moment, in the silence, computer powered down, as he ponders his evening's activities - going out on the date, seeming to be pushing toward establishing something romantic with Lilja. He is taken by it and quite obviously by her. He had not expected something like this at all, but he is also not inclined to ignore such attraction. He knows she is also experiencing it.

He had let the thought pass his mind of telling his mother, but he would not have anticipated the most positive of responses. He has been single for many years now, and though he knows she'd like him to find someone, she worries of his being hurt as he was before. She'd also

DANCE OF THE BUTTERFLY

likely be displeased with the age disparity between himself and the young curator-librarian, warning him that a young lady would be more apt to want children. He smirks to himself at that thought, as if she'd not want more grandchildren.

It is always a precarious thing when bringing someone new into the family, though such thoughts regarding that are obviously premature. He still ponders them, though, for he knows this is not some casual attempt at dating and pleasurable distraction while he is at work here. There is something about her which pulls at him deeply, a particular quality that he finds nigh undeniable. He shall continue.

CHAPTER FOUR

People mill about in the briefing room, some seated in the available metal chairs, which only provide a modicum of comfort and stability, others content to stand. The general level of chatter subsides as the captain enters. The older man walks to the front of the room, shirt sleeves rolled up, looking to already be under stress this early in the shift. The initial talk follows usual routine, many attentions focused elsewhere until something out of the ordinary perks everyone up.

"Kenneth?" the captain calls out, looking over at the so-named detective, "How are things coming with the vigilante?"

"No new sightings. We're still going through initial intelligence gathering, checking city camera records, sending out officers all over the place to talk to people-."

"What?" the captain interrupts, brow wrinkling, "We don't want the general public to know about this."

"Yes, sir," Kenneth affirms, nodding, "We're being discreet."

"Right, good," the captain says, pondering, then, "You've got enough help?"

"Yes, sir. In addition to the original Task Squad, Detectives Sladky and Contee have volunteered to help."

The captain looks over at Alec and Quain, "You two find out anything useful yet?"

"No, sir," Quain speaks up.

"Alright, well, keep at it. We need some results ... *soon*."

General nodding occurs from most of those on the special squad as the captain pauses, collecting his thoughts.

"Alright," he says, as an obvious preamble, gaining even more attention from the tone, "Some of you have heard, but last night we had a bad murder. A young lady, late teens to early twenties, was found dead, pretty much gutted, very messy scene. It's been given to Pasztor and Mahler, but here's the part that has to remain in-house," and this perks up the already poised focus. "It's not the first. Forensics has related it to another, similar homicide from almost a month ago. This one was another female, twenty-three years old, unlicensed sex worker. It's also looking like this most recent one was in the same trade, too. We're still waiting on all the necessary results, but we may have a serial killer here."

This gets a rise of murmured reactions from the group, some particular expletives piercing above the din.

"Alright, calm down, people," the captain presses. "This is being shared as a courtesy, and just in case anything comes up that could be useful. We don't want this getting out of control. We're having a press conference today."

"Is that a good idea?" chimes in one of the detectives.

The captain cuts his eyes over, the steel within them evident, "We're having a press conference today," he repeats. "You all know the routines. This is bad news for us, and with that vigilante thing ... well, we don't need it. Let's get out there and get results, or people will think we're useless."

*****

The media is a difficult beast to control, especially in this Information Age. The prevalence of such data, though, may present its own challenge with all the chaff hiding the promising wheat. There are those quite adept at monitoring such things, especially if they possess the acumen to properly coax and even manipulate the coded language riding the infrastructure of the data highways.

Articles and tidbits have been marked, cross-referenced, verified. There shows no tremendous effort to hide this story, but it certainly does not warrant the fanfare of some banner headline on popular news sites. What this may say of society is largely not the concern of the one who has taken note. Reliable conclusions have been discerned, even reports accessed that should not be available to the general public, but hacking is not out of the equation here. The trail of breadcrumbs is really quite visible if one only knows where to look.

The unfortunate young lady had been kidnapped three days ago. Tomorrow marks the deadline for her ransom, and her family may barely manage to come up with the money. They had been told, of course, to not go to the police, but they did. This afforded more information to those who may know how to find such. The modus operandi was quite regular for this criminal organization, what with their continued procurement of humans for ransom, or slavery. Another of their methods is to promise people passage from the East to the West, then charge them unexpected and exorbitant fees once they are away from home and support. If they cannot pay, they find themselves forcibly indentured, to put it mildly. This poor girl still stands a chance of joining many others as a drug-addicted slave in the sex trade, and she is barely seventeen.

The purring motorcycle rockets down the roadway, much further from the city for this jaunt, around 400 kilometers, a few good hours of travel, the trek begun well after dark, arrival slated for well before sunrise, though the window of opportunity is still narrow. Such parameters generally prefer to be avoided to mitigate risk, but urgency grows with this one.

The vehicle gets left some distance away, off the road in a secure area amidst a small, though thick stand of trees. After parking, the H&K G36C is retrieved from the bag slung over the rider's shoulders, fore grip, suppressor, and magazine affixed with the apparent ease of familiarity. The landscape out here is mostly flat and cleared as pasture, farmland in use or waiting for its chance to produce. The darkly-garbed rider jogs easily over the earth, coming in from the lightly forested northwest side, the jika-tabi giving forth short-lived, crunchy sounds from the soil and turf.

The single story farmhouse in the distance is a good choice, what with the easily observed angles of approach in all directions, it being situated here a couple of kilometers outside of the nearby hamlet. The lone figure, though, arrives in the dark of night, the special goggles strapped to the head giving excellent vision. Some sparse illumination does emerge from the small hovel, but it is obviously not intended to thwart intruders. Still, the vigilante is not reckless, and with the

DANCE OF THE BUTTERFLY

appearance of the sniper team and extra cameras and guards at the warehouse, it is obvious they are aware of the attention and taking some counter-measures.

The wooden structure is longer than it is wide, the front door off-center toward the left side as it faces toward the dirt road that leads to it. A meager porch raises up from the ground to the entryway. The small, southern face shows a single window. Two more are on the front, and the back is similar with a door in the center, three steps leading down from it.

The approach is slowed as the rider nears, stopping some thirty meters away, crouching, fingertips of one hand pressing against the ground to aid in stability, silently surveilling, listening. This position is held for some time, evidence of patience, until movement is spied within the small house, and the rear door opens. The figure lowers slowly and smoothly to the ground until nearly flat upon it, still watching.

The lone person, a man, comes out, a Skorpion SMG slung over his shoulder, the weapon at his lower back. It does not seem he is on patrol, merely stretching his legs. He ambles around, moving further away until he stops before a rise of scrub brush, squaring his feet and reaching for his fly with obvious intent. He manages to get mostly done with his urination before he loses consciousness, collapsed to the ground by the quick, silent approach of the figure, any noise made lost to the spluttering sound of his bladder relief. Zip-ties are applied, and the figure moves to the house.

It will likely not be too long before the knocked-out guard is missed, so the expediency rises. The window to the right of the door is somewhat obscured, but not completely blocked. The night vision goggles are raised, for the single light emits from this room, and a quick peer inside reveals three other men sitting about a dingy, wooden table, bottles, money, and cards giving clear indication of how they pass their time. They exchange quiet words, looking to merely be engaging in casual conversation as they await the return of their fourth. They are all armed. A pump-action shotgun is spied atop the table, along with more Skorpions, though they may be carrying pistols or knives as well.

The other window is entirely covered by what appears to be a thick, fabric secured from the inside, and it may be a reasonable bet to think the quarry is in this portion of the house. Still, assumptions may lead to danger. Time is short, but more quiet observation is conducted, the figure pulling forth a fiberscope and slipping it through a weakened portion of the window frame to peer inside.

Darkness cloaks the room, but a narrow cot may be discerned up against the north wall, tucked in close to the west barrier. A covered bundle lies atop it, the light colored hair visible on the portion of the head that is revealed just at the top of the dark blanket. It is obviously the girl, and the slow respiration shows she is alive. The rest of the room is obscured in darkness, but it is quite small and seems incapable of thoroughly hiding anyone from the view of the scope.

The vigilante retrieves the thin, lengthy tool, scurrying about to the south side of the house even as a plan of attack finds itself formulating. A small breaching charge is secured to the window frame, the fuse-wire lit, and the figure rushes to the rear, waiting at the southern-most window. The loud report comes quickly, mere seconds after the explosive is planted, wood and glass shattering into the room, bringing along an obscuring cloud of detritus along with the obvious concussive force of the tactical bomb.

The noise covers the coughing spurt of sub-sonic shots being fired through the window, assault rifle held firm, the stock of the compact weapon having been unfolded just before use, aim enhanced through the ACOG, the internal phosphor adding extra illumination. After a series of such expulsions, the attacker uses the barrel to clear out the glass from this window, leaping through with an obvious agility, moving in rapidly, kicking away noticeable weapons that may be in reach of the now supine men.

Two appear to have been rendered unconscious, the one nearest the window suffering the brunt, and a concerned glance is spared to the bloodied man, though he does breathe for now. The one who had been seated furthest away is splayed out on his back, also obviously breathing and bloodied. The third is in a heap a bit a ways from the toppled table, having fallen back from the charge then taking shots to his legs. He is struggling to move, leaving a thick trail of blood, grunts and moans emerging. He looks up, fright taking his wide eyes as he spies the assailant.

DANCE OF THE BUTTERFLY

"No, no!" he pleads, his right arm stretching out, the hand an ineffective defense to the pointed assault rifle.

The gun is held aimed, even as the vigilante's left hand drops from the fore grip, and the small, black-painted electroshock weapon is retrieved and used. The wounded man is rendered unconscious rather quickly, and the figure rushes over, momentarily setting down the main weapon in order to pull out the prongs and reset the small device before putting it away. The guard is zip-tied, then checked quickly for any life-threatening wounds.

Attention is now turned to the other two, and a pistol is noticed near the right hand of the man who had been on the other side of the table, the gun less than a foot from his waist. A few quick steps closes the distance, the H&K again in sure hands and ready to be used, as the handgun is kicked away.

And the man moves in that moment, motion like a blur as he grabs the ankle of the supporting leg to trip the intruder. Training is evident as the figure reacts instantly, rolling backward and rising in a practiced motion, aiming the G36C at the guard who had been lately playing possum. The gun is knocked away by a powerful kick that causes the other to reel back. The man proves very fast, springing his greater size and bulk to action with his own display of experience.

A powerful right hook curves forward, the eyes of the highly-trained guard focused like locked steel on his opponent, but it is dodged with a fast duck, taking advantage of the height disparity, bringing up a quick knee to collide sharply with the body. The man takes the hit well, delivering a fierce hook to the torso of the intruder, causing another backward reel and loss of breath, and before a counter-move may be done, the guard takes down his masked opponent, moving atop and choking with both hands, leveraging the weight of his upper body into the deadly hold.

The vigilante crosses arms atop the dangerous grip of the guard, pushing down, but the other proves too strong, resisting the attempt, hands squeezing off the much needed blood supply and oxygen. Making another quick effort, hips are raised up as high as they can go and brought down with force, striking down with elbows onto the choking arms at the same time, adding power from the abdomen into the movement. The guard's arms bend from this, and the pressure from the choke is released.

In that instant of opportunity, the vigilante quickly retrieves the knife strapped to the left shoulder of the combat harness, stabbing the guard in the upper right arm, burying the sharp, black blade in the bicep. The knife stays in as the man jerks away, and the masked figure brings a knee up high, then thrusting out with a sharp, driving kick to the chest, pushing him back.

The guard manages to get to his feet quickly, a grimace of anger given to his opponent as he jerks the blade free, holding it now as his own weapon, blood upon it catching the meager lamp light in the room. He rushes, and the vigilante rapidly pulls the 9mm Glock 19 from its leg holster, pointing, holding with both hands, pulling the trigger, and hitting the attacker three times in the chest in tight arrangement.

The man goes down, struggling for breath, blood spraying from his mouth even as the desperate attempts at respiration produce a horrible sucking sound from the wound. He does not have long.

Holding the pistol poised and pointed, the figure cautiously moves closer, bending down just enough to grab the knife and re-sheathe it. The pistol is then returned to its holster as the figure runs a quick self-assessment, checking for broken ribs, rubbing on the neck, the black, tactical gloves allowing for sensitivity and precision. Another moment is spared in checking on the mortally wounded man, but nothing may be done at this point to aid him. The other two are given a quick examination, making sure the zip-ties are secured and they are reasonably stabilized from any serious damage. Then, retrieving the assault rifle, the figure heads to the only other room, finding the door unlocked.

The girl is awake, but her appearance and lack of alertness indicates she is under the effects of drugs. The figure approaches cautiously, both to not needlessly frighten the young lady and in case of any further traps. The man who has been shot displayed awareness and skill far beyond the other sentries. A presumption is made that he was here in anticipation of this arrival, here with intent to kill.

Soothing, whispered words are issued from behind the mask, further attempts to reassure the girl. She shows signs of coming around, though

DANCE OF THE BUTTERFLY

the stupefying fog of intoxication still shows evident upon her. A pair of steel handcuffs hold her secured to the metal frame of the small bed, attached to her left wrist. The vigilante returns to the other room, finding the key on the one who had been rendered unconscious by the breaching blast.

"C ... call," emits a pitiful grunt and whine from the other man, the one who has been shot in the legs and shocked, "help ... need help."

He is no threat, and the figure moves back in to release the girl. Another of the disposable cell phones is used, summoning local emergency services. Their remoteness may result in some time for arrival, but they are not so totally isolated that it should take too long. It is quite possible they were already called in response to the noise of the explosion and pistol shots.

"The police are on their way," speaks the whispering voice from behind the mask, "You'll be fine."

The young lady blinks once, very slowly, having trouble with it and having to work to do so. Her head lulls to the right. She manages to weakly nod, moving to try to sit on the edge of the bed, and the person is quick to help. She rubs her left wrist where the cuff had been, then swallows, heavily lidded eyes moving to look again at her savior.

"Let me get you some water," speaks the voice, and the figure goes to the kitchenette in the main room, finding a reasonably clean glass and splashing some water into it from the faucet.

At least the water is clear, and the girl accepts it, needing help to bring it up and have a sip. Sirens are then heard in the distance, and the figure gently guides the girl's other hand to also hold the glass of water, positioning it in her lap. The reward is an attempt at a smile, and this is more than enough.

By the time the local police enter the farmhouse to assess the bloody scene, the vigilante is gone.

*****

Skot is greeted at the secure door to the Rare Collections room by an unfamiliar face, a young woman with dark blonde hair and something of a plain, if not utilitarian appearance to her.

"Good morning, Mr. Felcraft. I am Amanda Honeycutt. Miss Perhonen sends her apologies, but she took an unexpected sick day today."

"Aaah, I see," he replies, making a very good effort of hiding the sharp spike of concern which rises inside him. "Well," he smiles politely, "I do hope she gets well soon, and very nice to meet you."

She returns the smile, then leads the way into the room.

He offers her thanks, seating himself at his usual table, setting up his laptop, the advanced machine surging to life and readiness quite quickly. He is prepared when Ms. Honeycutt brings him the book. She also offers him coffee, which he graciously accepts, then gets to work.

After a time, he finds himself having difficulty focusing on his continued study and analysis of the book. Certainly there is some tedium associated with it, though he does enjoy the imbibing of the knowledge, and trying to piece together and cross reference the clues is quite stimulating, but if he is honest with himself, his thoughts keep drifting to her. He wonders if she is alright. Should he bother her with a phone call, maybe a text? He also is given to ponder why she did not text him to let him know she'd be out. Certainly their one date does not constitute a serious, personal relationship, but such a notice could have been delivered out of professional courtesy.

He realizes then what he is doing, even as he completely ignores the book and forgets that Ms. Honeycutt is in the same chamber going about some of her own busy work. He has grown attached to Lilja, and it seems, perhaps even a touch possessive. He smiles thinly, shaking his head. She certainly does not deserve that, but it does make him consider himself and the obvious affect she is having on him. He is disappointed to not get to see her and spend time with her today, and that is the crux of it. He hopes she misses him, too, in some small way, and he hopes she is well. If she is out again tomorrow, he will contact her. For now, he resolves to trying to put that sufficiently out of his mind to get back to his work.

The secrets of the book are not forgiving, the pieces of the puzzle hardly evident enough to cloud such things with other thoughts. He pours over diagrams, illustrations, categorization, even sections of more poetic verse. The mystery eludes him. He wonders at the sudden fortune that

DANCE OF THE BUTTERFLY

after so many decades upon decades, two of the Three are suddenly within reach, and though it had proven naïve, he had held hope that merely examining the contents would catalyze the revelation.

As it is now, he spends many hours of most days, since he has been here, collecting information, gaining familiarity, reading and rereading, and then he compares these to similar examinations of the other book. That one, of course, is not with him due to obvious security reasons, but he has a very good digital version as well as means of access to the original if need be.

After some length, he decides to call it an early day. He thanks Ms. Honeycutt, packing up his laptop and pulling the strap of the case over his shoulder. He holds a piece of scrap paper upon which are printed the locations of two books in the library which may help him. Lilja had given him a temporary pass, allowing him to check out the regular books of the library, though if any are needed by student or faculty, he has to return them right away. It does not take him long to find them, and he is in no rush, feeling rather comfortable amongst rows of books, and he heads to the front with the two tomes – a translated version of *Demoniality: Or, Incubi and Succubi* by Ludovico Maria Sinistrari and *Observations Upon the Prophecies of Daniel and the Apocalypse of St. John* by Isaac Newton. He has both of these books in his library back home, or did before the fire, and he suspects they may prove useful.

He comes up short when still some distance from the checkout counter, noting something of a surprisingly long line there, but this is not what causes his hesitation. A particular man stands with the others, who are obviously students, and he holds a few books of his own, intent upon borrowing them. Skothiam recognizes him by sight, one Denman Malkuth, the man bearing of fine, raven-black hair which he has coifed as though he were an actor or model, his entire presentation one of refinement. His wears a textured, dark gray tweed three piece suit, the shirt a lighter color to offset the even darker, solid tie. He appears alone until a trio of students near him engages him in conversation. He responds with instant and obvious charm as he speaks to them, seeming all the world like a lofty, accomplished professor who still has not lost touch with those whom he instructs.

It is all an act, of course.

Skothiam manages to turn away without garnering any notice, doubling back and moving over to some nearby shelves where he may silently observe. He notes than Denman only speaks to the students when he is spoken to, a subtle sign of his intent for any who may be carefully watching. The line finally moves enough for him to get to the counter, and he again puts on that disarming smile, going through the necessary protocol to temporarily procure the books he has brought forth.

Skothiam narrows his eyes, peering, but the distance is too great. He wants to know what books his rival may be getting. This might let him know if Denman is on the same trail as he, but if there were any doubt, such is shortly thrown aside, for the well-dressed man turns back into the library after completing his transaction. Skot maintains his silent surveillance, watching as the other strides unerringly to the downward staircase, heading undoubtedly to the Rare Collections room.

He curses mentally, but he does not give pursuit. He would assuredly be discovered if he were to do so. He also does not want to risk being found out, so he sets his own two books on a nearby cart, making a quick exeunt.

"Goodbye, Mr. Felcraft," bids a nearby voice, and he jerks his head up to see Marcel offering a warm farewell.

He cringes inwardly, though certainly the intonation has not been loud enough to carry all the way down into the lower floor. He nods his head once, putting on a polite smile, then heads out of the old building.

*****

Lilja's thoughts today have gone somewhat to Skot, but they have also travelled about and wandered in many other directions. She lies on the dark gray couch beneath a warm, brown blanket, ensconced amongst the rich red pillows in her comfortable pajamas, having some hot tea. Her clothing shows a warm, creamy white, somewhat in contrast to the other dark, earthy tones of the apartment, any invading light from outside succumbing to the dark curtains. A tall, black floor lamp gives gentle illumination to the living room, a warming cast spreading out from its place near her.

DANCE OF THE BUTTERFLY

She holds her drink close, letting the steam waft up from the piquant brew, inhaling of the black currant aroma before having another sip. She starts, sitting up straighter, her arm going out instinctively to balance the mug as her cat bounds up onto the couch.

"Dali," she chides, though her tone does not discourage the animal in the least, the large feline nuzzling up to her, purring quite audibly.

A warm curve traces her lips, though, as she settles back down, sipping more of the tea, her left hand petting over Dali, the cat rising up on its legs to press into the affection. She then moves her hand up to scratch behind his ears, something the long-haired, gray mackerel tabby cat obviously enjoys, focusing his big green eyes on her, giving a single meow.

"Miau," she replies in a cute tone, putting on her best cat imitation, scrunching up her eyes and nose and bringing her face closer to his as she continues the scritching.

She spares a glance to the television, the volume so low as to barely be heard, then she has another generous sip of her tea. She sets the mug on the nearby end table, then reaches for the open paperback which has been set facedown near her.

"Dali, I can't read this if you are on it," she smirks, for the large mongrel has indeed set his right front paw on the cover, though he moves it away as she pulls.

Her resuming of reading the science fiction novel is shortly interrupted as Dali butts his head into her once the petting has ceased for too long. She hardly notices, her left hand going back to stroking, and the feline settles down, close in against her, adding his warmth to that held in by the blanket. He does not display any disappointment during the short breaks that she uses her left hand to turn the page, though his colorful eyes pay close attention.

She eventually pauses in her reading, setting the book aside and picking up the mug, having more of her tea. She seems to just as quickly forget the novel, her eyes pointed at the screen of the forty-eight inch, high definition, flat screen television. The talking heads relay more news. She zones out, her hand resting against Dali's ample rib cage. He looks up at her, curious, silently pleading for attention. After a moment of this observation, he gives forth one, short, high-pitched mewl.

Lilja blinks, then looks down at him, smiling, "Miau," she says again, moving her head side to side, and he gives forth another vocalization, then rises up, stretching and he springs down, padding over across the living room to the kitchen. When he arrives at the bowl on the ground, he turns back, giving a more insistent noise.

"Fine," she exhales, eyes rolling, and she sets the book and mug of tea on the end table then rises from the couch, the blanket falling away, mostly onto the sofa, though a bit trails off to the dark, maple wood flooring.

She straightens on her socked feet, stretching gingerly, emitting a groan and grimace as though from body aches. She takes a moment to loosen up, though a light grunt and furrow of her brow indicates more sensitivity, so she stops, walking over to Dali, who rises up from having lain on the floor, giving out a series of talkative, impatient mewls.

"Joo joo, katti," she says, talking back in a higher pitched tone than her usual, angling her head forward, eyebrows raised, which only gets a louder, more demanding meow.

He then follows her as she opens the cabinet, weaving within her legs, nuzzling and headbutting as she brings forth the bag of dry cat food, shaking a serving into the bowl. Dali quickly gets to munching, eagerly snatching the small morsels into his mouth, then raising his head to eat.

She sets the bag on the counter top instead of immediately returning it to its place, and she leans up against it, cocking a hip into the closed door of the cabinet below, her right arm sliding down, a bent elbow also offering some support. Her eyes unfocus as thoughts again wander, her head moving in a barely perceptible bend to the left.

Her musings meander to him, and though she is not the best at recognizing her own feelings or admitting things to herself, she does wonder how he reacted to her absence at the library today. She also ponders if he may have found anything new or figured out anymore of the curious puzzle which lies shrouded in such mystery. She then thinks on how he may be in general and what has occupied his time, and then if he might would want to have another date sometime.

She does not immediately notice she now has a dreamy smile on her lips.

DANCE OF THE BUTTERFLY

*****

The three men stand on the loading dock, the rickety, paneled garage door opened. Coat collars are raised against the chill, residual precipitation hanging in the air like the tattered remnants of a gray curtain.

"How do you like this old warehouse?" Gnegon asks of the two police detectives on his payroll.

Alec peers over, eyes narrowing almost to a squint. Quain meanders out to the edge of the raised concrete, looking out into the misty afternoon, all colors muted by the gloomy weather. The man's beefy partner looks at him, but when it seems no one else will talk, he turns back to the gangster, pitching a comment.

"It's old."

"That it is," Gnegon chuckles, nodding slowly. "Ah," he turns as another man walks rapidly over, delivering a steaming mug of strong, dark coffee, from which a tentative taste is taken then an affirming nod given before he returns his focus to the other men, musing, "I retired this one years ago. It is small, too much inside the city, too risky. I prefer the larger, more secure warehouses on the outskirts ... or I did."

He takes another sip of his drink, "Are you sure you gentlemen will not have some?" he offers, slowly walking more toward where Quain stands. "Sasha makes wonderful coffee," and to emphasize, he has more of his.

"Nah, thanks, I'm good," Quain says, and Alec only shakes his head, his preference well known and apparently not being offered.

"It is difficult in a city like this," Gnegon resumes his musing tone as he joins Quain in looking out over the gray-cloaked, dripping wet environ. "Coastal cities have it much easier ... like Antwerp or Los Angeles!" he announces the last as though having recently come to the conclusion, giving something of an aside comment. "They have everything in abundance in Los Angeles."

He takes another sip of his hot coffee, the other two men content with waiting. "Shipping further inland is riskier and the logistics." He shakes his head, "And now with this *vigilante* giving me so much trouble," he says the word like a curse, his thin lips curving into a frown.

"It is beginning to cut into my profits," he adds, his eyes narrowing, then he pulls in a deep breath, turning, looking to the interior of the place. "So I have decided to dust off this relic, and it is not modern, no electronics, and I shall not use them. No cameras, no computers."

The two cops share a look, then Alec peers down into the depths of the building, noting that some men in jumpsuits are at work and some crates and boxes are on the shelves.

"Well, you've got something going on," he notes.

"Yes, I do," Gnegon nods, "Would it surprise you to know that there is coffee in those?"

"Coffee?" Alec wrinkles up his a face. "Drugs?" he posits.

"No," the other flatly answers. "The coffee is not camouflage. Coffee is a vastly traded commodity. I do engage in some legitimate business. Other crates hold cigarettes. Coffee and cigarettes, two things we've turned into quasi-necessities." He eyeballs the two men for a moment, taking stock of them, continuing with his own stimulating drink. "I understand you have questioned my men regarding the attack on the warehouse."

"Hey, if any of them are complaining, they should have been more-," Alec begins, but he stops as the other raises a hand.

"They failed in their duty. I spent money on better cameras, even hired in more guards, and they still did not stop the *vigilante*. They deserve more punishment than they have had so far."

"The intel is all over the place," Quain informs, turning to better face Gnegon, hands in his jacket pockets. "According to them, we've got a perpetrator who is invisible, a shadow, inhumanly fast, a ninja, short, tall, thin, large, hell the truck driver even said he thought it might have been a kid."

"What?" comes the gangster's incredulous response.

"Yeah, so we're still trying to get more solid information."

"That is a shame," Gnegon adds, "Well, as I said, this is cutting into my profits, so your pay will be reduced."

"Hang on a moment," Alec tenses.

"No, I will not," the other turns to face him fully, speaking smoothly, his naturally narrow eyes fixed unflinchingly on the man. "This is hurting me and my business, so why should I continue to pay you at the regular rate? But there will be a nice reward to you both if you stop this pest."

"Fine," Quain clips, the word serving to placate his partner.

"Besides, I have not been idle," Gnegon announces, reaching into the pocket of his dark topcoat to retrieve a basic looking, black flash drive, offering it to Quain who perks his eyebrows before removing his own hand from his jacket, taking it.

"What's this?" he asks.

"An unfortunate girl named Marina Potchak went missing from her home in Lviv," he begins, casting an offhand remark. "Probably nothing of note for the authorities here, but a great concern for her family and friends, of course. It appears she fled to a farmhouse outside a small town not far inside Poland, and it seems she was possibly there against her will."

"Okay. So?"

Gnegon turns to Alec, letting the moment stretch, having another sip of his dwindling drink. "There is information on that drive. Affidavits, photographs, reports from the local police. The poor girl was murdered along with an older man who may have been an accomplice, her lover, we are not sure, but both were found dead at the scene, from multiple gunshot wounds. Those of the girl were delivered by a P90 submachinegun, a known weapon of choice for our vigilante."

Quain gives the man a studied look before speaking, "Are you saying the vigilante murdered this girl?"

Gnegon blinks to slightly wider eyes, brow rising, "No, *I* am not, but *you* will take the information there and work in conjunction with *very* cooperative members of other law enforcement groups, and I think you will find that such a conclusion is inevitable."

"There's more than one P90 out there, Gnegon," Quain remarks, reasonably, "And a ballistics report would show that it was not the vigilante's weapon, since I am," he slows his speech, raising his eyebrows, "*assuming* this information is not entirely accurate."

"I am not concerned with such trifling details, and do not bore me with some idea that only those who deserve it are in prison. We are well aware of the system in which we operate," he adds, "Now then, I have handed you something that may well aid you in taking care of the pest."

"The vigilante is already breaking the law," Alec speaks quickly over the end of the other man's utterance.

"I recall saying something to the effect of 'do not bore me'," Gnegon presses, again setting piercing eyes upon the large man. "I am aware that vigilantism is against the law, and I am also aware of the politics involved in the execution of *law*," he iterates the last word with a noticeable measure of cynicism. "You policemen know how helpful or *harmful* the general public may be in that. Now, do you think the public would be more helpful with a person who fights criminals or one who is a cold-blooded killer?"

"We get the point," Quain interjects into the ubiquitous tension between the other two men.

"Do you?" Gnegon turns his focus, "This *vigilante* is very good at what he does. You must be aware of this and the potential threat it implies, and I presume you are also aware that this person could be very difficult to catch. So, if you continue to prove incapable of catching him, and if my own measures continue to prove incapable of thwarting him, then maybe the public will help stop a kidnapper and murderer of young girls. Hmm?"

"Right," Quain concedes, "We'll look into this," he gestures outward with his pocketed right hand, where the tiny storage device now reposes. "You say there is information on local police there who will be cooperative?"

"*Very* cooperative," Gnegon reminds, "And since the girl was carried over international lines, Interpol has assigned an agent. You will also find his information in there, and he will also be *very* cooperative."

"Interpol?" Alec perks his eyebrows.

"Yes," Gnegon quips, looking pointedly at him. "You don't think you two are my only 'friends', do you?" and the man adds a smirk after the loaded question.

CHAPTER FIVE

He brightens to see her here this morning, a warm smile taking his lips, just as one paints hers with a slightly coquettish tinge in response.

"Good day, Miss Perhonen," he greets.

"Good day, Mr. Felcraft," she returns, her head even dipping a bit, those deep, blue eyes peering up at him, "How are you?"

"Oh, I am fine," he informs, following as she leads the way into the room, his gaze traveling subtly over her figure, "You were out yesterday. Are you alright?"

"Yes," she nods, looking back at him.

He thinks he spies some satisfaction in her from his inquiry, but she is not the easiest person to read. He has noticed how inward she may seem, and he knows she is a very private person, also respecting the privacy of others. He finds that commendable.

"I was just feeling a little out of sorts," she expands, finding herself compelled to offer him something else.

She is, indeed, a very private person, an aspect she has learned from the culture in which she was reared, and though he has not pried further, she wants to give him more. She walks to the table, turning, standing with her hands held in that manner that seems a default state of hers, looking something like a hostess.

He sees that she wears all black today, not entirely out of the ordinary as he comes to learn her wardrobe and style whilst at work. She has on a form-fitting turtleneck, opaque stockings, a knee-high skirt and side-zip, taper-heeled ankle boots. Her lush, red hair holds in a high ponytail, a vibrant contrast to the dark clothing.

"Thank you," he says, noting that there is the usual thermal pitcher of coffee standing on a tray set on the table, along with the two mugs and additives they prefer.

"You are welcome," she smiles in return.

He walks very near her as he goes to set up his laptop, and he is pleased to note she does not step away.

He engages her in some small talk throughout the afternoon's work, mentioning the young lady, Amanda Honeycutt, who he learns is a newer member of the staff and serving as something of an assistant to Lilja as part of her general duties. He tries to indirectly find out what Denman wanted here, but he gets nothing of that from her. He is left wondering if it is because there is nothing to say, or if she is just adhering to a concept of professional courtesy. He wants to press, but he shan't.

He also finds himself equally relieved and worried. Her being out yesterday means Denman did not meet her, but he suspects the man will be back. He is imminently concerned what may happen between them. This makes him also consider formally announcing his presence to his adversary, something over which he shall mull.

The time finds itself inexorably passing, and he looks up at her as he is packing his computer. He knows she is also done for the day, as the two had exchanged such information during their sporadic conversing.

"Would you like to join me for some coffee?" he invites her.

She walks over to the table, smiling quite warmly.

"Or tea?" he adds, grinning as his eyes spot the pitcher then look back at her.

"Oh, coffee would be nice," she answers, noting his gaze, "We Finns drink *a lot* of coffee."

They share a further deepening of their grins at this, a light chuckle emerging from him.

It takes her a little more time to finish up and then the two of them take a short stroll to a nearby café, the weather proving nice enough after the recent rains. They soon find themselves seated at a small table, outside in the more exclusive rear section, their steaming coffee in front of them.

DANCE OF THE BUTTERFLY

"What brought you here from Finland?" he begins, once they have settled in and had an initial sip of their respective drinks, "If you do not mind my asking?"

"Oh, it's fine," she offers a polite smile, then, "It's really not very easy finding the type of position I have, especially if I stayed in Southern Finland, and I had some other ... personal issues that compelled me to want to get away."

"Ahhh," he nods, noting the hesitancy, not wanting to pry and thankful for her sharing, "I came here to examine the book, of course, but it is a very lovely city." He casts his eyes about.

She does the same, looking around the area, observing quite closely even within the calm motion.

"I served for one year in the Finnish Defense Force, with some subsequent refresher trainings," she announces, and he perks his eyebrows, looking back at her, "I was Military Police."

"That is impressive," he says with obvious sincerity. "I have never served in the military. My health disqualified me."

"Oh?" she bids, bringing her mug up for more sips, using both hands, the touching tips of her fingers noticed, her eyes staying on him.

"I grew up with quite a severe case of asthma, which does crop up from time to time in my family," he explains, "Though no one personally recalls as serious a case as mine. Still, it is well under control now, if not nearly gone. It bothers me very rarely."

"That's good to hear." She gives him a warm smile.

"I am also glad you found a place for your vocational talents," he says, and they both grin at this, and his cast takes on a bit more serious tone as he says, "Otherwise we would have never met."

She nods, looking down, a light blush trying to have its way with her smooth, pale skin. He finds it very charming.

"I suppose it keeps you rather busy?" he asks, bringing his cup up for more of its contents.

She looks back at him, her hands going to her own mug, though just holding there, relaxed, "Somewhat, I suppose," she shrugs, "I also spend two nights a week at the gymnasium teaching a self-defense class for women."

He blinks, eyes peering at her in a deeper fashion, "Very impressive, Lilja. You really are a woman of many talents, aren't you?"

And she gets that shy smile and threatening flush to her skin.

"I'm just me," she says.

He can do naught else but give her a warm smile at that pronouncement.

"How long will you be here?" she suddenly asks, eyes fully upon him, her mug raised, and she has another drink after asking.

"Oh," he replies, as though considering this for the first time, "I'm not sure. As long as it takes."

She nods, also savoring her drink, then swallows.

"You like books," she observes.

"I do," he nods, thoughtfully, "Something we seem to have in common."

"Who are some of the more interesting authors you've read?"

"Ah, well, I have spent a bit of time studying the works and life of the Marquis de Sade," he answers after a brief time of pontificating.

"Oh …," she comments, a moment of silence falls as she waits to see if he continues with the subject or moves on to something else.

"Are you familiar with him?"

"Some," she nods.

He notes the hesitancy, but he decides to push it further and gauge her reaction.

"I studied him in college in an Ethics class, of all things. I cannot say I agree with all of his .. philosophy, but he is an interesting man, and an excellent writer, even if his subject matter is not always agreeable."

"The word sadism is derived from his name and actions," she informs, "What was not agreeable to you?" and she turns those big, bright eyes on him again as her cup is tilted up for another sip.

"Well, not to spoil our conversation, but he did write about a lot of violence, even toward children and babies, as well as sexual acts performed without consent. He seems to have had no boundaries when it came to his writings. Some scholars think he was a revolutionary, testing society, which he still does to this day."

"And what do you think?" she quickly asks.

DANCE OF THE BUTTERFLY

"It's a very touchy subject," he begins to carefully answer, "If one is engaging in fantasy, writing, and so forth, then I do not think that many boundaries do apply, if any. We should not be convicted for our thoughts. Actions are entirely different, and I would never condone actually undergoing many of the activities about which he writes. Doing such things to people against their consent is abhorrent to me."

She nods, contemplating, looking away. She blinks, brow furrowing the tiniest bit, "I did not know all of that about him. I just thought he wrote about things like binding women and whipping … them," her intonation slows suddenly, and she looks back up at him, realizing what she is saying, and a blush does take her at this, though she makes an effort to keep herself together.

He smiles warmly at her awkward display. "He did, at that. He is the 'S' in 'S&M' after all." He watches her closely, and he is pleased to see that she does not show any signs of disgust at this. Instead, she looks back at him, a shy smile growing on her lovely lips.

*****

Detectives Pasztor and Mahler have seen many corpses in their day, both being veterans of not only the police force in general but also as homicide inspectors. They do not show any outward signs to the condition of the body, though their distaste is evident. The other person here, the well-fleshed Coroner McNeese appears most unfazed, and she should after her own education and experiences.

"The thorax has been rent quite savagely, initially torn open by three large wounds, ranging from ten to thirteen inches, the condition of the flesh indicating this was not a bladed weapon, nor were they done by the same hand."

"What?" Mahler asks, looking up from viewing the printed report which lies bound in a heavy stock covering.

"It wasn't a knife or dagger or similar bladed weapon. I consulted an old friend of mine who ended up getting into veterinarian medicine, and she agrees that this looks like it was caused by claws."

"Are you saying an animal did this?" Pasztor chimes in.

The examiner just gives a little shrug, her lips sort of edging up on one side, before she turns back to the remnants of the carnage. "Those three wounds sufficiently opened to the abdominal cavity, and further, similar wounds show the excision and evisceration of most major organs."

"Uhm," Mahler begins, and all eyes set on him; he manages to continue his train of thought, "Did anything look like it was done by teeth?"

"A good question, Detective Mahler," McNeese nods, "Open-minded, good, and I did check, but no, though it is obvious more than one weapon was used, none indicate teeth or bites."

"How many weapons were used?" Pasztor asks.

"It is difficult to tell, but I would guess at least four."

"So many?"

And another shrug before she goes back to the body, pointing with a ballpoint pen, "The face was gashed in all directions, the nose, cheeks, eyebrows, ears, and left eye being largely removed. The poor woman is virtually unrecognizable, but we thankfully had dental records for a match. Both arms have extensive and jagged wounds, hands showing wounds on top and inside, two fingers removed completely, two more hanging by a thread, as it were. This would indicate to me that the victim was taken unawares but had enough life to take a defensive posture. I would suspect shock and death were quite quick."

"Mmm," Pasztor gives a grunt and nod, which causes the coroner to look over; the man glances at her briefly, then she continues.

"The legs were not spared, either, the left thigh stripped of skin, fascia, and muscles as far as the knee. The right leg shows less serious wounds in more of a horizontal pattern across the thigh."

"She has been savaged," Mahler remarks.

"Indeed," she agrees, then exhales loudly. "It's all in the report there," she gestures toward it with that same pen, "With much more detail, of course, and pictures."

"Definitely a murder," Pasztor intones.

"Not if it was an animal, Detective Pasztor," McNeese is quick to point out, and the two men fix their eyes on her, which she merely returns with her own, steady gaze.

DANCE OF THE BUTTERFLY

"Was it?" Pasztor asks in the ensuing silence, a touch of demand to his tone.

"There is no forensic evidence to suggest it was an animal, but we're still processing. It is quite a mess."

"That's for sure," Mahler agrees.

"There also seems a lack of evidence from the killer. We've yet to find any hair, skin, blood, etcetera that was left on the body by the killer, and that would be reasonable to expect in this sort of attack. Even if the victim stood no chance, with this sort of savagery, one may expect the killer to harm himself or at least leave behind some sort of biological evidence."

"Or herself," Pasztor pitches.

McNeese looks at him a moment, then nods, a sort of concession within the obvious tension between the two.

"Or herself," she allows.

*****

It does not escape her notice that the collection over which she holds curatorship holds an unusual popularity of late. Certainly the compendium is well regarded within certain circles, but such groups generally prove rather small. There are showings of both a public and private nature from time to time, but her work is largely composed of care and management. After having spent so much time with Skothiam, she now finds herself speaking with another polished, well-dressed gentleman who shows similar interest.

"Nice to make your acquaintance, Professor Malkuth," she says, and Denman gives her a charming smile.

He then turns, looking about the room, and she flicks her eyes over him in a quick, studied observance. He wears a well-tailored, chocolate brown linen, double breasted suit, though this time he is without a vest. The shirt is a rich blue, though pinstripes of a cream color diffuse this rather than making the garment appear actually lined. His necktie is a darker blue, given over to not quite as dark red dots. He even has a matching piece of fabric sticking up from the coat's chest pocket. His shoes are obviously quite fine, polished, and bearing of such a dark brown as to almost appear black. She also notes that he is manicured, his nails quite long for a man's.

Beyond the notes of appearance, she senses an arrogance and aloofness from him, as though he always holds control. She does not garner that this is a lack of self-confidence, no, he is used to being in the possession of power. He is used to getting his way.

He speaks, not looking back at her, still gazing out over the books, "Where are the most valuable ones held?"

"In the rear, under lock and key, generally not out for viewing unless under prior arrangement," she says.

"A pity," he comments, then turns, looking at her.

He still wears that obvious charm in his expression, and she can tell he is trying to get her to agree to show the so-requested books.

"I dropped by the other day, but you were out," he tells her something they both already know. "I do hope everything is alright."

"You said you just started this session? In the Philosophy Department?" she changes the subject.

"Yes," he smiles further, taking a few steps nearer her, though still a sufficient distance away.

"What is your interest in rare books, Professor Malkuth?" she continues after a short pause.

"I am interested in the knowledge contained within them, Ms. Perhonen. I am not a bibliophile," he remarks, "But some of the more interesting knowledge is found in older, rarer books."

She offers no response to this, merely looking at him, holding place where she is, back straight, eyes taking note. He can tell she is being guarded, and he wonders why. Is it personal, or is she really just that much of a stalwart guardian of these tomes?

"Perhonen," he muses, "Such a lovely sounding name. Quite rare, in itself. I've never heard it before."

"Thank you, though I would think one knowledgeable in philosophy might realize the implication of thinking something is rare merely because it is out of one's awareness."

He lets a larger grin crawl over his lips, brought together now to hide his straight, white teeth. His hazel eyes narrow, flesh rising up and out near his otherwise sharp cheekbones.

DANCE OF THE BUTTERFLY

"Well said, Ms. Perhonen," he concedes, then he lets a deep breath pass through him, his expression dropping as he looks around. "I am interested, of course, in some books in particular, but I am generally eager to plumb the secrets of the old and rare. Such does not always result in anything worthwhile, but it is still a valuable effort."

He has wandered about a bit as he talks, then stopping to set his eyes back on her once he finishes speaking. He is trying to offer something to her.

"Which books?" she asks, dryly, though still being polite.

"Oh, I'll not bore you with that list, but perhaps I may send it to you sometime, and you could let me know. A woman in your position may even be able to help me find them if they are not here, hmm?" he puts on a shadow of his former charming smile, well-tended eyebrows rising slowly.

"I am generally rather busy, but if the school decides to pursue a particular book, then I would be involved."

"May I at least send you my list?"

"Yes," she offers a single nod.

"Thank you," he turns to fully face her, "And where might I send that?"

"I believe you know my work email address."

"Ah, yes, of course," he gives an affectation of an awkward grin. "Thank you for your time," he says, after collecting himself, which happens in nearly an instant.

She gives a single, silent nod in response, watching as he walks by, heading toward the door. He, of course, pauses, his hand in the process of reaching out for the handle, slender digits poised in the air, turning back to look at her.

"You are a very beautiful woman, Ms. Perhonen," he boldly comments, "Would you like to have coffee or lunch together sometime?"

"Thank you, Professor, but I do not date work colleagues."

"Ah, I see. Well, again, thank you for your time. I'll be sending you that list," he says, and then he is gone.

She takes a moment to process the interview. She wonders if he even knows the name of the Book, knows if it is even here, but it is still rather remarkable that this man shows up on the faculty roster this semester and also comes calling to her for this information. Of course, it may have nothing to do with the same book that Skothiam presently researches, but she finds that even less of a chance.

And now she wonders why she lied to him about the rarer tomes. They are in the rear of the room, in their display case as always. It would have been acceptable to escort him back there and let him look at them behind the glass. Why did she lie?

In the back of her mind, she knows exactly why.

*****

The report had been filed, and though it had taken some finagling, Detectives Sladky and Contee managed to procure the assignment to drive out to the small, isolated township to investigate a possible sighting of the vigilante. This sort of thing is most definitely out of the ordinary, but the local law enforcement there had shown that they were indeed very cooperative, filing the requisite paperwork and requests for assistance. All of it had been arranged and endorsed by Interpol Agent Gaspare Duilio.

They had considered just taking a day and driving out there, off the books, but it had been strongly intimated that they make it as official as possible. If they end up catching the vigilante, which they'd really rather not do, then they'd need this trail and evidence to get a conviction.

They are quickly passed through the small, quaint headquarters and admitted to the office of the man in charge, Constable Nedza.

"Come in, come in," he greets, seeming rather open and cheerful, his light colored, button-down shirt open at the neck, and he gives both hearty handshakes and offers them a seat, "Would you like a drink? Some coffee, tea, something stronger?"

"No, thank you, we're fine," Quain quickly answers for them both.

"How was the drive over? Not too long, I hope," he says with a broad smile.

"It was pleasant enough," comes a response from the same detective.

"So, about your ninja problem …," Alec says, and Quain holds his eyes closed.

DANCE OF THE BUTTERFLY

Still, the Constable shows amusement, breaking out into a healthy chuckle, "Yes, the 'ninja' problem. Very good. But it is not a problem we have, it is a problem of our mutual employer, no?"

The other two sort of blink, casting sidelong glances, then looking back at the ruddy, smiling man.

"Right," Quain acknowledges to a degree.

Nedza looks at them, then stands. "We're a simple town here," he begins, walking around, heading to the door, and obviously inviting the two to follow.

The visiting detectives rise up from their chairs, moving in the man's wake as he heads out into the main chamber of the small station. The few officers in here are engaged in the types of things one may expect – talking to one another or on the phone, filling out reports. The constable heads to a metal filing cabinet, opening a drawer, and sifting through the files. He then turns to the room.

"Where is the Potchak file?" he calls out.

"Right here, boss," responds a man at a desk, tapping on a file, then going back to juggling a phone call and a cup of coffee.

The three traverse the short distance to the desk, and the constable picks up the folder, handing it over. Quain takes it, opening to leaf through the contents, gaining an occasional glance from Alec. When he finally looks back up from his cursory perusal, he notices the constable looking at him with an expectant grin.

"Thanks," he says to the grin.

Nedza nods once, emphatically, as though he may have just done his best work. He then spends a moment looking between the two, waiting. "So, do you want to see the house where all this happened?" he finally pitches into the silence.

The two prove agreeable, so they head to the constable's vehicle, a white Dacia Duster with a luggage rack and floodlights, bearing of lettering and insignia that indicates its municipal function. It wears the dirt of many adventures, a caked-on brown coloring showing near the wheel wells, diffusing somewhat toward the windows.

They get an introduction to the town as they make the short drive over, and many of those they see offer friendly waves. It is apparent the man knows his district and that he is known. Quain begins to get the feeling that much of the town may be in Gnegon's pocket.

They walk up the creaky steps of the farmhouse and into a scene of obvious violence.

"There's where he blew in the window," Nedza points, "And that window is where he came in, shot up the place pretty good. Oh, one guard got hit out back when he was taking a piss." He shakes his head, sympathetic. "Your 'ninja' is good," he adds, smirking at the two.

"What about this assassin that was brought in?" Quain asks. "How good was he, really?"

"Oh, very good," Nedza pronounces, speaking low from his gut, his common smile dropped as though this were sufficient evidence to back up his claims. "Former Alpha Group, from Georgia, I think, trained in combat Sambo and Systema. From what I know, he did not come cheap."

Alec scoffs, which gains a confused look from the constable.

"Well, we're just a small little burg here, and this is a big event for us. Do you have many vigilantes in your city?" he asks, and if the short-tempered detective may be inclined to take offense, it is even apparent to him that the question is pitched with complete sincerity.

"Errr, no … just this one," he manages, blinking, then sharing a look with his partner.

The man nods, looking around, musing, "Well, I guess we'd better hope he doesn't take on a sidekick or start training others or whatever it is they do."

"Right," Quain replies. "So what else happened?"

"Well, the vigilante left the others alive, but he put three in the Alpha's chest. Poor guy was bled out when we got here."

"What about the girl?"

"Oh, yes," and the Constable leads the way to the smaller room, "She was in here," and he points casually, "chained to the bed there, or handcuffed, whichever," he waves the same hand dismissively.

"The report said handcuffed," Quain remarks.

"Yes, that was it, then," Nedza nods, quick to agree. "The poor girl was a mess when we got here. She even had a big glass of water held in her little hands. She was coming down from her usual dose."

DANCE OF THE BUTTERFLY

"She got up and got some water, then went back to the bed?" Alec asks, obvious confusion etched in his features.

Nedza shrugs. "Maybe the vigilante got it for her? He came to rescue her, after all. Then he called us the same as he called you back at the warehouse, using a cheap, disposable mobile, and there she was just sitting there on the bed, big eyes looking up at us. She was obviously scared, confused, but still under the effects of the drugs," he intonates, facing the cot, hands on his waist. "And then since Plan A did not work, Plan B, and we took care of her with a P90," he concludes, casually miming by pointing his right hand at the bed, index finger extended, thumb up, then lowering that digit in the unmistakable mime of a falling gun hammer.

After a brief moment of silence, which does not seem respectful in the least, he turns to the other two.

"No sign of the intruder, of course, but we got some real evidence. Looks like the P90 wasn't even used this time."

"Oh?" Quain looks back over at the constable who shakes his head.

"The vigilante has graduated to an assault rifle, used 5.56 by 45 millimeter ammunition, and he used a 9mm pistol on the Alpha. Doesn't really matter, though."

"Yeesh, what sort of arsenal does this guy have?" Alec asks, and Nedza nods to the rhetorical question.

"He's obviously also ex-military, like your dead assassin," Quain assesses, "Probably special forces, maybe even spent some time as a mercenary."

The constable nods to this, too, a very agreeable, cooperative man, his bottom lip pursing out slightly, then he lets forth a loud exhale, bringing his hands together in a light clap, "Well, that's about it here, unless you two would like to see more?"

"I wouldn't mind a little walk around outside," Quain says.

"Sure, then after that, we can get something to eat," Nedza offers, that big smile back on his face.

*****

"So, everything is coming along, then?" he asks, talking out loud in his hotel room.

"Yeah," comes the somewhat deeper, somewhat gruff voice over the speaker.

"Thank you, Jericho," he returns, a cooling glass of bourbon in his hand. "Clarence is adept at what he does, but I need your help with making sure everything is secure. It'll be good to have a home again."

This final remark is greeted with silence, though he knows the guardsman agrees. He just isn't as open about small talk or expressing himself. Skothiam takes a lengthy draw of his drink.

"I can send you some small arms if you'd like," the voice on the other end finally speaks into the silence.

"I'll be fine."

"You know there's something going on there," Jericho presses, "This is not just about the book. Denman is there, and even your sister senses something."

"Nicole always senses something," he retorts, smirking somewhat.

"This isn't a joke," Jericho chides. "You found the first one conveniently hidden in your own home, then the explosion. We could have all been killed. And now the clues your family has been trailing for so long lead you to the second, and the Malkuths also know. You know you're not the only ones. You know that."

"Yes, I know," he sighs, closing his lips during it for a more thoughtful exhalation through his nose, "And now the city seems to have a serial killer."

"Do you think it's related?"

"I am not sure, but let's look into it."

"Alright."

And more silence descends for a time, another drink had. He wanders around the room, pondering.

"How are things coming along with Holden?"

"Pretty good, but it could be better," comes the quick response.

"Well, he respects you more than most," Skot informs. "His extreme sarcasm is blunted in your presence."

"Not all the time."

DANCE OF THE BUTTERFLY

"Well, I suppose we can't expect the impossible," he says, and both men share a chuckle.

"He's doing alright," Jericho gives in, "Once I can get him to wake up and get out bed," and this brings some more chuckling, "But you know he's got more of a mind for this than the physical."

"Yes, I know, but he needs to master some basics, regardless, and as far as that brain of his, he is not touching its potential, either. He ought to be in college."

"College's not for everyone," remarks the guardsman, who only has a formal secondary education.

"I know, but it is for him. His mind is too keen. He needs further education."

"Then you teach him, or let Nicole have a crack at him."

He chuckles to himself, though it is not joined this time by the other. "Maybe," he concedes, contemplating, "Well, definitely, of course he will benefit from us, but I just think he needs a change and some other exposure and experiences."

"Give him time. Besides, he'll eventually get tired of me whipping him into shape."

"Right, or it will give him the discipline to be more motivated. Thank you, again, Jericho. You are a true friend."

"No problem," comes the matter-of-fact response.

"There's something else," Skot finally says into another bout of blooming quiet, then lets it stretch some more.

"Yeah?" Jericho finally prompts.

"I met someone, a young lady who works at the library."

There is another moment of quiet before the guardsman speaks. He knew that Skot would meet people on this jaunt, so to mention it thusly means something more. "So, what's going on with that? Who is she?"

"Lilja Perhonen, the Curator of the Rare Books Collection. We've gone out on two dates now."

"Huh," says the other. "What's she like?"

"She's very intelligent and very attractive. She's young, and she is from Finland."

"How old is she?"

"Mid-twenties."

"Whoa," comes another assessment, and Skot thinks he can almost see the smirk across the vast distance. "Well, maybe this will help with the book."

"I'm not trying to manipulate her," he is quick to point out.

"Yeah, but it might still help."

A moment of contemplation passes, then, "Hmm, well, maybe so, but she has not gift-wrapped it for me," he finishes with a light joke.

"Yeah, but you said you've only been on two dates," his guardsman retorts in his typical dry fashion.

Later on, as he is looking over some analyses on his computer, a book he has brought for entertainment lying untouched nearby, he hears the telltale notification of having received a text. He casually reaches for his sleek phone, thinking it may be Jericho, and he gets a little, surging thrill to see that it is from Lilja.

Hi, Skot. I hope I am not bothering you if you are asleep or something. I'd like to talk if you are not busy.

He smiles, warmly, and calls her.

"Hi," she says as she picks up the phone.

"Hello, Lilja, it's Skot."

"Hi, Skot," she says, "I hope I didn't bother you."

"No, not at all," he is quick to reply, a smile on his lips. "How are you?"

"Fine. How are you feeling?"

"I am fine," he replies, leaning back in the comfortable, leather chair. "I was glad to get your message saying you wanted to talk."

"Oh," she says, and he can hear the shyness, imagining her skin taking on a flush.

"Was there anything in particular you wanted to talk about?" he tries to gently lead her.

A moment of quiet passes. He hears her on the other end of the call, likely pondering, if not even hesitant.

"Would you tell me about your family?" she finally asks.

"Of course," he agrees. "My mother and father met when they were both very young. His parents did not approve, and they ended up eloping, believe it or not."

"Oh, that sounds romantic," she interjects.

DANCE OF THE BUTTERFLY

"It is," he smiles, "And fortunate they did so, as they ended up being very well matched. They were together over forty years until he passed away."

"Oh, I'm sorry to hear that," and he hears the sincerity in her tone.

"Thank you. It has been several years, so the pain has been blunted," he informs, and she gives a gentle sound of acknowledgement "My mother is quite spry and healthy, and she is presently living with my sister. We generally keep a family estate, and it has enough room to comfortably house many people. We had a recent fire, though, so we're in the process of relocating to a new one."

"Oh," she shows some surprise at this, "I hope everyone was alright."

"Yes, all we lost was the house and many valuables inside," he says, trying to efface the tragedy with sounding casual.

"Are you going to find a house in the same place? Maybe rebuild?"

"We thought of rebuilding but decided against it, so we have procured some new land and are readying the house there for our needs. It is in the same general vicinity."

"Do you like living in the United States?"

"I do, though I very much enjoy traveling."

"Do you get to travel a lot?"

"I do, yes," he says, then as the silence resumes, he goes back to telling her of his family. "I have a younger sister, though we are very close in age, almost Irish Twins."

"Oh, that's neat."

"Yes, and quite the surprise for my parents," he says, and they share a short laugh.

"Do you have any children?" she asks, and he knew the question was inevitable.

"I do. One son. Holden. He's nineteen."

"Oh, nice," she says, and he wonders if it enters her mind that she is closer in age to his son than to him.

"His mother and I divorced over fifteen years ago. It took many years, but things are usually amicable enough between us now … for the most part."

"Good," she remarks, the single word and how she delivers it telling much - she accepts the situation and does not wish to pry further.

"My sister has three children," he relays.

"Wow, that's a lot," comes her evaluation.

"Yes, just like my own parents." And since he realizes he has only mentioned his one sibling, he carries on, deciding for further disclosure, trusting her and hopefully generating bonds, "I had an older brother. He died when he was twenty-eight."

"Oh, no," and again her voice mists with evident sincerity, "I'm so sorry."

"Thank you. That was a long time ago." he again returns his own honesty to her, "So, what about your family?"

"I'm an only child," she tells him, "and my mother and father are divorced. My father is a really nice guy, very supportive, and he travels a lot. My mom, though, well, she's a bit odd."

"Mmhmm," he gives forth the non-committal encouragement into the sudden silence.

"She's very much into New Age stuff and has a lot of strange interests."

This piques his curiosity, but he doesn't pursue it further.

"I ...," she begins, and he listens intently, noting the hesitancy, hoping she will open up to him, "I was in a long, serious relationship before I came here, but it ended very badly. He cheated on me."

"I am sorry to hear of that," he offers. "I have been treated similarly. I'd wish that on no one. Loyalty and respect are very important to me."

"Me, too," she says, her voice giving a distant, musing feel.

He hopes that she is alright, and that the conversation has not brought up old wounds. His time of being betrayed was so many years ago that he has sufficiently moved on, but he has no idea how recent hers may be.

"So, you said you've read a lot of the Marquis de Sade," she pulls a new topic from a random direction.

"Yes," he accedes.

"I did some research on him. You know he thought there should be no such thing as rape since he felt that if someone desired you, you should be obliged to give in."

DANCE OF THE BUTTERFLY

"Yes, I know. One of his less savory beliefs. Still, many who study him think he was not serious, that he did such things to challenge and shake up society, just as with his fiction."

"Maybe, but what do you think of that?" she presses.

"Well, I find it deplorable, just as I do the idea of rape. It sickens me," he continues, the very disgust of which he speaks beginning to somewhat color the sound of his voice, "Taking without consent is heinous."

"So, the things he describes in some of his stories," she proceeds, driving to a point all this time, "They are okay if there is consent between both parties?"

"Well, it depends on what it is and those involved. As long as someone is able to give consent, then I would presume that yes, it is okay. There are many … unusual, but safe and fun things in which any number of adults may engage if there is understanding, trust, consent, and above all, good communication," he expounds, feeling a touch like a lecturer.

"You mean like BDSM?"

"Yes. Do you know much about that?" he asks, feeling a tiny surge inside from her question.

"No, not really, but I am curious about it. Do you?"

"I happen to know quite a bit, yes, and I would be happy to help you learn more, if you wish."

"Thanks," is all she says, and they wind down their conversation, bidding each other good night.

After the conversation is over, she just lies there in bed, staring at the ceiling, replaying the talk in her mind, over and over again, her thoughts sometimes wandering in directions that are not even related to the telephone call. After some time, sleep eludes her as she continues to think about what they discussed and what it means between them. Dali wanders into the room, the large cat easily jumping onto the bed, cuddling in with her. She merely goes to absent-mindedly petting the feline as she continues pondering.

*****

The darkly-garbed figure crouches atop the rise in the distance, the gentle hill providing a decent elevation. The motorcycle idles quietly nearby, adding something of a gentle background lull to the noises coming from the nearby structures. The small binoculars held in front of the rider's eyes give a good view of the goings-on below, even offering extra enhancement if expected visual-spectrum light is insufficient.

This locale is again on the outskirts of the city, a part which has devolved into something perhaps less than desired, a place of immorality and crime. The latter concerns the silent, observant figure much more at this time.

The area's isolation is made more evident by looking at the lights from the nighttime metropolis, for they dwindle as one leaves the center, and darker patches of non-use or slumber show up before the dimness of this ghetto arises. There shows even some broken, flickering neon to draw attention to the various promises within. The police are certainly aware of this shoddy part of the city, but for whatever reasons, the illegal activities continue.

The figure spends some more time surveilling. Some of the buildings are so makeshift that their sides flutter, showing they are made of fabric or have been patched up so. The arrangement of them off the main avenues is also pell-mell, revealing that once away from the streets, traffic is generally on foot. Still, that is not the main concern, merely taken in for intelligence. The more structurally sound building nearer the center of this tiny district is the target.

The front of it shows what one may expect here – a small, neon sign in somewhat better repair than the others in the vicinity, two men out front, one of whom acts the salesman, trying to goad in potential customers, the other bigger, meaner looking, part of the security. Another sign affixed to the wall by the entrance advertises what one may expect to experience in the interior – drinks, girls, pleasure, and it displays a few low quality images of women purported to possibly be waiting inside.

The building, of course, has a back door, also easily observed from the vigilante's perch on the nearby, night-enshrouded hill. Made of metal, the rear access also shows no windows, a single, caged lamp hanging above it, two large trash cans nearby. It has been observed this

DANCE OF THE BUTTERFLY

evening opening once, divulging a man coming out to drop some bags into one of the bins, his dark wind breaker rising up with the effort to reveal a holstered pistol.

After a time, the rider mounts the bike, moving slowly closer, leaving the vehicle parked in an opportune place for speedy location and exit without being too near or exposed to be found. Movement is now careful, though as quick as possible, body generally crouched low, steps deliberate, the figure's eyes moving about within the near total coverage of the black balaklava, the minimal, exposed flesh covered in black paint. A spot is finally reached without incident, waiting in the shadows now in the crook of the building's perpendicular shift of its walls, near the metal back door.

Presently, the door opens again, though this time the emerging person is a different man, leaner than the first, dark hair somewhat messy, hanging down over his forehead. He takes a few steps out, the door still open behind him, and he lights up a cigarette. He looks up at the dark sky, taking a deep drag, then exhaling, as though trying to send the smoke into orbit. The hiding figure watching him notes a bulge that indicates this man is armed similar to the other, though he wears a shoulder holster as opposed to it being at his waist.

The vigilante takes the small, black CEW in sure hands, raising it and taking aim. The shot is aborted, though, as a voice calls out from within. The man turns, peering, exchanging words, then steps back into the building. A few more, somewhat muted words are heard, then the man re-emerges, cigarette angled upward in clenched lips as he carries two large bags, both distended with what seems a good amount of waste.

He sets one near a trash can, unknowingly now but a scant few meters from the hidden, observant figure. The plastic lid is set aside, and he gets one bag in, both hands now raising the second, when he experiences a completely unexpected weight and pressure on his back, strong arms about his neck, and within seconds he is unconscious. The vigilante zip-ties the man's wrists and ankles, then pulls forth a roll of duct tape, quickly wrapping it about the man's head a few times, gagging him for when he inevitably regains awareness, and then heads for the building. The figure leaves the door open, pushing the remaining bag of trash against it, giving little more than cursory notice to the bulky, heavy contents of the sack.

The suppressed P90 is taken in hand, slow steps carrying the figure further inside, peering down the one hall that runs most of the length of the building here on this outer edge, though a perpendicular branch adds another avenue just inside, heading right. Music is heard through the walls, muted, the bass thumping incessantly, the music obviously techno. This route ends in a door, leading to a small room used by the operators, not the guests. The other hallway leads to two doors, one on the left that opens to the main interior, then continuing to the other, the pathway disappearing right. The general layout is known, having been provided to the intruder once the target had been chosen. Changes may have obviously taken place in some respects, but the basic information is still valid.

The lighting inside is dim, yellowish, bulbs behind translucent coverings spaced evenly in the ceiling. The vigilante's goggles are perched atop the forehead. Finger held off the trigger, but near and ready, the infiltrator creeps down the hallway that affords more options.

A pause near the first door, leaning in to better hear, listening to the main room, the one that holds the bar, tables, chairs, stages for dancing girls. The music covers any potential sounds of those inside. An intrusion into this chamber seems a poor idea. A thought is given to whatever changing or ready room might be offered to the 'entertainers'. The other passage may lead there. This holds better promise for further investigation.

A slow turn of the knob on this door proves that it is unlocked, and just as it seems opening it this carefully may give no notice, the man just inside turns to see who is coming through. The casual tones of curiosity on his face instantly go to confusion and alarm upon spying the infiltrator. The vigilante springs into action, a quick chop of the hand to the side of the man's neck causing disruption and pain to the carotid artery.

He begins to collapse, even as he is reaching for the gun holstered at his waist. The P90 is released, its strap holding it close to the torso, one hand grabbing that wrist, applying force and twisting to keep the man from drawing his pistol, the other retrieving the stunner, going in and up,

DANCE OF THE BUTTERFLY

being pressed at the armpit. The noise is noticeable, though not overly loud, the man tenses, then slumps.

"Gregov?" bids a voice further in, and another guard steps into view, leaning forward, peering, some four meters distant.

He notes the situation, and he quickly snatches his own weapon from its holster, shouting out a challenging "Hey!", pointing the pistol and stepping nearer. He displays some training in how he holds the gun and in his movement, but not enough to have entirely avoided this method of approach.

The vigilante crouches quickly, nigh instinctively, bending the knees, body at an angle and now thusly lowered to provide less of a target and better stability. The P90 is raised, the approaching guard no doubt having difficulty discerning the situation, what with his colleague's unconscious form in the way, providing some occlusion to the passageway as well as shielding the figure.

The weapon coughs four times, quickly, the aim almost imperceptibly changing throughout the short barrage. The first two hit the guard in leg and hip, causing sudden pain, partial collapse, loss of precise aiming. A follow-up shot striking the right arm in effort to further disappoint the man's ability to shoot, or at least shoot well, the final hitting him in the right mid-torso, perhaps doing the most potential damage if it has not ricocheted off bone and been depleted of energy.

The figure goes in quickly, gun still poised, a fast walk, getting to the downed, cringing, bleeding man in mere seconds. The dropped pistol is stepped on, then slid away with the controlled movement of the leg, the P90 again released so both hands may be used to quickly drag the guard over to his comrade. Both are left zip-tied and muffled in similar fashion to the one outside by the garbage, their weapons unloaded, discarded. The infiltrator moves further in.

Another hallway is here, heading further left, the right quite short, ending at a nearby wall shared by the larger room in the rear of the building. There are many openings leading off either side, those passages covered by hanging fabric, and the vigilante feels fairly certain what will be found.

Peering cautiously inside reveals just what had been expected – bound women on minimal beds, all likely being fed drugs based on the presence and use of certain apparatuses. Some lull within the effects, some looking up with wide, frightened eyes, none acutely enough aware to do much else. One is found in the process of being used by a client, the portly man laboring with pummels of his hips between the slim legs of the girl.

He feels two sharp, insistent slaps on his back, and he turns, confusion in his voice and on his features, to see the figure pointing the P90 at him. The man's eyes widen. The gun is moved in a way that gives obvious command to the man to get off the girl and step back, which he does, getting shakily to his feet, hands held out in surrender, his slick cock bobbing with reluctant detumescence, despite the fear of the situation. The gun is again moved, the barrel pointing intent, and the man gets to his knees, frowning somewhat, lips pressed together, flesh taut with fright. To his great relief, he is merely left zip-tied and muffled, though such is surely not pleasant in his situation.

The girl chained to the bed is partially sitting up now, obviously confused, dazed.

"Calm down," says a whispered voice from behind the mask, "The police will be here soon."

"You …?" she tries to speak, brow wrinkling some, voice weak, "You're … you're a-."

"The police will be here soon," the figure repeats, then turns and heads back to the hallway.

One direction leads to a door, which heads back into the main chamber by way of a small utility room and thence to the bar. That way is ignored, more checks made in the cubby holes to provide interruption to any 'services' being rendered. Despite it being a Friday night, business is somewhat slow at this time, and that is as the intruder wants it. The point is to disrupt the operation, not perform a sting on customers.

The two guards at the other door sit now revived, the shot one giving an angry glare, though his wounds had been field dressed by the vigilante to thwart bleeding. The other stares with eyes partially lidded, still somewhat hindered by having recently been shocked. The figure gives them little more than passing notice, moving back into the hallway, firearm at the ready.

DANCE OF THE BUTTERFLY

    This portion of the passage stretches to the end of the building, stopping there at the exterior wall, a door in its side leading to another room. The intruder finds this portal also unlocked, and a sneaking peer inside shows no guard at the wait. Though unsecured, the door is insulated, a sealing gasket felt to release as the way is opened.

    As tentative steps are taken inside, it is immediately noticed that this larger area is broken down into smaller chambers, the air is also stale, and there is a chemical stench upon it. Quick glances about in efforts of assessment notice mostly darkness, though the glow of light and the obvious noises indicate something going on further within.

    Another careful glance into an adjoining room reveals a small space holding two gurneys bearing of shrouded forms. The vigilante moves in, going to the nearer shape, pulling back the covering to indeed find the corpse of one of the young ladies. The other holds a similar body. The crisp, off-white fabric over the two is not of respect, the obvious signs on the bodies removing any pitiful effort in that regard. They bear wounds and markings that tell tales of physical as well as drug abuse, death possibly caused by physical trauma or overdose.

    Returning the shrouds to their original places, the figure moves on. The final room proves the most horrific, and though the eyes and covered form of the infiltrator show no outward signs, much is stowed away for later reaction.

    There is a single man at work in here, a covered lamp on a moveable, mechanical arm bent to provide the proper angle and illumination to his efforts. He wears scrubs of the typical blue often seen on such garments, his hair covered as well as his mouth and hands. Upon the operating table lies the form of another dead girl, and the doctor, if that is indeed his title, turns away from the use of a saw, removing a face shield baring of blood splatter, similar fluid staining the nearby area.

    He then takes a scalpel, leaning over the exposed abdominal cavity, ribs splayed out and flesh held open by a series of clamps. Delicacy shows not his method as he digs in, his hands disappearing from view as his arms move with the motion of his efforts. The figure watches as the man finally comes up with what is obviously an organ, turning and dropping it in a nearby beaker, holding preservative liquid. It stands near others of various sizes, some of which are also occupied.

"Stop!" a voice finally calls out, the command delivered with force.

The doctor turns from having been about to continue the obvious harvesting, starting with shock and wide eyes, hands going up on bent arms.

"Wha-! Who are you?"

"Drop the scalpel," the vigilante growls out the order.

"Oh my God," the man quickly spurts, dropping the tool into the corpse's cavity, "Y-y-you're the one that has been causing all the trouble, aren't you?"

The intruder's response to this proves to be further steps taken inside, nearer the man, gun pointed unerringly.

"Oh my God, oh my God," the man sobs weakly, then he jerkily reaches up, dragging down the mask from his mouth, then holding out his hands to indicate no further intent, "Don't kill me, please don't kill me. I'm just doing my job here. I didn't kill these poor girls. I promise."

"Turn around. Hands on your head. Get on your knees," commands the voice.

The doctor moves to do so, his body shaking with fear. "I didn't ... I didn't kill them. Don't you understand?" he pleads, turning and dropping to his knees there amidst his trays, tools, and the collection from his recent work, "I *hate* my job, don't you see? But if I don't do it, they'll kill me. You see how little respect they have for human life." He moves his right hand toward the eviscerated corpse as if presenting undeniable evidence.

"Hands on your *head*," reiterates the repeated command, the voice leaking its own evidence of the effect the scene is having upon its speaker, while at the same moment, the vigilante steps in, using the left hand to grasp the wrist of the man's right, forcibly moving it back to his head.

In that moment, the doctor speedily reaches over with his left hand, the one in which he had lately held a scalpel, and he brings up a loaded syringe, turning his upper body and stabbing the large needle into the other's thigh, the plunger depressed in that same instant.

The immediate response is the figure's hand chopping down at the doctor's, pushing away the attack, but the doctor has already relaxed his hold, doing his intended damage, springing up and away, crashing

DANCE OF THE BUTTERFLY

through the nearby metal trays and instruments. Two of the beakers baring organs spill to the floor, evacuating their contents with the same seeming cold lack of feeling evinced in this place.

The vigilante removes the syringe, throwing it aside, taking a few steps back, raising the P90 as the doctor turns with the electric bone saw in hand, flicking it to life and lunging. The trigger of the submachinegun is pulled in rapid succession, delivering a quick half-dozen shots, and the man stumbles back from the force, falling into the already upset trays, causing more clatter and mess as he drops to the floor, bleeding from multiple wounds in his torso, more than enough of which will prove mortal.

"What was in that?" the vigilante demands, rushing in to the fallen man, gun still pointed.

The doctor grins, chuckling, the sound turning to a wet cackle and sputtering cough, spitting up blood.

"I'm dead," he diagnoses, his voice almost sounding singsong, "I'll see you soon."

"What was – shit!" comes the response as the doctor lapses into unconsciousness in the midst of the further question.

The figure rushes about, trying to find the thrown syringe but failing to do so within the chaos of the scene. A search is then conducted for bottles, perhaps being able to find the one holding whatever has been injected. And then comes the first spreading cloud of disorientation. The vigilante stumbles, vision blurring briefly, mostly resolved with a sharp shake of the head.

The alarm will surely be raised soon, if it has not been already. Giving up on the desperate search, the figure turns to the door, falling over feet when almost there, a sharply extended right arm all that stops a total collapse. Struggling, fighting, a physical and mental battle, willing muscles to work, willing vision to remain sharp. Once again to the feet, and fumbling fingers produce a cylindrical, plastic delivery device, an EpiPen, swinging it down and firmly pressing the tip against the mid region of the outer thigh, holding it there as best as possible for several seconds. The adrenalin disperses a quick stimulation, a small measure of time taken to massage the area after dropping the autoinjector, helping the drug to better absorb and be diffused into the blood stream, and there is hope that it will not make things worse.

Turning into the hallway, and no guards prove visible. A shuffling jog allows to nearly gain the turn when another wave hits, reaching hands on outstretched arms, one, at least, finding the wall, balance is tentatively held, breath coming short, sharp. Stumbling further, turning and the final length of hallway appears much longer than before, vision pinpointing to its end. It seems that now even the most meager of resistance would result in kill or capture. *Have to get out and get to safety.*

Have to get out ...

*****

"Inspector Duilio," Quain announces as he and his partner approach the man seated at the outdoor table in the raised, brick-lined courtyard of the fine café.

"Ah, you must be Detectives Sladky and Contee," the man says, rising from his seat after a quick wipe of his mouth with a cloth napkin, and though his eyes are shrouded from the late morning sun by a pair of dark sunglasses, it is obvious he has correctly deduced which is which based on the suggested ethnicity of their surnames, peering just over the top of the spectacles at each as he speaks.

The man is of average height and build, if not shorter than both of the others, the gray at his hair and goatee showing something of his more than middle-aged years, though he wears his suit well and carries himself with an obvious ease and surety. After quick handshakes, he gestures to the three available chairs at his table, and the men sit.

"Would you like something?" he asks, "I have quite an expense account at Interpol, though do not order the so-called *Sfogliatella*, it is a cheap counterfeit, but at least the coffee is strong, if not somewhat terrible tasting."

"I'm fine, thank you," Quain says.

The Inspector sets his eyes over to the other, "Detective?" he invites.

"No, I'm fine, too," Alec finally says after a momentary pause.

DANCE OF THE BUTTERFLY

"Ah, suit yourselves." He shows the palms of his hands in a sort of a shrug, lips pursed out, brow furrowed, then gets back to his food and drink, looking at the two after a moment, "So, all business, then, no?"

"Sure," Quain eventually agrees.

Duilio looks at the darker man, eyebrows raised, then he picks up his demitasse, sipping noisily before setting the cream-colored, ceramic cup back on its matching saucer.

"Alright then, to business," he announces, giving another generous wipe of his mouth with the cloth before leaning back, crossing his legs, perusing the men. "You have heard of the attack last night?"

"Yeah, we heard," Alec says, squinting at the man, the sun mostly affecting him.

"Terrible, terrible," the inspector shakes his head, somewhat melodramatically, then retrieving a pack of cigarettes from inside his jacket pocket, but only holding it in his gesturing hand as though he has just as quickly forgotten why he produced the cellophane wrapped item, "It seems this time the *vigilante* has murdered a reputable doctor when the man botched some vile surgery he was being forced to do."

"What?" Alec inquires, incredulous, head rising up and back, spine straightening at his neck.

Duilio nods slowly, assuredly, "Yes, yes, a *terrible* thing. We think the vigilante may actually be an enforcer in a rival crime ring, if not someone even higher up in the organization."

"And what makes you think that?" Quain asks.

"The evidence is being gathered," the man cryptically informs, "We have vast resources at our disposal which your department, though in this glorious city, may lack, hmm?"

"Right," Quain responds. "Thanks for the 'cooperation'."

"Of course!" the inspector smiles, seeming to miss the hint of sarcasm in the word, then remembers the cigarettes, shaking one out and plucking it between his lips, dropping the pack to the table, then fishing out a silver-plated lighter, holding it with both hands, though he pauses once the flame is sparked, somewhat unkempt, bushy eyebrows perking up again as he looks at the two, "Cigarette?"

Both of the detectives decline, which results in another shrug as Duilio lights his, then unceremoniously drops the item on the tabletop by the pack, leaning back as he inhales, turning his head to blow the smoke away from them.

"We have information on many *international* crime rings," he begins, slowly and emphatically speaking the word, "And we think this vigilante may be a powerful enforcer for one of them. So, you see, he is a rival criminal, not some … comic book hero trying to right the world's wrongs."

"Okay, then," Quain leans forward, resting his elbows on the table, entwining his fingers as he clasps his hands, "What's the next step?"

"Ahhh, good question, yes," the inspector points at him with a hand that now holds the cigarette, using two fingers to do so in order to not drop the burning stick, "We must tighten the noose, no?" he says, holding up his free hand, which he closes into a fist. "This vigilante is slippery. How does he know so much about the operations here, and not just here," he announces, holding out his arms, "He knew of the girl in Poland. What else does he know? *How* does he know, hmm?" perked eyebrows accentuate this, and the cigarette is placed back in the man's mouth, the end blazing brighter as he pulls on it.

"That's a good question, too," Alec offers, and he gets a quick snap of a smile from Duilio, smoke exhaled through his nose.

"Exactly," the man nods, "So, we find the leaks and set up even better defenses. This vigilante has an infrastructure just like we do, some network of support, and maybe we can use this to cripple him or find him."

"Okay, so how do we do that?" Quain persists.

"We deduce, we detect, we inspect, no?" the man replies, pronouncing each action with greater emphasis. "And it may be time to get this out to the people."

"Now, hold on a minute," the larger of the two detectives says, "The captain said to keep it out of the public."

"Ah, well," Duilio says, smirking a touch, still holding and not much smoking his cigarette, "This is not just up to the captain, is it? Besides, this was said before the vigilante was a murder suspect."

And he takes another drag on his cigarette, giving the two a self-satisfied grin, as though solidly settling any debate.

CHAPTER SIX

Trucks after trucks pouring into the city. Surely, it may not necessarily prove a plague, but if one were to somehow acquire all the transport manifests, even though many would be misleading or outright fraudulent, it would be evident that imports to the city have increased, especially in a particular niche.

As far as they know, the vigilante is one person, working alone, and one person, no matter how skilled, has a limited scope. The idea is that if they cannot completely stop the attacks, they will overwhelm the city so that something will escape notice and generate revenue for them. A war of attrition. There is also the idea that if the vigilante is forced to step up operations, perhaps even urgency, then more trails will be left, more mistakes mayhap made.

There are other obvious revenue streams, but the meat of the crime ring's money comes from operations that are being hit. Consideration had been given to minimizing those in favor of the others, but the more aggressive approach has won out for now. Procurement and acquisitions have been stepped up, further investments made, thus raising the risk and cost and importance that they win this war in which they have found themselves unexpectedly and quite thoroughly embroiled.

One thing that may help is the information that was recently "leaked" to the press regarding the police investigation into a serial criminal lurking in the city, one whom, according to the reports, may be somehow linked to the very organization that is now stepping up their own operations. The captain had been furious, of course, to find out about the news report, giving the entire department a serious haranguing. They all knew this was largely due to a similar chewing he had, no doubt, received from the director. Even as evidence was developing that shows the vigilante in a much less favorable light, the department still wants to exert as much control as possible over the flow of that information. Accusing eyes had glared out from the captain, seeming to try to peer into each person's soul under his supervision, trying to force a confession from the likely source. No one, of course, had buckled under this scrutiny.

And as if this would not be bad enough on its own, but with the serial killer, things were looking dark indeed for the metropolis. One of the newscasters of a more sensationalistic bent took it so far as to question the abilities of the entire police force, positing some coming chaos to the city, even suggesting this masked criminal enforcer may also be the serial killer. If the police could get off their lazy asses and catch this "monster", then all would be well.

The murderer does lurk out there somewhere in the settlement, eager for more victims when the moment is again right. The area has recently become a nice home, a nice haunt, the ancient buildings of some quarters giving a sense of familiarity to the creature. A beast, yes, as evinced by the savagery with which it kills, but still sapient all the same. Rules must be obeyed, of course, and so patience is embraced, claws sharpened and ready, for that precise time may be felt growing, swelling like a burgeoning wave, a seeding storm.

More change is coming, and the influx of semi-trailer trucks is not the only sign of increased activity on the part of the criminal organization, for they have sent out the necessary inquiries and requests to employ a part of the underworld they do not always engage, one that may be more aptly thought of as part of a shadow world.

There are many ways to surreptitiously and indirectly seek the services of freelance criminals, and the methods of employing hackers and other such cyber-outlaws may seem amongst the more cryptic. Still, Gnegon's influence is sufficient, and the calls are made, especially as there is involvement, however directly unrelated, from the local police and even Interpol. Some of the potential hires do not find this connection, but the more savvy ones are aware of the nexus, and they are able to bring clarity from the clouds.

One in particular, a young girl of twenty-one years named Yan Therese Stendahl, going by Therese in her offline life and the hacker

DANCE OF THE BUTTERFLY

handle "Sparrow" in her other life, picks up on the connections and finds the job request very interesting, indeed. The pale, skinny girl with her dyed black, short, spikey hair has other contacts in the "shadow world", and she figures one of them will be very curious to hear of this. She puts in her bid, indicating her interest in pursuing the job, then sends off a message to her other connection.

She waits, running some scripts and analyses, putting together some quick reports and finding out more information regarding the job and the webs behind it. She adds some of this to another message to her contact and sends it via secure channels.

Still, no response.

That is not entirely out of the ordinary, but she is a bit excited to share this, even if her typical aloof, even defiant exterior does not change in the physical world. She may give the appearance of a dark, goth-punk person who hardly gives a fuck, but this is somewhat due to the speed and acuity of her mind. She is often bored, her brain moving at a seeming inhuman pace in some regards, thus giving way to an impatience she hides behind many layers.

She runs some more checks, digging deeper, executing some of the typical actions she does for her other contact. She pauses long enough to gulp lukewarm coffee from the mug on the table, doing her work here in her small apartment, on her tweaked and protected laptop. She leans back, propping her naked feet in the only other chair at the tiny, metal table. Two of her toes bare rings, the silver metal duller than the gleam of her black-painted nails, and a rather elaborate, grayscale tattoo curls and twines on the top of her left foot, sneaking up beneath her tight, black leggings.

After a short time, she checks again, and still, no response.

*****

Another laptop is fired up in a dark room, the glow from its monitor received with some irritation and minor pain by the sole person here. Tenderness has not entirely left. Narrowed eyes look at the screen as a cup is raised, the strong, steaming brew sipped carefully, thankfully, for the stomach is also upset.

The sleek, state-of-the-art machine is equipped with top-tier security software and a firewall on a very high setting, connected to the internet through Tor-network and proxies, perhaps something one could even consider paranoid. It takes a mere moment to see that messages await, and these are checked, the eyes scanning over the contents not at their usual sharpness. As the person reads, a stiffer posture is gained, the mug forgotten, until finally a noisy exhale is emitted, teeth slowly coming together in its wake, and now the eyes narrow in further thought, analysis, planning.

The cup is set aside, ignored for now, as fingers move in a flash over the keyboard, right hand occasionally moving over to the mouse. The criminal organization is trying to increase the stakes, trying to falsify information and possibly get the reader into more legal trouble than one might expect merely from practicing vigilantism.

The stout drinking vessel finds itself picked back up, the coffee remembered, its contents sipped as the person leans back in the chair, watching a video from the sensationalistic news caster, speaking of the crusader and the alleged crimes attributed. Then there is the not quite subtle suggestion that the vigilante may also be the recently active serial killer, and this causes another stiffening of the spine.

A light moan emerges, a movement left, then right, trying to gently work out soreness.

Fortunately, the drug stabbed into the vigilante's thigh had proven to only be a large dose of a sedative. It could have been much worse, especially without the counter-agent and the obvious fitness coming into play. The doctor may have just been trying to get out some random final attack, or perhaps he hoped it would render his adversary unconscious, left for the guards, but that had been narrowly avoided. The ride back home had been scary, the administration of the dose of stimulant along with sheer will keeping the rider awake and alert enough to make it.

Many hours after arriving home had been spent in forced wakefulness, another EpiPen at the ready, observing reactions, a phone nearby if any life threatening symptoms had manifest. Such had proven unnecessary, if requisitely cautious, though a trip to the clinic would be in order as soon as possible to check for any possible negative repercussions of the syringe of the doctor's possibly being 'dirty'.

DANCE OF THE BUTTERFLY

The figure leans back into the laptop, composing a message for another person in the network of informants and contacts, deciding to do some digging into other counter-measures that may be used in case something like that happens again, maybe something to take pro-actively if such threats are suspected or known.

So, the crime ring is trying to employ hackers and other such cyber-detectives to aid in thwarting this "nuisance" to them? With the security already in place, it is doubtful that will yield any positive results. Thankfully, Sparrow is involved and providing the same sort of invaluable help she always has. Meeting her had proven very fortuitous. Though, depending on how things develop, she could also be the weakest link.

More things to consider … many more things.

*****

Lilja uses one of the library's public computers, having easy access to them due to her being on the staff, ticking away with evident experience on the keyboard, her nails in their usual very short, trimmed state, painted a mint cream. The information she seeks is readily available, which is good, because she is not logged in, just using the machine in its default state of protocols. She has chosen one toward the far end of the room, the position of the station facing toward the main entryway, allowing her to note anyone's approach. This may not be her usual sort of activity here, but she has decided to do some checking, and she'd rather not be found doing it.

The screen shows mostly text, immersed within some degree of aesthetic, the design is conservative, somewhat baroque, an economical menu bar down the left offers other choices, the school's name and insignia displayed at the center top of the page. An image of the recently hired Philosophy Professor, Denman Malkuth, shows toward the top right beneath another header bar providing pathways to other areas of the website. Basic information is offered, and Professor Malkuth shows quite the curriculum vitae, receiving his PhD at Oxford, though he is obviously not from England, unless he has made very exacting effort to remove any regional intonation, speaking with a rather Transatlantic accent. Of course, she also knows how one's accent may not necessarily be that immediately indicative of place of birth or rearing.

He shows to have spent time teaching at Humboldt University of Berlin as well as Duke University. He has published many papers, and not just in his field, also encroaching into art history and linguistics, also serving as editor on a compendium of German philosophers, paying particular attention to the works of Lazarus Geiger. He also seems to hold much interest in the work of Rousseau, penning essays of his own regarding the 'noble savage' and human avenues of development. His course load for his first semester shows him teaching classes in the interpretation and meaning of communication, an advanced study in perception, and an introductory session in early modern philosophy.

It all looks very accomplished and in order.

A quick search on his curious surname does not reveal much, cross-referencing mostly to the sephirot of the Kabbalistic Tree of Life, referring to matter and the physical world. It also means royalty, royal power, and to reign. It appears as deliberate as his entire image. She wonders if it is truly his last name as well as how much of his listed credentials are legitimate. She also wonders, again, at the curious timing of his arrival, his curious nature, and the new things lately afoot in the city.

She considers why he is wanting the book and what ties he may have with Skothiam. Should she mention him to Skot? She also finds it interesting that she knows of the Felcraft name and its obvious position in the world of book collecting, but she can find no mention of Malkuth as either a rival collector, dealer, or agent. All she is able to locate is mention of a philanthropic foundation tied to a Malkuth family, but she is unable to locate anything that links this to the new professor.

And she finds herself also burning with more curiosity about the tome itself.

It is surely not just a matter of authenticating a valuable publication in hopes of acquiring it for a personal collection or profitable resale. It must have something to do with the contents of the book. She possesses access to the item as well as enough knowledge of Latin that she could likely navigate through it, but she figures it would take more than that to begin to plumb its secrets.

DANCE OF THE BUTTERFLY

Though, in the back of her mind, she knows she shall not so isolate herself. She has already chosen a side.

She looks up to see Amanda approaching, and a fuller raise of her chin and fixed stare upon the woman brings her to a nearby halt.

"Ah," she says, implying much in that word, "Mr. Felcraft is downstairs, waiting for you."

"I'll be there shortly. Thank you, Amanda."

The other woman gives a lengthy look, then a single dip of her head before turning and heading back.

*****

Later that evening, they walk together to her parked car. They've had another dinner date after a day of work. She had subtly inserted herself more into his activities, asking about his research, and he had proved receptive. This pleased her, not only due to her growing curiosity about the book, but also because of her growing feelings for him.

She had quietly sat there in the chair next to his, listening as he gained steam and became something of a lecturer, talking not only of the rare book's contents but other subjects to which they relate, touching on physics, metaphysics, mythology, religion. He relayed how some parts of the book read like poetic verse, speaking of worlds and dimensions, seeming to be as much an occult text as the flowery framework of fantasy. She had listened with rapt attention.

It had been enlightening, and she finds his knowledge attractive, especially the passion he evinces of it and the way in which he expresses it and himself. She even found herself gently interrupting every now and then to ask him the meaning of a word. Her knowledge and use of the English language has been for many years now, making her quite fluent. Though she occasionally comes across an unknown word, in the short time they have known one another, it crops up more and more often, his vocabulary rather more robust than most.

They had drifted into discussing music whilst enjoying their evening meal together. They both share something of an interest in dark, melodic tones, but they also both have rather, broad eclectic tastes. They had mentioned artists of which the other was lacking familiarity, sharing grins as they texted each other names and songs to investigate at a later time.

She asked him his favorite, and he had trouble narrowing it down, trying to give as best an answer as he could muster, and just as when they had initially discussed preferred foods, he had returned the question to her. She had again given a very broad response, her gentle, innocent-seeming charm coming through. He finds it interesting, as well as deeply attractive, that she displays moments like these, as though she were an open, curious, and courageous child in search of the world.

And now the night has fully drawn its canopy over them as they meander back to her vehicle. It brings a mystery and romance to the moment that might otherwise show lacking under the full blare of the sun. He walks on the side nearer the street, the occasional car moving past at the slow speeds generally kept here so close to the university grounds. Her car is no more than two short blocks away, the black 1989 BMW M3 parallel parked there on the street in one of the more prime spots reserved for those with a staff permit.

She speaks into a moment of comfortable silence that has recently blossomed between them, "So, how *much* experience do you have with BDSM?"

The question comes on the tail of their phone conversation the other night, and he smiles very lightly at the delivery. He hopes it means that she trusts him, and herself, enough to have brought it up in such a way.

"A decent amount, though quite a bit of that is speculative."

She turns her head to him, eyes moving up to his, as they continue the relaxed stroll. The question she poses is evident enough, so he carries on.

"I've studied many books, even one that purported to be a comprehensive list of 'unusual' sexual practices, but that doesn't mean I've directly experienced all, or even most, of those."

She nods, her face turned back to see where they are headed, the gesture indicating her contemplation.

"I also try to be very open-minded. I was at a party one time, and there was a young lady there who seemed to be interested in coprophilia, and when I say 'seemed', I am being polite, for she assuredly was." He pauses for a moment, expecting her to ask after the word, what it means.

DANCE OF THE BUTTERFLY

She does not. "We shared a short, private talk, and she expressed surprise that her particular fetish did not cause me to recoil or judge her. As I openly explained that it did not, she then tentatively invited me to join her in it. I declined that," he finishes, smiling when her eyes move briefly to him, her own lips curling into a similar expression.

"What kind of stuff have you done, then?" she asks more pointedly, though her tone is still rather casual, obviously curious.

"Well, I have engaged in light bondage, denial play, corporal discipline-."

"You mean spanking?" she asks, glancing over, still wearing that sincere, open expression on her face and in her eyes.

"Yes," he affirms.

He watches as she returns her gaze forward, noting a barely perceptible curve to her mouth.

"Were you the dominant or the submissive?" she then asks, showing some of her own knowledge of the subject.

"Dominant."

And she gives him another glance of her beautiful eyes, and he sees yet another light curl take her lips, this one showing her bashfulness.

He wants to say more. He experiences another surging thrill within, a tempt, a tease at anticipation, but he shall keep this to himself for now. It is yet very early in their budding relationship, and rushing would possibly produce negative results.

They finally reach her car, standing by the passenger door to say their farewells. She has her back to the vehicle, having stepped forward as he slowed at their arrival, and she looks up at him. He returns the gaze, letting their eyes lock, sharing a moment. It is thrilling, intense, even as it is silent and short in duration.

She looks away, her eyes moving in a quick blink, glancing down and left and then blinking back up at him. She pulls in a slow breath, and he sees the motion and rise of her chest in his peripheral vision. She seems to be gathering courage, and he is very eager to hear what she is about to say.

"I didn't expect this," she finally speaks, "I had kind of written off this sort of thing when I was hurt so badly in my prior relationship. I don't want to be hurt again."

He nods slowly, a short motion of his head, the warm smile on his lips dropping a bit to show sympathy to her seriousness and her memories of pain.

"I have also been hurt," he reminds her, "And I cannot say as I was actively looking, but I am glad we met."

She smiles openly at this, another breath going in, and she rises up on her toes.

"Me, too," then she blinks twice, heavily, a slight moment between each, "I really like you … a lot," she finally offers.

He sees the courage this has taken, even as she holds her eyes to his, a flush slowly rising through her cheeks.

"I like you very much," he returns, speaking with an easy, smooth tone of voice, smiling further.

"You do?" she asks, and he can sense the humility in her, even the hints of doubt that she would believe such a thing.

His smile grows, and he nods, slowly, assenting to her that he, indeed, does. And her own lips curl into a broader grin at this. The sight of her thusly is a vision, her bright, open eyes at his, giving of herself to him in expression and words.

He leans in to her, bending at the waist, closing the small distance between them, moving slowly but with obvious intent, lowering his face to hers, and her eyes widen, pupils dilating, even as her chin raises, her own possibly subconscious response and desire showing itself as she makes the rendezvous easier. He tilts his head to the right a small degree, bringing his lips to hers.

She does not shirk away, her own face moving a touch to the right, as they kiss. He presses further, and she returns it, and they melt more into one another. His right hand glides over, gently, placing against her upper left arm, and she raises her own hands, elbows bending, giving tentative exploration to his waist.

When he feels this, he brings his other hand up, sliding his arms about her and pulling her closer, the kiss continuing, growing in intensity, sensations coursing through them like a cascading flow pushing behind an initial surge. His pulse increases, just as her own heartbeat rises, thumping in her chest as they move their mouths

DANCE OF THE BUTTERFLY

together, savoring, tasting, parting to exchange a passage of warm breath, an exploratory touch of tongues.

He pulls her even tighter, and she responds in kind, her arms about his waist, beneath his jacket. The kiss continues, their jaws moving with it, still a relatively slow pace, taking their time to experience one another, and finally, slowly, they part, still embraced in each other's arms, lids languidly opening. It feels like resolving back into the real world from a dreamlike hiatus, and they gaze into one another's eyes, content smiles on their recently kissed lips, showing their arousal and evident need.

CHAPTER SEVEN

The four men sit about the round, darkly colored, wooden table, playing poker. Judging from the way the cards are being dealt, they engage in hold 'em, being on the turn round of this hand. They are using quality clay chips, the color spectrum showing mainly red, green, and black, a growing pile of them collected in the center.

"Fold," Quain says, tossing down his two cards and picking up his nearby drink, bubbles rising through the lightly flavored tonic water as he has a sip.

Gnegon looks at him, taking stock, then he throws in more chips to call and raise, commenting casually as the checks leave his hand to clatter atop the pot, "It appears our efforts are finally showing fruit, hmmm?" he perks his eyebrows, his narrow eyes widening, which makes them almost as wide as the average person would appear in a relaxed state, the dark pupils focused on the one who has recently folded.

"It's all your 'ace' there," the detective says, still holding up the drinking glass, perking his own eyebrows and indicating across the table from himself.

"Ahh, no, I am but one man," Duilio comments, a smoldering cigarette in the glass ashtray to his right, taking a moment to study his cards, then squinting at Gnegon who merely smirks. "We are all in this together," he concludes, then, "Call," as he throws in the requisite amount, picking up the lit stick for a drag.

All eyes move to Alec, who bears a self-satisfied smirk of his own.

"What about you, Detective Sladky?"

"Hmm?" the large man blinks, eyes raising to look at the others, casting about, "Oh, yes. Reraise," he grins, splashing in more chips.

Gnegon grumbles, reaching toward his own stacks.

DANCE OF THE BUTTERFLY

"Not the hand, Detective," Duilio says, "Our efforts against the *vigilante*. We are doing much better."

"Oh, yes, yes, we are," he nods, clearly more focused on the hand, "And it is your turn," he says to the inspector as Gnegon calls.

Duilio keeps at his cigarette, merely staring back, a little curl to his lips, "How much to call?"

"Thirty-five to you," Gnegon says.

"Ahhh, too rich for me," the man replies, eyes never leaving Alec, as he slips his cards over toward the current dealer.

Quain sets down his glass, taking up the nearby deck to discard the top one in the other small pile of those already used and flip over the next, adding it to the end of the row of community cards, thus making it the fifth, the river, and ending what cards will be in play this hand. He spares a glance to the his partner, noting the somewhat subtle, though obvious signs of excitement, then looks to his left. Gnegon is as intent as ever.

"There have not been any more recent attacks, and since we brought in so much merchandise, we are actually experiencing a net gain," he says, still looking at the final card, no doubt trying to decide his next move in this battle, then settling back in his chair, looking over at Alec, brow furrowing slightly, then he picks up two of the green chips, tossing them softly onto the pile.

"That is good," Duilio remarks, still savoring his cigarette, eyes moving almost surreptitiously from the crime boss over to the heavy detective, "But still, lack of evidence is not evidence of absence."

"Raise," Alec says to this, throwing in more chips, which gets another simmering scowl from Gnegon.

"I don't think anyone's saying that," Quain replies to the inspector after sparing a moment to watch his partner and Gnegon.

"Of course not," Duilio is quick to exclaim, nodding slowly, emphatically, "I was just being ... romantic, no? Philosophical, hmm?"

"Right," Quain somewhat humors.

"Call!" Gnegon all but shouts, tossing in the needed chips, then shooting a stare at Alec.

The barely suppressed grin slowly spreads over the fleshy lips of the man as he reveals his cards, showing he has a full house, achieving the powerful hand on the turn card. A quick analysis of the community cards would indicate he is in possession of the most likely top hand possible.

"Gah!" Gnegon resorts to a louder voice at this, throwing his two cards down without any formal reveal, a clear indication of his loss, and Alec beams as he rakes in the pot.

"Though we have had a breakthrough with our counter-measures," Duilio interjects.

"Oh?" Quain perks up to this, sliding the deck and the corresponding 'dealer' marker to his left.

The inspector spares a glance to Gnegon who picks up the stack of cards, beginning to shuffle it with effectiveness if not some evident lack of dexterity.

"Yes, we have discovered a contact within the police that is feeding information to an outside source."

"The vigilante?"

"Which department?"

The two detectives throw out their respective questions almost on top of each other, clearly piqued at this revelation.

Gnegon's eyes shift between the two, then to Duilio.

"Not your department," he says to Alec, then, "And no," to Quain, "We do not think so, but the information is too similar to have not gotten into the vigilante's hands."

"Why don't you think so? Maybe this guy *is* feeding intel directly to the vigilante. We could trace that and-," Quain presses, but he is cut-off.

"We don't think so," Gnegon clips, firmly, then he looks up at the approach of a man within his organization.

They exchange a few quiet words as the visitor leans in to speak quietly and quickly into the boss' ear, leaving once a few nods are returned. Gnegon looks out at the other three at the table with him.

"I am sorry, gentlemen, but business calls me away."

"Oh?" Alec tries.

Gnegon looks over after he has risen from his chair, reaching for his coat from a nearby wooden, standing coat rack.

"I am sorry to deprive you of more of my money, Alec," he quips, then grabs his garment, bidding them goodbye as he walks away, several of his men in tow.

DANCE OF THE BUTTERFLY

Alec smirks at this, stacking up his checks, counting them in preparation of cashing them out here at one of Gnegon's illegal gambling establishments. He finally looks up to see the Interpol man staring at him through narrowed eyes.

"What?" he demands.

"You are not very good at this game."

"I am, too," he protests, puffing up his chest somewhat, "Look at how much I won," gesturing with a jerk down of his head to the stacks.

"Oh, I am sorry, Detective. Forgive my poor communication. I was not asking a question," the inspector charmingly replies, throwing a somewhat patronizing, though not too obviously insulting, smile on the end of his statement.

Tension resolves itself rather quickly onto the hefty officer, face pinching up as he stares at the calmly smoking man. He then glances at Quain, who seems mostly nonplussed, keeping only a casual eye on the development.

"You didn't win the most," Alec finally declares, sounding like a petulant child.

"Ahhh, you think I meant merely this game," Duilio says, smiling good-naturedly, gesturing with his hand to encompass the table, the cigarette now in the right, leaking a lazy trail of thin smoke as it is moved. "No, no, no. Though," he sparks, poking that same hand up into the air, "It is an apt metaphor for life and the games we play in it, hmm?" he perks his eyebrows, pushing away and crossing his legs to be more comfortable, showing the dark crimson, silk socks he wears, "This game is about bluffing and reading the other players, and I have 'read' all of you."

Alec rolls his eyes, but those of Quain just look over at the man, somewhat amused but also inquisitive.

"You," Duilio points at Quain, "You play like a regular person who doesn't really care, yet you are cautious and still aware," then he shifts his position, "You," speaking now to Alec, dropping his propped foot to the floor, leaning forward onto his knees, pointing with both hands, "You play too aggressive. You are a sore loser, and a sore winner. Is that the correct expression?" he asks, aside, "A *poor* winner, yes, *that*," and he stabs his left hand toward Alec as emphasis, "You should learn to lose sometimes to Gnegon, but do not let him know you are doing that, hmm?"

He looks between the two, leaning back, eventually moving his eyes to the other, "You, though, Detective Contee, you give me the most trouble to read."

"What about Gnegon, then?" Alec challenges.

"Oh, he is almost as easy to read as you are," Duilio dismisses.

"Hmph," Alec scoffs, "Then why didn't you win more?"

"Because the game is not just about the paltry money on the table," Duilio says, like springing a trap, "*That* is why."

*****

Gnegon stands inside the open bay of one of his many warehouses, this one large enough that a truck can be backed up completely inside to be loaded or unloaded of its cargo. Right now, though, it is devoid of any such vehicles. The single lit light, hanging from the tall ceiling by its long, rigidly encased cables, gives up the figures of several men lingering on the raised area of concrete flooring next to the empty vehicle space.

After a short amount of time, a trio of other men enter, a particular one amongst them that the crime boss has come to personally see. That man is shorter than average, stocky from muscles and strong from hard physical labor as well as his own life experiences. He keeps his hair shaved very close, thus giving a bit of a muddled, shadowed appearance to his pate, the edge of the receding hairline noticeable but reduced in contrast.

"Maral," Gnegon speaks the lieutenant's name, the man standing uneasily before the boss.

Maral nods, shifting his weight nervously, eyes moving from Gnegon to the others, all of them part of the same organization.

"I wanted to let you know that our trouble with the pest has lessened of late."

The man stops moving for a moment, eyes shifting about more, then he nods, almost his entire upper body going into the gesture. "That's good, Boss. Good, good."

DANCE OF THE BUTTERFLY

"Yes, but we shouldn't slack our guard, no?"

"Oh, no. No, Boss," and he vigorously shakes his head.

Gnegon nods slowly, contemplatively, "I am glad you think so," then takes a moment to just look at the man before speaking again, "The pest is very annoying. He has caused us much trouble, as you know, especially to the club you oversee."

And more of the emphatic nodding comes at this statement, "Yes, yes, Boss. I'm sorry about that."

"I can see that you are," Gnegon responds, speaking smoothly, "We know of the attacks. We're learning more all the time. We know how dangerous he is, no?" he perks his eyebrows at this, getting more nods from his man, "We should be on high alert until we are sure we've killed this pest."

"Yes, Boss. Yes," nods the lieutenant.

Gnegon reaches into the right pocket of his dark topcoat, pulling forth a small, black oblong object, which fits neatly in his gloved hand. Though Maral stiffens somewhat at this, he makes no other movements.

"He uses something like this as part of his arsenal," Gnegon raises his hand, fingers loosening somewhat to better display the object, "It is a stunner."

The other man peers, eyes narrowing to try to better make out the dark device held within the hand, then he nods.

"It is quite effective. We should begin giving them to our guards. Are you aware of what it can do?"

A furrowed brow comes after this question, before Maral gives answer.

"Well, yes, Bo-," is all he gets out before Gnegon turns his hand, bringing the item to life with a press of the button and hitting his lieutenant in the face, just below his nose.

The two beside the man, the ones who served as escort, quickly grab him, holding him up, bracing, and Gnegon leans in, holding the stunner there before finally releasing. He then looks at the two men, and they also release, the lieutenant collapsing to the ground. His resilience is shown as he does not take long to begin moving, moaning.

Gnegon then nods, and the man on Maral's right pulls a Glock 17 from within his jacket, pointing it and firing two close-range shots into the lieutenant's head, effectively ending any writhing and groaning, the bullets impacting their target, causing a noticeable eruption of blood and other internal matter.

The steely-eyed crime boss looks down at the dead lieutenant, the moment of silence stretching, then he finally sighs audibly, a forced exhale of breath through his nose.

"Get to it, then," he orders, and others join in to help picking up the corpse for disposal, also cleaning the area of any signs of the punishment that has just occurred.

*****

They are out in a nearby park area, enjoying each other's company, again strolling leisurely, somewhat taking note as the day reluctantly gives up its hold.

"So, lots of fresh berries, then, hmm?" he iterates, smiling warmly.

"Yes, I miss that from my home," she replies, smiling just as pleasantly, "I used to be able to go not far from my front door and pick all sorts of wild berries. It was nice."

She looks out toward the setting sun as she says this, and he notes a slightly melancholic tinge to her expression, especially as brought out by the reflection of light on her shimmering eyes. Whatever it may have been is gone when she blinks, though he dared not disturb this moment for her. She then turns to look at him, her smile brightening, and he cannot help but return the infectious expression.

"Do you like dancing?" she asks.

"Oh, yes, very much so, though I have not received any formal training in it," he informs as they resume their walk.

"I have, but it was just part of the curriculum at school, basic dances and moves," she explains, then grins further, "I start everyday with some music and fun dancing, though. It gets my motor running."

His grin increases sharply at this, and she eventually pauses, looking up at him, smirking.

"What?" she demands, though the tail end of the word is more drawn out than sharp.

"You are adorable," he answers, gazing fully upon her.

DANCE OF THE BUTTERFLY

"No," she says, looking away, a blush taking her cheeks as she smiles deeply.

"I'm afraid so," he smirks, speaking with mock seriousness, and she looks up at him, a similar playful twist now also on her lips.

They make their way to a stone bench, hardly anyone else out in the area, despite the nice weather, sitting in the middle, right next to each other. He extends an arm, wrapping it about her shoulders, and she accepts this, leaning in toward him. They spend a short measure of time like this, just experiencing one another's closeness, looking out over the colorful sky.

"I would like to tell you something about the book," he eventually speaks, and his tone is enough like a serious pronouncement that she sits up from where she had drifted into a comfortably relaxed state, resting against him.

"Okay?"

"It is one of three," he informs.

She blinks, obviously pondering this, bewildered, eyes moving away as she drifts into the annals of her mind before re-focusing on him.

"I understood there to be only the one copy. There are three?"

"Oh, no," he quickly expounds, "It is part of a trilogy."

"Oh," she says, the word drawn out into a whispering suggestion of contemplation before she again returns her focus, "I didn't know that, either," and he waits as she appears to again be thinking deeply, then she looks into his eyes, "How could this not be known? Well, obviously *you* know it, but that is in none of the major listings or references? This is remarkable."

He smiles warmly, her personality and openness so contagious, made even more so by the seeming fact that she is not doing it to impress or charm. It is just how she is.

"So, how do you know this? What are the other two books? Where are they?" she suddenly pummels him with questions, and he reels back, chuckling, which causes her to shrug up her shoulders, that bashfulness rising. "Sorry."

"No, it's fine," he says, giving her a snug with his arm, "But," he gets more serious, gaining an increase in focus from her, "the answer is complicated," and she furrows her brow, "Well, the answer is not, I suppose, but proving it is."

"Okay?"

"You are obviously aware my family is a known collector of books as well as other art and artifacts," he begins, and she nods. "We've had … knowledge of the Three Books for some time now. Their whereabouts and the true depths of what they hold is still a mystery."

"Well," she starts, and he can veritably see the wheels turning, and it pleases him that she so quickly rushes to help him rather than be suspicious or contrary, "You know of at least the one in the collection here."

"Ah, yes, well, my family is in possession of the first."

Her eyes widen at this, face moving as her chin raises, looking fully upon him.

"It's not in our published list, of course, for obvious reasons."

"This really is remarkable," she says, her voice like a breathy whisper, as she goes back to her thoughts.

She had received Denman Malkuth's 'list' via email, and if there had been any doubt he did not know the name of the book, such was erased when the title appeared, almost casually, within the short index of others. She recognized the names of those, too, noting, though, that no others were in the school's collection. She figures this is by design, so that if the book is in their possession, she may rush to offer the one positive she is able. He is playing off the oft times natural inclination of humans to want to give some sort of answer or 'good' response, something she generally has in abundance, but she is also aware and wary. She sent him a short reply that none of his requested tomes were in the library's possession.

She looks back over at Skothiam, her blues eyes given to his own, and she again ponders telling him about the other suitor, but instead, she holds it to herself for now.

"So, what do the three books do? Are they like a puzzle?" she asks.

"Yes," he nods, "Very much so, and a rather difficult one, at that. I've ...," he begins, brow furrowing, lips pursing a bit with thought, his right hand even coming up to absently toy with the short hairs of his goatee, "I've not even spent as much time with the first as I have with the one in your collection," he muses, looking off into the distance, falling into his own thoughts. "And we're still trying to figure out the location of the third. It's daunting, really, and-," he stops speaking as she reaches over, gently taking his hand in both of hers, bringing it closer to herself with no resistance from him.

She guides it into her lap, her fingers moving with a soft caress. Her eyes travel from this up to his gaze, and she smiles beautifully, a hinting tinge of pink at her cheeks.

"We can do this," she says, and it touches him deeply, the gesture and words and obvious sincerity, "It may just take some time and work."

He returns her smile, nodding, "Yes, of course, you're right, and thank you. Thank you so much for your help, Lily," he says, using the nickname he has just recently adopted and found out she seems to quite enjoy.

Of course there is much more to it than that, but he is still reluctant to speak further. He knows there are others out there who also want the book, and they will be much less inclined to be courteous, even law-abiding, in gaining possession of it. There is a sense of urgency, but he does not wish to so worry her.

She does not deserve that.

*****

Pello Halkias does not cut in line as he patiently waits to pay for his bagel and coffee. He well could, but he does not. He is not that kind of police officer. He traded his uniform for his less obvious clothes a few years back, working his way up through the ranks, perhaps slowly, but surely. His partner is not with him right now, as Pello is using this time of the morning to patronize the local shop, as he is often wont to do, before heading to his car and in to the station. The older man behind the counter smiles broadly, going through his normal routine of trying to offer the wares for free or at least with a deep discount, but as usual, Pello has none of it, paying full price.

One may make a reasonable argument that giving such grace to the police is a good way of doing business, just as one may make an equally valid point that this may lead to an assumption of privilege and even corruption. Detective Halkias hails from a land deeply steeped in philosophy, but that is not his forte, so he opts for the safe, cautious route. He stays in the good graces of the people of his neighborhood by doing his job, being courteous and friendly.

Still, he is not naïve. He knows the myriad levels of corruption, ethics violations, or minor infractions that go on. He knows it is all part of the machine. Some bend the rules, some break them. He compartmentalizes the dynamic, filtering it through his brand of pragmatism, maintaining focus. He has a strong sense of justice, and sometimes, he does not see everyone on the force heading in that direction. He tries to do what he can to make up for it.

He glances at his metal watch, noting he has more time than usual, so he decides to take a seat at one of the few outdoor tables at this small eatery. He generously spreads the creamy tzaziki sauce over the bagel, which has also been flavored with caraway, bringing the stirrup-shaped bread up for a deep, deliberate bite, chewing away as he raises his mug to follow with some strong coffee.

His attention drifts to his smartphone, which he has set nearby on the tabletop, interfacing with the screen with deft use of his extended little finger, trying to keep any other potential spills or bits of his breakfast from bothering the device. He checks the news, some messages, mundane things, as certain other operations need be left for more secure equipment.

He is a more than halfway through with his breakfast when he sits up, his attention gathered, and he turns to see a quartet of police vehicles has rushed up and surrounded his parked white Škoda Rapid. Two are unmarked, but the lights whirling on their dashboards remove any subtlety, the others obvious patrol cars. The various officers rush out, some going to his vehicle, others noticing him as he turns in his chair, rising, and they move in his direction. He has no idea what is going on, and he just stands there, flummoxed. He recognizes at least two of the plain-clothes officers coming toward him, though he does not know them very well. They are both from the Homicide Division.

"Detective Halkias?" one of them says, and at least they have not drawn their weapons.

"Yes?" he replies, keeping still, hands visible.

DANCE OF THE BUTTERFLY

"Would you please come with us to your vehicle and unlock the trunk?"

He blinks, head moving back, obvious confusion.

"What's this about?" he demands.

"Please come with us and open your trunk."

He wonders if they have a warrant, wonders what is even going on, but he knows that the best way to handle it will be head-on, so he complies, keeping his hands out, held somewhat away from his torso, always in view, as he walks slowly to his car.

"I am going to get my keys out now," he announces, and the Homicide Detective nods, understanding, and Pello retrieves them, depressing the button on the activator that releases the lock on the trunk, resulting in an audible click and the lid coming free.

"Please step back, sir," the detective says, and he does, his heart beating rapidly, though not enough to debilitate him, as he waits to see what will be in there.

In that split second, he lets any number of possibilities crash through his mind, many options of contraband, but then, Homicide would not be here if that were the case. He sees the bundled form, the irregular shape beneath the shroud, a large and obvious enough item. One he knows full well he did not put in his trunk.

He is being cuffed and led away. There is a corpse in his trunk, and he is being taken in for questioning. It is an obvious set-up, and he wonders what evidence there may be that could even damn him. Breaking into someone's trunk and planting items is really quite simple, so he wonders who is doing this, why, and what else may be in store.

He doesn't yet know it, but he will soon find out that the body in the rear compartment of his vehicle is a known member of a local criminal organization, a lieutenant named Maral, executed with two shots to his head.

Another person is off in the distance, watching behind sunglasses, despite the early hour, his cultivation evident in his fairly decent suit and the refined look of his graying hair.

"It is done," he speaks into the mobile phone, "Yes, yes," he says, speaking slowly, "The vigilante is down one contact … for now," he iterates, then pauses as he listens to the phone, "Well, no, this will not stick, but it will put Halkias out of the picture for a time, and then maybe we have a 'talk' with him. We're not trying to get him locked away as some corrupt cop, we're trying to get him to stop feeding information to our pest."

He pauses, listening more, rolling his eyes behind the shaded spectacles, tucking the small phone against his ear with the use of his shoulder, using his now free hands to pull forth a pack of cigarettes, managing to get one in his mouth before he talks again, holding the lighter ready.

"Oh, calm down, please. I know he has leaked information that hurt you, but this is not a vendetta. Do not go down that road. You handle your punishment with your own, but for Detective Halkias, we just need to plug the leak, hmm?"

He further perks up his shoulders, holding out his hands, then brings them back together, flicking the flame to life and igniting the cigarette. It bobs up, stiffening at a high angle, the end flaring to an obvious brightness as he inhales, putting the igniter away and holding the phone again in his hand.

"We're working on that. This is not the usual interrogation and investigation. Questioning Halkias will not help. We need to use this to get into his flat and do some searching. You let me handle this, okay?" and he pauses, exhaling, flicking the ash of his cigarette into a nearby trashcan, "Good, good. Yes. Leave this to me."

And so said, he ends the call, sparing another glance to the scene, where the processing is underway, and Detective Pello Halkias has already been taken away for booking. Duilio's own special investigator will be here soon to check out Halkias' electronic equipment. Then, maybe, they will get something to help them trace the shadowy trail back to the vigilante.

*****

He lies upon the thin mattress, the meager offering upon the rickety metal frame, staring up at the ceiling. He sees patterns there, images resolving within the texturing of the sheet rock, mingling with the tiny cracks of age and disrepair, the flaking of paint.

DANCE OF THE BUTTERFLY

He wants to sleep. He doesn't want to sleep. His pale blue eyes remain open, rarely blinking, staring at the ceiling. His thoughts are taken by pathways and strange images, shadows and flashing glimpses of an invisible world. He see things he does not understand, does not want to see.

He finally rises up from the bed, his very thin form moving to sit on the side of that mattress. He runs his skinny, bony fingers through his short, light blonde hair, adding more disarray to the chaos. He then holds them out, palms down, just looking at his own hands, digits splayed. Some nails are long, some are cracked, some torn away. They tremble slightly, and he looks upon them as though lost, taken by a brewing fright. He then suddenly clenches them into fists, the shaking intensifying, lean muscles, tendons, veins standing out on his naked arms as he does this. He is obviously possessed of a powerful, potential energy.

He releases his tension just as suddenly, leaning toward the simple, wooden nightstand, barely worthy of even being called furniture, and he fishes a small pill out of a cellophane bag, popping it into his mouth and chasing it with several deep gulps from a large cup of room temperature coffee. He sits there then, just breathing, eyes again unfocused.

His name is Ernst van Zyl, and he is from South Africa, though he has lately arrived in the city from Switzerland, where he lived for a few years, studying at the prestigious University of Zürich. He had excelled at mathematics, physics, but he had been just as gifted in the arts, showing promise as a violinist. He seemed well poised to attain his Bachelor of Science degree when everything tumbled away, sliding down a hungry fissure that had merely laid in wait for him, patient, unseen.

Unseen …

He does not remember exactly when it all started, but he eventually realized things were not 'right'. Perhaps it was the stress, perhaps it was his brain finally filling with enough of the measured, exacting science and trying to process it on deeper, unconscious levels. Stress and weight cause fractures. He knows this.

His attendance at classes had faltered. He spent much of his time locked away in his quarters at the dormitory, scrawling in his journal, using a thick, dark graphite design pencil when he had quickly broken away the all too fragile and thin lead in his mechanical one. He could have used a computer, of course, or an electronic touchpad, like so many of the other students, but he felt compelled to do all of this in a large, black casebound journal he had procured from one of the school's many bookstores.

The pages were covered in work that belie the innards of a simmering mind. Some of it was lengthy equations, geometric designs, some of these harshly struck through, deemed worthless, others retained in a pristine state. There were words upon words, some more legible than others, some like a sprawling prose, some like poetic verse. Which were dreams, which were the fancies of his mind, which were real? As the pages became more and more filled, he could not be sure. Perhaps some part of him had hoped that dumping the contents of his mind into this notebook would help to ease the load. Judging from the progression, things had only worsened.

Some of the sheets bore crudely indicated music, and these tunes he had played on his violin, filling his small chamber and the outside world nearby with the strange, weird music that made use of singular harmonies unheard of in other compositions. It proved to be this, as much as his lagging academic achievement, that led to his expulsion and eviction. He became less of a shut-in and concern and more of a bother as this music intensified, becoming a shrill, mad, frantic playing that shrieked about, seeming to make sounds impossible of such an instrument.

He had found quarters in a hostel, ignoring the incessant calls, emails, even telegrams from his family back in Port Elizabeth. They were obviously concerned, wanting to know of his state, wanting him to return home and get help. He would not. He could not. He had seen things; he had done things. People were hurt now.

Ernst felt the splintering of his mind like a compulsion, and he realized he had begun sleepwalking, or perhaps just wandering about at odd hours in such a hypnogogic state that he assumed he had been taking a stroll in the midst of his slumber. His odd, haunting dreams lured him into depths he'd just as soon not visit, but even in his alleged waking moments, he began to glimpse the flashes of images, the sharp blink of

DANCE OF THE BUTTERFLY

something that seemed to be there, to be very, very real, and yet proved missing just as quickly, no focus or scrutiny of his eye capable of revealing the truth.

The things he heard, the things he saw.

He began to try to fight the sleep, which just made things worse. He dissolved his bank accounts, taking everything he could in cash, selling his books, what items he had that held any sort of negotiable value, and his health deteriorated, his usually trim form lessening as he began to subsist largely on coffee, cigarettes, amphetamines. He held on to his diary, buying a generous handful of the pencils along with a cheap sharpener, and since he had few blank pages left, he bought two more empty journals. If he managed to fill them all, he'd have a cryptic trilogy documenting his descent into madness.

He sold his violin for the train ticket. It should have pained him, but the power that now compelled him proved all that mattered. For a time, this force had given him to create these unearthly compositions and render them unto the air with his playing, but now merely the writing of them was sufficient. He heard them quite clearly in his mind. He pawned the instrument, thinking nothing of it, and he boarded the train to come here. Why? He did not know, nor did he ask. He merely followed his compulsion.

He has been here now for over a month, reaching an odd plateau with his physical condition, mummified in life in order to complete his work before he will likely fall to dust, grated up and chewed to mulch in that gaping fissure which waits to finish him.

CHAPTER EIGHT

She is good at knowing things she is not supposed to know. This is part of her talent, her skill set, her job. She figures those that employ her are aware of this, and if not, that's their tough luck. To assume may make an ass out of 'you' and 'me', but she is determined to not be the 'me' in that.

She finds the initial information easily enough. It's on many of the public news channels, and keywords are set to trigger one of her sniffer scripts, anyway. It looks like a classic set-up, and it is being handled fairly well, not going too overboard, thus causing suspicion, almost delicate, apologetic – the way to properly handle the disappointment from the fall of a hero.

She digs deeper, and though she does not so easily find everything she wants or suspects is out there, it's obvious to her why this is happening. She knows things she is not supposed to know.

She pauses in her work to take a sip of the steaming café mocha, slurping at it, then sucking slightly on her lower lip, as though in thought or perhaps realizing the drink is hotter than she expected. She sets the mug away without taking her eyes from the screen, data streaming over it with such rapidity as to give one to wonder how she processes any of it, open windows like a chaotic-looking mosaic, some showing video, none of it appearing to impede the computer or its operator in the least.

She absently plays with the left ring of her snake bite piercing, the hoop quite tight over her lip, then dropping her hand, still moving the metal about with a suck on that lip and movement of the tip of her tongue. She slowly brings up her right leg, pulling the knee to herself as her eyes continue to funnel the information. She is wearing black boxer

DANCE OF THE BUTTERFLY

shorts, with a style of print on them that a gamer might recognize, as well as a white tank top.

Her girlfriend, Akua, had spent most of the day here, sleeping over after a fairly late evening out last night, but Therese had finally shooed her away, so she could get some work done. The girl had been reluctant to leave, putting on something of a big sister approach in her obvious care for her friend. Therese figures it is likely due to the mystery within which she surrounds herself, keeping even her close friends, like Akua, at some distance out of necessity. Akua probably thinks she's a drug addict or maybe even a dealer. She smirks lightly at the thought.

Just as quickly, she wills that from her mind, concentrating on what she is learning from her searches. She'll distill this down to the important stuff and send it to her contact. She figures it will reveal something about herself, but she doesn't mind. She has measures in place for all sorts of protection, some electronic, some more mundane, but no less practical.

This is about the vigilante. She knows that much, and that is one of those things she is not supposed to know. This also means someone else who was not supposed to know does, otherwise, the unfortunate man would not be in this predicament. Someone good had to have found this out. She knows of the connection, but she is *very* good. Still, the compromised detective is not quite in the same league, obviously. She does some more digging, fingers flying over the keyboard with a speed that may make one wonder if she has not melded with the machine on some level.

She eventually pads over to the counter here in her tiny kitchen/dining room, deciding to make herself a bowl of instant oatmeal, pouring some water from the tap into a bowl and shoving it into the microwave. She chews more on that left hoop as she waits, eyes still showing a lack of focus as the beep is heard, and she moves her hands to open the door.

She hisses as the heat transfers to her fingertips, resolving more attention to the task at hand, setting the bowl down quickly, then pouring the oatmeal into the near-boiling water and slowly stirring with a spoon as she walks back to the table, her work station, such as it is.

Cross references have produced further information, and she does more digging, running a script on a somewhat secure site as she follows the data trails. What she finds causes her to forget her oatmeal and coffee as she sits up straighter in the chair.

"Shit," she curses, eyes widening, lips thinning as she draws them in with a sudden tension.

She then works quickly to compose a message, adding in relevant information, applying the necessary encryptions, then firing it off to her contact. She stands up, looking about, then runs a hand through her short, black hair, obviously worried. She knows risk comes with the territory, but she does not like what she has found. She hopes her contact is able to handle it. She wonders if her contact may be the person she somewhat suspects they may be. If not, they have to be close. Something has to be done with the information she's found before those using it get what they want.

This is big, very big.

*****

They have accessed the place through a non-descript blue door. There is no sign, but the door is open for those who would pass through. The building looks old, though it is actually one of the more modern ones in the particular area. This is not an attempt at pretentiousness or mystery, though one may easily assume such, it is a result of the limitations on dreams, the daring chance to cultivate a deeper temptation that holds and lasts if but found.

Inside, the place is dimly lit, of course, the walls of creamy, rich brown wood save for some areas where it has been painted a warm red. The tops of these walls shows a change to a milk chocolate coloring, textured, almost marbleized. A large, wide painting hangs over the length of the bar, water color on parchment, laid out in panels within the plain-seeming frame, a study of a simple outdoor scene, one that lures one to fantasy in order to provide detail to the open spaces.

The furniture is a mélange, though not confusing, merely a palette of many offerings for the various tastes of the place's clientele. One may sit at the bar, or at tall tables with similarly tall chairs. There are lower tables with several seats, some with few, many couches from various

DANCE OF THE BUTTERFLY

periods, offering a multitude of aesthetics and means of comfort. A few stained-glass lamps populate the place like art nouveau sentinels.

It is called Frelankse, and it is a lounge primarily for lovers or those perhaps seeking to become so.

"How did you find this place?" she asks him, looking about, open curiosity in her expression and demeanor.

"The Internet," he smiles at her, giving the smallest of shrugs with his shoulders and the twist of his lips.

She gives him a very short, airy chuckle at this, her smile rising. He is entranced. He manages to raise his stout glass, a vodka-based cocktail, looking at her as she goes back to somewhat studying the environ.

"I did a search for the city's most romantic bars," he expands, just as the rim of his glass gets to his mouth, following up with a sip.

Lilja looks back at him, the warm smile returned.

"You did well."

"Thank you."

Her own drink, a rich amber held in a somewhat bulb-shaped glass. Next to it, a serving of water and a spoon take up some small amount of space. The piece of cutlery is ornate, sterling silver, and looks as though it would be equally at home beside a bowl of sugar. She reaches for this, sampling the scotch with a raw sip, then using the tiny utensil to precisely add a couple of drops of water to open up the flavor of the liquor.

They share a moment of just looking at each other, their banter generally smooth and easy.

"Have you had a lot of experience?" she asks.

He smiles gently at her, "With …?" he leads, eyebrows slowly rising.

"This sort of thing," she elaborates, holding out a hand in a casual way, indicating the sultry bar, "Romance. Women."

"Some, yes," he openly admits, and he notes the ever-so-slight narrowing of her eyes and the subtle twist to her lips, so he decides to do his own elaboration, "I have been in three relationships that I would consider serious – two resulted in marriage, the first of those produced my son."

She nods, thoughtfully. "I have only been in one," she informs, looking away, seeming to get lost in memory, then she looks back at him, "The one I told you about."

Skothiam moves his own head, indicating he recalls this, "I suppose relationships that came to an end are not generally the fondest of recollections. Still, if they had not ended, we'd not be here now."

She nods slowly, giving this very real thought, instead of just taking it as some charming point.

"Yes," she finally does say to him, smiling warmly.

He returns it with one of his own, feeling that fluttery surge inside that she so often causes.

"Is there anything else you'd like to know about me? Please, ask me anything," he says.

She smiles further at this, a different sort of tone to it, but a positive expression nonetheless. "You can ask me anything you want, too."

"Thank you," he replies, sincerely.

"How many lovers have you had?" she decides to take advantage of his offer, raising her drink for a very dainty sip.

"Oh," he thinks on this, mulling it over in his mind, then, "Thirteen."

"A coven," she casually remarks.

"Ah, yes, well I had not really thought of it like that," he admits.

"Were any of them witches?" she follows up, and he blinks a change in focus to her, studying her, but he cannot tell if she is joking.

"Only one, actually," he decides to answer with a mingling of serious and whimsical, "Though several had potential."

She grins at this, nodding, her glass again back in her lap, held by both hands. They have chosen a comfortable couch of dark fabric, sitting next to each other in a somewhat secluded area, turned toward one another so that their knees barely touch.

"What about yourself?" he asks, "How many lovers have you had?"

"Just the one," she says, punctuating this revelation with a sip of her scotch.

He nods, contemplatively, many thoughts coursing through his mind about her. He decides to also have another taste of his cocktail, his dwindling at a much more rapid pace than her own. The ice shifts back down once he is done, the clear liquids mingling with more of the tiny, floating particles from the fresh lime.

"Have you …," she thinks for a moment, "*done* BDSM in all your relationships?"

"Oh, no," he is quick to say, though he pauses to think, "Though I am sure I developed such inclinations long before I lost my virginity."

"And when was that?"

"When I was sixteen."

She spends a moment taking this in, not looking shocked, just absorbing.

"I was also sixteen," she reveals.

He nods, "We seem to have a lot in common."

She looks up into his eyes, then, smiling, taking a moment to just do this, then she exhales through her nose, smiling further, her cheeks becoming more noticeable.

"Well, except that my sixteen was much longer ago than yours," he segues in a not terribly subtle fashion, "Does our age difference bother you at all?"

"No," she shakes her head, easily, "Though I wonder what others may think of it."

"Hmm," he muses, "I am more inclined to be worried what you and I think of it."

"I know," she agrees, speaking somewhat softly, "but I wouldn't want people to think I was being a Gold Digger."

He grins, then blunts it to more of a gentle smile as she looks at him.

"If anyone we care about thinks that, then we can point out their misconception," he offers, and her somewhat serious expression resolves back to the smile at his words.

A moment of silence begins to brew between them.

"You have such a wonderful smile," he says, and she looks down and away, that expression widening a bit, teeth showing, and though the lighting in here is indeed dim, he can somewhat make out the rising flush to her face.

She finally looks back at him, raising her chin to firmly focus on his face. "So do you."

"Thank you," he replies, just looking back at her, not as prone to blushing as she.

He leans down then, covering the short distance between them, to offer her a kiss. She accepts it eagerly enough, a movement of her face showing this, and they both melt into it, moving their lips together, slowly, until the union is broken, and he pulls back, sitting up again. They look into each other's eyes, smiling warmly.

"That's very nice," she says.

"It is," he agrees.

He slips his left arm about her, holding her close, feeling her lean into him. It is a lovely contact, warm, sincere, and stirring. They sit there like that for a moment, his left hand moving lightly at her arm, her right hand moving out to tentatively touch at his knee, grazing him gently with her knuckles.

"So, you said you have a lot of speculative knowledge about BDSM," she begins a new avenue of discourse for them, and he nods, "Will you give me an example?" she asks, peering up at him.

"Of course," he agrees, still holding her close, thinking for a moment before answering, "I know that there are certain places on the body that should not be spanked, even if you are familiar with the use of the chosen tool."

She glances back up him, silently bidding him to continue.

"Like the joints, knees, elbows, hands, lower back, for example. It also depends on what you are using."

"Ah, yes, those are sensitive places in combat."

He nods, having some knowledge of these things but deferring to her likely more extensive experience.

"Why does it depend on what you are using?"

"Well, a crop is a lot different than a bullwhip," he elucidates, "I don't use bullwhips, as those require a good deal of training and practice to not hurt the submissive or even the wielder."

She nods, thinking, then stops, looking into the unfocused distance, and another blush takes her face, enough that he easily notices it this time.

"What?" he asks, smiling.

DANCE OF THE BUTTERFLY

"Oh ...," she says, blinking, looking up at him, "I was just thinking on what you said."

"About crops and bullwhips?"

"No, about the submissive," she answers, and though she blushes more, she holds his gaze now.

He sees strength there, even in her obvious desire to yield. It is like a sure arrow into his heart.

"Do you want to be my submissive?" he asks her, deciding to be forward, like a well-aimed dart.

She takes a moment to answer, and he wonders if he has moved too quickly, asked too much too soon, but he does not falter now, merely waiting for her answer.

"Yes," she finally says, surprising him somewhat, even as it was the word he longed to hear, "I think that could be fun," and she leans into him.

"Thank you," he says, hugging her with his one arm. "Of course, this requires a great deal of trust and communication."

She pulls back a bit, looking up at him, fully, "I trust you," and in so saying, he realizes how much she trusts herself; she is indeed a strong woman.

"Thank you," he says again, "And I trust you."

"Thank you," she offers her own sincerity.

A couple of hours later, and they walk into his hotel room. She knows where he is staying, asked him about it before. She recognized the name of the quite fancy place, though she had never, personally, been there for any reason. He does not waste time giving her a minimal tour of the suite, for that is not the pressing need. Instead, he shows her in, then closes and locks the door and extends his hand without a word. She takes it, and he leads her to the bedroom.

He walks her a few steps inside the expansive chamber, very little expense spared in these rooms, and releases her hand. Candles hold place here, and he sets a small few aflame, giving flickering illumination to the space. He looks over at her, offering her a warm smile. She returns the soothing expression. Her pulse is faster than usual, her skin taking on a different flush than her sometimes usual reaction.

He walks over, moving behind her and reaching around, setting his hands on the lapels of her jacket to take if off her. He parts the garment, her own arms going down and loose, angled back so as to aid him. He notices the prominence to her chest as she does this, her breasts pushing against the fabric of her light-colored, button-down shirt.

He lets the coat drop gently to the carpet.

He adds his own to the pile, then moves in behind her, very close but not pressing in as yet. He moves his hands underneath her arms, touching at her waist, then going up, causing the tapered shirt to tighten in further, his hands then slowly gliding to her belly. She sighs, moving her hands over his, letting them sit there, trailing with his motion. She arches her neck up as she feels him touching his lips to her flesh there, the kisses beginning delicately, inching up to just behind her ear. He notes her smooth respiration as he does this, paying close attention to her, taking in her scent and taste as well.

He moves his hands up, softly touching over her chest, letting the palms graze lightly over the curve of her breasts, then pausing as his fingertips work at the buttons of the shirt, slowly undoing them in a downward progression.

The shirt is added to the pile.

He moves back to her, still behind, touching over her shoulders, hands moving up along her flesh to her neck. She sighs again, a fragile, ethereal wind, as more of the delicate kisses find the back of her neck.

He draws his hands down, along her back, turning his wrists and moving then to her waist and about to the front. He leans in, pressing against her, and he feels her pushing back as he flatten his hands over the tops of her thighs, then brings his fingers in, holding her more firmly, drawing upwards with the pressure of the tips, moving inward, the material of her black skirt bunching up somewhat. She lets forth a very light sounding moan, almost more of a sigh given voice as his hands release, moving around to undo the metal fastener at the back of her garment, then slowly apart, coaxing the zipper downward. So released, he uses but the barest effort of his hands to ease the skirt down, and he feels a shift of her hips to aid this as the garment falls to the ground, leaving her in her thigh high stockings, black tanga, and her black, four inch pumps.

DANCE OF THE BUTTERFLY

He holds her waist more firmly now with his right hand, still kissing over her neck, though more intently, as he slips his left hand about to cup her panty-shrouded pussy, pressing in and upward with his fingertips, massaging her, palm pushing down onto her mons Venus. He feels the yielding of that soft, inviting flesh, the friction of his movement added to by the fabric of her underwear as it is moved over her pubis.

She lets a gasping, hitching breath pass through her parted lips, chin raised now, neck more taut, her head leaned to the left, giving him better access. She reaches up with her hands, her left going over the one of his between her legs, the other seeking back to grab him, up high near the hip, fingers clutching with growing need, her knees bending, body tensing in response to his touch.

He looks down at her as he continues kissing and suckling and nipping at her neck, pressing in with his teeth, causing another lengthy note of pleasure to flow from her mouth. He sees the increased intensity of her breath in the rise and fall of her blooming cleavage within the alluring clasp of her brassiere, the top of the molding cups lined with a touch of lace.

He then pauses, lifting his chin to whisper warmly in her ear, "Just stand here. Hold as still as you are able."

She nods, the gesture almost unnoticeable, another deep breath passing through her lightly parted lips as she remains in place, hands coming away from him as he moves, her arms held out, poised but unsure. He places his hands on those slim limbs, sliding down, gently encouraging her to just relax hers to her side, which she does.

He then brings his hands up behind her, sliding the knuckles of his bent forefingers over her smooth flesh, upwards to either side of her spine, until he reaches the clasp of her bra. He undoes this quickly, pushing it in with a pinch of fabric to release the hooks, then sliding his hands under the lengths of delicate material, pushing up and forward to her shoulders, which she shrugs in to aid him. He leans in, hands going down the length of her arms, and the bra is added to the pile.

Her breasts are lovely, enticing, nicely shaped toward round, not overly large or small. The pink-hued nipples stiff from the attentions she has been receiving, firming up within the circular enclosure of her perfectly sized areolae. He then places his hands on her hips, just in front at her pelvis, and slips the fingertips inside the edge of her tanga, then slipping it down easily with a bend from his waist. She dutifully raises her heels, and he also gathers up the skirt, adding both pieces of clothing to the pile.

He stays behind her, looking at her lovely form, the flicker of the candlelight caressing her shape, her slender legs and pert rear end, as though licking over the smooth, enticing skin. He begins to undress himself, taking his time, just gazing upon her, letting her wait, thoughts no doubt careening through her mind of what may be about to next transpire. She holds her place well, displaying her own patience, her own eagerness, perhaps, to do as he has bid.

When he is naked, his own garments added to the pile, he moves back in behind her, reaching his hands about and up to hold her breasts, cupping and fondling them, moving his fingers slowly over her soft flesh, tips moving up to take her nipples, applying a slow, steady pressure, but not too hard as yet. She inhales a slow breath in anticipation of some shocking sensation at her nipples, and the smoothness of the respiration barely hitches as he closes his fingers together.

His arms are now about her own, and she reaches her hands back to clutch at him as he increases his touching of her; he stops what he is doing, leaning in to whisper, "No, be still, dear Lily."

She gives another little nod, complying to his wishes, letting her arms hang again at her sides within his embrace as he resumes touching her bosom, kneading the flesh, even as he presses into her with his crotch, feeling the return push of her firm derriere. He says nothing to her about this movement, deciding to wait until a further time to press more diligently with any restrictions, instead reveling in the electric feel of her rear end against his still thickening member.

He again reaches down with his left hand, keeping his right in a firm hold upon her breast, sliding down along her taut belly, tracing the outer edge of her navel in its downward progression, fingertips moving between her legs again. She emits another moan, this one at greater length, her eyes closed, her arousal evident in her breathing, the flush of her skin, tilting her pelvis outward, eager for the exploration.

DANCE OF THE BUTTERFLY

He stops then, moving his hands away from her, and he senses her confusion. He moves to her right, taking her hand in his own, guiding her the short distance to the bed. She looks upon him now, for the first time since he has disrobed, seeing his slender form, noting the shadowed definition of his abdomen and ribcage, the curve of his rear end, the outthrust rod of his erection. He is possessed of lean muscle. She looks up, seeing him gazing back at her, an inviting smile on his lips, a need in his eyes, just as she shows the same in her own.

She follows his lead, going to the large bed, and he moves a hand along her extended arm, guiding her. His hand moves down to the upper curve of her buttock, continuing to give her suggestive pressures of his touch and motions.

She pauses just at the edge of the bed, so close to him, looking up into his eyes, "Do you want me on my back?"

He smiles more, feeling the lovely thrill of hearing her question, her offer, her willingness. "Yes," he answers with a languid blink of his eyes and single nod of his head.

She accedes to his bid, moving onto the bed, the dark duvet remaining in place, its sheen belying the tempt of slickness to it, something she feels against her skin like a cool coax. She crawls fully atop it, then turns, reclining to her back, legs parted just slightly, looking up at him.

He slips into the bed next to her, his left arm pressing into the yield of the bedspread and mattress, and she raises up a bit, sensing his intent as he puts his arm about her, getting in close to her, his body now against hers. He is on his side, looking her deeply in her eyes, a gaze which she returns, the smiles gone from their lips, her breath still increased from their recent foreplay and further anticipation. She looks up at him with a pleading expression in her beautiful eyes, and it thrills him.

He leans down, and she pushes upward with her face, leading with her chin, and their lips meet. She emits a sigh, even as he lets forth a deeper sound of pleasure, though still mingled with audible exhalation of breath. They kiss hungrily, though still savoring one another, their lips moving with it, tongues slipping out to feel of one another, the slick sensation adding to their arousal, more light gasps and buzzing moans adding to the score of their engagement.

She does not move her arms or try to use her hands, still holding herself mostly still, either from bashfulness or adherence to his bid, he is not sure, but he places his own right hand against her face, delicately stroking over her jaw, then down to her neck, as though weaving the air, like a conductor with no baton, luring and enticing further feeling from her. That hand travels down, over her collarbone, touching it lovingly before drifting further to her left breast, cupping and fondling the lovely flesh, and again finding her firm, erect nipple, applying a slow pinch with the pads of fingertips, his index then brought up, curled, pressing into the end with his fingernail.

She moans at this, her body tensing, and he feels her own fingers curling into claws, pressing into the bed, even as her spine arches somewhat, causing her chest to push up even more into his hold. He releases, moving his hands out, still against her flesh, grasping her breast more firmly, massaging before moving down.

Their kissing does not stop, breath becoming more rapid from both, especially her, warm gasps traded into each other's open mouths, tongues lapping together, tasting, giving way to the closure of lips, only to part for more. He presses more into her side, leaning his face over her, directing the angle and intensity of the kissing. She follows this easily, eagerly.

His hand again finds the focal point of her moist arousal, fingertips gliding up along her petals, middle pressing in to find the opening, feeling the gathered honey of her enlivening. He pushes in, less delicate this time, easily moving his index finger to join this one, sliding both fully inside her. She gasps again at this delving, her lips pressing sharply into his, and he grips her more strongly with his left arm, holding her as close as possible.

His fingers are moved in and out for a time, travelling the silky depths of her, giving her more sizzling stimulation, until he slips them away, candlelight reflecting off the glistening shine of them, his hand then finding its way back to between her legs.

Their kiss breaks, her head going back against the pillow, her breath more intense, rapid. He looks at her, her eyes yet closed, her body drinking in the sensations, and he brings his fingertips up, finding the

DANCE OF THE BUTTERFLY

engorged bud of her clitoris and pressing over it, moving in smooth, tight circles over the sensitive nub.

Her eyes snap open at this, mouth held with further parted lips, the muscles of her thighs standing out in a rigid response. He feels her hand on him tighten, and it shoots an electric feel through his being.

"Oh, gods," she exclaims, looking at him, "I want you inside me. Please," she pleads.

He moves then, getting atop her, between her legs, which spread out further. Her willingness and accommodation is but one of the myriad layers to her lure for him. Her chest moves with her breath, nipples still firmly pronounced atop the soft pillowing of her breasts, her eyes all but stuck on him, and his are no less magnetized to her intoxicating form. He presses inward, and she moans lightly, more of an inviting hum, eyelids going down somewhat, her hips writhing. He continues pushing, sliding inside her with little effort, penetrating her to the hilt.

She gasps, a sound answered with his own throaty moan, and he leans down to her, sliding his arms up outside her. She begins to reach up to him, but he props himself with his left arm, taking her right wrist in hand and pulling her arm to the bed then out and up, keeping hold as he does the same on the other side. He then completes sliding down to atop her warm body, the sheen upon her ambrosial flesh brought forth from the flickering illumination of the candles. He pushes her arms up over her head, lacing his own within hers, holding her down in this embrace as he begins moving his hips.

She brings her slender legs up, wrapping them about him as they move together, and he feels the touch of her thighs like a fervent addition to the bouquet of sensations. His thrusts are met eagerly with her own, if not more so, his attempts to dictate a more thoughtful pace overridden by her vehement responses, engulfing his every departure with a needful push. It is a bliss unmatched, and he can feel his own conclusion approaching.

He holds her tightly, feeling a similar firmness from herself, their eyes again locked into a naked channeling of their lust, their faces so close as they gyrate their hips. She gasps more openly now, punctuating each driving thrust, her breath evidence of her quickening.

"Please," she murmurs again, her brow knitted with her burgeoning approach, "Please, Skot," she adds, "I- I," she says, her voice needful, yet stammering from that very intensity.

He grits his teeth, adding his own increased vocalization, both of them matching their heightened breathing to the pace of their union. He feels his heart practically exploding in his chest, his body all but quivering with it. Her own hot craving also courses within her.

He barely manages to contain himself until he feels her body tense, taut like a bow string, and she cries out, her fingers interlaced with his, curling into iron claws. She continues the movement of her hips, grinding over him now, her muscles fluttering as her orgasm takes her. He feels the clutching, and he is unable to resist, his own spasms erupting as he expends himself inside her, the several jerks of his organ finishing before her own climax finally calms.

They lie there together, their bodies now released of tension, though still burning with the sweaty heat of their culmination. They kiss, and she slips her arms down to about his torso, holding tightly just below his chest. He brings his own arms down, slipping them about her petite frame, a firm grasp. He stays inside her, just experiencing their continued union, the basting feel of their bodies against each other.

*****

He sits alone at the small wooden table, the round top holding the stout glass bearing a double vodka on ice, the edges of the surface marred by cracks and splits, one large enough that he grazed his finger against it and felt a painful pinch, then shifted the position of his chair to avoid it. He suspects this drink will not help his continued attempts at staying awake, but he also knows he cannot put that off indefinitely. Besides, he chewed up and dry-swallowed two more of the small, candy-like, red pills before venturing out. He is not sure if that may diminish or enhance the effect, nor exactly what mixing alcohol in may do. He isn't the most cautious since his life changed so drastically and coming here from Zürich.

Ernst's downturned eyes gaze out from beneath his prominent brow, his face long, narrow, perhaps giving him a look of intensity that he does

DANCE OF THE BUTTERFLY

not intend, of which he may not even be fully aware. He feels lethargic, lost, wrapped in a sleepy buzz as he sits here. He gazes out over the dark landscape of the place, the techno music driving, though it sounds as if it is behind a wall, even as he sits right here in the midst of it, occupying this place somewhat on the outskirts of the room.

There is a large main stage here, and two smaller ones that are really not much more than podiums, though there are poles on each. Using these are scantily clad girls of generally youthful appearance, some topless, but none fully nude, what with the very thin g-strings and impossible-seeming high heels. Others meander through the crowd, dressed more than their sisters on stage but still showing off their bodies in very un-subtle displays. He has turned down three thus far who have shimmied by, offering their company and services.

There is a plastic ashtray at his table, and he has lit one cigarette, the length smoldering, untouched now within one of the four grooves cut out of the edges. The thin tendril of its smoke bleeds upwards, languourously, matching the mood of its owner.

He is not sure why he came here. There are more reputable places in other parts of the city, though his appearance and pocketbook would likely preclude his patronage. He followed his new compulsion here, feeling less and less capable of resisting it. His evening had begun with some aimless wandering before he found himself in a less savory part of the city, the neon shape of a curved body and the large lettering outside the place doing less to entice him inside than this incessant call he feels like some constant white noise in his mind.

He raises his glass, downing the remaining contents and settling it back to the tabletop, ice clinking in place. A waitress comes over rather quickly, just another of the girls, picking up a tray to perform one of many duties expected of them.

"Another, sweetie?" she bids, leaning down over the table to give him a nice show of her cleavage, pressed together and thrust upwards by her halter top.

"Yes, please," he says, almost robotically, not looking at her.

"Can I get you anything else while I'm at it?" she pushes, "Some other sweets for you, sweetie?"

143

He looks over then, and she glances from his eyes downward to her chest then back up at him, causing a slight jiggle to her medium-sized breasts.

"Just the drink, please," he says, dryly, and though he does not mean the rejection as an insult, she sort of curls her heavily painted lips as she turns and heads to the bar, still giving a saunter of her thin hips in case he is watching her ass.

He is not, already turning back to look out over the playscape of the locale, not really taking anything in, yet managing to somehow absorb everything through his seeming hypnotized awareness. The waitress comes back somewhat quickly, showing the less than busy nature of the evening to this point, though she did spend some time talking with the bartender. She sets the drink down near him.

"Here you go," she announces with less enthusiasm than her earlier attempt.

"Thanks," he mumbles, slipping her a note which is more than required for the amount, and when she goes to make change, he holds up his right hand, "Keep it."

"Thanks," she grins, resolving back to the temptress with this gratuity.

He doesn't have a lot of cash to spare, but the appearance of nonchalance is more of his lack of concern for things outside the pull of his obsession. He glances past the stripper on the small stage nearest him, eyes moving to see another sitting in a customer's lap, trying to seduce into further transactions. He has seen others walking into more secluded areas, some booths where he sees the unmistakable bobbing of heads in the midst of fellatio. Still others have disappeared through the side door, and he figures they're getting the full treatment in the rear of the place.

Another of the girls walks by, her bleach blonde hair tied into two long pigtails on either side of her head, the darker roots of her hair visible at the part. Her blouse shows off her belly, the somewhat puffy garment clinging firmly to her small chest, giving it some lift, then leaving her shoulders bare to travel about her biceps. She also wears similar high heels as the others and a very short skirt, one which barely manages to cover most of her alluring behind. Though she looks attractive enough, perhaps one of the overall better looking ladies in here, that is not what catches his sudden attention. She notes this, almost as though the girls here have built-in sensors, as her eyes go to him, peering from within the heavy, dark make-up. She alters her course quite obviously, sauntering over to him.

"Hi," she says, giving a sort of half-grin, seductive smirk of her lushly colored lips, the liner about them to make them appear even fuller, more inviting, "Want some company?"

He peers at her legs, seeming transfixed by the slender, coltish appendages. She notices this, of course, posing herself in such a way as to better display them.

"What's that tattoo?" he asks, getting closer, eyes squinting to enhance his focus.

"Oh, that," she says, grinning more openly, even emitting a very short, almost silent giggle, and she turns to better display her left leg, raising up her skirt, thus showing off her entire hip, and the suggestive stretch of her g-string, angling herself in such a way as to also give up the luring curve of her rear end.

She has moved closer for this, and he leans in even more, peering with a great intensity. She continues to grin, not at all bothered by his scrutiny. With this closer inspection, he can tell the tattoo is fresh, some of the nearby skin showing pink, the thing shining with ointment, likely just received in the past couple of days at most. It is of an intricate pattern, almost chaotic, abstract, with many intersecting lines, some straight, some curved. The design is also mostly black, though some coloring blossoms out from intersections of lines. It covers a decent portion of her upper left thigh, having shown itself peeking out below her skirt.

"Do you like it?" she asks, still grinning, shifting her hips so as to sway into a slow luring motion.

"Where did you find this design?" he asks, oblivious to her question, even reaching up with his hands to gently place them at her waist, trying to stop her movement, so he may better study the marking.

"I dreamt it."

He looks up at her, slowly moving back into his chair as he straightens up from having been somewhat bent forward, thus diminishing the relative distance between their eyes. She just keeps smiling at him, though the degree of the expression does lessen some from his behavior.

"You dreamt it?" he asks, his face pinching inward, something a very careful observer might note as dread.

"Yeah," she nods, pursing out her lower lip, giving a subtle shrug, "I had a strange dream, and when I woke up, I remembered it, so I sketched it out and went to the tattoo shop. Do you like it?" she tries again, smiling up to a greater luminescence, showing her teeth, back to the gentle sway of her hips since he has dropped his hands.

"I understand it," he replies, and this gets her to fully stop moving.

Her smile drops, traded for bewilderment, "Huh?" she says, brow furrowed.

"It's makes geometric sense, though it is definitely not conventional, non-Euclidean," he expands, his voice sort of turning to a musing murmur toward the end.

"Uh," she wrinkles her top lip, "I thought it just looked kind of like a strange, neat web."

"You sketched this?" he looks back up at her, speaking more clearly. "From the memory of your dream?"

"Yeah," she nods, her smile back, interpreting his attention as something positive directed at her.

"This is rather complex," he says, looking at it again.

"Well, I used to draw and paint when I was younger. I kind of wanted to become an artist, but … here we are," she presses her lips inward, eyebrows perked, hands moving out upon bent arms, presenting herself and making a joke of her own lot in life.

"This is just remarkable," he comments, back to looking at the tattoo.

"Well, thanks," she says, perhaps having finally reached her threshold of indulgence, "I'm glad you like it. I'm working here, so," she leads, looking down at him.

He does not look up, still transfixed on her body art, so she playfully taps him on the top of his head. Her lengthy nail does not feel the unwashed greasiness of his hair, the shine and angles of it done with a

DANCE OF THE BUTTERFLY

casual application of cheap styling gel he managed to acquire, using the travel sized bottle sparingly. He peers up at her.

"You want to go have some fun together?" she pitches, putting on her best, seductive smile, thinking this is his last chance.

He gives this some thought, much more so than the flippant negatives given to the other girls who tried before. He feels a swelling of the compulsion and opens his mouth to answer.

*****

Death has come to this building, the pale stucco walls of the small complex like slowly decaying bone, the 'L'-shaped structure holding just less than two dozen rooms, all small, cramped, but possessed of the minimum requirements to get by. Every one even has its own shower, which is more than most might expect from such a place. This is luxury, some have said, but they say so in order to manipulate, control, indebt.

Each of the residents is a prostitute, answering to the local crime ring, though allowed the "freedom" of a private living space, occasionally doing business out of her apartment, some working at the nearby club, a short walking distance away, no more than four blocks. Some of them keep their quarters clean, some do not. If they are too clean, it may even catch notice from the men in charge, and that is not good. If most time is spent working, partying, doing drugs, sleeping, then who has time to clean?

Cleanliness was not a concern for death. The killer did follow a scent here, but that particular smell was of vibrancy, a dazzling array like underwater light reflected by a metal fishing lure, but this fish has proved a shark. The shark swam in, its sensitivity practically overloaded from all the headiness, these waters clouded with a richness that might give one to swoon in so many ways, but rules are rules, and all of these other temptations had been ignored. Many other potential lures were hardly seen, worthless to this killer.

The one had been marked, chosen, and she had been rent, laid open and now devoid of life, her gruesome remains waiting to be found, the door carelessly left ajar, as if the killer does not try to hide in any expected way, thus expediting her discovery.

The other girls would express their own selfish luck, some even feeling a small twinge of guilt, at having been spared, but there was no luck involved here. This had been a choosing as sure as any act of Will. The timing had finally dawned, birthed unto this night like a screeching, blind babe come to announce a presence of evil, something known, felt, even if not seen. Each death like a sacrifice, a feeding, all meant to convey a transference of energy, an emergence from change.

Rules are rules.

*****

He reclines in the antique French gilt Aubusson upholstered armchair, one of a pair in this exquisite sitting room, three of the four walls bearing of expensive works of art, each canvas rather large, held in thick, gold-painted, wooden frames, the corners pushing out further, somewhat bulbous. He relaxes, looking over the comprehensive list on his touchpad, most of the information there having little to no value to him. He had already run a search on the names, and the title he seeks had shown up, and so like a beacon, that one draws his attention. He sits there in the expensive chair in this fine house he has rented for his hopefully short stay in the city, and he runs a lengthy, polished nail across his bottom lip.

She lied to him.

Why did she lie, he wonders.

He ponders this calmly, not letting it anger or otherwise disrupt him. It is far too interesting to figure out why than to take personal offense. Though he does wonder if it is personal. Personal for her, or perhaps personal toward him? Either way, whatever the reason, he wants to know.

He sets the slim device on the nearby rich cherry wood end table, the legs of the Victorian piece curved in a gentle shape, the gilt bronze accentuating it, culminating in the intricate face of a gargoyle as the centerpiece.

He delicately takes up the handle of the bone china tea cup. He sips of the creamy tea, hints of lavender wafting up. The vessel is very ornate, the bowl of it like the outer tracing of a fully bloomed rose. The top inner

DANCE OF THE BUTTERFLY

edge of the cup is a deep blue, gold designs of a very intricate nature extending throughout. A softly painted rose, also of the same blue, holds place at the center of the saucer, a no doubt matching flower also at the bottom of the cup's interior.

He savors the taste of the tea, letting it help to calm him even further, giving willingly to its embrace as he ponders more on the situation. No, the *revelation*.

The book is there. The second one of the Three. And the curator of the collection, Ms. Lilja Perhonen lied to him about it. Why? What is she protecting? Surely not the book. It is under lock and key and quite the robust security system, he has discerned. It is, of course, not proof against all efforts, but still, it is a quite valiant effort that could offer sufficient deterrence. He does not think this is exactly the case of some guardian having gotten too drunk with power. He could even go over her head, if he wished to take that somewhat complicated route, and gain access to the book, but that option does not seem the most attractive at this time.

What does she know, he then wonders.

Could she possibly be aware of the powerful secrets the book holds? But if so, why lie to him about it? She'd have to somehow perceive him as a challenger, a threat. Could that be possible? He blinks into a very slight furrowing of his brow, following the thread of this thought.

She would have to know that he intends to possess the book, if he is able, but still, it needs be more than that. If she knows he wishes to have it, then she has to figure he knows it is there, so lying of its presence seems foolish. She must think this sophomoric deflection would actually throw him off the scent, and if so, then she has no idea who he is, no idea of what he is capable, and if that is the case, then why would she know he wants it as he does?

He briefly entertains the idea that perhaps another collector has offered her some tremendous bribe to purchase it, and she might be considering breaking the law and selling it. He almost as quickly discards this idea, for though he is not psychic, he can read people fairly well, and he does not think she is the type to do such as that. Besides, the other potential competitors for this book would not likely take such an avenue for its acquisition.

And what of the other interested parties? Is it possible they have also learned of the tome being in this city, perhaps even in the school's collection of rare books? He ponders this more, but measures have been taken to alert him to such things. These are, of course, not full proof, but he feels fairly confident he'd know. Unless … no, he decides to remain confident.

He has another sip of his drink, slurping it very lightly, eyes off in some other realm than the corporeal one in which he sits. Whatever it is he may see, he still travels within the maze of his thoughts, thinking of the book, of its sentinel, of its other defenses, and why she has done as she has. Her actions almost seem desperate to him, knee jerk, but again, he is not sure why he picks up on such threads. Her control appeared almost impeccable, and that does not mingle with being reckless.

She is quite the enigma. He will have to find out more about her. And he thinks an "accidental" rendezvous may be in order.

He sips further of his tea. Nothing outward changed, but then a very slow curl takes his lips. Yes, he has come to a conclusion, a course of action, another domino to gently push and see what falls – the expected or the chaotic? He appears rather satisfied with his decision.

*****

"Lots of blood missing on this one."

Officers Pasztor and Mahler are again getting a report from the coroner, and both look at each other, then to McNeese.

"How can you tell?" Mahler asks her. "The prior two were pretty much completely gutted."

"Yes," she says, "but our analysts on the scene are generally able to make a decent determination, looking at blood spatter in addition to what is left in the victim. The state of this one was actually less of a mess, and there is a sufficient lack of blood volume for what is expected in the human body."

"Wait, what?" Pasztor rumbles. "The killer took the blood?"

"I am not saying that," McNeese tries to be patient, speaking slowly, emphatically, eyes peering at the detective like a frustrated teacher with a headstrong, ignorant student.

DANCE OF THE BUTTERFLY

"Then what are you saying?" he persists.

"There is sufficient lack of blood volume for what is expected in the human body," she repeats.

He throws up his hands, scoffing, turning away. The other gives her something of a sympathetic look. She is not needful of either reaction.

"Detective Pasztor, I am the coroner. *You* are the detective," she reminds him.

"I know that," he snaps, turning, glaring at her, "What did the killer do with it? Are we dealing with a vampire?"

Mahler, generally the diplomatic one of this duo, loses his composure at this, letting lose a few chuckles, looking at the floor and bringing a hand up to somewhat cover his face, in a mostly symbolic effort to conceal his amusement. He receives a look from his partner, but before he may speak, the coroner does so.

"I do not know if the killer consumed the blood. I am also not a profiler," she reminds him. "What I can tell you is that sufficient lack of blood volu-."

"Yes, yes, I heard you!" Pasztor interrupts, throwing his hands up again, then looking at the other officer, who is jittering with the diminishment of his chuckles. "Shut up," he delivers, not amused in the least.

Mahler wonders if the two ought to get back together, or at least have a few good, savage rows. The tension between the ex-lovers is always so palpable. He looks between them, Pasztor still looking challengingly at him, the coroner rather exasperated.

"Let's continue," he leads.

"Similar wounding, same weapon," McNeese falls right back into her role, certainly no lack of professionalism on her part, "Well, weapons," she points out, emphasizing the plural. "This one had an approximately five centimeter cut across the throat, which was effectively the cause of death."

"Effectively?"

She spares a single shooting glance to Pasztor. "It was the cause of death ... as best I can tell. There is another, very deep puncture wound, just underneath her sternum that pierced the heart, causing enough tissue damage to disrupt normal rhythm. If she were alive at that time."

151

"Well, can't you tell from the arterial spray from when her throat was cut or something?"

"I am not a field blood spatter analyst," she repeats to Pasztor, "And the documents are being studied to determine better information, but as I said about the lack of blood volume at the scene ..." she sends a narrowed gaze his way, making her point.

"Wait," Mahler bids, getting two pairs of eyes on him, and he looks up from his pondering, showing surprise to have so gained the attention of the other two, "If the victim was dead prior to the throat being cut, then there would not be the arterial spray, and if there was a lack of blood at the scene ..."

"That is a good point, Detective," the curvaceous woman concedes, "But the lack of blood, and *arterial spray*," she says, looking pointedly at both, "at the scene just tells us that there is a lack of blood at the *scene*. One reason for the lack of blood could be that the victim was killed elsewhere then deposited where found."

"Ah, right," Pasztor chimes in, "So, the killer may not have taken blood as trophy or some sort of bizarre fetish but just killed the girl in one place and left her in another."

"Yes, Detective," McNeese nods, and Pasztor looks up at her, not sure if she is being sincere of patronizing.

He will remain unsure, as she has turned to the corpse in question, gazing at the cleaned and autopsied remains atop the table, consulting the touchpad in her right hand. She extends the ballpoint pen, a constant tool of hers, using it mainly as a pointer rather than a writing instrument, and raises the covering sheet.

"I thought you two might be interested in this," she says, revealing the victim's left leg.

The two move closer peering, noticing the intricately designed tattoo high up on the corpse's thigh. It looks rather fresh, an abstract pattern, and left entirely untouched by the brutality which has taken her life.

"That's an interesting tattoo," Mahler remarks.

"Yes, something that looks very unique," Pasztor adds, both serious and focused now. "I am sure we could check the sort of parlors that these girls frequent and get some leads, help us with identifying her."

Both rise up from examining the marking, looking at McNeese.

DANCE OF THE BUTTERFLY

"Interesting, isn't it, that the killer avoided this area entirely," she poses, eyebrows very subtly perked. "This killer has shown a savagery unlike anything I have ever seen, and yet it seems they deliberately refrained from marring this tattoo."

"Well, it seems that way, yes, but we can't be sure," Mahler points out.

"Of course, you are correct, Detective," the coroner concedes, "but still, the other bodies have been shredded so thoroughly as to almost hinder identification, and yet this somewhat sizeable area of the thigh has been left untouched."

She looks between them both, light colored eyebrows raised more openly.

"What are you driving at?" Pasztor demands, though his tone is somewhat tempered.

"An animal would not be so exacting," she says.

"Ah, yes," Mahler nods, thoughtfully, but the other sort of furrows his brow.

"We're not entertaining that option," he quips.

She shrugs. "Suit yourselves, Detectives, but in case you wanted to leave open *all* possible avenues until proven otherwise, I thought I might try to offer some help."

"We need to get this one closed, like the others," Pasztor says, moving away a bit, hands on his waist.

"Others?"

"Well, yes, there has been an unfortunate rise in deaths of young ladies like … *these*."

"And what are *these* like?" McNeese somewhat puffs up, going on the defensive.

This gets a roll of the eyes from Pasztor.

"Runaways, missing persons, prostitutes, drug addicts, some combination thereof," he elaborates. "We're not *judging* them, Harriet," he says, giving a little shake of his head to emphasize his point, "We're trying to catch who did these things to them."

She takes a few moments, glaring at him, her eyes narrowing, a slow inhale giving rise to her chest within the white coat she wears. She then exhales sharply through her nostrils.

"Good," she finally says, "You do that."

DANCE OF THE BUTTERFLY

CHAPTER NINE

Skot sits at the same place, the one that feels like "their" table now. It has, of course, become something of a desk for him during his time of study here, his own inclination for routine bringing him to sit in the same seat each time he arrives to further examine the book.

It is quiet in the room, a simple slurp of his coffee like the sounds of a gurgling brook, and he continues to look at the pages of the rare, open tome. The assistant, Amanda Honeycutt, is also in here, appearing to be engrossed in her own task of putting away some of the books that reside in the more crowded shelves toward the front of the room. They are much less valuable than the ones deeper within, being lent out or available for access under much more generous restrictions than the one he examines.

He flips a leaf, the short, generally unobtrusive sound again seeming something louder than usual in the quiet room. He draws the pads of his fingers along the resilient paper, smoothing it down gently, feeling the ridges formed by the lettering, his eyes on the recto page. The cabalistic information is almost entrancing, perhaps made to even be so, covering an abundance of subject matters and styles, a sure-flowing river as opposed to a maelstrom. It is as though an arrangement of matters that may immediately be thought of as too conflicting and presenting them in such a way as to expose the constant communion, not create it, merely move veils aside to reveal. He becomes lost in it.

"Is this the chapter on mathematics?" asks a soothing, alluring voice.

He looks up to see her there, having walked up behind him, placing her hands gently atop his shoulders to lean in and peer at the cause of his fixation.

"Geometry," he says, smiling warmly into her similar expression, "Physics, perhaps … or metaphysics. Cosmology."

They both grin further, then bubbling into a light chuckle. The sound is just as quickly dissolved as he turns to look about the room.

"She's gone," Lilja informs, leaning in further to speak this, giving it in the tones of an almost suggestive whisper, then sneaking a quick placement of her lips at his upper jaw, just beside his left ear.

"Ahhhh," he nods, "I didn't hear her leave."

"I noticed," she says, still speaking in that quieter tone of voice, leaning in to him, hands sliding down his shoulders to his upper chest before she wraps her arms together, snugging him.

He turns to look at her, smiling warmly, and they share a kiss, lingering at it a short time, but not too long lest they be discovered in such an amorous exchange.

"Don't you have video surveillance in here?" he asks, looking about at the tops of the walls of the room, "To protect the books?"

"Only for the more valuable ones in the back of the room," she reveals, still holding onto him, though having relaxed into a more comfortable embrace.

"So, we're not being spied upon, then?" he smirks, the expression appearing slowly, subtly, then growing, even as his eyes narrow slightly.

"No," she says, grinning back at him, and he merely continues to return the expression she wears. "What are you thinking about?" she presses.

"You," he says, giving length to the word, letting it taper at the end into a breathy hint.

"What about me?" she continues, that curve still upon her inviting lips.

"You obviously do not weigh much. I am certain this table would easily support you."

She blinks, her eyes going wider, then she tucks her chin in a bit, and that lovely flush rises to her skin, "Oh…" she realizes his implication, then cuddling into him again, another kiss to his cheek, "We can't do that."

"Well, we *can*, but I suppose we shouldn't."

DANCE OF THE BUTTERFLY

And now it is her turn to smirk, rising up and giving him a playful smack on both shoulders with her hands. She then slides gracefully into the chair beside him, scooting it very close, her right hand going to his left leg under the table as they both lean in to look upon the book.

"Geometry and cosmology?" she tries to lead him back to less salacious subjects.

"Yes," he smiles lightly, managing to tear his eyes from her and look down at the open pages.

"I am not as familiar with cosmology," she informs him.

"It is something like studying the history of the cosmos through its physical properties, trying to discern and understand those 'laws', then even using that to predict its future."

"Like geology is for the Earth?"

"Somewhat." He gives her another small grin, and she glances up at him for that brief moment to share in the expression before they both return to the tome.

"So, using the geometry of the … cosmos," she says after the brief pause in thought, "You can deduce its history and its future?" she posits, shifting her eyes to him for an answer.

"I would presume that is the point, but I am not a professor of either subjects, and this is not exactly an accepted academic text."

A brief smile traces over her lips at this, but then she as quickly looks serious, that same expression of open curiosity on her that she often wears. He thinks it is fearlessness, though he suspects she would disagree.

"We know next to nothing about the author, Domitus Caelum," she muses, "It sounds like a pen name, anyway. Who would have been named Domitus Caelum at that time?"

He nods, weightily. "We've come to the same conclusion. The name may be translated as 'to tame or dominate the heavens', which could merely allude to the idea of trying to understand the universe through the means presented in the text."

"Knowing something doesn't mean dominating it," she remarks.

"Not necessarily, but it may connote a form of possession or control, or it may even be giving an even more subtle commentary on the presumed power that comes from knowledge."

She nods further at this, obviously giving his words some thought, then looks back at him. "But knowledge is power."

"Well, that does seem to be a popular saying, and I would agree with it to a degree. We may certainly gain some power *through* knowledge, but does knowing something, like knowing this book, for instance, gives us dominance over it?"

"Not over the book, I suppose," she carefully, if not somewhat reluctantly, admits.

"Our general presumption at this time is that it is to be taken metaphorically or that the author or authors may have been rather arrogant."

"Maybe both," she somewhat murmurs.

"Maybe," he offers her a smile, which she returns as she looks back at him.

"So, what is this, then?" she gently touches the woodcut figure on the right page with the tip of her index finger.

"It seems to be the plotting of many confluences, a schematic, as it were, or a map, showing connections between ... well, passageways," he looks at her carefully after he says this.

She finally looks back to him as the silence grows, noting his attention on her. She merely nods, accepting of what he has said and desirous of more.

"The book purports to document different dimensions of existence, such as we may sometimes consider there to be a corporeal and spiritual realm, for example."

"Who is 'we'?" she asks, giving her eyes fully to him.

"Oh, humans," he expands, showing something of a sheepish smile.

"You were using plural pronouns earlier when referring to the book, so I wasn't sure."

"Oh," he says again, his smile increases, "I meant my family then, but now I was just using a general example from human history ... for comparison."

And again she gives that simple nod of open acceptance.

"So, this book talks about such different dimensions and how to travel between them?"

DANCE OF THE BUTTERFLY

He just looks upon her for another lingering moment, and as before, the increasing silence finally scratches at her mental focus, giving her to look back up at him. "Well, yes, some parts of it do," he gives her.

She smiles very lightly at this, and he continues to just stare. Not sure what exactly to make of her incredible open-mindedness. She notes the gaze, not looking back at the object of their study this time, and the pleasant curl at her lips increases, no bashfulness this time, just smiling at him. She then leans in for a kiss, which he willingly accepts, their lips meeting briefly, almost casually within the comfortable intimacy such implies.

"So who travels between these gateways?" she asks, and he notes the particular choice of word, 'gateway', and the instinct and understanding it suggests on her part.

"When they are open," he qualifies, "Those who are able," then going to the book, moving through its contents with a sure familiarity, though still being mindful of its rarity and value, "This part spends some time describing the various denizens who dwell in the dimensions, though, there do seem to be more dimensions listed than populations …"

"Are they uninhabited, or did the author just not know?" she asks, showing more of her astute insight.

"We're not sure."

She nods, thoughtfully, realizing what it means for them to not know. "And you said 'when they are open'," she continues, "So, they are sometimes closed, and does that mean that opening them is not very easy?"

"Not easy at all." He nods, continuing to be impressed by her, "Imagine it is like a tunnel with ends that may be open to varying degrees," he says, holding up his right hand and making a fist, the side of it angled for her perusal, and she watches closely. "It may be closed entirely, and no one gets through, but it may open some," and he relaxes the clench, allowing a tiny opening through his fist, "So, those that would fit may get through, and it may be compelled to open further," and he makes a larger opening, "Allowing more through."

"Compelled?" she asks, "Are the gates alive?"

"No. But they obey their natural law like anything else."

"So, compelling them means that if you know how, you can open or close them when they otherwise would not?"

"Well, something like that," he thoughtfully answers, "It would be more like causing the normal stimulus that would naturally open or close them. Without that, they will not move."

"Amazing," she says, her lips curving into an appreciative smile, "It sounds like a fantasy or science fiction novel."

"Yes, I suppose it does," he grins, "But I assure you," he adds with a perk of his eyebrows, "The author did not intend it as such."

*****

Several people are gathered in the office, not so many that it is uncomfortably crowded, but the tone of the meeting contributes far more to the unease than the number of bodies. Most of those are male, which seems to belie the continued current trend in gender dominance of these positions, though the few women present indicate a potential change.

It appears quite possible, though, that only one person wants to be in this room right now.

The man behind the desk is not the most powerful in here, though from day-to-day, he may be. Right now, he sits behind this piece of furniture, and such is typically not a position from which he takes a haranguing. The man who has come this morning has chosen this place to let the director know that even on his home ground, he is not immune.

The visitor had been seated, the others standing about as informal audience to the main event, but as he has picked up steam, he has risen from the comfortable chair offered to him, set just across from the director, the only other chair in here, as though an honor. The decent upholstery on the seat, back, and arms may have even been meant to possibly lull the man, but if that were the case, it has failed.

He wears a dark blue suit, obviously tailored, not too expensive, but certainly not cheap. His shirt is an off white, the tie bold, powerful. They all know who he is, and they all know he makes a rather good living. His sole income certainly does not come from his position on the City Council, and if his past record is any indicator, he is primed to rise much higher.

DANCE OF THE BUTTERFLY

The man's short brown hair is parted on the left side, thick and full enough to give indication of the waviness it would have it not so carefully controlled. His nose is broad, his face almost square, though his strong chin does provide something of a tapering effect. His dark brown eyes appear alight with a fire.

"Ten dead girls in barely two months," he says, the words uttered carefully. "*Ten*," he emphasizes, narrowing his eyes into something of a glare at the man behind the desk, "That is not acceptable in this city."

"Councillor Keller, we are a city of some size, and we, unfortunately get dead girls quite often," the captain tries to help, and the director closes his eyes, all he'll show of the cringe at this attempt.

The so-addressed politician, Dominik Keller slowly looks over at the captain, his eyes leading the way. The intense glare gets various responses from the ranking detectives standing near their commanding officer, some wanting to defend the man, others wanting to move out of any potential range of those eyes.

"Ten dead girls in two months," the councillor repeats, taking a few steps toward the man, "Pardon me, Captain, for not being more specific, but these ten girls are all linked to the human trafficking and sex slave problem we seem to be plagued with in this city, and of those ten," he continues, picking up pace and more steam, "Two died from overdose, one of questionable cause, of the other seven, five are definitely murder. That is a one hundred and fifty percent increase over this same month last year, and if we include the others, since they seem headed in that direction, we have a three hundred percent increase. *Three ... hundred*."

The man does not shout, but the force of his words is undeniable.

"Councillor," the one behind the desk summons the other's attention, "Forensics is still working on those, and they are all open cases at this point. We're taking this very seriously."

"I hope so," he asserts, "because I am."

"We can see that, Councillor Keller," the director finally speaks into the heavy silence.

"I've read the reports, all of them," the political man continues, going quickly on the end of the director's words, "Even those that may not seem directly related to the victims. We have a very serious problem in our city, and it is trending upwards. This *will* stop."

161

"Of course, sir."

"This city will not be known as Central Europe's prime destination for human trafficking and sexual slavery. Is that clear?" he pushes, and his question is greeted with several nodding heads, "I cannot fathom that you all are not more aware of and focused on this very serious problem."

"We are, Councillor," the captain presses in, whether out of recklessness or bravery, it is not clear. "We've put together task forces in addition to the normal method of assignments-," he continues, but is cut off by one of his own men.

"Maybe it's the vigilante," this one blurts, "We're working on getting him," though if more were to be said after this, the beam of Keller's eyes setting upon the one talking halts any further words.

Once the officer has shut up, the councillor looks back at the captain.

"The vigilante is not part of this," he iterates.

"Sir, with all due respect, we have reports linking the-," the captain tries, but he is again interrupted.

"Do you mean the report from that … *town* in Poland?" the councillor interjects, having thought better of whatever adjective he may have had in mind, "I've read that report, Captain. Have you?" he continues, drilling his eyes into the other's face. "It's bullshit."

No one says anything to that, but many pairs of dumbfounded eyes stare.

"We have reports that the girl, Marina Potchak, Ukrainian, seventeen, was murdered in cold blood while chained to a bed and coming down from drugs," he begins, "She suffered several gunshots wounds inflicted by an FN P90, at least three of which would have been sufficient to cause death, and there is a statement from a survivor that someone fitting the vigilante's possible known appearance was there. Does that sound correct?"

He is greeted with a few nods, though most just continue to stare.

"The vigilante uses an FN P90, we know that from the attack on the warehouse here, an attack which resulted in several incapacitated *guards*, and I use the term generously. They were criminals, mercenaries, armed killers, and they would have intended lethal harm to such an intruder, yet he did not kill a *single one*. They were disabled and secured, much like

DANCE OF THE BUTTERFLY

would happen at the hands of a law enforcement officer who was trained to only use lethal force under certain circumstances.

"So, why, then, does the vigilante, if indeed he was even there, kill a non-threatening young girl?" he pitches, pausing a moment, "He leaves three alive, including the 'witness'?

"Same ammunition," he continues after another weighty pause, "We know it was a P90, but where is the ballistics analysis that links it to the vigilante's weapon? Our offices have some of those for comparison, so where is the analysis? Same caliber bullet does not mean same gun."

He pauses, eyebrows raised, daring anyone on this impromptu jury to contradict him.

"I have my doubts if he was even there," he continues. "What the vigilante is doing is giving a lot of trouble to the crime ring in our city, and they are going to *push back*."

"But what about the murdered doctor?" a detective pitches.

"We've wasted enough time talking about this vigilante," he dismisses, turning his focus back to the man behind the desk. "The Task Force put together to investigate and find the suspect is a waste. I want it dissolved. Pursue the vigilante for *vigilantism*, just like any other case, and assign it a priority, just like any other case, *but*," he nears a climax, "The very limited resources of this department need to be better focused on busting up this human trafficking/sex slavery operation. *That* is a blight on the city, and it needs to stop.

"There are families of those missing and dead girls back in other countries," he continues, extending the fingers of his left hand in succession as he ticks off the information, "Ukraine, Russia, Romania, and I am not going to act like this is less important because only two of the ten dead girls are from here. This *will* be handled." He pauses again, looking around, giving a steady, pointed gaze to all those in the room before going again back to the man behind the desk.

"Director, I thank you and the others for your time. I will also expect regular, frequent reports on this matter delivered to my office." And thus concluded, he turns to make a smooth exeunt from the chamber.

It takes a moment for the silent tension to relax, but once it does, it is like a growing splinter in the dike. People begin moving, some throw out quiet chuckles and wide eyes as signs of their anxiety. Some appear angered.

"Captain, can he really tell us how to conduct our business?" one asks, and the captain looks over at the speaker, then turns and angles his questioning eyes at the director.

The man behind the desk takes a moment to collect his thoughts, pulling in a breath, but trying not to seem too shaken up in front of his subordinates. The large-sized lenses of his round spectacles take on a reflection of the overhead lights as he lowers his chin, obscuring his eyes from view before he looks back at them fully, preparing to speak.

"Councillor Keller is a powerful man in this city. He may not be the Mayor … *yet*," he adds after a split second of afterthought, "but he has many powerful friends. He has the Minister's ear," he informs, and they all know he refers to the person to whom the director answers.

A moment of tense silence stretches out, a cacophony of shuffling feet, moving hands, murmured words exchanged.

"Alright, everyone," the director refocuses, "The Councillor is right, even if I do not care for his methods. We have an obvious problem here. I'm bothered that it has come to this and even gained his notice. He's going to hammer on this; I can assure you of that."

"It'll help his political career," says one cynical voice.

"You can bet on that," the director quips, staring at the one who has spoken, "And that's why he'll be in this to the end now. So," he closes, "that end better come soon," and he looks about, then sets his eyes directly on the captain.

"Yes, sir," the man says after a moment of enduring that stare.

"Alright, you're all dismissed." And the group funnels out of his office with the meandering energy of a stunned herd.

*****

"What do you mean the Task Force is disbanded?"

The crime boss does not even look up from where he is standing, wearing a dark blue track suit, throwing out hunks of meat to the chained Rottweilers, the light of the descending sun catching off the red shine.

DANCE OF THE BUTTERFLY

The dogs are eager, fighting over the treats, wolfing them down as quickly as they can move their powerful jaws.

"Look at that, huh?" he grins broadly, "I bet my dogs would make quick work of that *vigilante*," he all but spits the word.

The others just watch as he takes up a few more pieces of the meat, tossing them to the powerful animals before brushing his hands off, using a nearby towel to finish his cleaning, turning his eyes to the men.

"I asked you a question."

"The Task Force was disbanded," Quain says, meeting the other man's gaze.

"Why?" Gnegon pushes, perking his eyebrows, his slit eyes widening, his entire aspect as one who is reluctantly dealing with a child.

"A particular City Councillor has taken an interest in dead girls," speaks a voice, but it does not belong to Quain.

They all look over to Duilio, who is still watching the animals, and still wearing his ubiquitous sunglasses despite the imminent gloaming. He even looks to have raised his chin, peering at the feeding dogs from beneath his shades, his lips pursed somewhat to hold the burning cigarette.

"What do I care if some city councilman is a necrophiliac?" Gnegon asks, perplexed. "Are we trying to bribe him or something?"

The inspector pushes off from where he had been leaning on a large, wooden crate, taking a few lazy steps toward the other three, his face now downturned as he looks at the men over his sunglasses.

"No," he flashes a grin, "This councillor is taking an interest in young girls who have turned up dead, some murdered, in this very city, and I would suspect that the ones who were not born in this city were brought here against their will, made to become dependent on drugs, forced into a sort of sexual servitude …" and the eyebrows have been perking up this entire time.

"Get to your point," Gnegon growls, and the two dogs look over from where they have lapsed into a somewhat contended recline, ears perking up, but they do not take to their feet.

"This councillor is a powerful one, not just some old seat warmer who casts occasional votes," Duilio continues, "He's *fierce!*" he emphasizes, shooting his hands out, splaying his fingers, then he plucks the cigarette from his mouth after a quick drag, and he shows another grin from which emerges a short, bubbly chuckle, smoke puffing out with it, as though amused with his own telling. "He thinks that a bunch of unfortunate girls is a problem, and that it means *bigger* problems. Much bigger than some *vigilante*, no?"

Gnegon just stares, any good mood he may have experienced from spending some time out here in the nice air, feeding his dogs, having now completely dissolved. His face is pinched up with concern, frustration, a brewing anger.

"But that doesn't mean we will stop what we are doing, hmm?" Duilio says, finally removing his sunglasses, after slipping the cigarette back between his lips, folding the arms of the black shades and tucking them in his inside jacket pocket, angling his now exposed eyes to the other two.

"Right," Alec blurts, though Quain just stands there, giving a slow, nearly undetectable nod.

"Who is this *councillor*," Gnegon finally speaks, some spittle erupting as he does. "Why don't we just kill him?"

"No!" Duilio exclaims, eyes going wide, hands held out, fingers up to display his palms. "Do you want to bring an end to yourself?"

"He is that well connected?" the crime boss asks, more thoughtful.

"He is, he is," the Interpol Agent nods, emphatically, "He will probably skip right over the local avenues left before him and end up on the national legislature soon, and who knows, maybe even higher than that someday."

"Shit!" Gnegon curses.

"Yes," Duilio nods deeply, "Shit," he agrees, though uttering the word in a very calm fashion.

"So, I step up imports to counteract the vigilante, and he disappears, so this results in a glut, too much supply-."

"Which will lower value," Duilio points out, and the crime boss nods, not bothered at all by this interruption.

"And because there is always going to be some amount of *dead girls*," he iterates, looking between the three men, his sarcastic tone evincing exactly how much he dehumanizes the young ladies. "There are too many!" He throws up his hand in exasperation.

DANCE OF THE BUTTERFLY

"Three hundred percent increase from last year," Quain states, he and his partner having been two of the detectives summoned to the meeting that day.

"So much?" Gnegon asks, perking his eyebrows.

"Yeah," Quain nods, "But three of them are victims of the serial killer."

"What?" Gnegon almost shouts. "That *súka* is also hitting *my* girls!?" he exclaims, then scoffs loudly, throwing his hands about, and the dogs finally rise up to their paws, one of them giving a clipped, inquiring bark.

Gnegon turns to this sound, emitting a short kissing sound with this lips, and the two animals go back to relaxing. He then turns his frustration back to the three men.

"So, I have the vigilante, this councillor, and the serial killer all harassing me?" and he shakes his head, pressing his lips together.

"You are the big fish in this lake, Gnegon," Duilio says, having finished his cigarette and disposed of it, and he clamps a hand on the man's shoulder. "You know you will have enemies … troubles."

The gangster nods, pursing out his lower lip. "I do, yes, and I need troubleshooters, hmm?" He looks pointedly at the three.

"Of course, you do," the inspector releases the hold, moving, turning his back to them momentarily as he talks, "We have to change tactics on the vigilante," and he turns back, holding out his arms a bit, "I am sorry to say that, Gnegon, but this councillor is a bigger issue, and if he decided to focus on *you*, that would be a much, *much* bigger problem."

"He *is* focusing on me!" Gnegon exclaims, bringing up semi-clawed hands on bent arms, shaking them.

"No, no," Duilio soothes, moving back over, this time actually draping a consoling arm over the man's shoulders. "He is not focusing on you. He is focusing on dead girls."

The crime boss gives this some thought, moving his gaze from the agent over to the officers, both of whom nod.

"Alright," Gnegon says, moving away from Duilio. "So, then, what do we do?"

"Well," the inspector gives a shrug, pursing out his lips, "Trim down your operations, take more control over what happens to your girls, and if they do die, for whatever reason, dispose of them better."

"Not as much 'official' help with hunting the vigilante, either," Quain adds.

Gnegon just shakes his head, obviously displeased but more accepting of the developing situation.

"If I do too little, the vigilante cripples me," he muses. "If I do too much, the government comes after me," he says, throwing his hands toward the two detectives.

"It is a careful balancing act, yes." Duilio nods slowly, purposefully.

Gnegon glances over then adds his own nod of agreement. "When I was new in this town," he begins, "I had to be very careful, and not just because of the police, but because of rivals. I had to spread out, not too thin as to be unable to protect myself, but not so centralized as to be an easy target, eh?" he continues, getting agreeing nods from the trio, "Now, I have no real rivals. The city is mine." He turns from the expansive backyard, looking toward that very place. "Being spread out helps to keep the police off my back," he spares another glance to the detectives who give no outward reaction, "But it also gives many targets to the lone vigilante. He is one man, and how do I stop one man?" He pauses again, looking at the three, "I give him one target."

"Hmm?" Duilio somewhat asks, eyebrows rising.

The crime boss just smirks.

*****

Outside the city, not too far, but far enough to be in this field, the rolling hills swooping away, the trees like ancient heralds, even the thin ones, even the stubby ones. Some hold the colorful leaves of autumn, others have eagerly shed this weight, preparing for the coming winter, their branches like grotesquely elongated fingers with too many joints.

Mist caresses this place, the wispy tendrils thickening in some parts enough to perhaps seem a fog. The enshrouding like a haze even as much a filter, softening some things, heightening others. Noises travel through where vision meets confusion, scratchy calls might be from an insect,

DANCE OF THE BUTTERFLY

shrill turning to throaty, the croaking of frogs, something else, something odd and unknown.

He blinks, almost a casual gesture, even reptilian such is it so slow, deliberate. His eyes linger in the direction of the most recent piping call, trying to discern more of its origin. As such mysteries are left unanswered, he moves his focus forward, eyes like the steady, slow sweep of a lighthouse beam. He tenses the muscles of his right leg in preparation of taking a step, but he halts, just looking out over the gloom.

How did he get here? When did he get here?

He remembers being back in his dingy room, again just staring at the ceiling. His mind was somewhat preoccupied with the tattoo he had seen on the prostitute. He had returned that evening and done his own sketching from memory, adding the image to his journal.

He starts then, lean muscles tensing, rising up to resolution within his all-too-thin frame, eyes jerking over in the same direction from which he had heard the long, throaty call. He saw something moving, or thought he did, but it seems gone in a blinking flash. Though he is obviously immersed in confusion, fear, he takes tentative steps in that direction, holding out his right arm, hand up, fingers curled, as though the distorted cane of a blind person.

"Who's there!?" he calls out, demanding, for he has seen the shifting shadows and hints of a body moving deeper in the covering mist.

He receives no answer, sees nothing else there.

He jerks his head about, dread growing. How did he get here? Where is he?

He fell asleep, back in his room, and now he is here. Did he sleepwalk all the way to this place? He looks around, trying to find lights from the city, and yes, he sees something off toward his left, not really far at all, though feeling a world away. He jerks his head back right as he hears another animalian noise, and there is another bright flash in his peripheral vision. Something there, but not.

His compulsion has brought him here, as sure as if he is a dumb dowsing rod. He even parts his thin, cracked lips, trying to defy this and speak, but he is not even able to manage the most pathetic squeak to add to the creeping noises of the area. His tongue somewhat pokes out with the effort, a discoloration and coating upon it that bespeaks of his ill health. He gives up, after some measure of strain, shaking his head, eyes squeezed shut, taking in lungsful of air.

That air is so wet upon his skin, giving a chill to his already sickly pallor. He looks down and realizes he is barefoot, taking this subconscious jaunt in his nightclothes – a stained, white tank top and thin, gray sweatpants. His feet are covered in the detritus of his travels, no doubt leaving behind a trail of his explorations. He looks back, wondering if anyone is indeed following him, but other than the eerie sounds and occasional glimpses of movement, it seems he is alone out here in the mist.

He doesn't feel alone.

It is curious to him, in the deeper recesses of his analytical, rational mind, that some people seem to lose their hold on sanity, reality, whatever one may wish to call it, by feeling alone, isolated, but he would much rather feel alone. It is the things he senses, the things he sees, that are driving him to this horrible point in his life. He wishes they were not real.

He'd rather just be alone.

*****

"SSC."

"SSC?"

He smiles lightly at her, nodding slowly, chewing his food. They sit at a somewhat secluded table in this nice, small café, enjoying a late morning breakfast, or even a brunch, if one were so inclined. They had spent last evening together, she staying again overnight in his hotel room. She'd even brought a bag with her, a change of clothes, some toiletries, though the scarf and hat proved unneeded as the unseasonably warm and dry weather continues to bless the area, the relative humidity below seventy percent.

"Safe, sane, and consensual," he expands, after having swallowed his food and followed that with a taste of his fresh fruit juice, "A core tenet of healthy, mature practice of BDSM."

She nods, taking this in, keeping herself in a mainly polite, quiet repose, enjoying the meal and company, paying attention to him.

DANCE OF THE BUTTERFLY

"There are obviously a lot of activities in which people may engage that may *seem* non-consensual, this may even play a part of the fantasy element, the exhilaration, but ultimately, everything is consensual. That is also why people use safe words and signals."

She looks back up at him from having gathered another forkful of food, perking her eyebrows. He hears the question plainly enough.

"Another core tenet is openness and communication. This all comes from mutual trust and respect. We should be able to talk, meaningfully and maturely, about anything. It doesn't mean we will be okay with everything or do everything, but being able to talk of it is important."

She nods to this, for it is something about which they have before spoken.

"In relation to this, neither of us should take it personally if the other does not want to do something." He looks at her, that gentle curl still on his lips, and she nods lightly in understanding, bidding him to proceed. "We know we are sexually attracted to one another," he states, and this gets a grin on her lovely lips, and that ever-ready blush tickles at her features, though it does not claim her as much as usual, "So we should not take it as a rejection if one of us does not want to do something. A safe word or signal may be used by the submissive if they are being asked to do something they do not want to do. The signal is given, everything is stopped. No bad or hurt feelings. It's not a personal critique; it's just about preferences."

She nods, picking up her mug to have a few swallows of the milky coffee. "But what if I want to be pushed?" she asks.

"Yes, well, we *will* push each other, I suspect," he smiles, "But that goes back to open, honest communication. I'd rather us talk about something instead of, perhaps, my springing it on you in the depths of a session."

She nods to this, pondering, and he waits for her.

"I like that you push me," she finally says, looking into his eyes. "This is new to me, and I am very shy, anyway, so I need the push. But not too much. You are patient, and you nudge me just the right amount, in just the right way."

He smiles even more at this, the expression warm, loving. "Thank you, Lily. You deserve to be treated well."

And this does get the blush to arrive as she grins deeper, those shoulders scrunching up a bit, though they settle quickly enough, and her lips part to reveal some of her teeth as the smile broadens.

"So, we choose a safe word and signal," he carries on after spearing some more of his meal on the fork.

"Signal?" she peers, wiping her mouth with the cloth napkin, "And why both?"

"Well," he answers, a smirk taking his lips in a subtle suggestion, "If one is gagged, they may not have clear use of their voice."

"Oh." She blinks, and the blush from before looks calm compared to the one that takes her now.

"A signal may be a rapid series of blinks or a tapping of the fingers, any number of things that does not require a distinctly heard word. Some even use the humming of a particular tune. The idea is to have many options agreed upon by all parties."

"Ahh, like tapping out in a martial arts bout," she compares.

"Yes," he agrees after a split second of consideration, "Just like that. If you tap, it stops. And tapping is a good one to use, because if you are blindfolded you cannot very well use your eyes to give a particular sort of blink," he adds, then pauses, staring at her, his grin one of bemusement, for she has looked away, somewhat scrunching in to make her petite self even smaller than usual, and the healthy flush of her skin manages to increase even more. "Lily?" he gently tries.

Her grin curls up then, more to the side, becoming its own smirk, her eyes shifting about, then moving up to give him a tentative look, before she blinks and averts her gaze again. He just watches, continuing to give his own warm, accepting smile.

"I think I would really like to be blindfolded," she finally says, leaning forward somewhat toward the table, her hands down in her lap now, arms pressed in tightly to herself, unwittingly giving a press to her bosom.

He watches as the moment lingers, not disturbing her, for it is her discovery. She lets her thoughts take her, still looking forward and down, not focused on the physical. After a moment of this, she looks back up at him.

DANCE OF THE BUTTERFLY

"It's scary but exciting. Not knowing exactly what is going to happen next."

He nods slowly. "It very much includes the mind, and people like we make generous use of our imaginations."

She smiles sweetly at this, giving a blink of her eyes.

"So, what might you like as a safe word?" he asks before resuming the use of his held fork.

"Oh," she ponders for a very brief moment, "I don't know. What do you suggest?"

"I tend to go for flowers or plants or some such. You'd not want to use a word that might normally come up in the context of a session, not even one that might normally be useful in such a situation, due to the aspect of roleplay. It is not a good idea to use 'no' as a safe word, for instance, but 'banana', well, that stands out."

He offers her a teasing grin at this, and she chuckles lightly, nodding.

"Oregano," she suddenly says.

He looks at her, in the midst of chewing his food, then he nods as he finishes, applying a wipe of the napkin to his mouth as he reaches for his own coffee. "That is a good one. May I ask why you wish it?"

She looks fully upon him then, "Oregano is known to repel some butterflies."

He nods, after swallowing the strong, somewhat bitter liquid, "Oregano it is, then."

They share a smile, letting a quiet take them, working through more of their respective dishes. It is not terribly crowded here, though the weather on this Sunday is very nice. It could likely well be contributing to people being out and active as opposed to sitting in a café, lingering over a meal and pleasant company.

"There are also often rules agreed upon by all participants."

"Oh?" she leads, having a generous sample of her water, the glass standing next to one of milk and another of fresh fruit juice.

"Yes, such as how to dress or behave, how to address one another, certain tasks that may need to be done, certain protocols followed."

"Oh, that sounds involved."

"Well, we don't need to go so far at this time, if ever. Those are just examples. It is entirely up to us." He smiles warmly at her.

She smiles back, thinking. "How would you make me dress?" she asks, and he senses the playful flirtatiousness to it that he so adores.

"Well, it would depend on the circumstances, but you have a remarkable body, which I find very pleasing and attractive, so, if you are willing, I would probably dress you in ways that show that off, again, depending on the circumstances."

She nods, taking it in. "For us, right? Not to show me off like a trophy?"

"Yes, for us, though may I have a bit of pride at knowing someone such as yourself chooses to be with me."

And she blushes again, though it is lighter, more a warm soothe. "Yes," she manages, then she sits up straighter, collecting her thoughts. "I get bothered a lot because of my looks," she says, and he gives her his full, serious attention. "I get emails sometimes of a very unpleasant nature, people wanting sexual things from me, some even outright offering me money."

"That's terrible." He blinks, brow furrowing.

She looks at him, lips pressed together. "My email is public, so it happens," she says, "And so I sometimes distance myself, and that makes some people think I am just a stuck-up, cold bitch. I work out and train for myself. I make myself look pretty for myself. It doesn't mean I am doing it to catch a man or something. I want to be healthy, and sometimes I like to wear pajamas all day, and sometimes I like to do my hair and put on make-up and nice clothes."

He nods, slowly, still just watching and listening. She then looks back up at him, and where she had just worn a somewhat open, almost casually determined expression, she now has on one of her wonderful smiles.

"I'd like that, though, wearing what you want me to wear, sometimes, depending. I'd like to look good for you, for you to think I look good."

"Thank you," he says with utmost sincerity, "That is a wonderful gift you give me, and I do think you look good. You are a very beautiful person, Lily, inside and out."

DANCE OF THE BUTTERFLY

"Thank you," she says, smiling back, that normal flush that may have threatened from such a compliment not taking her now as she stalwartly returns his gaze. "Likewise."

His own smile increases, cheeks pressing out to greater prominence, "Thank you."

"What other sorts of Rules?" she asks, cutting into the dwindling remnants of her breakfast sausage.

"Well," he ponders, finishing up a mouthful of his own food with a quick swallow, "Sometimes people that are not living together agree to send a good night and good morning each day."

"Wouldn't people in a 'vanilla' relationship also do that?"

"Yes, but in this case, there might be consequences for the submissive if they break a Rule."

"Oh," she says, blinking into that lost stare she sometimes gets, thoughts again taking her.

"It is meant to be a way to make those involved feel close, of course. It's nice to know you may be your partner's first and last thought of the day."

She smiles up at him. "I think about you a lot."

"And I, you," he returns.

"You also said something about tasks," she leads, now just interested in coffee and talking.

"I did. There may be tasks, or even chores, if you will, given, and again, if they are not done in a proper and timely manner, there could be consequences."

"May I have an example?"

"Of course." He smiles at her, very much enjoying her manner, and he fixes his eyes on her, deciding it is time for a push, "I want you to choose a time, *soon*, and somewhere in public, whether your office, a bathroom, wherever, I want you to pleasure yourself and think of me, and then I want you to tell me about it, in detail."

Her eyes have stopped blinking as she just stares at him, and they slowly grow wider, and as if on cue, the lovely flush rises over her flesh.

"Oh," she finally says, the sound somewhat meek, breathy, "Okay."

He smiles. "Good," reaching over to gently place a hand atop her nearer thigh, "Don't get caught, and …," he leans in closer, and she rises up on a subtly stiffening spine, shoulders going back a bit as he brings his mouth to her ear, whispering, "Don't orgasm. You may not orgasm without my permission."

When he has finished slowly moving back to his own upright position, she is covered in a riotous blush. He merely looks at her, his lips curled into a subtle grin. She finally meets his gaze, and she nods.

"Okay."

DANCE OF THE BUTTERFLY

CHAPTER TEN

The darkly-garbed figure has arrived here on foot. It had proven a lengthy trek, and much of that time had been spent pondering. The intruder has to be careful of possible cameras, even those carried by most people nowadays on their mobile phones, and so shadows, height, care find use to minimize this potential exposure as much as possible. It is not just fortunate that the buildings in this part of the city are so close together, but the layout is known and thus taken advantage of in the planning of the night's excursion. Few people bother looking up, and even if they did, they'd have to catch the precise moment to be lucky enough to see a passing shadow. Some people hear odd sounds, like footsteps or scurrying through their ceilings. They presume this to be pests of some kind, hoping it does not become an issue requiring further intervention.

The email in-box had been rather more full than usual, some messages sent with a high importance. They had been waiting too long, and now, with a simmering feeling of guilt, the vigilante is out again. One of them, in particular, had held big news, big, found by the contact known as Sparrow.

They are trying to pin the murder of the girl, Marina Potchak, on the very person who tried to save her. It had struck deep in the gut to read that information. All that effort expended to rescue the girl only to have her slaughtered there in that farmhouse. And it had been an obvious trap, and now the figure feels guilt at having been so lured and that an innocent life has been extinguished. Casualties must be expected in this war. It won't be easy.

The vigilante crawls up a tight collection of cable pipes outside an apartment building, moving up to the roof of the tall structure, the metal brackets placed well, supporting the weight of the climber as the length is traversed. Quick, quiet footsteps, and the other side is reached, and from this vantage, the target proves easily seen.

The building to be watched holds one story, across the street and down a ways, not far at all. The enhanced binoculars are brought out, placed in front of the eyes, and the spying begins.

Messages had also been received regarding Detective Pello Halkias, and though this is far less disconcerting than the news of Marina, it had still been a blow. More information had been unearthed, and it seems a fair assumption that Halkias will eventually have the charges dismissed, if any get filed at all, but that source has likely dried up. He will feel less compelled to so risk himself, whether by choice or coercion. Hopefully, no further misfortunate will befall the detective. He is a good man, and he deserves better.

It is a war, and there will be casualties.

Five minutes of surveillance reveals nothing. The location appears empty, dark, devoid of any activity.

The dark-suited figure scurries down to street level, choosing a place to sprint across that is lacking in any real coverage of light. There is little presence of pedestrian or vehicle traffic here, but even one sighting could prove too many. Once near the other small building, all is dark, all is quiet.

Eyes peer in, being more careful at first but finally openly peeking in windows, scanning the interior as best as possible. Nothing. This building had been a small way station for the crime ring, a place to temporarily store certain goods, generally not human goods, but the locale and its possible purpose had been documented. Now it looks to have been abandoned.

This is a further bother. What opportunity may have been missed? It has been too long since this work has been done. Too many messages, too many developments; must be more diligent.

A rear door is easily forced open, and the figure carefully enters, goggles down over the eyes to enable seeing quite well in this dark environ. The place is largely empty, though some used crates and boxes and some broken furniture still dot the region like discarded heralds with dust-filled mouths. The P90 is held at the ready, finger near the trigger

DANCE OF THE BUTTERFLY

but not on it, as the vigilante carefully checks the building, realizing it has, indeed, been vacated.

Some time is spent giving the place a thorough looking over, mostly done due to curiosity. Why was this establishment abandoned? Was anything left behind that may indicate where they have gone? There are always trails; no one is invisible.

Back outside and easily atop the roof of this place, crouching, hidden in darkness and shadow, thinking, waiting, watching. Some digging has also been done as regards the serial killer haunting the city, especially as a few of the more sensationalistic news outlets associate that murderer with the vigilante. It's ludicrous, of course, but the implication is more of a concern.

The serial killer seems interested in the same girls, but as prey, not victims needing help. A passing moment is spent pondering this, but there is as yet too little information. Unfortunately, young ladies in just these sorts of situations often end up as victims of violent crime. It could just be a coincidence. Still, if anything may be done to stop it, it will be done.

The war is intensifying. The crime ring is trying many avenues to thwart this work. It would be amusing, if it were not pathetic, that the criminals are manipulating the police and the media to help them instead of those two same institutions working more fervently to stop the expanding activities of the criminal organization, that influence spreading like a dark mist throughout the city.

What is becoming?

*****

He takes a moment to get settled in before turning to the package that has recently arrived for him. He is alone here in his rooms, and he finds that it feels empty now when she is not here. As he disrobes, he thinks of her, a gentle smile taking his lips.

He has not felt like this in years, having been lost in dealing with so many other issues that courting has not come up. Certainly he has felt its lack from time to time, and other moments, he has found himself taking note of someone he may see, but such has never been seriously pursued.

His mother and sister had joked about trying to set him up, but, of course, nothing had ever come of that, either.

And now, there is her.

He realizes the potential challenges to what they seem to be about to pursue, but he will not let that stymie him. And what will he do when he has concluded his business here? He cannot just abandon this, abandon her. This is not a fling or a passing fancy. He feels it deeply, taking him, and he eagerly embraces it. He wants to give it every chance to bloom to its fullest. He senses such amazing potential between them, and he finds himself experiencing a sense of happiness, eagerness, that he has not felt in so long.

He scoops some ice cubes into the round, stout glass, then splashing some of the whiskey over them. He swirls it, letting it cool, bringing the glass up, but he pauses just before it reaches the mouth. He thinks on how she drinks her scotch, and another little grin takes his lips. He ought to try it that way sometime, he decides, then he samples of his own, enjoying the heady taste and subtle burn.

Now in his black silk pajamas, drink in hand, he heads back to the table and looks at the small package. It is from home; he notes that easily enough from the label. They use a special encoding to ensure proper delivery and so the recipient knows the parcel is to be trusted. He wonders what it is, since any sort of information could be sent electronically. He had not requested anything. He sips again of his drink, then sets the heavy glass near the parcel. He takes up his ornate letter opener, really more of a small knife, the entire piece made of Damascus steel, somewhat in the style of a tanto, the whirling pattern upon it adding to its aesthetic.

He can feel the reasonably weighty contents as he opens the box, and within he finds several things – a small data key, three 10-shot magazines, two boxes of specially made bullets, a shoulder holster, which is no doubt tailored to his specifications, and a custom-modified pistol. He supposes Jericho decided to ignore his comment that he did not need any more weapons. He has his cane, after all, and he has not even bothered to begin carry that around with him, even knowing Denman Malkuth is here.

DANCE OF THE BUTTERFLY

He picks up the handgun, admiring it, a two toned Walther P99, chambered in .40 S&W, fitted with an Insight X2 light and laser sight. He pulls the slide, noting how smoothly it moves, also making sure the gun is empty, though he would have been rather surprised had it not been. He tests the trigger, pulling on it delicately, and he feels the ease, the force necessary to fire having been reduced. Jericho has many roles and duties, Weaponsmaster being but one of those.

He takes the data key, then moves to put the rest of the package in the room's safe. Once secured, he walks back over and boots up his laptop, slipping the key in its port. The information contained within tells of the weapon, giving some basic specifications and things to note regarding the customization of it and the bullets. The majority of the data pertains to the serial killer.

He sees reports, analyses, photographs, many of which are from the Police or Coroner's office, information he likely should not have. He becomes engrossed in the information, his brow slowly furrowing as he takes it all in, skimming over some parts, giving much more attention to others. He has not completely forgotten about his drink, picking it from time to time to partake of it.

He sits back, letting the knowledge absorb into him just as he swallows more of the liquor, feeling the simmering burn caused by both. He ruminates. An outside observer might wonder if he has lost vitality, such does a stillness settle over him. He finally blinks, once, heavily, breath returning to his body in the motion of his chest beneath the dark pajama shirt. He picks up his sleek, thin phone, placing a call, but as expected, the ringing resolves over to the voice mail. He does not leave a message, instead he switches modes and sends a text to the caller, hoping this will result in gaining better attention.

His sister, Nicole, is notoriously difficult to get a hold of, being a woman of many talents and pursuits. He could call her husband, but he'd rather not involve anyone else at this juncture. He just wants information, the sort which she is best suited to provide.

His thoughts wander again to Lilja, for she is a caretaker of knowledge. His lips slowly curl up into a smile, a subconscious gesture as he ponders more on her. She brought up Nicholas Rémy's *Daemonolatreiae libri tres*, and though it could have been the results of mere cross-referencing, he wonders how much more she might know of the particular subject, namely that regarding witchcraft, the supernatural, the infernal.

He sips further of his drink, wondering how much more of the veil he ought to lift for her.

*****

"That day, the witches are wandering around, gathering supplies for their journey to Mount Kyöpeli, a sacred magical shrine for magic users. They go door to door, selling spells and good luck charms. It is like Halloween, but a much older tradition. Children dress up as witches and sell spells and lucky charms for candy and goods. It is basically similar to trick-or-treating from Halloween in the USA, but instead of the subtle threat of a 'trick' if a 'treat' is not received, the children provide good luck magic to people and receive the treat as payment."

Lilja pauses in the lecture, looking out over the small gathering, for this is not a formal class, but she had been asked to give a short presentation on lesser known holidays, something with a voluntary attendance. She knows some professors had offered their students a form of credit for attending, and some people are genuinely interested, so she is not speaking to a nigh empty room.

She wears her usual dark colors, but instead of black, she is dressed in deep reds and rich browns, almost as though she represents the fullness of fall even as she discusses an obscure day that is more a harbinger of the vitality of spring. Her form-fitting turtle neck is crimson, the neck of it somewhat loose, hanging in a gentle swoop of drapery, revealing a portion of her throat. She has tied up her hair into a rather utilitarian-seeming bun.

Her skirt tapers down along her slim hips, stopping just at her knees, the color of dark chocolate, sometimes even catching a sheen when hit properly with the lights. She also wears stockings, adding a smoothness and the whisper of a darker hue to her pale skin. She moves about atop her four inch heels, a graceful surety in the motion within the dark pumps.

DANCE OF THE BUTTERFLY

She pauses, the small device in her hand which may advance the presentation or even emit a beam to point out certain portions of the visuals, looking out over the gathering. She raises her chin as she spies something.

"Yes?" she looks in the direction of a raised hand, perking her eyebrows as a bid to speak.

"Is it always that day?"

"The last Sunday of March. Always," Lilja answers, then going on to intone in her mother tongue, her voice rich, sure, even lilting a bit as though adding a hint of song to the verse:

'Virvon varvon
Tuoreeks terveeks
Tulevaks vuodeks
Vitsa sulle
Palkka mulle'

"That is the most common spell, and it means - I make you, or this household, fresh and healthy for this upcoming year. Lucky wand for you, price for me. And thus the 'witch'," she continues, raising her hands and making the unmistakable 'quotes' sign with her fingers, "receives the price, usually sweets, and gives the wand as a lucky charm. Wands are made from the willow tree, a magical tree for Finns, and decorated by the witch themselves."

She nods toward another raised hand.

"So, in Finland, witches are not automatically treated as bad?"

"No," she shakes her head once, more of a slowly shifting movement, "Witchcraft is a very big part of Finnish history, culture, and religion. Though we had good witches, and black magic was not allowed."

"Where is Mount Kyöpeli?" asks another, not waiting to be called upon but pitching the question in the ensuing silence.

She turns her eyes in that direction, still meandering as she talks, the images on the large screen changing in a series of slow dissolves, giving backdrop to her words.

"You can only get there by flying and magic. It is said to be located in a secret place, close to the border of Tuonela, the Finnish land of dead.'

"It is also said that it is actually possible physically, or even mentally, to travel in Tuonela and go have a chat with your dead friends and relatives and other people," she carries on, a curve to her lips. "There are tales that witches and sages have traveled there to learn long lost lore and spells. Only problem is that it's very hard to get back from there. There are many guardians. Cats are but one example in our own world."

And before long, the lecture is concluded, and everyone is filing out. She had hoped he would be here, but he had an unfortunate timing issue with an appointment he could not miss, one that had been arranged long in advance. He even toyed with the idea of cancelling or rescheduling, but she had begged him off of that, not wanting to inconvenience him too much for this. He had asked to be allowed a copy of her presentation, along with a write-up, which she had happily agreed to provide. He had also suggested she might give the lecture again, to him, as a private lesson. She smiles a touch bashfully lost in that thought, as she gathers up her things.

"Well done, Ms. Perhonen," says a voice, and it carries well, for they are the only two now left in the chamber, and the man speaks with a clear, deliberate intonation.

She looks up, knowing who it is by the sound of that speech, her enjoyable thoughts and mood gone completely.

"Professor Malkuth," she greets, her eyes on the well-dressed, handsome man as he wanders toward her, having obviously been sitting in the rear, "I did not realize you were here."

He lets his lips take on the barest of curls at this admission, though it does not last long, resolving back to his more congenial expression.

"I do hope it is alright that I attended, though I am obviously not a student," he says, and he tries a grin on her which fails to yield any sort of positive response. "I heard mention of your lecture, and I must confess, the subject matter appeals to me, and I could not pass up a chance to watch you at this sort of work. I had no idea you were such an accomplished public speaker."

She says nothing, for he has not asked any question, so she continues gathering up her things, powering down her laptop, placing it in the small black carrying case, finally looping the single strap over her shoulder. She then sets her eyes back on his, for he has also not seen fit to move away or say any goodbyes during this time.

"I am glad you enjoyed it, Professor," she finally says.

"Mmm," he nods, thoughtfully, eyes drifting away in contemplation, or the appearance of such, before looking back upon her, "I also wanted to congratulate you on your recent, quite amazing acquisition to the Rare Collection."

She just looks at him, her eyes steady. After a moment, she blinks.

"What acquisition might that be?"

"Ah, well, yes, one of the books I asked about, one on my list, the one I emailed you," he persists, and she finally gives him a sort of reaction with the nod of her head, "A rather important one on that list, if I may say, perhaps even *the* most important, well it seems it is now in your collection, so I presumed you must have made that acquisition *very* recently, hmm?" he finishes, his hands having gone together in an interlacing clasp of fingers, his well-tended eyebrows perked up above his self-satisfied smile.

Despite her easy tendency to blush in certain situations, there is no response at all to indicate she may have been ensnared, but her mind is reeling. She had to have known he would find out, but her recent distractions of late have perhaps made her willing to accept less than general avenues of approach to potential problems. She begins trying to figure out how he found this knowledge. The inventory of the collection is certainly not that much of a secret, but she had actually taken some recent precautions on how that particular title may come up in more public inquiries. And if he knows they have the book, he may well know when it was brought into the fold.

"It was not a recent acquisition," Lilja says, still giving him that impartial look.

He blinks, his brow wrinkling, head moving to the side, "Oh?" he says, playing the consummate actor, "I wonder, then, why you told me it was not in the collection?" and he throws that perk of his eyebrows back on the end of the question, as though he is harmless and deserves all answers.

"I suppose I missed it when I glanced through your index," she offers. "I am sorry. I have been very busy lately, so I did not give your list that much time."

"Ah, a pity, but no matter, I was able to rectify this ... oversight," he says, his speech as polished and premeditated as a skilled politician's, his hands now separated as he talks. "I do realize you must be a very busy woman, Ms. Perhonen, and they even have you giving lectures now in addition to all your other duties," he announces, smiling.

"It is something I do from time to time," she intones.

"Indeed," he says, pondering a bit before his smile grows to show some of his teeth. "Well," he clips, inhaling a sharp breath, "Is your interest in witchcraft just academic, or is it personal?"

"Regardless of the answer to that, I am here, giving this information in an academic capacity," she answers, still just standing there, facing him, eyes not wavering, her right hand on the top of her case, ready to leave at any moment.

"Ah, yes, I see, well, I was just curious," Denman says, putting on the touch of an apologetic smile, and she can see the intent of this, hoping to give her reason to think she has over-stepped and needs to make amends.

"Curiosity is something with which I am quite familiar," she speaks, and though it is not the hoped for reaction, she can sense she has given him a morsel, and she inwardly, and silently, curses herself for it.

"Ah, yes, *curiosity*," he tastes the word, "Are you curious about that book in your collection?" he asks, his fingers again interlaced, his eyes not giving a centimeter of ground in their staring battle.

"I am curious about every book in the library's Rare Collection."

"Well, yes, of course," he somewhat dismisses, releasing his right hand for a little wave to that effect, before slipping them back together, "But this book is *unique*, extremely valuable, does it not warrant more than the usual amount of curiosity?"

"It has been thoroughly authenticated. We know of its rarity and value, and thus it is under the most secure protection we have available."

"How very nice," he says, letting his statement take on a tone of condescension. "You must realize that a book of such rarity and value would be coveted by others."

DANCE OF THE BUTTERFLY

"There were other interested parties when it was made available. The school won out."

"Indeed, and I do offer my sincere congratulations, even if it is not a *recent* addition," he replies, still just looking at her.

The moment lingers, and she can tell he wants more, but she has decided she is not inclined to give it.

"If you'll excuse me, Prof-," she tries, but he cuts her off.

"I would imagine that some of those interested parties, as you put it, may be unhappy that they do not have it. There may be, even now, new interested parties who want it ... badly."

"Professor Malkuth," she says, sternly, "If you do not mind, I-," and she is interrupted again.

"The Book is a danger."

Lilja shakes her head very slightly, eyes blinking from a wrinkling of her forehead, and she figures he misspoke or she misheard.

"How is the book in danger? We have it under very tight security, even water and fireproofed-."

"The book is not *in* danger, Ms. Perhonen, it is *a* danger," he reiterates.

"What?" she finally gives in, the word clipped, demanding.

"It is a danger because there are people who want it, people who will stop at nothing to get it, and it is a danger because of the knowledge it holds. You were lecturing on witchcraft just now, magic, spells. Do you believe in any of that, Ms. Perhonen?"

"I don't see how that is relevant," she says, eyes widening somewhat.

"You are correct, of course, it isn't, but what is relevant is that those who covet the book do believe in it, and they will not let you stand in their way to acquire it. Are you willing to give your life for that book?"

"Professor Malkuth," she says, using some effort to keep a calm tone of voice, "I am leaving now."

He watches as she walks away, the clicks of her heels very steady, though she does not rush or storm out. She continues to show that measure of control, though he knows he cracked it a bit, just a bit.

"Goodnight, Ms. Perhonen," he calls out after her, not even sure if she has heard it, but he adds a little teasing tone to the end, just in case she is still in earshot.

He remains there after she has left, looking about the room, pondering, seeming to almost try to focus in on residual energies that may not be so easily visible to the common senses. He wonders further at her guardianship of the book, for he assuredly thinks of her thusly. She is no mere curator, but a *protector*, a fortitude and drive that appears inherent in her very nature. And now this curious, intriguing morsel – the very subject of her lecture, paganism in Finland.

She hails from a land with an interesting culture and a quite tolerant attitude toward the practice of witchcraft. She spoke of being able to travel to worlds beyond the corporeal one in which humans live, and though that land may be conveniently referred to as a Land of the Dead, there was mention of witches being able to go there in life.

How much do you know, Ms. Perhonen, he finds himself pondering yet again.

He had already begun to think of her as an enigma, and that idea only strengthens. There is much more to her than he had initially thought, and now he knows he must learn as much of that as he is able.

*****

Therese sits in the chair opposite the desk, watching as the other woman looks over the printed sheets that had lately been stuffed unceremoniously into a manila folder. She sucks on the left inside of her lip, darkly-lined eyes peering about as she waits, somewhat impatient but almost bothered. Her black jeans cling so tightly to her thin legs as to appear more a textured paint than pants, giving greater contrast to her clunky, black boots. She also wears a black leather jacket over a hoodie and t-shirt, despite the continued warmth in the air outside.

The woman behind the desk, one Ilona Salomon, appears a vision of professionalism compared to the other in here, though in truth, she opts for practicality in her appearance – sensible shoes with rubber soles, basic button-down shirt tucked into her trousers, somewhat masculine-seeming even, a point that has sometimes been used to disparage her.

DANCE OF THE BUTTERFLY

She finally looks up at the hacker, "I assume there's more than just this."

The other moves her eyes to meet those of the older woman, and she nods her head.

"There's always more with you, Therese," she says, somewhat as an aside, somewhat laced with exasperation, then, more pointedly. "What are you hoping to do with this?"

"Make a difference," comes the almost muttered response.

"Since when do you care?" the reply shows quickly, not pitched as scathing sarcasm but actual curiosity.

Therese just keeps looking, boring her own eyes into those of Ilona's, whose eyebrows finally lower as she realizes how serious the other is.

"This is dangerous stuff, Therese," she continues, gesturing with the now closed manila folder, "We normally work on deep background check, insurance fraud, aggressive validations-"

"I know that," the almost muttered words cut her off.

"Then why bring this to me?" she presses, still holding onto the folder, which Therese takes as a good sign,.

"Because I trust you," comes the simple answer.

The taller, stouter woman pulls in a stabilizing breath, then exhales it smoothly. She is not unused to potentially troubling, even confrontational situations, but she still likes to be careful.

"I trust you too, Therese, and that is one of the reasons I take this seriously, why it worries me, and why it doesn't seem like you."

The goth-punk girl just looks back, though Ilona's body language indicates wanting. She sets the folder down, but instead of doing so to distance it from herself, she opens it, going through the slim contents again.

"You've got information here about the human trafficking and forced sexual slavery of young women being brought into this city," she begins, "And not just that, but information suggesting the police know about it. I presume this means they are turning a blind eye to it, if not outright helping, but that would be in the other information you've yet to share with me, hmm?" she looks upward toward Therese, eyebrows again raised, her face still mostly angled down toward the open folder, and when she gets no verbal response, she continues, "Information that this *vigilante* is actually focusing efforts on stopping the human trafficking, and here is where it gets really good, that the police are fabricating evidence against the vigilante to stop these efforts against the criminals." She finally breaks physical contact, sitting back in her chair and moving away from the desk with the momentum, "Wow, Therese. This … this is … *insane*."

"It's all accurate," Therese flatly declares.

"I don't doubt that," Ilona states, "Your information is always good. Anytime we've peer reviewed you, you've come out spotless. I mean this whole … *thing* is insane."

Again, another stretching moment of silence. The petite girl just sits there, shielded in her layers of clothes, make-up, attitude, saying nothing, just looking at the other.

"Okay," she nods, moving forward again, leaning over her desk, placing her elbows down atop it, hands clasped, and Therese recognizes this as a thinking position of the other woman's, good, "You've brought this to me for a reason. What do you want me to do with it?"

"I've got more," she says.

"Yes, I'm *sure* you do," Ilona quickly speaks on the heels of those words, eyes widened, head nodding.

Therese just stares for a moment, but it proves clear that Ilona is now willing to wait longer, or if necessary, end the meeting entirely.

"And I can get even more."

"Okay," more nodding, , "And then what? What's to be done with this information. Who's the client here, Therese?"

"I think this information should be given to someone who cares or could make a difference."

Ilona's eyes narrow slowly as she peers, the moment lingering. She eventually closes them, pulling in a slow, contemplative breath, then she opens her eyes again.

"Forgive me, Therese, and I am not trying to insult you, I'm just not used to seeing you so … worked up over something like this. You don't exactly strike me as a social crusader."

Therese just sits there, staring.

DANCE OF THE BUTTERFLY

"Who, then?" the P.I. demands, though she takes some of the edge off the question, "This information is rather potentially damning to the police."

"The media, Internal Affairs, the Office of the Interior," Therese begins a dangerous list.

"The Office of the Interior!" Ilona raises her voice for the first time since this excitable engagement has begun. "Therese, are you trying to get yourself killed?"

"Someone has to care about this," she mutters.

Ilona calms, sighing.

"Yes, yes, someone does," she admits, then offhandedly, even gesturing casually with her right hand toward the open file, "It seems the vigilante does," then as though struck with a moment of revelation, Ilona freezes in place for a moment, then angles her eyes at the hacker. "Do you know who the vigilante is?"

"No," comes Therese's clipped response.

Ilona more openly studies the other, leaning forward slowly as she scrutinizes. "You are either lying, or you are upset that you don't know that information," she postulates, but she does not push further in that regard, sitting back into a more relaxed repose. "Okay, so why involve me, Therese? You can just put together your package, gift wrap it, and deliver it to all those places."

"I need more."

"Okay, so go get it. Isn't that what you do?"

"Not just electronic information."

And this brings another moment of silence, this one heavier. Ilona again studies the skinny young woman, and her jaw flexes as her teeth press together.

"No, Therese, no."

"Why?" the hacker demands, speaking the word calmly, slowly, drawing it out to fill it with greater weight.

"This is seriously *dangerous*," Ilona responds, "You are talking about investigating professional criminals and potentially corrupt policeman. You know I used to be in law enforcement, and you partially know why I left it. There's also a reason my little practice here is limited to what we do.

"I don't want any part of this," she concludes, seeming to have to steel herself to make this statement.

And again, Therese just stares.

After a sufficient time of this awkward silence, she rises and quickly leaves the woman's office, disappointment, even some disgust, obvious on her generally aloof features.

*****

The music is loud in here, but not so loud as to eliminate the possibility of talking, so long as the participants in the conversation are in sufficient proximity. These two here in the dark booth have no trouble with being close to each other. The place is called simply The Garden, an ultra lounge, a place in between a bar and a nightclub, though it does have a small dance floor, currently unoccupied. It is a place meant to cultivate a particular feel, what with the wavy, deep tones of the electronic music, not too slow or too fast, the darkness weaving throughout the place to be interrupted by a deep, inviting blue that rises up in spots that need more illumination – the bar, the foyers of the restrooms, the entryway, some brighter, white lamps hanging down, their cones more precise to give further luminance to areas that have such need. The clientele looks polished and well-dressed, some might even say chic, but the two at the dark, secluded booth only have eyes for each other.

She is wearing a satiny-looking shirt, the collar and cuffs of which are a lighter tone than the creaminess of the blouse, a stiffer form even, giving prominent accentuation. The shirt is unbuttoned enough to give a tempting glimpse of her cleavage, the view of which he has graciously partaken. Her skirt is black, quite short, stopping at her mid-thigh, her legs bare as they end, enticingly, in her black, high-heel pumps. Her red hair is out in all its vibrancy, matched only by her glittering eyes which appear to take on many different shades depending on how they catch the available light in this place.

He is garbed in all black, his French-cuff shirt also showing an open neck, the collar widened from the lack of fastened buttons at the top. His cufflinks are silver wrapped about ruby, though the gems, somewhat

DANCE OF THE BUTTERFLY

subtle in their presentation, appear generally black in the dimly lit establishment. The dark trousers are simple in their elegance, ending in a narrow cuff over his buffed, black leather shoes. She smiles at him, running a hand over his left ear.

"What are you thinking?" he asks as she sits there, grinning gently, eyes moving away to survey the place, her left hand about her glass of scotch.

She sets her eyes back on him.

"I've been living here for two years now, and I have seen more than I ever have of the city's nightlife in the past few weeks because of you, a visitor."

"I hope that's a good thing," he smiles.

"It is," she smiles in return.

"Is this place not to your liking?" he pursues, picking up his drink, turning to look out at their environ as he sips of the cocktail.

"Oh, it's fine," she says, "Very nice, just … not my usual thing, really," then she looks back at him, smiling warmly. "It's nice being here with you."

He turns his face back to her, giving her a similar expression, "Thank you, and likewise," he returns, then leaning in to bring his lips to hers.

She meets his readily, their kiss slow, lingering, savoring, as they move their lips over each other's, feeling the softness, the simmering touch. He gazes upon her as it stops, pulling back.

"Did you have anything specific to tell me?"

She looks at him, inquisitively, "Uhm," she ponders, "The scotch here is good."

He shakes his head slowly, "I meant about the task I gave you."

"Oh," she blinks once, then her eyes are held in an open state upon him, and though it is dark, he feels certain she is blushing; she licks her lips, drawing the bottom in with the tip of her tongue, holding it beneath her teeth, giving a gentle bite, and her eyes shift in a barely perceptible movement to fix fully on his. "I did my secret mission," she whispers.

His grin increases, "Secret mission," he all but tastes the words as they emerge from his mouth, "I like that. Tell me about it, please. How did it go?" and he punctuates his bid with a further taste of his drink, eyes yet upon her.

She somewhat retreats into herself, her bashfulness coming forth, her shoulders rising up slightly, going inward, her arms coming to her sides, chin angling down. He keeps looking at her, warm, open, his left hand going over to gently stroke behind her shoulder, touching soothingly with his fingertips.

"I did as you asked of me," she says, glancing up at him at the end of her sentence. "I went into the bathroom at work," she continues, looking away, then back, as she speaks, "I ... touched myself ... uhm, starting at my neck." As she says this, he moves his hand over, extending his index finger to gently touch at her throat; she grins, showing a bit of her teeth, looking at him as she continues, "Then I ... moved my hands down and stroked over my inner thighs."

"How did it feel?" he gently interjects, still moving his fingers lightly at her neck.

She moves her eyes, her smile growing as her lips press together, her shoulders coming up again. "It felt nice. I imagined it was you doing it."

He nods, slowly, encouragingly.

"And then I played with myself, and that felt really good, and I slipped my hand inside my panties, since I didn't want them to get too wet, I didn't have another pair at work with me, and ... I ..." She glances at him, her grin again rising with her embarrassment. "I played with myself more, and ... I had to stop or else I would cum."

"But you didn't?" he checks.

"No." She looks at him, shaking her head, "You said not to, not without permission."

He grins warmly, leaning in to give her a nice, short kiss on the mouth.

"You did very well," he says. "Thank you."

She basks in this, smiling more openly, feeling wanted, sexy, settling in more comfortably. They sit there for a moment, taking in the place, ensconced in their sense of privacy within the darkness and the somewhat buffering effect of the music. She turns and sees that he is looking at her, and she meets his eyes.

"Did you like doing something I asked you to do?"

DANCE OF THE BUTTERFLY

"Yes," she nods once.

"Would you like to do more?"

"If you want," she offers, openly, and as he continues looking at her, his grin twists subtly into something suggestive, and she averts her eyes, smiling coquettishly.

"I do want," he says, his eyebrows barely rising up, slowly, as he continues looking at her. "I want you to do two things for me," he says, and she looks fully upon him, expectant, even perhaps anxious. "Remove your panties."

She just looks back at him, eyes on his, and she pulls in a slow breath.

"Okay," she agrees, "Do you want me to go into the-?"

"Here," he says, still wearing that subtle curl to his lips, "I doubt anyone will notice."

Her eyes lightly stretch their sockets, but with a movement about of those same, checking her immediate surroundings, she gets to the task, worming and squirming quite deliciously as she manages to work her dark underwear out from under her short skirt. She holds a closed fist out to him, the barest hint of the lacey garment peeking out at the sides as she offers it.

"Just set them on the table," he says, and though she seems again a bit reluctant, bashful and blushing, she does so, setting the panties down there, and they partially unravel, the dark, suggestive pile of fabric now sharing a small space with their drinking glasses.

She moves her hips and thighs, trying to get comfortable again, smoothing her skirt, perhaps feeling the sensation of her nudity beneath the short item. His grin grows as he watches, feeling also another sort of stirring inside himself.

"Thank you, my dear," he says.

"What was the second thing?" she asks, still looking somewhat awkward but also obviously eager.

He slowly looks out onto the area, commenting, as though giving a casual notice, "The dance floor looks neglected."

"You want to go dance?" she asks, and he knows she likes such activity, but she shows some measure of embarrassment at the idea of the two of them taking the floor alone.

"No," he says, then he moves his steady gaze back to her, "I want you to go out there and dance, by yourself, but dance for me, know that I am watching. I want you to entice me with this. You are to dance with no one else, just alone, for me."

She appears to have frozen in place, looking up at his face, eyes open, though not stretched, just unblinking, as she absorbs the bid. He begins to wonder if she will refuse.

"Oh," she finally says, then, "Uhm," eyes moving to the small, empty floor, then back to him, "For how long?"

"One full song," he says, and she nods slowly. "Or longer if you wish. If I think you are out there for too long, I'll come fetch you."

She looks at him, the idea of staying that long not even a consideration for her. He takes her right hand, squeezing it, and she offers him a bashful smile. He then leans in, whispering to her.

"Put everyone else out of your mind," he suggests. "This is just for us, just us. Just think of yourself and me watching you. You'll do fine."

She nods, and he can tell she is obviously nervous. And it seems the current song ends all too soon for her, but she gives him a glance and then courageously slips out of the booth and walks over to the floor.

He watches, noting the shift of her trim hips, even as she shows somewhat stiff from her anxiousness. There are not that many people in here, as the evening is yet young, but she does get a few notices as she covers the short distance to the area designated for dancing. It is not yet obvious, of course, what she intends, but she is attractive enough to garner looks merely from her presence.

He notes a change in her cadence as she takes a few steps within the barrier created by the different look of the dance floor, not going too far in, keeping this place somewhat close to the edge, and then as she plants her feet, she begins to sway in place, mainly moving her hips as she warms up. He brings his glass up, sipping of it, his eyes on her, hungry. She lets herself get lost in the music, moving about sinuously, raising her chin, her long, red locks falling down her backside. She moves her head slowly, causing her hair to sway, catching the light, adding to her charming dance.

She turns in place, and he sees her eyes are closed. She brings her hands inward then, having extended her arms, bent, fingers out, waving

DANCE OF THE BUTTERFLY

gently on thick currents in the air, but now she places them on the sides of her face, low, aside her jaw, then slowly glides them down, tracing over the contours of her shape, turning her wrists as she moves them over the top of her chest and outside her bosom, down over her ribcage, then out.

And then she opens her eyes, and they catch his as sure as any lure. Her lips are just barely parted, he can see from here, and her heart is hammering in her chest, though she does not falter from her enticing dance, continuing to move her body in a way designed to elicit arousal from him.

She brings her feet closer together, planting them firmly, the motion of her body like a waving slither, shoulders moving in the alternate direction of her hips, all of it slow, hypnotic. He spares enough awareness to note that some others have now taken notice, and it seems some of the women are showing some interest in also moving to the dance floor, some bidding of their companions, some perhaps ready to venture out alone.

He returns his focus to her, noting as she widens her step, her skirt riding up just slightly, not nearly enough to threaten to reveal her lack of panties, but it still thrills him all the same to know. Her back now to him, she arches, perking that lovely, firm rear of hers in his direction, moving it slowly side to side, a tempting invitation, and then the song bleeds away, dissolving into another, and she stops, looking around, a shy smile on her lips as she regains awareness of her surroundings, and she walks back over to their booth.

She slides in, gracefully, moving over until their hips touch, and he envelopes her in his left arm, and she snugs in quite readily. He gives her a kiss, exchanging a smile with her.

"Very nice, my sweet Lily," he says. "Very enticing."

"Did you like it?" she asks, looking up into his eyes.

"Oh, very much so. You arouse me to no end."

She grins further at this, and they resolve back into enjoying their company, the drinks, their continuous flirtations, touching, kissing, all part of the simmering play and build-up for the evening's culmination when they return to his hotel suite.

CHAPTER ELEVEN

He's seen stars before when he's orgasmed, if it proved a particularly powerful one. In truth, he's experienced visual distortion and various nerve stimuli associated with the tension of muscles, restriction of respiration and flow of blood in his body. Still, during those more amazing moments, he feels like he's gone out of body, seen things, had his mind blown. The girl at work between his legs is about to send him into one of those.

He's had blowjobs before, many of them, paid for many of them, just like this one. He's never used this girl before, but there was something about her that pulled him in, and she seems very eager, very into it, and he is feeling it. It is *amazing*. Her experience and expertise is undeniable, like a hot stoking that travels through his loins, fermenting at the base of his spine.

She got in the car with him, and they drove the short distance to this abandoned parking lot, one whose entrance is somewhat tucked tightly between two buildings, very easy to miss if you don't know the way. He's been here before, driven down the cheekily referred to "Lovers' Lane" to enjoy some private time with the lady of his choice.

This lady has shown to be a good choice. She's not even making him wear a condom, and the feel of her talented lips moving up and down over him is about to make him burst much sooner than usual. He pushes back against the inside of the front door of his car, having turned sideways to give her better access and send him to heaven, the windows down enough to let in the outside air but not so much as to invite undue intrusion.

She stops, looking up at him, and he opens his eyes, moving his gaze to her.

DANCE OF THE BUTTERFLY

"You like it?" she asks, almost pleading with that doey look.

"Yes, yes," he says, quickly, "Don't stop."

And she doesn't.

He moans as she gets back to it, her head bobbing at his crotch.

The parking area is decently sized, though not huge by any means, surrounded on all sides by buildings. It sometimes sees use during the daylight hours for more legitimate purposes, but it now has largely given over to these less legal pursuits, transitioning as it has become forgotten.

There is no one else here now being serviced, the other working girls just down the street, hoping to find some clients and have their own excursions in the parking lot. Things have changed lately, too many girls, too many choices, having to try harder. Certainly the many deaths of young ladies, even the serial killer preying on a subset of those, ought to enter their minds, but it doesn't. Not all of this information has even been shared with the general public, and even if it has, not all of these ladies partake of such outlets.

Though the two in the car, the driver tensed up and about to blow, and the girl working diligently at getting him there, may be the only here engaging in such transactions, they are not the only ones in the parking lot. Another has snuck in, unseen, bent on secret observation of the goings-on, perhaps even more.

The car moves on its shocks, creating a noise like a large metronome, the man's steady grunting muffled from within but still an extra instrument to the unusual symphony. The other watches them, waiting, taking it all in.

The man tenses further, the muscles of his legs going taut, and a deeper, longer noise emerges through his bared teeth. One hand shoots out and grabs the steering wheel, moving it, locking it in place, the other grips the top of his seat. The girl's humming adds to the noises, encouraging him to arrive at the tune's crescendo.

His eyes bug out as the sensations hit him strongly, and he knows that boiling culmination is near. He's already seeing things, flashes of bright light, images popping into his awareness. This girl is *good*. He keeps his eyes wide as his moaning rises in volume, his hips lifting off the seat, those eyes seeing nothing, everything ... something?

Whatever it was is lost to his concern as he ejaculates. The girl moves her mouth away just before this happens, experienced enough to know when a john is about to blow, and she pumps rapidly with her hand, and she feels a generous splash of fluid, then more, and it doesn't take long for her to realize it is too much.

She looks up to see a horror, something that should not be, something that doesn't quite register in her mind. The guy's head is gone, cut or torn away, and the stump of his neck spews blood in time with his struggling heartbeats, the convulsing of his body, even as his climax continues, the involuntary clutching at his loins, expending him.

She sees something else, a shape, a movement, but it is dark and fast. She releases her hold on the guy's spurting, twitching member and brings her hands up like claws, rising up from her tucked in and bent over position, and she prepares to let forth a huge scream. Hardly any of it gets out before she feels a vice-like grip on her head and throat, and then she is also dead.

If anyone else is there watching, they certainly wouldn't remain much longer after that.

The police are out in force, responding quickly, searching, dropping a figurative net over the area. They feel confident this time. They've never gotten a call so soon afterwards, and they have a description from a witness. Someone happened to be walking down the street that runs near the narrow turn into the parking lot, and they heard the noise, and then shortly after, saw a large, dark-skinned man running out of the parking lot, heading away down the street, running fast, not caring of his surroundings.

The witness had gotten only the barest glimpse of his face as he peered in their direction, then took off the other way. Clean shaven, short hair, probably about 1.9 meters tall, hard to tell with how he was sort of flailing as he ran, clearly distressed and in a great hurry. He'd been wearing a green jacket over a white t-shirt and jeans, white athletic shoes.

The police scour the area, looking everywhere, knocking on doors, asking everyone they can. This is the break they need to stop this serial

DANCE OF THE BUTTERFLY

killer. They have an eyewitness description of a suspect. They *have* to find him.

"Sir?" the patrolman in the passenger seat calls out from the slowly moving car as it brakes to a stop, shining a flashlight at the man's chest, trying to illuminate him but not blind him. "Sir?"

The man looks over, squinting his pale blue eyes, left hand brought up to block the beam, the raised hood of his gray jacket covering the unwashed disarray of his very blonde hair.

"Yeah?" he says, speaking in a noticeable accent that seems somewhat singular even in this cosmopolitan city.

The beam of the policeman's torch moves over him. The man is obviously Caucasian, very thin, doesn't match the suspect's description.

"Have you seen a black male, approximately …" and the officer lists off the aspects, hoping to get a hit from this guy.

"No, no, I haven't," he replies, hands now stuffed in the front pockets of his hoodie, bloodshot eyes narrowed against the beam, staring at the cop car.

"Are you sure?" the patrolman persists. "You haven't seen anyone that looks like that, maybe running, looking distressed. Heard any unusual sounds around here recently?"

"Around here?"

"Yes, around here, maybe in the last twenty minutes or so?" the cop reiterates, moving the beam of the flashlight about as though encompassing the potential area, though one would assume he means a much larger vicinity.

"No," the guy says.

"What's your name? Where're you from?" the cop tries.

"Ernst van Zyl," Ernst says. "I'm from Port Elizabeth. South Africa."

"Aaah, so that's the accent," the cop nods.

Ernst just looks at him.

"Alright, well … just be careful." The car pulls away; the two cops exchange words about the guy's obvious appearance as a drug user, but they have a bigger fish to catch right now – a shark.

Ernst turns, watching as they drive off.

If you could see the things I see, Officer, he thinks, *hear the things I hear. It doesn't matter how careful you are, they'll find you, anyway.*

*****

"There's been an interesting development."

"Oh?" he speaks into the small, mostly unobtrusive earpiece, opting to not use the visual component during this conversation with his mother.

"Things are heating up there."

"I know that."

"We received a request for assistance," she finally reveals.

"What?" comes his genuinely perplexed reply.

"A City Councillor, Dominik Keller, has put out a call for aid that has been relayed to us through one of our channels."

"Why did this come to us?" he asks, and she cannot help but make note of the question.

"There has been a rash of young women there turning up dead, most attributed to homicide, and what with that beastly serial killer on the loose, it triggered enough criteria for us to be notified. You know we'd rather be safe than sorry."

Of course, he knows this, he's had a hand in modifying those protocols.

"Well, I am already here, obviously, so-," he begins.

"But you're busy with the book, which is taking a lot of time, so I wondered if you might need some more help."

He waits a moment, feeling like he is being set-up. He loves his mother, dearly, but she can be overbearing sometimes, even manipulative and judgmental, and he also notes her little jab at his continued lingering here in study of the tome.

"I can easily run some checks to see if there is any reason why we'd need to get involved."

"Well, yes, but I wondered ..." she begins, letting her voice trail off in a very characteristic lure of hers.

"Yes?" he bites.

DANCE OF THE BUTTERFLY

"If we did get involved, maybe helped with this problem, that Councillor would likely feel grateful, and maybe he could help *influence* a very liberal loaning of the book to us, if not an outright procurement?"

"I don't want to take that route."

"Why not?" she throws back, sounding exasperated.

"I have very good access to the book right now."

"Yes, but what if someone else manages to snatch it away? You know Denman isn't there to polish up his lecturing."

"I know."

"You seem distracted, Skot," she says, "Is everything alright?"

"I'm not distracted," he replies, trying to sound calm, "It's just that figuring out the book is taking more effort than I had imagined."

"Well, how could we have imagined at all how much effort it would take?" she posits. "Which is why we need better possession of that book. If we had it in our collection-."

"That would be optimum, yes."

"Then maybe this councillor can help us, if we help him."

"I'll keep it in mind."

"Well, here's something else to keep in mind," she begins, and he can hear it in her voice, her rising upset, her disappointment at how he has reacted to her idea, "You know we are not the only ones there that want that book. You know how crucial it is to get that book and not just for its secrets but to keep it from the others."

"Yes, I kno-," he speaks, his own exasperation evident, though his is more resignation than indignation, yet he still gets cut off.

"May I finish, please?"

"Yes, Mom, please do."

"Thank you," she clips. "The book is there, you are there, Denman Malkuth is there, and the city is also suffering from that serial killer, and now there have been enough dead girls that this Councillor has sought help through national and international channels. Have you been paying attention to the news? There is a serious problem with that city being the focal point for sex trafficking. "And there is that vigilante."

He lets the silence linger, making sure she is done before he speaks again.

"Yes, I have been paying attention to the news," he says, feeling like he has had this conversation before.

"Do you really think it is coincidence that all of this is happening there, right now, in *that* city?"

"No, I do not."

"Well?" she pitches into another lengthening silence.

"I tried contacting Nicole, but she has not returned my messages."

"Hmph," she somewhat snorts, "That's not unusual. If I see her, I'll have her call you."

"When was the last time you saw her?" he asks, for his mother is still staying with her as the new manor is being readied.

"She's very busy."

He knows that is not an answer, but he does not press.

"I could send David there. You know he'd go if I asked. He's always looked up to you," his mother suggests.

David, his first cousin on his mother's side, a stalwart member of the family, nine years his junior, and definitely suited to certain situations.

"I really don't think it's come to that," he opts.

"He could just be there in case something happens. Wouldn't that be better than you needing help and having none?"

"It would."

"Good, then I'll tell him-."

"No," he stops her, and he can feel the tension in the silence, "I don't see the need for that now. I'll talk with Nicole, and I'll put out some other checks. If there is a real reason to get more people here, I'll call them in."

"Alright, Skot," she gives him, and he can sense her disagreement, but he *is* the Head of the Family.

She stands there for a time after the call has ended, still in her fine pajamas and robe, a steaming cup of coffee near at hand, thinking. She senses there is something he is not telling her. He certainly has a huge task with not only trying to figure out the book but also in working to acquire it. That must be the ultimate goal. Knowing its secrets is one thing, but it must be kept from the others. He just seems distracted. She

DANCE OF THE BUTTERFLY

brings the mug of coffee up to her lips, having a sip, wondering what has him so preoccupied.

*****

They return from a lovely evening out together, the time spent in tease and tempt, smiles and flushes of skin, tentative touches, some more daring than others, all designed to produce the simmer that will not boil over until they return to the privacy of his sumptuous suite. And now they stand in the bedroom, naught but candlelight to illuminate the chamber, causing a flickering fluctuation to the accentuating shadows. They have disrobed one another in the breathless heat of still-rising passion, removing the dark, elegant garments until he is fully nude and she stands only in her high heels.

"Stop," Skothiam bids, gently taking Lilja's arms by the wrists, and she complies, looking at him with eager eyes.

He moves around behind her, brushing his hands over her shoulders and down her back, leaning in to kiss her on the nape of her neck. Her scent is lovely, intoxicating, but he must resist the urge to partake too quickly. She fuels and inspires him to such need, but it must be savored.

She arches her neck, a breath escaping her lovely lips, and she reaches back, her hands seeking his crotch even as he presses in, but he again takes her wrists.

"Wait," comes the commanding whisper, and again, she pauses.

He moves away, and though she dutifully holds her place, her eyes move to follow him. He returns to her shortly, the dim lighting in the room revealing little more than their bodies. Again behind her, he raises his hands to place the blindfold over her eyes. She takes in a breath, and though it is quiet, even stifled, its intensity is easily sensed. He knows she wants this, as does he. Both of them feel a quickening as the blindfold fixes securely.

He stands there a moment, close behind her, sure that she feels his presence. Her lips are parted a bit as she breathes, an increase of arousal from the mere placing of the blindfold upon her. She has instinctively moved her right hand up.

"Caress your lips," he says, and she raises that hand further, obeying by touching lightly over her mouth, her breath rising from this just as his own excitement increases.

He moves in closer, though still not touching, "Stop," and she does, "Lower your hand to your side."

He then reaches around with arms over hers, moving slowly, bringing fingertips in to teasingly touch of her breasts. She emits a soft noise, which increases as the moving digits finally take her nipples, pressing in slowly yet firmly until pinching both.

She gasps and as he does not release, a tiny whimper emerges. Her body in response to the sensation, her rear brushing against him. He then lets go, feeling a light shudder from her. He leans in to kiss more on her neck, moving slowly in the attentions until he presses in with a hard, deep kiss. She tenses, another breathy gasp emerging.

"Get on your knees, please," he bids, and she lowers herself.

He looks upon her, moving about, taking in the lovely sight, breath kept slow, steady.

"Take hold of your heels," he adds, and she reaches back, carefully, her ability to control herself, her muscles, her balance, quite evident.

She is now somewhat arched as she holds the spiked heels of her shoes, her breasts thrust out. She is beautiful, strong, alluring. He lets her wonder what shall happen next, and she knows he is looking at her. Her breath continues, slightly rushed, just as her skin holds a light coloration.

"You are beautiful, Pet."

"Thank you," she manages, her voice touched by a quiver, accepting of the sudden nickname, and he gently strokes her bottom lip with the tip of his left thumb.

She dares to place a kiss on his finger, so he slips the thumb further into her mouth, and she suckles. He reaches up with other fingers, cupping the side of her face as she sucks, and she tilts her head, nuzzling into that hold.

After a time, he retrieves his thumb. A moment passes, her breath the loudest noise in the quiet room. He is rocked by the beating of his heart, but she does not hear that.

"Do you know what I am doing, Pet?"

She shakes her head.

DANCE OF THE BUTTERFLY

"I am stroking myself as I look at you," he tells her.

A breathy moan leaves her, so much like a sigh, a beautiful sound, and she bites her lower lip, murmuring.

"What, Pet?"

Another shuddering exhalation leaves her, and he watches as that breath moves her displayed breasts, her hold on her heels tight from arousal more than anything else.

"I want to taste you," she pleads, louder, though her voice is still more of a forced whisper.

He steps closer, still stroking himself. She knows how near he stands, and she emits another quiet whimper. She again licks her lip, the tip of her tongue sneaking out almost as though of its own accord, tugging her bottom lip up for her teeth to again bite on it.

"Please..." she begs.

He feels her hot breath, such is his eager organ so close to her. It gives him a shock of pleasure, just looking down at her, such a salacious sight.

"You may," he grants, then experiencing the exhilarating feel of her succulent mouth over him.

She gently suckles, moving over him, lips pushing delicately against his holding fingers as she moves down. He then drops his hand away, giving her the full length and she takes it eagerly. She maintains the hold on her heels, her hands gripping tightly, her body moving, trembling as she continues to drive him to greater heights. She moans, her voice producing a buzzing hum, a light whimper. He eventually steps back.

Her breath comes out louder now, her body all but gasping, moving with the respiratory need, and he eats up the sight.

"Thank you, Skot," she says, and those words almost make him melt.

"You are welcome, Pet," he returns. "The bed is to your left, crawl up onto it, hands and knees, point your rear out away from the bed."

She nods, and he sees the suggestion of a shudder to the expression as she moves her lovely, lithe body, steadying her lack of sight with her left hand, moving atop the bed, crawling slowly until she is fully atop it, on all fours, her firm derriere presented outward.

"I want you, Pet," he eventually speaks.

She nods her head, "I want you."

"Are you mine?"

And again she nods, her voice not much more than a heated whisper, "Yes, I am yours, Skot."

He then reaches forward, and she feels hands on her buttocks, touching softly, moving fingertips about until the digits splay, palms going in to caress of that silken skin, squeezing, moving in so that the tips of his thumbs tease so very close to the outside of her delicate folds. Her breathing again increases.

He then moves his left hand up, taking a tighter hold on the side of her trim waist, using that as leverage to pull back with the other hand and deliver a sharp, loud spank to her right butt cheek. She yelps, and he rubs where he has struck, only to pull that hand away and deliver another sharp slap, and this one brings forth a stunted exhale of breath, almost a groan, and he caresses the area again.

"Do you like that, Pet?"

She nods, "Yes … yes" her words rushed out, carried on the hot breath of need.

He moves his hand back and another loud strike is delivered to her right side and another and more until he has spanked her several times in quick succession, bringing a pink response to her already flushing flesh.

She has gasped and moaned many times, her breath now coming even more rapidly.

"Ahh, beautiful Pet," he says, his own voice terse with the breath of obvious arousal as he rubs his hands over her, finally again taking hold and delivering a spank to her left side.

She cries out, more in surprise at having been lulled with the gentle pettings. And then he resumes, delivering spank after spank to her lovely left cheek, each hitting harder, louder, giving forth a buzzing sting.

Then he stops, leaving her breathing heavily, again just looking at her there atop the bed, on elbows and knees, her rear presented, her delicate flower swollen and wet with a nigh undeniable invitation. He somehow manages to resist.

He walks around to the other side of the bed, eyes on her the whole time. She realizes some time has passed, her breath coming in a more manageable way now and not as loud. She cranes her head about as if to

DANCE OF THE BUTTERFLY

see through the blindfold or perhaps hear better, feeling the pressure as he sits on the bed, across from her head. He slides in closer to her, stroking her hair with his left hand. She moves her head into it, returning the gesture as best she can from her position.

"Give me your hand, dear Pet," he says, touching her right, and she does, raising hers in offering.

He takes it, a smile on his lips, guiding her gently.

"Good. Now lie on your back," he bids, and she does, now resting in the center of the bed, her head atop a pillow.

He leans over her, coming in close, slow, to place a deep kiss on her lips. She responds readily, pushing up against his mouth, tongues entwining, more hums and moans emerging to accentuate the kiss.

He then pulls away, retrieving the lengths of bindings already affixed to the headboard, and he secures her wrists. She whimpers a bit, the sound barely audible, but he hears it, and it gives a thrilling surge. Once both wrists are held tight, arms stretched out at an angle but loose enough to not hinder circulation, he binds her ankles, securing a nice part to her slender legs.

He moves away again, standing beside the bed, just looking at her. The sheen of her arousal mingles with the motion of breath and candlelight, such a beautiful sight. He then retrieves the nearby crop, and he brings it over, moving the tip of it along the contours of her torso, the tongue descending atop her belly, off to her left side, touching gently.

"Good girl, such a good Pet," he compliments, for she has not instinctively tried to pull away from the feel of the tool, merely giving forth a shudder of movement and breath.

He moves the crop, the tip gliding down below her navel then back around to the left side over her hip and to her leg, further down and inward, stroking back and forth lovingly along her inner thigh. She emits a breathy gasp, her breathing again beginning a slow, steady rise, her lips parted with this needful passage of air.

"Do you like that, Pet?"

"Yes," she manages, the single word almost becoming a moan.

He brings the crop back along her thigh, but this time he draws the leather tongue inward over her mons, bringing forth a light gasp from her. He lets it sit there, moving it against her sensitive folds with the

209

motion of his wrist. She begins to move her hips in response, a lovely sight to behold.

He stops just long enough to bring the crop up and slap it down against her, and she jerks, yelping, and then he slides it back down and in, resuming the wiggling against her. But before she may settle back into this pleasure, the crop is back up, and again, her delicious pussy is spanked. Another whimper and moan comes forth from her, a writhing of hips.

She brings her tensed thighs together as much as possible as though to shield herself, but, of course, the bonds keep her legs spread sufficiently. He sees a rise to her tendons as she experiences the pleasurable pain, her hips twisting as she moves her body, and then he finally stops, moving the crop to his left hand and reaching down to gently touch her with his right.

"You are very wet, dear Pet."

She nods, her breath coming out in short gasps, accenting the motion of her head. He adds to this by leaning in more to her, sliding a finger inside, and her head arches further back, her lips parting more as she feels the penetration.

"Do you like that, Pet?"

"Yes," she gasps as the finger continues its motion, sliding in and out, then once all the way back in, curling up, moving about to seek other sensitive places within. "Oh, gods," she adds.

"Mmmmm, yes," he agrees, nodding, and he pulls his finger out slowly, causing a tension to her bound form.

He gently slides his hand up, still pressing against her, stopping fingertips over her clitoris, the delicate nub of flesh risen to prominence in the carriage of her delectable folds. He rubs there in short, circular motions, and her tension rises further, her body pulling taut, head pushing back again into the pillow, her luscious lips allowing another building gasp to escape, her breath coming out faster, much more audible even as he increases the rapidity of movement.

"Oh, gods," she calls out, "Gods," again, and he keeps at it, looking at her as her body shudders, "You're going to make me cum."

DANCE OF THE BUTTERFLY

He stops, leaning in, close, looking her over, watching the passage of heavy breath within her. He lets her feel his breath, so close to her now, and she tilts her head, angling her blindfolded face at him.

"We can't have that yet," he whispers to her, "Though you are welcome to beg for it as much as you like."

He then moves to between her bound legs, knees moving up under her legs as he leans down, taking hold of her, moving in closer to kiss her hungrily, deeply on the lips. She moans into it just as he emits his own humming sound of pleasure, lower, more guttural, even as hers takes on a somewhat similar cast. Together they emit sounds that make up a universal language that grants depths of understanding. Their senses are tuned, heightened to each other.

The kiss lingers, his hands on her neck as he moves his head about through the exchange. She greets it with as much hunger as he shows, their tongues writhing sinuously together as lips move in a quickly increasing desire. He has begun moving his hips, grinding against her, and he feels a similar return from here, a motion of her pelvis in response to his own as best she can manage in her bonds.

He pulls back from the kiss, leaning over to undo the bonds at the footboard, releasing the hold on her legs. He then reaches down, gripping her thighs and pushing up her legs. Her own flexibility evinces itself in how easy this is done, and he presses her legs up and out, bent somewhat at the knee, feeling the backs of her heels brushing against his shoulders.

She moans at this, gasps coming out as he presses his crotch against her, letting her feel his own turgid arousal.

"Do you want me inside you, Pet?" he asks, teasing her in more than one way.

"Yes," she breathes, her need as evident as his own, "Please."

And so he grants her desire, and his own, sliding inside her.

She takes in a lengthy breath at this, her chest then slowly falling with the release of that respiration, and he takes better hold of her legs, beginning to slowly move in and out of her. Their breath rises, moans and hums escaping both as they continue this movement. He leans more over her, pushing her legs back further, going as deep as he is able. She pulls her arms against her bindings, and he cannot resist, so he reaches out to release those ties. She immediately grabs at him with newly freed hands, grasping out at his arms, moving over them, then to chest and abdomen, as though she has gained vision anew through her fingers, and she wishes to desperately partake of the sight.

He continues to move in and out of her, savoring the feel, faster, then slow again, leaning down atop her, and she moves her hands aside, wrapping him in her arms, her legs also going tightly about him. Her hands rub over his back, even becoming claws with the surge of more intense moments, scratching into flesh.

"Do you wish to see, Pet?" he asks, breaking free from kisses just enough to pitch this near-desperate sounding question.

"Yes," she breathes her own need, nodding, and he slips his hands up to remove the blindfold.

And then he sees her eyes, and the sight is almost enough to take his breath away. He smiles, and she returns it.

But the hot call of their loins shall not be denied, and they soon trade smiles for the tensed-up expressions of coaxed arousal, eager to explode. Their eyes stay locked as they continue moving together, their need burning. They are so close, holding each other, and she hitches, gasping in a stuttering fashion, and this almost sends him over.

"Do you want to cum, my Pet?"

"Yes, please."

"Cum for me."

She nods, "I will, and I want you to cum. Will you please cum for me, Skot?"

And it is his turn to nod, "I will, all for you, dear Pet."

Their motion continues anew with a fresh intensity, and he feels her take an even stronger hold, pushing herself against his movements, a deep clutching over his member, a feeling like no other.

He looks her deeply in the eyes, losing himself in that promised world of beauty and love. Her face is enshrouded by her vibrant red hair, her lips parted, her culmination so very evident, her breath rising to a frantic pace, and her orgasm finally takes her amidst moans and sharply pitched intakes of breath, tightly clutched hands, arms and legs. He feels the pulsing climax within her, the spasmodic flexing of muscles at her loins, and it is more than he can bare, and he groans, tensing, feeling the undeniable surge and clench within as he expends inside her.

DANCE OF THE BUTTERFLY

It takes some time for her orgasm to pass through her, hips bucking, and the pulsation of it is a torturous lure to his spent member still held within her. She holds tight, hugging him, and he returns it, both trying to catch their breaths, feeling the hot mingling of flesh against each other.

"Thank you, Skot," she says, amidst the warm, eager kisses they now share.

"You are very welcome, Lily, and I thank you," he replies, looking her deeply in the eyes.

Again, they share that warm smile, and then kiss again, and it feels as though they melt into one another.

It is bliss.

*****

This is not her first night out doing this, and though it has not yet been that many, she is quickly beginning to realize why she is a much better cyber sleuth than more conventional detective. She just doesn't have the patience or talent or whatever it is that makes this sort of investigation useful.

She knows the parts of town that may yield the most potential, and thus armed with the intelligence she is able to gather from the digital domain, she prepares to disembark from the subway to venture forth this night into a less than savory part of the city.

First, though, she'll need to do something about the two guys who have taken an untoward interest in her.

They boarded a few stops back, and their exchanged words and grins mark them not only as good friends but also troublemakers. Something in their glances, their attitudes, and she knows they are not just putting on a show. For all her social isolation, she is decent at reading people. Still, though, she finds more comfort in the electronic, finding bits of data to be firmer and much easier to coax than the muddled, confusing chaos of the offline world and its all too human inhabitants.

These two noticed her, despite her being huddled over within the raised cap of her hoodie, covered in the usual, bulky layers of black leather, thick cotton, worn denim. She peers over, wearing no make-up tonight, though her piercings are still evident as is the angling of her black hair from beneath the edges of the gray hood. She could probably pass just as easily for a teenage boy as a young woman, but whatever those two see, they think of her as potential prey.

They whisper, sometimes speaking louder, though they are still far enough away that she does not make out much of anything tangible. Their looks, though, their grins and smirks and laughter, that is all evident enough. These two bullies intend something for her.

Of course, they also exit the tram when she does, obviously intent on following her. She stabs her fists into the front pockets of her leather jacket, the heavy garment zipped and buckled up, encasing her skinny torso, and she moves at such a fast walk as to almost be running. She notes out of the corner of her eye, giving a quick glance to her right as she speeds up, that one of them has nudged the other, motioning toward her with jutting chin, and they also pick up their pace. She's carrying a small blade, but she'd rather it not come to that. As she prepares to reach the stairs, looking up to see what lies ahead, she spies the camera. Of course. She is quite familiar with these, having even hacked into some before.

She stops, turning, defiant, daring, boring her eyes into the two, and they shuffle to their own halt. They are confused, for a very brief second, then they return to their hyena-like nature, grinning, moving closer. She notes the flexing of fingers on the part of one, likely the more dangerous of the duo.

"You see that camera there?" she bobs her head up, indicating the device hanging high up on the wall, light blinking to signify its life, as she now stands below and forward of it a few steps.

They pause, eyes going up, and it is obvious they do indeed see it.

"It's a police camera," she continues, "Put down here for security reasons," and so said, she reaches up with her left hand, pulling her hood down and turning, putting on a faux smile and waving to the camera for a short moment, then looking back, "And now it's gotten a good look at me ... and both of you."

They blink, looking from her to the camera then back. She just stares.

"So, now, if anything happens to me, they'll run a routine check on these records, assuming I took the tram to get here, and they'll see me."

DANCE OF THE BUTTERFLY

She turns and gives the camera another look, though this time without the fake smile and movement of her hand, then looking back at them, that stone expression, which seems much more natural for her, still on her face. "And they'll see *you*."

"They'll see you two standing here, squaring off at me. If either of you have an ID, any sort of license for work, driving, school, anything, any sort of records, fingerprints, prior arrests, they'll find you, and they'll come looking for you."

And so declared, she stands there, silent, staring.

After a moment, the two head up the stairs.

She's not stupid, though, so she walks over to a nearby bench, sitting in full view of the camera, calming and collecting herself, waiting for a good half hour before carrying on. She's not on any sort of schedule, anyway.

She's careful as she leaves, going to street level, keeping an eye out not just for those two but anyone who looks suspicious. She doesn't see the two guys from the subway, which is good. She spies plenty of ladies who look like they might be in the line of work that brings her here tonight, but she wonders if she is just seeing what she wants to see. She finally notes a somewhat decent concentration of them in a particular area, so she finds an open coffee shop, heading in to find a spot from which she can observe.

The place is better lit than she'd like, hearkening somewhat toward an American diner aesthetic, but she does manage to find a booth against the wall, giving her a nice view through the large window of the goings-on outside.

She sips of the strong, overly bitter coffee, not seeing much of interest out there, save the mundane passage of people, some stopping to talk, cars driving about - the very things one might expect to see in a busy enough part of the city at night. She again realizes why she is not a conventional private investigator. Ilona had told her once about all the waiting, and if you're not the type of person for it, you're not the type of person. She feels a stab of disappointment at thoughts of Ilona, though it has blunted somewhat since the P.I. refused to help her. She supposes she can't blame her, but she'd much rather have the assistance. Ilona's also a lot more intimidating in person than she is, despite her gruff bravado.

She sent some more messages to her contact, even drifting toward some pointed conclusions, though those had still been hints, just not as subtle. If her contact has the answers she suspects, she hopes she'll get a response. She stopped short of declaring her intentions, though, not wanting to invite any more risk or exposure to this endeavor than already awaits. She's received no replies beyond the scant, usual requests for particular types of information and analysis.

She finally sees the guy, not sure exactly when he showed up, but finally drawn to notice him, perhaps inevitably, as she has been sitting in here for a while now, still trying to get something out of her time spent in amateur surveillance. He's also wearing a hoodie, his head presently uncovered, his unkempt, light blonde hair in an obvious unconcerned array. Like her, he is also very thin, though he looks sickly, his pale flesh almost gray or ashen, his blue eyes washed of color.

He sits there, uncommonly still, as though his motionlessness is a shroud. She wonders, then, why she has noticed him, and he certainly seems to not notice her, if he sees much of anything at all. He looks lost to this world. But then, he moves, bringing a cigarette to his lips, followed by a lighter, and she can see the shake there, the simmering jitter, and his eyes sort of bug out. He fires the cigarette, puffing on it, then brings up his coffee cup, somehow not spilling any, taking a shaky gulp before setting it down, another deep, puffing intake on his cigarette before he lowers his hands, the moldering stick between his fingers, then he almost imperceptibly resolves back to that statue-like state.

She figures he doesn't care about the ordinance about not smoking inside public places. The waiter comes over, intent on reminding him, and Therese pays close attention, wondering how this may play out. The server is polite, quiet, maybe too quiet, because the guy does not respond. He leans over more, getting closer, intent on gaining the guy's attention, but the smoker only stares off with that vacant look. The waiter finally dares to set a gentle hand on the guy's shoulder, and this brings a slow blink and obvious rousing to him, as he looks up, that brewing tension back to his appearance. Some quiet words are exchanged, and then he uses a napkin to put out his cigarette, leaving the crumbled,

DANCE OF THE BUTTERFLY

barely used thing sitting atop the table. As the waiter leaves, he blinks a few more times, then goes back to the stillness.

Something is very off with this guy. She wonders if he is just another washed out piece of human refuse, lost in mind or body or both. But he doesn't seem that common, which is sad in and of itself. She's seen addicts and the homeless and the mentally unbalanced, and though he appears to have characteristics in common, he seems somehow discrete from them. There is something in his eyes, something that fills her with a discomfort at not only what he may possibly see but also what is going on in his mind.

This goes on for a while, her watching him as he will suddenly break from the spell, going into a buzzing, jittery animation that had previously been totally lacking, partaking of his coffee. She even observes as he fishes in his pocket, unworried at all at anyone's possible notice, bringing out a tiny red pill, almost like a piece of candy, slipping it into his mouth and chasing it down with the caffeinated brew.

By the time he finally does get up to leave, she has decided to follow.

She's spotted something else, for even as his lingering moments of stillness are occasionally interrupted by his stuttering motions, when he does finally slip out of the booth to make his exit, that aspect has gone. Though his appearance is still of that almost otherworldly pallor, he looks to have better control of himself now, somehow compelled to a calm focus. She gives some passing wonder as to what type of pill he took, but her main concern is to follow him without giving the appearance of doing so.

This proves easy enough as he meanders down the street, a trail of smoke from a fresh cigarette like the misty expulsion of a mechanical pipe atop the tall fellow, as though the biochemical process gives him his motive power. He hardly seems to even be taking notice of his surroundings, any oncoming foot traffic moving out of his way, and he certainly doesn't look to his rear.

He finally does stop, and so does she, hanging back a good fifty feet, pulling out her phone to seem less suspicious. She keeps an eye on him. He looks around, though his gaze still does no more than pass over her. He peers across the street, and she wonders if he will move down and take the crosswalk, or maybe he'll just stroll across here, now, not a care given for vehicles on the road. He then looks left, doing a double-take, as though someone may have called his name, though she has heard nothing. She peers, seeing naught that may indicate a compatriot or otherwise trying to get his attention.

She does see what has gathered his notice, though, the space here at the corner occupied by a strip club, words and neon shapes on the outside speaking of the promising erotic, sexual visions of girls inside. A deep drag on the cigarette, then a careless toss of it aside, and he heads within. She lingers but a moment before following.

She pulls her hood down, trying to better obscure herself, and she knows the burly doorman is eyeballing her. She hopes he figures she is just some thin, young guy, perhaps out for his first taste of such teasings and temptations. She see the cover charge cost posted clearly enough, and she hands over an amount that includes an obvious extra. If he had been inclined to question her, he now just takes the money, waving her inside.

The place looks as one might expect – dark, seedy, though not so insufferable as to be covered in spills or grime all over the area. The wood walls are painted, that dark coloring only peeling away in a few places. The art on the walls, what there is of it, is abstract, amateur-seeming, even somewhat grotesquely-proportioned, erotic paintings of women. She can't tell if it is even more demeaning or perhaps an eloquent commentary on what is going on in here.

She wanders to a small table, one against the wall, not near the stage with its poles and nigh naked girls upon it. She glances about, looking for her quarry, but she doesn't easily spot him. Maybe he went to the bathroom, but she'll give it a better study once she's settled. She sits, then looks into the expectant eyes of a girl who has followed her to the table.

She blinks, a bit startled, as the young lady smiles, her make-up overdone, just like the tight squeeze of her breasts pushing up from within her demi-cup bikini top. She also has on a very short skirt and lime green fishnets going down into clear platform heels.

"What can I bring you?"

DANCE OF THE BUTTERFLY

Therese looks down, "Beer," she grumbles, trying to sound gruff, coming off perhaps more awkward, which she hopes is interpreted as her being a young, shy guy.

"D'ya have any particular flavor?" she asks, and from the downward angled gaze, Therese sees movement at the girl's ankles, a sway of her body, the underlying meaning of the question obvious enough.

"No," another gruff response, and the working girl heads to the bar, the click of her heels heard for a short time within the overwhelming barrage of the guitar-heavy rock music.

When she returns with the bottle of cheap beer, Therese has already placed a note on the table top, which proves barely enough to cover the inflated cost. She peeled and cleaned the black paint from her nails, but she still keeps her slender fingers hidden in the pockets of her jacket. She lets the change stay there as she takes a shallow sip of the ale. She doesn't respond in any way, expecting a foul taste, but it turns out to not be that bad. She's had worse.

The place is deceptively larger than what one may quickly deduce from outside, stretching back, away from the entrance, having a few doors and doorways that lead to other places, as well as a staircase toward the rear that rises up to a partial second floor, more like a very large balcony. She wonders if maybe the guy went there. She also wonders what goes on up there, if it's any different than down here, and what may be going on beyond the doors. One of them obviously leads to the restroom, but the other, and the open doorway, well, she does not know, and he may have disappeared via either of those.

She decides to play it cool, something she feels she has done a poor job of to this point. She takes another sip of her beer, looking at the girls on the stage, trying to act like she is just another customer. If the guy went to any of the more secluded areas, she hopes he'll have to come back through here eventually.

She then wonders why she followed him at all. What does she hope to discern? She knows there's a serial killer out there somewhere in the city. Does she think this is him? And if so, why is she putting herself at such risk? She wants to get more evidence of the rampant problem with human trafficking, sexual slavery, and the police's complicity in that, not single-handedly chase down the serial killer. She's not the vigilante, and if the information and suppositions she has prove correct, the vigilante is not after the serial killer, either.

So why is she - and there he is, sitting across the room, eyes locked on her.

She has to fight to not visibly react, though her own ocular orbs do widen in shock. She doesn't move, doesn't make any other reaction. She now worries of what she ought to do. She should surely look away, but she keeps staring. She blinks, eyes still latched onto him. He does not break the look, does not even see to blink. He is a statue again, though instead of the placid lack of focus, he is quite thoroughly drilled onto her. She also senses some animosity, but she as quickly dismisses that as paranoia.

She finally tears her eyes away, managing to pick up her bottle of beer with a reasonable amount of normalcy, finding herself guzzling quite deeply of it. She sets it down, and when she looks back over, he's still staring at her, but this time, once the returned gaze is met, he does finally look away, taking his time with it, quite deliberate.

"Ready for another?"

Therese almost starts again, really thinking she is not cut out for this, her eyes snapping over to the waitress, well, a waitress, as this one is yet another of the girl's at work in here. This one is healthier of flesh, her rather large breasts almost cupping her chin, such are they contained and pressed in and up by her top. She stands there, hip jaunting out, waiting for a response.

"Uuuhh?"

The girl's penciled eyebrows rise slowly, and she finally pitches, "Want another beer?"

"Where ...," Therese stammers. "Where's the bathroom?" she asks, knowing full well where it is.

The girl points, "Through that door."

"Thanks."

"Want another for when you get back?" the waitress gives another try, but Therese is up and scurrying away, trying not to move too fast, but still looking rather rushed and awkward regardless.

She goes through the door and down the short hallway, through another portal at the end, which is thankfully unlocked, the small

DANCE OF THE BUTTERFLY

bathroom unoccupied, and she shuts the door, locking it. The last thing she needs is some drunk or horny guy coming in here to try to take a piss.

She turns on the cold water, holding her hands under the spigot and splashing water on her face. She looks up in the fractured mirror, taking in slow, deep breaths, trying to get a hold of herself. She likes to play it cool, even handled those guys in the tram station pretty well, but she knows she is out of her element. She needs to calm down. She has no idea if that guy out there has anything at all to do with the serial killings, and if he does, she's not his type. She just needs to get control of herself and get out of this place.

She'll go back to Ilona, tell her what she's been up to, ask for help again. She knows another P.I., too, though she'd rather not work with Macar, the guy always seems to want to get in her pants, but maybe she can exploit that. Yeah, yeah, she'll get out of here, get some sleep, then try Ilona one more time, and if she still won't help, she'll go to Macar. That sounds like a plan.

She instinctively shuts off the light, though just like the door is probably meant to be left unlocked, this is probably expected to be left on, and she exits to a fairly dark hallway. She remembers light in here, but she can make out the lit outline of the door at the end of the passage, part of it obscured.

She almost manages two steps, then she collides with the person in here. She didn't hear anyone try the door while she was in the bathroom.

She yelps, tensing, "Shit!" and makes to mutter an apology and move to the side and make a beeline to the exit, but she is hit, losing consciousness almost instantly.

She wakes in darkness, though it somewhat dissipates as she focuses, revealing that there is some scant source of light. She feels lost, reeling, lethargic, disoriented. She has trouble even remembering where she is, when, how, even. She takes a very slow blink with her eyes, her lids seeming to prefer staying shut, as though she has to pull them back up with an arch of her brow.

Her head hurts, throbs. She feels like she just wants to lie down and sleep, but as she tries to raise a hand to hold behind her skull where she feels pain, she realizes she is bound. She freezes, a sharp spike of realization like adrenalin, bringing her to greater wakefulness and focus.

She tries to sit up, noting that she is in a small room, on the ground, wrists tied together, arms behind her, ankles also bound. She feels a grittiness to the floor. She tries to calm herself, tries to keep her heart from hammering out of her chest. She looks around, seeing shelves, noting some products on them. She sits in some sort of utility closet, judging from the silhouetted shapes and the somewhat permeating chemical smell.

She is not gagged, so she figures yelling will do her no good. She cannot be sure of that, but she decides to remain silent, trying to take stock of the situation. She's still dressed. She doesn't hear the music, so she wonders if she has been moved, or if perhaps the place is now closed, the soundtrack gone silent. She's been relieved of her small knife. She was not carrying a wallet or any identifying documents of any kind, just some cash. They've also taken her cell phone, of course, she can feel the absence of that insubstantial weight. She doesn't expect she'll get it back, but she has protective measures in place that will keep any of the data within it from being used against her or others. Still, she supposes she ought to be more worried about her skin than electronic information. She still has an option, and she hopes it will work.

To that end, she curls the fingers of her hands, using all of them to try to brush against that particular place in the lower, center of her left palm. She has a tattoo there, too, a decent-sized, rather intricate design, and beyond its aesthetic and meaning, it helps to hide the implant. She manages to find the end of it, a different texture than her skin, somewhat like an old blister, and she presses into it, hard, harder, and finally she triggers the tiny mechanism. A signal is sent, and when it reaches its destination, a script will run, and a very important message will be delivered, periodically, until receipt is confirmed.

She keeps pressing over the inorganic material there in her palm, toying with it, like a nervous tic, though she knows such is not needed. She's tested it before, but she's never had to trigger it for its intended use. It's a long shot, but she hopes it will work.

She hears footsteps then, growing louder, and before long, it is obvious they are coming toward her.

DANCE OF THE BUTTERFLY

She hopes it will work and work fast.

*****

The rider has arrived here as quickly as practically possible, taking chances when it proved worth the risk, mostly adhering to traffic law, mostly. There is confidence in the ability to elude the police, if need be, but running from them to get away would be much different than running from them with a specific destination in mind, especially when there is need to be in a very real hurry to arrive at said location.

The place is passed, speed significantly lowered for this surreptitious drive-by, the motorcycle purring. Once done, a secluded, somewhat hidden parking space is found, counter-measures engaged. Hopefully the vehicle will be out here when this is all done. Leaving it where it is holds greater risk than usual, just like this entire outing.

An even more hidden place is located, making sure no one is watching, and then the casual enough looking outfit is changed for the all-black tactical suit, slipping into it as quickly as possible, the Glock and P90 checked, loaded, ready, handgun holstered at the thigh, suppressed submachinegun strapped tight to the torso, in front, angled downward. Other items are in their respective pockets and pouches, all ready to go, and the figure now moves out of the dark area, a shadow in motion, covering the short distance to the rear of the destination.

It is very early in the morning, just a few hours before dawn, and the place is closed. The driver is not sure if this is a normal time to be shut down, or if it is so due to the prisoner they have inside. There is also very little traffic in the area, but the stillness makes any sound or movement that much more a potential risk.

The figure holds place now outside one of three casement windows in this rear wall, crouched low. A small mobile phone is consulted, the face giving up information on the trace, and yes, as so confirmed, the target is inside. This is not the preferred method of approach, not at all, but expediency is required, so after a peer inside to be sure that at least no one appears in the immediate vicinity, an automatic center punch tool is retrieved, pressing into one of the panels close to the crank until a soft pop is heard, the glass shattering, though staying in place. Muscles tense, ready, but no alarm sounds, no signs of anyone nearby to check on what is going on. The small fissure is then widened with quick, gloved fingers, allowing the hand through to open the window. Deftly, the infiltrator slips through, crouched low again, a quick, nearly silent sweep of motion, P90 pointed. The area looks clear.

Waiting a moment here, in this smaller room, looking about. It seems a mostly unused part of the building, some portion given over to casual storage, a table also showing signs of some use, though it all holds sign of neglect. Noises heard then, coming from outside the room, from within the hallway, two men walking by, glimpsed through the ajar door, dim light seeping in. The vigilante dares to peek out as the guards move further down. They are both armed with holstered handguns, and a stunner is spied attached to the belt of one, also in its own special holster. Exchanged words are heard in passing.

"He's nearby now," says one, putting away a cell phone.

"Hmph, well, too bad for her, hmm?" the other replies, giving forth a rumbling chuckle which is not returned.

They turn, heading through a door and back toward the front. Another short moment is taken, waiting, listening, then the darkly-garbed figure moves into the passageway, going the direction from which they came, carried upon quick, silent steps, covering the distance carefully. The bend is taken after a quick peek to be sure no one else is down that way, and this short distance ends in another chamber larger than the one which was used for entry, though a quick peering with goggles in the darkness shows movable racks of clothing along with mirrored stations and even some small sections on one side for the hanging and storage of clothes – an obvious room for changing and making one's self ready.

There is no one else in here, but there is another door, and a quick consulting of the mobile phone confirms that the signal originates from behind it.

There is no window, but there is enough space for the fiberscope, and the snake-like device is slipped in. There, sitting in near total darkness, is a bound person, mouth now gagged with some dark material that has been stuffed inside, eyes peering about, and she seems simmering in a mingling of fear and anger. An angling of the camera

DANCE OF THE BUTTERFLY

shows that it appears the door is not wired with any alarm or trap, so the vigilante pulls the probe back.

The door is opened, some meager illumination from the hallway coming in. The rescuer moves in quickly.

"Message received," is all that is said, the words coming out in a gruff, forced whisper, as the vigilante moves with sureness in the darkness, goggles still over the eyes, pulling forth the simple and rugged military knife to cut through the bonds, saving removal of the gag for last.

"Holy shit. You came," is blurted into the quiet, and though it is not yelled, it is loud.

"Ssshh," comes the response.

"I can't see," Therese whispers, very low.

She feels as her hand is grabbed, then guided to a rigid canvas strap. She holds on as her rescuer, who obviously can see, leads the way out. She tries to be quiet, but she seems to be making all the noise as they head forth, her clunky boots shuffling and creaking as she walks. Then other noises arise, and the vigilante picks up the pace, pulling Therese to the other room.

"Stop!" shouts a voice, and they are seen just as they duck through the doorway.

Therese is whirled about as the figure turns. She manages to hold onto what is obviously a combat harness, then her rescuer reaches back, giving a sign to let go. The other points, jabbing a gloved index finger at her then toward the corner, then pointing down with all four fingers. Therese takes this to mean that she ought to get back there and hide, so she does. She is just in time, as rushing footsteps result in the two guards from before bursting into the room.

It all happens very quickly, and Therese peeks up enough to watch the whole thing as best she can in the dim lighting. The first guard rushes in, pistol held forward, both hands wrapped about the grip. There is a chaotic movement of dark shapes, some glistening reflections of metal, stunted shouts, dull thuds, nothing at all like one may be inclined to expect from over-dramatized action films.

The vigilante moves in front of the guard, using the first man as something of a shield, the second coming in with the stunner held at the ready. The guy's gun is forced upwards, in a direction away from where Therese hides. A few more hits are heard, movement seen in the darkness, though the intruder is smaller and nearly invisible within the all-encompassing suit. The gun has been removed from the man's hands, the other coming around, sparking the stunner to life.

The vigilante is fast, very fast, and another duck, shuffling sound of quick feet and a push, and the first man is shoved toward his colleague, resulting in the wrong person receiving the shock. The man tenses, though his partner releases the trigger, but enough damage is done, and the man's weight falls toward his fellow, aided by a quick side kick from the figure.

The vigilante moves with the falling pair, scrambling over them, much more in control, and a quick stomp is delivered to the one sentry's wrist. He grunts out in pain, not the least of which comes from the weight of his comrade, and the intruder rises up with the stunner in hand, springing it to life long enough to deliver further shocks to both, causing a settling shift to the bundle of men, weak moans emerging from them.

The device is then tossed aside as quickly as it is used, the P90 taken in sure hands as the vigilante whirls, taking a low shooting stance, pointing the submachinegun expertly at the doorway and the other person standing there, the laser sight flicking on, settling on the man's sternum.

"Don't shoot!" he calls out, holding out both hands, arms extended, palms out, "Please, please," he begs, "I am not a threat."

He speaks with a Latin accent.

The two lock eyes for a moment, a deep degree of study there. Calmly, still holding the P90 locked on target, the left hand retrieves the electroshock weapon from its small pouch, pointing it.

"No, wa-!" the man tries, but the trigger is pulled, the electrodes flying out, hitting him, the shock delivered, and Inspector Duilio of Interpol crumbles.

The vigilante moves rapidly, collecting the prongs, reeling in the wires to reset and holster the device, glancing at the disoriented man, then turning to Therese, gesturing an unquestionable message with the jerk of a hand, pointing to the window, then heading there to use it.

DANCE OF THE BUTTERFLY

She follows, scurrying out from her hiding place, taking the proffered aid to get up and through the opening. The figure seems to not need this, springing easily through. Now outside, Therese looks the person over.

"You're as small as I am," she notices.

Another quick jerk of the hand, unmistakable, and the figure scurries off, Therese following. The pack is retrieved from its hiding place, and then they move to the motorcycle.

"Oh, wow, this is nice," Therese comments, looking over the black bike.

Still silent, the rider secures the pack, weapons now unloaded and safely inside, then gets on the vehicle, firing up the quiet, purring engine, looking expectantly at Therese.

"Oh! Right," the hacker starts, blinking, then climbs on behind, the two speeding off to safety.

CHAPTER TWELVE

Frustration runs high with Detectives Pasztor and Mahler. Not only does the captain want very regular updates, but the director sometimes comes straight to them, and they know he is adding their progress as part of his own status reports to Councillor Keller. A high profile case like this can make or break a career.

They were poised to think they were onto a good opportunity when the call came in about the double murder at the 'Lovers' Lane' parking lot. Patrols convened quickly, scouring the area. The scene had been very fresh, but nothing had resulted regarding the "eyewitness" account of the suspect. They have decided to re-visit this, talking to each and every patrol group who had been there. The work is tedious, but they know that such careful prospecting can occasionally yield a glimmer.

They've been at it for hours, on this the second day of such work, when they get to the current pair.

"Yeah, the guy looked suspicious enough, and we would have probably asked him more questions, but he didn't fit the description."

"Well, we're beginning to wonder how accurate that description is," Mahler relays, and the two patrol officers look back at him, inquiry in their eyes. "The witness saw a black male running from the area. The witness did not see this individual kill anyone or even directly interact with the victims. It's possible this person happened on the bodies, maybe even saw the murders, and then ran away. We're hoping to find him, of course, but he may not be our killer."

The other two nod, taking this in, then the original speaker continues.

"This guy looked high," he resumes, "Not all there, hmm?"

"Physical description?" Mahler asks, pen poised over his notebook.

DANCE OF THE BUTTERFLY

"Caucasian. Tall, very thin, but that was judged from his face. He was obviously slender, his clothes kind of baggy."

"What color hair, eyes?"

"He had on a hoodie," the other offers.

Pasztor tries to help, "Did you see his eyebrows? Facial hair?"

"He was kind of scraggly, unshaven, but not a full beard or anything, but yeah, now that you say that, it almost seemed like he didn't have any eyebrows at all."

"So, they were shaved, or he had light blonde hair."

"Oh, *very* light blonde. Really pale blue eyes, too. He said he was from South Africa."

"He did?" Mahler peers up from his pad.

"Yes, I asked his name and where he was from," then he looks at his partner, "What was his name?"

The two ponder a moment, then the other muses, "Erik … was it? Erick … something with a Z."

"South African white guy?" Pasztor throws in, "Van something? A lot of their last names have van in it."

"Yes!" the first jumps in, "That was it – *Ernst*, not Erick, Ernst van Zyl."

Mahler jots this down, nodding, "Good, good, so he was tall, thin, light blonde hair, pale blue eyes." Then he looks as the officers, desirous of more.

"He looked ill," one of them says, "His face was very bony, prominent, sunken in."

And this sets off its own bulb, and the two detectives look at each other. Pazstor reaches for a folder, pulling out papers, leafing through them, just as Mahler grabs an electronic notepad, going through its contents rather quickly. The two patrol officers share an inquisitive look, then silently watch the detectives.

"Here it is," Pazstor declares, gesturing with a piece of paper, just as Mahler is nodding, coming to the end of his own search.

"Yes, yes," he says, still looking at the device, "A person with a matching description was seen at one of the victim's places of work the same night she was murdered. The two interacted, though no one could say if they left together."

Then the detectives look at the other two. It takes a moment, but under such scrutiny, the patrol officers both slowly tense, eyes widening a bit.

"We were looking for a large black male. That was the description given from dispatch."

"This guy was at both places," Mahler says. "You may have been talking to our serial killer."

"Shit!" one declares.

"Eh," Pasztor grunts, "We have a name to go with the description. We'll find him now."

"Yes, we will," Mahler agrees, then looking at the other two, "Thank you, gentlemen."

*****

He walks up to see her bent into the engine of her car, black sweatpants pulled over the contours of her lower body from her extended position, the vehicle parked in the small, private garage she has rented to go along with her apartment. He is expected, but it seems she has not heard his approach. He takes a moment to admire the shape of her as her petite form is half-disappeared from his approaching view.

"Hello," he calls out.

"Oh! Skot," she replies, still under the hood, "One moment."

He smiles warmly, nodding, as if she could see, "Okay."

She finishes up, rising, turning to him as she grabs a nearby towel, wiping her hands. She is wearing a loose t-shirt, her hair tied and held up with a cloth headband. She smiles brightly, oblivious of the black mark on her right cheek, rising up on tiptoes as he steps nearer, and they exchange a kiss.

She hums into it, and he returns the sound, then she settles back onto her feet, smirking playfully up at him.

"Were you looking at my butt?" she teases, giving a rakish shift of her hips.

He perks his eyebrows, "Yes, I was," he admits.

She gives him more of that smirk, then leans in and up for another kiss.

DANCE OF THE BUTTERFLY

"Though now I am noticing that mark on your cheek," he says.

"Oh," she says, reaching up to her face.

"Other side," he says, grinning, and she brings up the rag, wiping it somewhat away. "So, how is it going?" he looks over at the exposed engine of the BMW.

"Fine," she says, "Just checking the oil and changing the spark plugs. What have you got there?"

He brings up the plastic bag in his right hand, "I brought you something to drink."

"Oh?" she responds as he fishes out a plastic bottle of Gatorade, presenting it to her. "Thank you," her smile warms as she accepts it, "This is meant to be drank during a hard exercise, to compensate the loss of electrolytes you get while sweating. *This*," she nods toward the straight-4 DOHC piston engine, "isn't really that hard," then, with a grin, she pops the cap of the bottle, taking a good sip of it, "Thank you."

He notes the sheen to her flesh.

"It's still quite warmer than usual for this time of year, isn't it?"

She nods, swallowing, then drinking more, finally replacing the cap, "Yeah," she confirms, then looks about for a place to set the bottle, and he holds out his hand, and she places the drink there with a light, gracious smile.

He watches as she gets back to work, noting the sureness and focus as she resumes her task.

"I've never changed my own spark plugs before," he comments.

She glances up at him, smiling, "No? Why not? It's not that difficult."

He shrugs, "I just never have. I'm not really that adept with automobiles."

"I like taking care of it myself," she says, "If something's wrong, I do research, and I fix it. I've never taken this one to a mechanic. That's one of the things I like about this older model. I can handle it myself."

He just watches, smiling, until she rises up for another short breather, and he hands her the bottle.

"Thanks," she says, that casual smile still on her lips.

As she has another drink, he moves in closer, slipping his hand to the small of her back, pressing her inward and leaning down for a closer, deeper kiss. She returns it, but as he brings his hand to her waist, getting in nearer, she pulls back, her grin widened to show teeth, the bottom lip barely caught there.

"I'm all sweaty," she informs.

"I don't mind."

"I do," she chuckles, "Let me finish."

"Is that an order?" he perks his eyebrows.

"No," she purses her lips, a playful pout, "May I finish, please?" she asks, throwing in a teasing, coquettish air.

"How could I refuse that?" he grins, "Of course, you may."

He watches, gone back to holding the bottle for her, then he meanders toward the open doorway, peering out, noting a few people going to and fro in the parking lot, some vehicular traffic, though not much. He can hear the nearby sounds of the city.

"Have you been following the news about the serial killer?" he asks.

"Yes," she calls out, her answer taking a bit to arise, "Have you?"

"Some," he remarks, then he turns, working his way slowly back toward her, again letting his eyes drink in the sight, "Terrible enough as it is, but to prey on unfortunate girls like that."

"Not just girls," she says, "There was a man killed in the last one."

"Yes, the recent double murder, but I suspect he was just in the wrong place at the wrong time, and the girl was the main target. She suffered much worse treatment. And the others … just gutted like that. It's horrible to think about."

She rises up, wiping her hands, peering at him in a particular way. He hands her the bottle, and she drinks more, holding onto it this time.

"Yes, it's terrible," she agrees, "To think a human being could do that to another."

"Maybe it wasn't a human," he pitches.

"What?" she furrows her brow, looking at him. "What makes you say that?"

"Oh, nothing," he is quick to reply, "Just thinking out loud. Besides, the wounds certainly seem like they could have just as easily been made with claws as a bladed weapon."

She stares at him, though he doesn't notice. She certainly does not linger on it, else she'd likely garner his attention, but she wonders why

DANCE OF THE BUTTERFLY

he has said this. Why make a comparison to the use of claws and the killings perhaps having been caused by something non-human? She wonders if it is mere conjecture or something more. She does not recall anything in the typical news outlets that have made any allusions to such as that.

"I suppose it's possible that the killer does not think he is human," he continues his musing.

"I don't know," she finally says, her own eyes off now on other thoughts, her right hand holding the bottle close to her mouth, uncapped, but she just sort of presses the tip against her bottom lip, not drinking more as yet, then she glances up, seeing that he is looking at her, and she gives a grin, "I'm not a profiler."

"Neither am I," he admits, "But I've read a bit on it, and I did take some courses on Criminal Psychology when I was in college. Of course, that doesn't qualify me, and I am just reaching at threads, making conversation."

She nods, contemplatively, "The whole thing is sad, really."

"Hmm?" he gently pushes, raising his eyebrows, still looking at her as she has gone into her thoughts.

She looks up at him, her large eyes drinking in the available light, the tip of the bottle still held at her lower lip, though the grin is now gone for a look of seriousness.

"The human trafficking," and he nods his agreements as she adds, "I wish there was something more that could be done."

"Yes, it's terrible," he says, looking at her, then away as he drifts into his own musing, "It's unfortunate that that sort of negative action still goes on. There are many ways to satisfy one's need for 'vice', so to speak, that does not involve causing such pain. Don't people give any thought to what it does to generate such negative energy? It doesn't just disappear. There are repercussions."

She has looked over at him as he has spoken, her eyes studying him, watching as he shows a measure of his own personal investment in the situation. She wonders if this means anything, if he's perhaps experienced anything directly related to these sorts of crimes.

"I realize it is not as if the human traffickers are deliberately bringing these girls in here as a sacrifice of sorts for the serial killer, but it just ... bothers me that people seem so callous to others, so ignorant of the wider damage they cause beyond the focal point of their original crimes."

He then looks over at her, noticing her intent focus on him.

"Sorry," he says, smiling thinly, "I'm a little too upset about this."

"It's okay," she says, smiling in return, hers very warm, sympathetic.

"I know we can't let these sorts of things consume us, then it becomes even worse. I talk about negative feelings, and I am letting that very thing cause more in me right now. Of course, the opposite of that spectrum may lead to trying to be a crusader, which may be equally difficult and unfulfilling."

"Why do you say that?" she asks.

"Well," he glances at her, taking a spare moment to collect his thoughts, and she chooses that moment to slip an arm about his waist, and they resolve easily into a close embrace, "How do you right all the world's wrongs? How do you even know if what you are doing is 'right'? It's very complicated, and just having the power to influence or even compel others in very real ways does not mean one should exercise it."

She nods, thoughtfully, then speaks, "But if you do have the power to make a difference ... at least against those things you know to be wrong, why wouldn't you do something about it?"

He gives her a good snug, nodding slowly, "Yes, you are right, of course."

She returns the hug, cuddling into him somewhat, then rising up again on her tiptoes, chin forward, and he replies to the obvious request by meeting her kiss. She then gets to tidying up.

"Let me get cleaned up, then how about some lunch?" she pitches.

"Sounds wonderful," he smiles, watching her, very happy to be with her.

*****

DANCE OF THE BUTTERFLY

"Maybe she was just some dyke?" the large man suggests, and he brings a flask up, but it pauses, held there, as he notices the look he is receiving from one of the other two with him here at this barbershop.

"Detective Sladky, pardon me for saying, but you are a *fool*!" the inspector says, the sentence beginning with his characteristic calm only to spike at the end. "The vigilante came to rescue her. She is important to him."

Alec takes a moment, trying to decide if he will be offended, the decent-sized flask with the dimpled leather covering still held open near his mouth but not used, "The vigilante rescued other girls."

Duilio rolls his eyes, sighing, causing another pause in the developing difficulty the detective appears to be having in getting his drink to his lips.

"The vigilante arrived and almost had her out by the time I got there. Doesn't that tell you anything?"

Alec looks at the Interpol man, trying to figure this one, now curbing his generally impulsive tongue.

Duilio mutters a short sentence in his mother speech, something that doesn't seem terribly flattering, then, "She has a way to contact him."

"What?" Alec's brow wrinkles further.

"He's right," casually quips Quain, still reclining in a chair, receiving a nice, close shave from one of the two older men working in here, the straight razor wielded with calm expertise, the uttering of this single sentence not hindering the barber in any way.

The rotund detective looks toward his partner then back. Duilio gives a slight, apologetic shrug.

"Gnegon has everyone on very high alert, and he has instructed his men to notify of us of *anything* suspicious," Duilio proceeds, and Alec gives something of an exasperated nod, for he knows this, but the Inspector presses anyway, his own non-verbal commentary on the other man's comprehension skills, "So, this 'dyke', as you so eloquently call her, was apprehended, and Gnegon was called."

"I was there," Alec says, his growing agitation showing itself, the flask's cap returned without anything from it having been consumed.

"You were there in body, Detective, but were you there in *mind*?" Duilio asks, tapping his own brow near the temple, narrowing eyes at the man to whom he speaks. "I decided it was worth pursuing, since we all know the vigilante is getting his information *somehow*, and before I can even get there and question the girl, he has already arrived and set to rescue her ... which he did!" he concludes, throwing his hands forward, gesturing with them toward the officer.

"I know all that!" Alec all but huffs.

"Ah, yes, but you think the girl was just some 'dyke' who snuck in to look at the strippers," Duilio fixes a steely glare upon the man.

Alec returns it, his own eyes narrowing, but he stays seated, says nothing.

"Let's all calm down," Quain tries, rising up from the chair, looking and smelling very fresh and clean, "Why don't you try a shave, Alec? It's very refreshing."

The portly detective grumbles out an obvious negative to the suggestion. Duilio rises up from his place, though, going to sit in the barber's chair, a large drape placed around him with the casual flair of a matador's cape.

"Just a trim," he says to the barber, gesturing with his right hand toward his hair, content to remain with his salt and pepper goatee.

The white-jacketed man nods once, setting to business.

"She is the link to the vigilante," Duilio says, and a tenting forms in the fabric about him as he works his arm free, holding up the index finger of his now liberated right hand, "Or *a* link," he amends, "but she can be *our* link, hmm?"

"Right," Quain nods, signifying his own travels into thought, then he blinks, looking over at Duilio, "But you said she had no ID, and her cell phone was locked. Our guys lost the data when they tried to get in."

"Yes, yessss," Duilio contemplates, the finger of that right hand brought to his own lip, "To have a protection like that, she must be someone who is smart with electronics and computers. I wonder ..." his voice trails off.

"Hmm?" Quain pitches into the growing silence, still watching the inspector.

"Well, we put out some requests of our own into that 'hacker' community," he says the word as if it is foreign, "And we know the

DANCE OF THE BUTTERFLY

vigilante is a hacker or has people of such *proclivities* helping him. It is possible that someone who works for him saw our requests."

"Right, but then wouldn't they be warning the vigilante, not out at one of Gnegon's places?"

"Yes, that does seem to make more sense, regardless, this girl is a link. *Our* link," Duilio repeats himself, "We have to find her."

"How?" Alec throws out, his voice simmering with pain from the earlier exchange.

"This is your city, Detectives," Duilio says, "I am sure you can find her, and imagine how pleased Gnegon will be when you do, hmm?"

And so said, he quiets, content to now just enjoy his haircut. He has his own thoughts on the situation, despite seeming open to sharing most of what crosses his mind. He got a good look at the vigilante before he was shocked, and now he feels he better understands. It is all still suspicion, supposition, but this new information may make things clearer for him. He feels a resolution is much more in their potential grasp than it ever has been before.

*****

The group is gathered at this area of the otherwise empty gymnasium, the time into the early evening this weekday, and this smaller arena chosen due to its not being used as much by others. Some of those in this small collection are students, some are not, but the college had agreed to offer this instruction for free. Still, the attendance of this woman's only self-defense class does not generally prove to be that abundant.

Lilja has already completed her warm-up, and she mostly looks over her students, observing as they get themselves ready, offering any advice or pointers as she sees fit. There will only be eight of them today, only one new face, the others comprised of semi-regulars and a core group of four who manage to attend nearly every session.

She tries to keep these somewhat relaxed, more about practical combat than martial proficiency, also in effort to attract students, and so she wears a black t-shirt over black gi pants, her feet bare. The shirt shows an insignia of wadoryu emblazoned on the back - a stylized dove, its small oval head in profile, as the bold wings go up and around, forming a circle, in which is held the front view of a fist. Those who attend show mostly garbed in sweat pants and t-shirts, also barefooted. Lilja walks over, greeting the new person with a warm smile, introducing herself, obviously making the woman feel more comfortable about being here.

She is just about to gather the group's attention and begin the class, walking to a place she likes to use for just such a purpose, when she sees another student rushing over, trying to get in before being tardy. The woman is obviously very young, her dyed black hair mostly just brushed back, held in place with an obvious sheen of styling gel, too short to be tied, and the chaotic juttings of some portions indicate her possible usual style, the top holding most of the length while the sides are shorter.

She wears a black t-shirt over black track pants, and though it has been some time, she has been here before, some months ago, as memory serves. She had started then, wanting of learning and had attended several classes for a length of time before suddenly failing to show up anymore. As she recalls, something had happened to the young woman to compel her to want to take up self-defense.

"It's Therese, ma'am," she reminds, "Sorry for being late. I used to take the class."

"I remember," she replies with a very light, polite curl to her lips, "And please just call me Lilja."

"Right," she nods, and the look on her face seems to indicate she is ready to get started.

"Alright, everyone," Lilja says, looking out to the others, and those that have not already begun to, move in closer, "Please gather to a half circle, so you can all see me." She watches them, patient, as they do so.

The group warm-up is then begun, going through some jogging in place, jumping jacks, sit-ups, and stretches. Once this is done, she addresses them.

"There is one new person here, and a returnee from some time ago, and some of you are pretty regular, so you may have heard this, but I am not teaching this to teach you to fight but to teach you so you don't have to fight, and that the main key to self-defense is not to get into the risky situation, and the best defense is running away and diplomacy.

DANCE OF THE BUTTERFLY

"This is about risk management. 'Risk' is something manageable and avoidable. You have to somehow deal with the risk before it becomes a threat. 'Threat' is something you can't avoid and is immediate and you need to eliminate such threat. Keep up your situational awareness; don't make yourself an easy target. Be aware of your surroundings, sometimes just making eye contact with a potential assailant can get them to change their mind and move onto different prey," she continues, letting her own eyes move from person to person, fully meeting their gaze. "Practicing against pads or a bag is great, but when someone is coming at you, trying to hit you, trying to throw something at you, that's different, so what we do in training has to be relevant to a real, potential situation."

This, of course, brings up some questions from them, all of which are fielded for a short time until going on to some self-defense techniques, basics about body language and positioning along with a few pair exercises. After a time of this, she calls out for the next task.

"Okay, let's move on. Miranda, step forward," and the so-named woman, one of the core regulars and a decent-sized, healthy specimen at that, moves over to Lilja. "Let's assume that Miranda is some guy who grabs my wrist and I don't want that, what should I do to stop her from doing that or how can I get free?"

"The weak point of the grab is here where the thumb meets the fingers," she informs, pointing out that very spot where Miranda has a hold of her left wrist, "So we rotate the wrist in the direction so the palm is facing down, keeping the elbow low and bent and then apply pressure away from the grip. That's it," she says, slipping her arm free. "Then you take a step back to get some distance, raise your hands up to show your arms are empty, this also creates a barrier between you and your attacker, then firmly tell them to stop and leave you alone. Use power in your voice, speak from within your chest. Intimidate them, not the other way around." And so instructed, she steps back, raising her arms and speaks, "Stop! Leave me alone!" The words are uttered with such force that several of the woman start, eyes going wide as they exchange looks, grins, even smattering of somewhat embarrassed chuckles.

"Of course, if they will not stop, then we can follow up with a controlled strike to any number of vital areas, such as a quick and powerful step forward and arm straight with your palm on their face," she relays, demonstrating the very move toward Miranda, "That forces them to stop or even back away, tilts their head back and prevents them from seeing properly, even confusing them. There you can follow with a knee, punch, elbow, or kick if needed." In quick, controlled succession, she demonstrates all of these, coming very close to but not touching the taller woman. "And then just run away."

She looks out at the others, holding her hands out a bit, looking to see how they may be absorbing the lesson.

"Strike locations are eyes, nose, throat, diaphragm, and groin. The priority in that order," she carries on. "Alright, let's pair up and try that."

Therese has been paying close attention, feeling quite interested based on her recent 'adventure'. She's come back after her long absence due to the change in her life and her decision to try to get more information in hopes of helping the vigilante. She now realizes how risky that is, and after she got over cursing herself for her naïveté, she remembered the self-defense classes and decided to come learn how to better protect herself.

Her recent foray and resultant rescue has been running through her mind quite a lot. She noticed the vigilante's small size, hanging on and having that motorcycle ride to get somewhere safe. She's come to a startling conclusion – she thinks the vigilante may be a woman.

It baffles her, though, for how could a woman compete with a crime ring, much less the large, experienced men that would make up those ranks? Wouldn't it make more sense for the vigilante to just be a small man? Bruce Lee was a very trim, very skilled, and powerful guy in a smaller than average package. Still, though, he had been five foot seven, and the vigilante looked her own height, and she is barely five foot three. It had been dark, everything happening very fast, but there is some gnawing feeling in her that says this person is female. Perhaps it is just because she *wants* the vigilante to be a woman.

But now, as she watches, Lilja, a very petite lady, shows them moves and practices with a sure confidence and skill. Therese begins to realize what a trained, self-assured woman could do. Still, stopping and escaping an attacker is quite different than taking on an organized crime ring. Of course, so is taking and teaching a self-defense class.

DANCE OF THE BUTTERFLY

Once the class is ended, Therese sits on the bench in the changing room, just holding place there, having had a quick shower after the other ladies have left, her hair dripping. She's deep in her own thoughts, eyes focused on nothing as the droplets of water gather at the tips of her hair, then fall into small, splattering puddles on the floor. She finally shakes herself free from her reverie, eyes blinking, and she quickly gets her clothes on, packing up her small bag and preparing to head out.

She pauses once she's back in the gym, turning to the dull sounds of thudding and the accompanying grunts. She pulls back to instinctively hide herself, and there, across the way, is Lilja punishing a punching bag.

Therese silently observes for a while, noting the wobbling and movement on the part of the heavy thing, dangling from its thick chains. It is obvious Lilja is possessed of strength and force of focus as well as speed. The hacker begins to imagine if that punching bag were instead an armed guard and how quickly and effectively Lilja might disable him. Just at that moment, she delivers a loud cry and a powerful kick, pushing the bag away more than anytime yet, and Therese starts, blinking as she tenses.

She's seen enough for now, deciding she'd rather not risk being caught spying on the teacher, so she puts her head down and walks out as fast as she is able without seeming to be fleeing.

*****

There is a knock on the door.

After a rather short wait, another, more insistent knock arises.

He blinks, rousing from whatever place he had been journeying in his mind. He cranes his head over in the direction of the portal, moving slowly, as though his silent, still repose has caused him to become something of a statue, and he must now break free from that solidification. No one knocks on his door, ever.

And then there is another knock, again loud, insistent.

His rent is paid. He has no friends. His family does not know he is here. No one ever knocks on his door.

The two detectives outside in the hall wonder if they should loudly identify themselves. They know there is a window leading to a fire escape. They also feel very confident in the information they received from the desk clerk that the guy is inside. They don't want him to think the arrival of the police ought to be responded to as a fire.

They managed to gather a good deal of information on one Ernst van Zyl, hailing from Port Elizabeth, South Africa, promising student of mathematics and the arts, having been accepted to the University of Zürich, only for his grades and attendance to suddenly slip, and then he had been expelled and disappeared from the grid until his passport was used for his travel to this city. He certainly was not trying to hide himself that much.

Some of the consensus seemed to be that he got into drugs, thus resulting in this downward spiral, the brightening light burned out before it could reach its peak, but that explanation does not entirely sit well with others who may better understand the psychology of a serial killer. He may definitely be into drugs, but that would not be the cause.

Still, his involvement in such a 'hobby' had allowed them to eventually pinpoint information about the parts of town he frequents and where he might live, and it had not proved too difficult at that juncture to locate his room here at this dingy hostel.

Pasztor looks at Mahler, giving a sort of simmering expression of exasperation, then pounds again, his fist giving forth a loud thump, and he keeps at it much longer than before. The door finally opens, the emaciated young man looking out, eyes squinting as though he were peering out into the sun from some cave. He doesn't even say anything, just looks at the two.

"Ernst van Zyl," Mahler says, not a question, "I am Detective Mahler. This is Detective Pasztor." They both hold up identification, which Ernst proves disinclined to inspect, "We'd like to come inside and ask you some questions, if you don't mind?"

He looks the two over, briefly, his expression one almost more of passivity than any indication of being bothered, and he steps back, leaving the door ajar. The two Homicide Detectives exchange another curious glance, then head inside.

The small space is a picture of dusty neglect. It is not trashed, but it is obvious that its occupant feels no great compulsion to clean. There are some bits of refuse, but the trained eyes of the detectives spot a waste

DANCE OF THE BUTTERFLY

basket, bearing of some items, along with a white trash bag in the kitchen area. Its top hangs open, like a drooping aperture, about as listless as the room's occupant, just waiting for more to occupy its innards. Pasztor wanders over, bending down for a sniff. It doesn't smell as bad as he had expected, certainly not reeking in a way to suggest the decay of human parts.

Some of the room's corners are occupied by spider webs, areas of discoloration or punctures showing in the sheet rock walls. The only area that has any personal touch at all is the small part that is meant to be the 'bedroom', judging from the closed notebook, open soda can, and other small items that must belong to the occupant, all cluttered together on the tiny side table near the glorified cot.

"How long have you been here, Mr. van Zyl?" Mahler finally asks, after they have let some silence ferment from their ambling in and observing the surroundings.

Ernst has taken a seat on the side of the bed, and Mahler pulls one of two chairs over from a small table in the kitchenette, seating himself near the young man. Pasztor continues to look around, peering in cabinets, but there is not much to see, no closets, no private bathroom. The seasoned detective notes that the man appears to not shit where he lives, literally or figuratively.

"Uhm," Ernst finally speaks, his eyes blinking once, slowly, licking his dry lips, then lapsing into a silence that makes Mahler wonder if he'll continue, , "A few months," he says, still not looking either of his visitors in the eye.

"A few months?" Mahler repeats, "Do you not know how many? Two … six?"

Those pale blue eyes finally look at the speaker, boring into him with a casual study, and then the head slowly nods, "Yes. Two."

They know they can get this information from the desk clerk, but they're here to question van Zyl. Two months, if that is precise, would not have him here long enough to be responsible for all the killings, but they don't give his answer that much credit.

"What brought you here from Switzerland?"

And with this question, Ernst looks over at Pasztor, the man having ended his brief search and now just standing nearby, hands on his waist.

He did not ask the question, but he seems to be getting a much deeper draw of those haunting eyes than his partner. After a moment of silence, the two detectives exchange a glance. Something is amiss with this guy, that much is obvious, but he is not displaying the exact sort of signs they'd expect from someone under the influence of intoxicants. He acts more like someone unable to fully wake from a deep sleep.

"I had to come," he finally says, having moved his eyes away and now just slowly pitching words out for anyone.

"What do you mean you 'had to'?" Mahler presses, "Did you get a job? Are you employed, Mr. van Zyl?"

"No," Ernst answers, his eyes back to Mahler.

"Then why did you have to come here?" he keeps pushing after waiting a moment and realizing the man does not seem prepared to speak further.

"I had to," comes the eventual reply.

Mahler closes his eyes for a moment, taking in a breath.

"Why did you *have* to, huh?" Pasztor asks with more intensity, eyes boring into Ernst, brow furrowed.

"They made me."

"*Who* made you?" the more forceful officer continues.

"You wouldn't understand."

"Ernst?" Mahler speaks, gently, and the young man looks over. "You don't mind if I call you Ernst, do you?"

Van Zyl takes a moment to give a slow shrug of his shoulders, his eyes still rather droopy, "No."

"Ernst," Mahler carries on, "I'd *like* to understand," and he tries on a warm smile, "Would you help me understand?"

"That's not a good idea."

"*Why* isn't it a good idea?" Pasztor pushes, his tone of voice very much marking him as the 'bad' cop, if the two are engaging in such a routine.

"You don't want to know the things I know."

"Well, you're wrong about that, Ernst." Mahler picks up the ball, still wearing that curve to his lips that implies he is just looking out for the sickly youth. "I do want to understand you, and if I can, I'd like to help you."

DANCE OF THE BUTTERFLY

"You can't help me."

"Why can't I help you, Ernst?" he asks with utmost sincerity.

"Because you don't understand."

Mahler looks over, receiving rolled eyes from his partner. He glances back, noting Ernst's gaze, and though it still lacks any intensity, it is quite locked onto the detective.

"I'd like to understand," he tries.

"No, you wouldn't."

"Now, how do you know that, Ernst?"

"Because I know what you're asking, and you don't," the ill-looking man replies.

Another moment of silence stretches between them, as though Mahler has lost his own voice from the steady stare of the young man he is questioning.

"What's that supposed to mean?" Pasztor takes another turn, his inflection still much more demanding.

He finds the aspect of van Zyl to be very discomfiting, especially with that silence on the part of Mahler. Mahler is good at interrogating people. Pasztor has seen enough of that to know, and though he sometimes may play the 'bad' cop or even get too heated for his own good, Mahler generally handles these sorts of things quite well. He takes a couple of steps closer to the young man, and as he does, Ernst slowly turns his eyes to look up at him.

"You don't want to know the things I know."

"Oh, stop talking in circles," Pasztor throws out his hands, showing his growing frustration.

"Not a circle," Ernst says, speaking in a somewhat musing tone, "Circles are too simple. It's all an interconnected sphere, like a round web that spins back upon itself."

"Here we go," Pasztor comments, rolling his eyes again.

"Have you heard about the serial killer in the city, Ernst?" Mahler interjects, and this gets more of a reaction from the young man as he looks back over with more speed and focus than he has evinced thus far.

"Yes," he says, his voice still sounding flat, but obviously uttered with more firmness of intonation.

It is apparent to both detectives that they may have hit a nerve.

"What do you think about that, Ernst?" Pasztor chides. "Some guy going around cutting up those poor, defenseless girls, even taking their blood? Maybe he's some twisted, messed-up person who thinks he's a vampire."

"It's ..." Ernst begins, "It's horrible," he says, and the sincerity in his voice is evident to Mahler, and he notes that the fallow-looking fellow has suddenly grown agitated, his body displaying some animation now as opposed to the almost zombie-like aspect he has shown up until now.

"It is," Mahler agrees, nodding, gathering Ernst's attention. "We're working on the case. We're trying to stop him."

"You won't be able to."

"Why not, Ernst?" Pasztor asks, and the young man looks up, his attention now lobbing back and forth between the two, his own indicative body language and small movements of tension growing. "Why won't we be able to stop him?"

"You *won't*," he pushes back, his tone taking on something of a challenge, "You just won't. You ... you *can't*."

Pasztor makes ready to say something, but Mahler raises a hand. Once his partner has held his tongue, he looks back at the other.

"Ernst?" he bids, getting that attention returned to him, "Why *can't* we? What makes it impossible?"

"You," he begins, and Mahler sees a sudden flutter of eyelids before those pale orbs are back open on him, and the tension spikes, tendons rising up on the parts of Ernst's frail, thin body that can be seen within his dirty clothes, "You don't want to know."

And another roll of the eyes comes forth from Pasztor, and he scoffs, then begins to talk, "Yeesh, Ernst, we're ti-," but he is cut off by the continued speech of the one under interrogation.

"Protect your sanity," he warns, "Protect your *souls*. Stay blind to it. Once you walk through that door, you *can't* go back. You don't want to get lost in the fog ... with *them*."

"Ernst, what are you talking about?" Mahler tries, his brow furrowed, his own genuine desire to understand etched on his features.

"I know who's doing it."

"What?" comes Mahler's surprised response.

DANCE OF THE BUTTERFLY

"You know who's responsible for the serial murders?" Pasztor as quickly asks.

And the sickly-seeming man nods, "I do."

"Is that a confession?" Pasztor quips, and he gets a disapproving cut of the eyes from his partner.

"What?" Ernst throws back, his head snapping to Pasztor with a bird-like quickness.

"You say you know who did it, so I say *you* did it." He points an accusing finger at Ernst.

"I didn't kill those people," he says, eyes widened, his spine stiffening as he somewhat rises in place, still sitting there on the side of the thin mattress, then he looks back at Mahler, "You don't think I killed them, do you?"

"We don't know yet who killed them," Mahler tries to placate, "But you said *you* do, Ernst."

And a slow, steady nod emerges, "I do."

"Well?" Mahler bids into the growing silence, "Who was it?"

"I-," Ernst begins, and just as it seems he has gone back to being a statue, he shakes his head, and a pained look wrinkles onto his skeletal-like visage, "No."

"What do you mean 'n-?" Pasztor begins.

"No!" Ernst looks back over, raising his voice, and it looks like the young man is about to burst forth in tears.

"Ernst," Mahler tries to summon the attention back to himself, but now the stressed man is just looking at Pasztor, his head slowly moving side to side, "Ernst?" He looks back over, "Just calm down, okay?"

"No!"

Pasztor takes another step closer, much more threatening now, and again, Mahler halts him with a raised hand.

"Ernst, if you know who did this, we have to get that information from you, and it would be much better if you helped us willingly, don't you think?" comes out the very calm question.

"No!" and Ernst is all but trembling, his head still moving back and forth, lips curled up in a grimace, teeth bared, not signs of anger but abject fear.

"Now, look-," Pasztor steps closer.

247

"No!" Ernst repeats, holding up his arms, palms shown, an obvious instinctive attempt at warding off a perceived attack, "Stay away from me!" he yells, scrambling back into the corner against which his bed is placed, hugging his knees up, now openly trembling, eyes wide and looking between the two men.

"Whoa, whoa!" Mahler stands, his hands now out, placating, and he gives his partner a 'look', then he transfers his eyes back to Ernst, "We just want to help-" And he stops, peering.

One of Ernst's legs has dropped, still bent at the knee, but now angled out from his body, the other still up, though it is obvious the arms holding it do not possess the same tension they did a mere moment before. The eyes are still open, but the face now looks smooth, blank, mouth slightly agape, and a length of saliva drools out.

"Ernst?" he tries, and there is no response.

It is obvious the young man is breathing, but he just sits there, unblinking.

"Shit," Mahler curses, going over, "I think he's having a mild seizure."

And just then, there is a knock at the door.

"Who the hell could that be?" Pasztor asks, looking back, not too perturbed by the developing situation, but he does not know that no one ever knocks on Ernst's door, that is, until today.

"You see who it is. I'll call for medical," Mahler says, and he pulls out his mobile phone.

When Pasztor gets to the door, opening it, there is no one there. He is obviously perplexed, so he steps out into the hallway, looking left and right, then further out, looking up and down the staircase, but there appears to be no one about.

"There was no one-" He announces as he walks back into the room, but he stops, eyes widening in shock, and he jerks out his firearm, aiming it at the form of Ernst who looks to have not moved at all since the onset of the petit mal seizure, "Don't move!" Pasztor orders, and were in not for the crumbled body of Mahler on the floor, leaking a profuse amount of blood from his open neck, it may seem comical.

There is a large, arced spray of blood on the wall, obviously having erupted from the hideous wound as the detective had been preparing to

DANCE OF THE BUTTERFLY

call for medical emergency. Pasztor does not know if he completed the call, or if anyone is coming, so he keeps his pistol poised on the immobile form of van Zyl, trying to stop any potential trembling in his hands, as he reaches for his own phone.

"That won't be necessary," speaks a very deliberate-sounding voice, the words delivered in a cultured, Transatlantic accent.

Pasztor whirls, moving to face the direction from which the voice emerges, trying to point his gun in that same angle, but he is stopped, the pistol removed from his hand. It transpires so fast that it takes him a moment to realize what has happened, and just as he comprehends that the black-suited figure has deeply sliced his wrist with a straight-edged, single blade knife, pain not quite caught up to him, though he is bleeding profusely, the same weapon is expertly moved again in an arcing flash. The detective tries to clutch at his own open throat, trying to stifle the forced ejection of his vitality, only one hand working properly. The awkward, quick clutching of his hands to his neck just redirects the jettison upwards, and after a terse moment, he collapses.

Denman Malkuth watches the man as he dies, then he just as calmly looks over at the only other person in here who still draws breath.

"They almost discovered our secret, didn't they, Ernst?"

There is no answer from the young man on the bed.

"But we still have more work to do, don't we?"

And so said, he reaches for his own phone.

*****

She brings up the mug, its contents steaming, having a sip of the vanilla-flavored black tea. She wonders if she ought to make something more stimulating, maybe brew up a pot of coffee. She's been at this for only one hour, and she can already feel the boredom setting in.

She then again wonders why she is even doing this. What has compelled her to want to watch this security footage? She didn't know if her position in the library would even permit it, but she did not see the harm in asking, she is the Head Curator after all, and the security personnel had appeared more surprised by the novelty of any request at all as opposed to having any caution at giving out copies of the video.

So, here she sits, wearing comfortable pajamas, sipping her tea, watching a very boring show of the camera angled onto the display case of the library's most valuable books.

She looks down at the sudden noise, Dali looking up at her, and she gives him a warm smile, leaning over to scratch behind his ears.

"Kiskiskis," she says, patting her lap, "Dali, hyppää," and the large cat springs up onto her, "Miau," she coos to him, scritching more behind his ears, and he responds in kind as she pets over his back, and he rises up into it, his purring quite loud.

He eventually settles, making himself comfortable there, and she keeps up the somewhat absent-minded affection as she watches the video, letting it play on its fastest speed. If it were not for the rapidly advancing numbers in the bottom right corner, it would almost seem like a still photograph.

Her thoughts wander to him and their recent experiences together, and the curl to her lips slowly changes from something a bit dreamy to more of a suggestive smirk, her eyelids becoming a touch heavier. She thinks on their more erotic adventures, also pondering her own exploration into it. She likes being his submissive, his pet, especially because he does not expect her to lose her own identity and strength in doing so.

She had asked him if he wanted that all the time, wanted her to be so completely subservient to his will, and she had been worried when she asked, hoping he wouldn't take it negatively. He had not, understanding her point. He explained that some people do indeed engage in such a relationship to that depth and constancy, but even then, it is not meant to compromise one's Will. The submissive has just as much power, if not sometimes more so, than the dominant, he had explained, again mentioning the safe words and signals.

You have the power to stop it, anytime. You are just as much in control as I am, he had said to her.

She smiles further, remembering the conversation, and as she reminisces more on their actions, a light coloration begins to spread upwards from her neck and about her face, increasing in its redness. She has not felt like this in so long, and it makes her feel very wanted, very sexy, to know that he desires her so.

DANCE OF THE BUTTERFLY

She glances at her phone, noting the time, figuring he is likely still awake, wondering what he might be doing. She could easily message or call him, and that would make this boring chore much more endurable, but then she might -, and then she freezes, locking her widening eyes to the screen, having reached over to slow the video to its normal pace. Her other hand still holds her phone poised, but it is completed forgotten.

Dali looks at her expectantly, for the petting has stopped, and as she leans closer to the monitor, he seems to understand what is happening, and he easily jumps to the floor, wandering off to his own pursuits.

She observes, noting that what she is watching happened earlier this very evening after she had left for the day. It appears the new Philosophy Professor, Denman Malkuth, stopped by to visit the collection, and Amanda Honeycutt accompanied him. There is no sound, but the two are obviously exchanging words. She sees that self-confident smirk on the man's lips, and it brings the beginning of a scowl to her own. Why had she not thought of him going through her assistant? Amanda is much less experienced and equipped to handle someone like this.

He is impeccably dressed, as usual, his hands in the pockets of his trousers, watching as Amanda disengages the locks on that particular book.

"Oh, Amanda," she empathizes, looking a bit saddened, for she feels badly that the man is indeed taking advantage of the junior lady.

She watches as the book is retrieved from its place and Amanda presents it to him. Lilja leans close to the monitor now, her attention rapt on the display. Denman gives a cursory examination to the item, holding it in one hand, so he may open it with the other, flipping through a few pages, looking them over. Once done with this brief interaction, he closes it, handing it back to Amanda with a pronounced grin, one more predatory than gracious. Amanda is all smiles, looking much brighter than her usual demeanor as she returns the book to its place.

Lilja feels a very real sense of relief when that locking mechanism is again engaged. She had been filled with anxiety that Denman would walk out with the tome.

Any relief she may have felt is quashed just as suddenly as Denman places a hand on Amanda's arm, turning the woman to face him, stepping in close to her. Amanda looks up at that charming face, eagerly accepting as he lowers his head, and they embrace in a passionate kiss. Lilja's eyes seem glued to the window, though she finally blinks once the two have finished their amorous exchange and walked out of view.

She has to get the book. It is no longer safe.

*****

She was correct in her assumption that he is not yet asleep, and he evinces happiness in his surprise to receive her as an unexpected visitor, but that beaming exuberance almost instantly dissolves as he looks her over.

"Lily?"

"May I come in, please?" she asks.

"Yes, yes, of course." He moves back, holding the door open wide, and she enters his hotel suite.

"Lilja," he says, trying to remain calm, for she is obviously agitated, "What's wrong?"

"Did you lock the door?"

"I ... yes," he says, then narrows his eyes, obviously confused, burning with curiosity, but he contains himself, walking closer to her, and he places his hands gently at her arms, putting on a comforting smile. "Lily, what's got you so upset?"

She then reaches into the satchel she carries, and he moves his hands away, giving her room. She pulls out a bundle, wrapped in cloth, and upon exposing it, he sees that it is the Book.

"Here," she says, moving it toward him, "It's not safe at the library anymore."

"Lilja?" he tries again, that continued war of consolation and confusion in him. "Why not? What has happened?"

"Denman Malkuth," she says, speaking the name slowly, the usual sparkling blue of her eyes looking darker now in the dimly lit room, as though they had become portents.

"He's trying to get the book," he states, speaking in a low, smooth tone, his expression now changed to a stalwart stone.

DANCE OF THE BUTTERFLY

"So, you *do* know who he is," she says, and he is not sure if her statement comes with relief or suspicion, though quite likely a mixture of both.

"Yes, I do," he admits.

She nods, a bit weakly, and he gently reaches up to take the book. Once she has been relieved of the burden, she exhales audibly, then walks over, slowly, and takes a place on the room's love seat. He watches her closely, then takes his own steps to the nearby table, setting the tome atop it, still looking at her. Her eyes are away, her thoughts inward, then she finally, after a time, looks back at him.

"How do you know him?" she asks.

"He belongs to a powerful, prestigious family that is something of a competitor, a *rival*, even, to my own."

She nods slowly, taking this in, looking away, going into her thoughts. He again waits, letting her ponder, and then she gives her eyes back to him.

"He is your enemy?"

"Something like that, yes."

"He came to the library not long after you did," she relates, "He tried to get me to give him information about the book and access to it. I was not cooperative."

A subtle pinch of confusion takes him, his head tilting slightly to the left as he asks, "Why?"

"There is something about him that is … disingenuous, untrustworthy, manipulative," she says, turning back to focus on him as she finishes, seeing him nodding slowly.

"He is, at that, though few seem astute enough to ferret it out so quickly, if at all."

"Did you know he was here?"

"I did," he admits, and he suspects he knows where this line of questioning is headed.

"Why didn't you tell me? Why didn't you warn me about him?" she asks, as he expects.

"Lil-ja," he begins, changing his inclination at the last moment from using her pet name, for he does not want her to feel he is trying to disarm with charm or familiarity, and he walks over, sitting down next to her;

thankfully, she does not move away, turning to face him, open, accepting, willing and wanting to hear what he has to say, "I knew he was here, yes, but what if I had come to you and mentioned him, asking you to keep the book from him? You might be suspicious of me for asking that. You would have wanted to know why. And why, then, would you have any more reason to trust him than you did me? He is a member of faculty. I am not."

"A new member," she points out.

"Well, yes," he agrees, "A station procured merely to get at that book."

"I know you much better now," she says, and he feels a rush of relief as she places a hand on his leg, just behind the knee, smiling. "I trust you."

"And I trust you," he says, also smiling in a similar manner. "And as I grew to better know and trust you, I suppose I began to assume you'd let me know, even if only in passing, if someone was trying to get the book out of the collection.

"I also, perhaps somewhat naïvely, began to hope that he did not realize the book was in the collection, that he might be on the wrong trail. What has recently happened?" He tries again, "Why is the book no longer safe in the library?"

"You know Amanda Honeycutt," she begins, and he nods, remembering the assistant, "He's gone through her, using her, seducing her."

"Oh, no," he breathes, eyes going wider, "Is she alright?"

"I-," Lilja begins, confusion taking her with a furrowed forehead, "I guess so. Why ... why do you ask that?" and then her confusion wipes away to widening eyes as she sits up straighter, "Is she in danger from him?"

"Denman Malkuth is a dangerous man. I don't think he'd harm her, but he is capable of it. As long as he thinks he is getting the cooperation he wants..." his voice trails off as he ponders, her eyes on him. "I don't think he'd measure the reward worth the risk of harming her, unless she stood in his way of getting the book once he'd decided to take it."

"I am."

DANCE OF THE BUTTERFLY

His eyes slowly move to hers, and he sees a fortitude there that does not surprise him in the least. He extends his arms, wrapping them about her, and she accepts this, slipping hers up to about him, leaning in to his embrace.

"I am sorry, Lily, I should have told you. It was a needless caution."

"I could have told you, too," she says, though he knows she'd have much less reason to do so than would he, "Besides, I am more than capable of assessing threats."

"So it seems," he gives her, obviously impressed.

"I feel stupid, though, that I didn't see his angle of using Amanda, but now that we know." She looks back at him, showing strength as well as a degree of imploring in her eyes.

"You aren't stupid, Lily," he says, hugging her close again.

She accepts this, very subtly, more desirous of proceeding in the relevant direction, "We can better protect the book now."

He nods, looking over at it, deeply touched that she has done as she has, though it still invites questions and concern.

"Won't the school wonder where its valued tome has gone off to?"

"Oh, well, as Head Curator, I am given some privileges, so I just put in the paperwork that the book needs to go out for special cleaning," she says, rather matter-of-factly.

"No one will follow up with the cleaner?" he asks, looking at her, and she moves her eyes to his, "I can't imagine there are too many artisans who handle this sort of thing."

"I doubt they will," she says, "I left the name out, 'accidentally', so someone would have to ask around or come to me, anyway."

He nods, then, "How long do we have?"

"Two weeks."

And he continues nodding, then he muses, "Two weeks to deal with Denman Malkuth."

"What are you doing to do?" she asks, and as he looks back at her, he doesn't just see concern there but also an indication of intention – she wants to know not just out of any worry of his safety but also to evaluate, to help.

"Well, the enmity between our two families goes back many generations, and it is not entirely unheard of for us to sit down at a negotiation table and come to some conclusion that both parties are able to at least swallow ... for the time being."

"You're going to *negotiate* with him?" she presses, a tad incredulous at the suggestion.

He gives her a grin, something that wants to trend toward a smirk. She wastes no subtlety, curling her lips into just such an expression, her eyes narrowing.

"I *could*," he says, trying to explain an obvious position not so easy to defend, "Besides, I don't think he knows I'm here. If I were to formally announce myself to him, then he'd know, and I think that would make him less likely to try to outright steal the book.

"And you are Ms. Honeycutt's superior. I daresay you could have a little talk with her about this. Things like this sometimes even lead to someone losing their job."

"I don't want to *fire* her over this," Lilja retorts.

"Of course not, but if she is made to worry that her behavior could lead to demotion, disciplinary action, possible loss of her employment, then that would likely give her good reason to cease her cooperation."

She nods, her lips moving a bit as she thinks, pressing together and out lightly, causing a gentle purse. He sees this, and despite all that is going on, it makes him want to kiss her.

"There are other options as well," he says, and she looks over.

"Oh?"

"We could both confront him," he says, "Once you have your talk with Ms. Honeycutt, he'll re-focus on you as the main barrier to his access, anyway. If he perceives us as a united front, and if ...," he begins carefully, "*perhaps*, my family ... were to provide a public endowment, indirectly declaring ourselves to the Malkuths as something of ... watchers over the book as it remains in your collection-"

"It's not my collection," she reminds him, smiling warmly. "You're sweet," she adds, and he blinks, "You're trying to spare my feelings. Thank you. I have great pride in my work, but those are not *my* books. And that may be a good idea. The Felcrafts are known collectors, so it would make sense. If your family did give a donation, maybe some books and money, then that somewhat publically declares your intention over it. Is that what you mean?"

DANCE OF THE BUTTERFLY

"Yes," he nods.

"So," she says after a moment of silence, looking back over and their eyes meet, "I've avoided the biggest question, you know?" and he nods. "I won't press now, but eventually, I'd like to know what it is about this book that has two such powerful families trying to get at it. This is not just a case of acquiring a rare book for its own sake."

"It most definitely is not."

"Alight, then." She stands, turning to face him, and he remains seated, looking at her, not having to raise his eyes all that much to meet her own, "You don't mind hanging on to the book until we get this sorted?"

He shakes his head, lightly smiling at her.

"Okay. Thank you."

"Thank *you*."

And she smiles further.

"I'm sorry to have come unannounced like this and bother your evening," she says.

"Lily," he smiles warmly, taking her hands in his own, "You are always welcome to visit me."

"Thank you," she says, and now that blush does rise up, though still a subtle coloration, especially in the low-lit chamber, "But it's late, so I had better get home."

He squeezes her hands, "Stay with me tonight," he asks, still just holding her eyes with his.

He sees as she thinks on this, notices even as she wrestles with her initial reaction of declining, but then she smiles more, her beautiful eyes blinking wider, and she nods, murmuring, "Okay."

CHAPTER THIRTEEN

She zips through the streets with the practiced assurance of a veteran. She's lived here all her life, and though she may spend more of her time indoors in front of a computer, she does get out from time to time. Just like now, engaging in her other form of occasional income – working as a courier. She navigates back streets and lesser-used throughways with ease, even sneaking through traffic as she is able on her black Mac Pea Shooter, the "thumper" engine giving her good acceleration and agility without being too much for her to handle.

It does not take her long to get to Cody's, a small place tucked away within others, ostensibly a tiny storehouse, but really proving to be little more than a hangout for some guys and a place for the passing through of information and the occasional holding of "something". There are boxes and some disused items about, empty air tanks, small file cabinets and the sort, but nothing of any importance stays long here.

The conversation between the five guys inside stops as she walks in, holding the black motorcycle helmet in her right hand, her worn pack strapped tight across her torso. She gazes at them, returning their looks with a steady one of her own. A couple stare at her cautiously, but most have that leering male look a lot of guys use on her. It doesn't matter much, anyway, as Cody jumps up to greet her.

"Therese! Great, great," he says, holding a can of large size and brilliant coloring in one hand, an energy drink of some sort, "Glad you made it back so quick. What a day, huh? Busy, busy day. Got another delivery lined up for you. Man, this one is *hot*. They really paid premium."

DANCE OF THE BUTTERFLY

He moves behind the makeshift countertop that sort of serves as the barrier between his more private area of business and the rest of the space, setting the drinking can atop it with a high-pitched clink.

"They asked for you specifically," he comments as he rifles through some papers.

"They did?" she asks, mingling subtle surprise, even perhaps suspicion, within her normal tone of nonchalance.

She wonders why he still deals in paper at all, but he likes to print-out the jobs and hand over slips to them. They have the tech to make it easy and digital, but he sticks to the thin, vellum hard copies.

"Yep," he says, shoving the paper toward her, his eyes too wide underneath the extremely short hair of his head, "Guess you've made positive impressions on some people. Heh," he short of chuckles out, the sound almost more like a hiccup.

One of the other guys laughs, and she cuts her eyes over, not moving anything else, just letting the narrowed orbs within the heavy black eyeliner stare him down until he shuts up. She takes the paper from Cody, then goes over and grabs the package, something rather small, having barely any weight as she tucks it into her satchel, zipping up and heading out without another word.

The money she makes from this side work, as she thinks of it, really isn't that great, but it's still not a bad form of extra income. She mainly does it for two reasons – it gets her out of her hovel of an apartment, letting her have some fresh air and good time on her bike, and the freedom. She'd found out about Cody through some other contacts of hers in the "shadow world" of her online life as Sparrow, though he doesn't know that. He calls himself Cody Violin, an obvious fake name, but that suits her just fine. His business is also not always entirely legitimate, but that also helps, keeping her from having to go through the regular bonding and licensing to be a more official courier. So, she gets to keep her privacy, working freelance for him, and only when she really feels like it. He had sent her a request to come in today, a rather more insistent message than his usual, and as it turns out, it has been a very busy day, indeed. This will be her third delivery, and because this one has asked for her specifically, she'll make extra.

She guns the engine of her café racer, zipping by some cars and barely missing a scrape at an intersection, gaining some flashing headlights of angry drivers in her direction, along with a short, high-toned beep from one car's horn. As long as it's not police, she doesn't care.

When she gets to the small, rather recently built warehouse, the gate is open, no guard or any other sort of barrier in place. She figures the metal fence must be to just keep people out at night when the business is closed. She's done a lot of research on warehouses lately, in her other pursuits, but this one has never been on those lists. She casually wonders what they handle here, but there is really no way to tell. There is also a sign that indicates deliveries should go to the rear, but she figures they mean larger trucks and the sort, so she heads on in the front door.

The receptionist, if that is what the person is, turns out to be a guy, and he seems much more interested in what sounds like a football match playing on the computer screen. He might be security, but he is not wearing anything that would indicate such. He barely gives her any notice as she informs that she is there to make a delivery, so she waits, then waves the paper at him.

"Do you want to sign, or is there someone else?"

"Oh," he says, still looking at the monitor, "Yes, I will-" He pauses, hands brought up, held tense, ready to turn into fists, and he cries out, "Yes!" giving a short laugh and pump of one fist, before turning back to her, "Delivery?"

"Yeah," she says, perking her eyebrows up and looking at the small parcel.

The guy is somewhat young, probably not yet hit thirty, dark hair, thin, and she sees him taking her in. She has a moment to wonder if he is going to hit on her, already dreading it, but he just looks once at the tiny package then grabs a pen and signs the vellum.

"Who's even using paper anymore?" he comments.

"We are," she says, though making it more a critique of Cody's business than being sarcastic.

"There you go," he says, and she takes her copy, noticing that the guy is already absorbed back into the game, so she heads out.

DANCE OF THE BUTTERFLY

There is a somewhat tall, portly man standing out beside her motorcycle, looking it over, and she wonders what this is about as she gets her key in her hand, positioning it between two fingers to be used as a weapon if need be. He turns as she walks over.

"This your bike?" he asks.

She nods.

"It's nice, though that motor looks pretty small, but," he gives a little grin with his leech-like lips, "you're small. I guess that makes sense."

"Yeah," she mutters, and she wants nothing more than to get on the vehicle and get out of here, but he is in the way.

"You came here to make the delivery?" he asks, just staring at her, and as she looks up at him, she notices that the clouds are growing grayer and heavier, threatening rain.

"Yeah," she gives another flat retort.

"It was very important," he comments.

She just looks at him, not sure what to make of this. She knows it was important. They paid a premium for expediency and to have her as the courier.

"Yeah, I've got others to make today, too, so-," she begins, and she hears the sound of feet behind her, so she moves to the right, keeping the big guy in view.

"Hello, Therese," comes a voice, speaking with a Latin accent, and she turns to see Inspector Duilio from Interpol, a cigarette jutting from his mouth.

It takes her a moment to remember him. She doesn't like her name being used. That already sets her on edge, but still, it had been dark, and their seeing of each other had been very short, brief, before the vigilante had sent him into unconsciousness. Her darkly-lined eyes widen.

"Shit," she manages, just as she feels the steel embrace of the other man coming in from behind, wrapping her in a bear hug and picking her up off her feet.

Shit, shit, shit, she repeats to herself, mentally, going through the paltry parts of self-defense she remembers, but she doesn't know of a way to get out of this. She struggles, but she is no match for the size and strength of Detective Alec Sladky. She tries to use her heavy boots to kick at him, but it proves ineffectual.

"Calm down," Duilio says, taking a drag on his cigarette.

She doesn't seem inclined to take this advice, still fighting. Alec squeezes, and she grunts out in pain.

"Come now," the inspector tries, "We don't want to hurt you."

"How did you find me?" she demands.

He grins, noting the almost professional pride that has cracked in her having been duped in this manner, and even now, she wants to know those leaks, so she can stop them. He imagines she is somewhat like himself in this way.

"You know the police are helping us," he says, giving a brief moment to his smile, almost sincerely apologetic. "We found a very good picture of you from a subway camera. It did not take much more work, then, to find your file. You used to be a ward of the state, and even though Mr. Violin's work is not entirely legitimate, it is official enough that we learned of your … *employment* there."

He then gives a subtle shrug after this, as though asking for pardon of his own involvement, then he brings his cigarette back to his mouth, inhaling, the tip flaring with brightness.

"Stop turning me into the fucking damsel in distress," she grates out.

He leans in closer, though staying out of range of her feet, turning his head to expel a stream of smoke away from her face, then speaking to her, "Why, Miss Stendahl, that is *exactly* what you are – the *bait*. We did not know it the first time, but this time, well … we do."

He then gives her a look before finally nodding to Alec who moves his right hand up to cover her mouth, and he carries the slight woman with ease, following Duilio as they leave the area, her muffled cries and continued resistance not helping her in the least.

*****

"Two missing detectives …," the man says, as though the words in his mouth are the most foul food he is being force-fed. "How do you have two .. missing … *detectives*!?" his frustration bubbles forth at the end as he changes nigh instantly from a calm repose of contemplation to one of tense anger, his emotion funneled out at the man behind the desk.

DANCE OF THE BUTTERFLY

"Councilman Keller," the director begins, maintaining a smooth, calm tone, "I can assure you we are just as upset, if not more so, by the disappearance of Detectives Mahler and Pasztor, and we are concentrating quite intently on finding them and discerning what happened."

"I certainly hope so," the councillor says, eyes still drilling into the bespectacled man, and then after a moment, he backs away, returning his posture to less one of focused intimidation and more of neutrality. "I need information. The pack of wolves is out there waiting for me. You know that, and it'd be you being fed to them if I had not stuck my neck out and made this cause my own," and he turns those intense eyes back onto the director, "I will *not* go down because of this."

After a moment of very tense silence between the two, the man continues.

"They went to question this Ernst van Zyl?"

"Yes, sir."

"Alone. No back-up?"

"Yes, sir. At the time, Ernst van Zyl was just a person of interest. They did not even have a search warrant, much less an-" and he stops as the other has raised a hand.

"And now...?" he leads.

"Well, yes, sir. We've questioned the clerk at the hostel, and the detectives were seen going up to van Zyl's room. And now van Zyl has also disappeared. The room had been quite thoroughly cleaned, but our forensics team found traces of blood."

Keller slowly shakes his head, "Nothing from their mobile phones?"

"No, sir. We've found no signals."

The councillor nods slowly, contemplating, then, "I trust everyone is on alert. The suspect's photo has been shared across the entire department?"

"Yes, sir, we've even sent out the information to other agencies, even Interpol."

"Ah, right," he nods, "Interpol … I ought to speak to them directly," he says as an aside to himself, then re-focusing on the other man. "I want this arrest to be ours, Director. You put a net over this city and you find this Ernst van Zyl.

"At least the dead girls have stopped," he concedes, and the other man gives the barest hint of a nod. "I can throw that bone to them," and he shakes his head, "Just when it seemed this whole things was getting under control, this happens. *Dammit.*"

The director cannot help but feel that this is more an inconvenience to the councilman as opposed to any real sympathy he may feel toward the missing, quite probably dead, detectives. They *are* out there, scouring the city. They do not take kindly to the murdering of their own. But he sits here, trying to keep his calm, playing the political game that is oft required of him due to this position. But then he sees something in the councillor's body language that makes him think that maybe the man is taking it more to heart than he had allowed.

"This is a very big deal, Director," Keller says, "This is the sort of thing that rocks families, the department, the city. We have to be able to count on our forces here. You protect us. You are supposed to be inviolate. Do you understand me?"

"Yes, sir. Of course, I do."

"Good." He just looks at the other man, "We carry a heavy weight, Director, a sometimes terrible weight, but we will not falter under it."

And so said, he heads out of the office, walking with a determined speed of foot to his next engagement, hearing the milling, hungry crowd as he nears the area that has been designated for the press conference. Some of his own people have gathered in his wake as he quickly moves to the gathering, and the director is not even that far behind.

There is a quieting to the din as he arrives on the scene, walking unerringly to the platform, his Public Relations Officer ceasing her own talking and silently moving away so he may take the podium. He looks out over the crowd as lights flash and beam at him, indicating still and motion photography focusing on his person, actions, and words. He is used to it.

He begins explaining the situation, starting with pointing out the success in the reduction of young ladies being found dead in the city, the efforts of the police to thwart the influx of such victims through human trafficking as well as successes in the finding of places that use the women, arrests being made, those businesses shut down. He then moves on, none of his reluctance evident, to the serial killer and the

DANCE OF THE BUTTERFLY

disappearance of the two officers who went to interrogate the suspect. The crowd is chomping at the bit when he finally opens up to questions.

Even the initial positive point does not hold up long as someone asks that couldn't it just be that the disposal of the bodies of young ladies has become more effective. The question irks the councillor, as such theoretical often does, and he spends little time on pointing to the futility of such a line. More probing questions arise, and though the man is very good at his job, holding his fortitude and poise, it is obvious there is something terrible going on in the city.

Skothiam watches the live press conference with rapt attention, having spent a good portion of the day today in his rooms, getting some work done. He finds, though, that he misses going to the library and spending the day with Lilja. She had gone into work, of course, not wanting anything to look out of the ordinary, so they have spent the time apart. It has distracted him somewhat, as his thoughts often turn to her.

He has not bothered to yet call his mother, worrying she might advise him to just leave now that he has the book, just take it. He will not do that. Formal, legal acquisition of the book is still a complicated situation. Lilja does not even have a say in something like that. But the things his mother pointed out to him are weighing on his mind. There is something going on in the city, something more than just these two rival families trying to get the book. He now greatly worries over what that may fully entail.

He watches the councillor closely. This is the man his mother wants them to help, even though he likely would never know how much they would aid him. This is the man his mother wants indebted to them, so they might use him as leverage to get the book. Skot sees a power there, and he can easily tell why Keller has done well in his career. The man has promise, ambition. It might be a good idea to get him as something of an ally, but he'd rather have a sincere compatriot, not someone manipulated into their grace.

And now it seems probable that the serial killer has added two law enforcement officers to the tally. Skot sighs, shaking his head slightly. He knows the negative forces are merely growing in this city, coiling about, putting a shadow, a fog, over the area. This will not have a good outcome if it is not somehow thwarted, dissipated properly.

He still has not heard back from Nicole, which bothers him more now than usual. She often is very difficult to catch, and it is not out of the ordinary for her to take some time to get back to him, but now, with this brewing, boiling even, he feels more desperate to speak to her. He also gives thought to his mother's suggestion that he get more help here. He could phone David and get him en route quickly. His cousin always seems ready to drop everything and help when the family is in need, his wife very supportive, even helping out when she is able to contribute.

He mulls this, looking back over at the screen, listening as the members of the media hammer into the councillor. He handles it well, not cowed but very accepting, as though the civil services deserve some of this reaction and interrogation by the very public they purport to serve.

The conference finally ends, and he shuts off the television, getting back to work, opening the tome to a place he had noted with a leather bookmark, though with much less eagerness than usual. His thoughts, of course, go to her. He glances at his phone to check the time. He suspects she should have ended her work day by now, but he has received no message from her. It could, of course, mean nothing, but with recent developments, worry claims him. He picks up his phone, about to send her a message, when it buzzes forth, the dark screen rousing with a message from her.

He reads it with no sense of small relief, as she explains that her day went well, no questions, no untoward visits from any curious parties. She says nothing of any talks or interactions she may have had with her assistant. He presumes that Miss Honeycutt noticed the missing book today and informed Denman. Perhaps it will prove a benefit, as Denman may think it an opportunity to acquire the book, busying himself with discerning to which cleaner it has been shipped.

She also mentions feeling tired, stressed out by the recent events, and that she plans to just go home and relax. She'll be available via her phone or computer, of course, but she just wants some rest. He will not begrudge her that. This must be a much bigger deal than she is ever used to having to handle. He'll do his best to not fret, and leave her be.

Some hours pass, and he has managed to lose himself in his work, the remnants of a meal nearby. He has not plumbed anymore direct clues

DANCE OF THE BUTTERFLY

to the nature of the contents, but he has gotten deep into some allegorical history, mythology, and he finds it fascinating. It also seems to perhaps verify some of his family's own conclusions, but he wonders how much he may be manipulating his own interpretations. These are symbols, forms, and he must be wary how he lets them filter through his own perceptions.

It is then that the beeping interrupts him, and he looks over to his computer, noting that one of the 'checks' he put in place after his phone conversation with his mother has had its alarm triggered. Before he can fully bring up the information, another alarm goes off, then another, and soon, the monitor of his laptop is blinking in several places.

Anxiety claims his features, though he does retain some calm, his fingers flying rapidly over the keyboard, then one hand going to the mouse. He executes another program, some quick analysis from the sudden influx of data, and a particular spot of the city reveals itself, the coloration provided by the filter indicating a vibrant red.

"Shit," he says.

He takes some short minutes to change clothes, fire off some messages, and put on his shoulder harness, making ready his loaded Walther P99, the two spare magazines also filled and held on the opposing side of the holster. He then shrugs a jacket over this, not wanting to be detoured by unwanted attention before he even reaches his destination, and grabbing his cane, he heads out in an obvious hurry.

*****

Everything has been properly prepared, laid out atop the short table, the surface covered in a dark cloth. The air holds a charge of incense as the person here kneels, knees somewhat tucked under the piece of furniture, an aspect one of respect, meditation. Amidst the smaller items, a sheathed katana rests across the entirety of the tabletop's length, as though the dimension has been customized especially for it.

The tsuba is designed to appear as two butterflies, their wings going up, the tips of each pair delicately touching so as to form an encirclement. The artwork is fine, eloquent, the ridged bodies of the insects stretching back, various lines and curves going out to give more detail to the spread and flow of the large wings. The fuchi shows more intricate work as curves and coils and stretches of delicately detailed metal surround the handle like overlapping currents of stylized air or the flow of water. A similar pattern is shown at the kashira, though this looks more indicative of a firmness like the precisely tilled soil of a rounded hill. The tsuka-ito is black, matching the general overall dark coloring of the sword and its sheath.

Then holding the weapon with care and reverence, the blade is pulled forth smoothly from its saya, the scabbard set aside, vertically, over the shorter width of the covered surface. The right hand is kept about the hilt as the left picks up one of the small white cloths arranged nearby. Taking care of the sharp edge, the material is wiped over the moderately curved length, paying close attention even at the blunt no-hi edge. Once completed, the uchiko ball is picked up, and slowly tapped along the length of the blade, depositing its powder in small puffs. This is done carefully, slowly, also along the top, and the other side, the right hand sure and deft in its grip and handling. Another cloth is used to clean the powder away, its purpose having been to pick up and allow the removal of any residual oil. Now cleaned, exposed, bare, the sword will be anointed anew, and a final cloth is picked up, already doused with a small amount of choji oil, and it is drawn along the sword, leaving a thin coating.

Thus cleaned and prepared, the sword is re-sheathed and placed back in its holder, stored horizontally, edge up. It will not remain so long, for it shall be taken on this evening's mission. Though it is regularly maintained and sometimes used in practice and training, it is rarely taken along on operations. Tonight, though, shall likely prove one of the most dangerous outings ever, and so it shall be brought, carried in its special place over the back, a pragmatic necessity for many reasons. The vigilante is well trained in its use, though a reason for that shall hopefully not arise.

The data has been gathered. Reconnaissance has been conducted. Informants have been consulted. It is obvious things have been changing, and it is not a slow change. It is, though, rather expected, in retrospect. The crime ring has turtled. They have gathered themselves into a more centralized location and concentrated their raised defenses.

DANCE OF THE BUTTERFLY

Not only had some more abandoned locations been found during other outings, but the recent increase of product influx had tapered. Since they had not proven capable of stopping the vigilante, they had changed the locale of their operations. This sort of adaptability and dynamism must surely not be a foreign concept to those in their line of business, and so the effort had been set to finding these new sites. The analysis suggests there is now one compound, one place that is handling most, if not all, of the operations, one-stop-shopping, as it were.

Some time has been spent verifying this, for even as it may seem convenient, it also means a concentration of strength. Once it had proven accurate, a method of approach had to be developed, if such an attack saw the light of day at all. It was one thing when the vigilante had been less known, the targets smaller, more numerous, more like guerilla hit-and-run tactics on less important targets. Now, this would be an assault on the main fortress. Some very serious consideration had been given to not taking this approach at all, to putting everything together and delivering the information to the police. The files have been so collected, and if this evening's foray does not prove adequately successful, the messages will be sent. And not just to the police. If worse comes to worst, other parties will be notified.

A reason for that shall hopefully not arise.

*****

"Maybe we ought to just kill the girl," speaks a voice, the tone one of calmly discussing the possible mowing of a lawn.

"No, no, that should not be done."

Gnegon looks up from swirling his glass, the clear contents not interrupted by any ice or other flavorings, the expensive vodka not so delicate as to change its subtleties of taste from this mere motion. He also wears a very fine tuxedo, looking all the world like he is ready to head to an evening of celebration and entertainment, which he is.

He fixes his narrow eyes on the inspector, the Interpol man also dressed very nicely, more so than his usual daily flair, also holding a preparatory drink in advance of this evening's festivities.

"Why not?" he asks, then after a short moment, "Do you like this girl, Gaspare?"

Duilio smirks, a subtle curl to one side of his lips, "Oh, no, she is exciting, to be sure, but she is not exactly … my taste. Perhaps if I were twenty years younger."

The two share a short laugh at this.

"No," Duilio repeats on the tail end of the shared chuckling, "The *vigilante* will come again."

"How do you know?" the crime boss presses, any trace of levity gone from his features.

"A hunch," Duilio finally answers, and then he brings his drink up to his mouth, pausing as he notes those steely eyes still on him, so he shrugs. "What harm will it do, Gnegon? Are you so scarce of space in this compound of yours that you need to do away with her so urgently?"

"It has been three days," Gnegon points out, "Last time, the vigilante came to rescue her within hours."

Duilio perks his eyebrows, tilting his head a bit right, another sort of shrug, then drinking from his glass of wine, swallowing with a nod, "I know, I know, but what harm does it do, hmm? You could keep her as a prisoner for a few weeks, even, then do with her as you will." He casually waves his free hand.

"It's a risk keeping her alive."

"A risk?" Duilio retorts, releasing a short series of low chuckles. "Oh, Gnegon, how so? She is a fellow pest, just like the vigilante, and now you have caught this one and put her in a cage. And what a glorious cage," he holds out his hands, "I must congratulate you. This location is quite wondrous."

This seems a genuine smile to the other man's lips, and he raises his glass in a subtle toast, which is returned by the inspector.

"Yes, I suppose there is no reason to be hasty," the man concedes, "Things are looking good for us. We are centralized, well-defended, and we are in the process of culling our unnecessary supply. Things are looking better than they have in quite some time."

"There. You see?" Duilio grins, "And you stand to make some good money tonight."

DANCE OF THE BUTTERFLY

"Hmm, yes," Gnegon mulls, "Some of our finest specimens are up for auction. I don't like keeping the beautiful ones around very long."

Duilio smirks more openly, letting forth another quiet chuckle, nodding slowly, "You are a wise man. They are more a danger to you than this other pest you have as bait. You will be rid of them and make a bundle in the process. Let these others fight over the pretty birds, hmm?"

"Yes, yes," Gnegon nods, another grin trying to take his generally dour face.

"They will fight with their checkbooks instead of guns, no? And you will reap the reward!"

And the two share another short bout of laughter, this one more boisterous than before.

"Good, good." Duilio nods, then he glances at his watch, "Shall we be getting on to the festivities, then?"

Gnegon ponders a moment, still deciding executions and the potential stays thereof, then he blinks, moving his eyes to the expectant ones of the agent.

"Alright," he agrees, downing the rest of his vodka and leaving the empty glass on a nearby end table.

*****

Ernst's shod feet move slowly over the cement walkway. He doesn't pay too much notice in his almost zombie-like shamble, but he ought to feel fortune he is wearing shoes this time. Most of the people hereabouts pay him little mind. He pays them even less. He knows they are there, knows they are people, but beyond this base recognition, they do not concern him at all.

He knows something bad happened at his room recently, and he has now found a new one. He doesn't remember exactly what happened, nor how he came by his new place, but that also does not concern him very much. What does compel him is the growing feeling in his mind, a feeling which spreads out and encompasses his entire body then leak free from him like a glowing effluvia, seeping out toward those beginning hints of haze that he sees.

His trek takes him along a meandering route, but he is finally interrupted in his reverie by another of the blinking flashes in his peripheral vision. He looks up, not too quickly but still moving with more rapidity than typical, and he sees nothing. He then feels an acute, growing pressure in his head, beginning in the upper left and spreading. He spies more glimmers, then, some like a dancing buzz of static, but with a few blinks and shakes of his head, all is gone. He stands there for a moment, his left hand brought slowly up, as though moving through some syrupy morass, to rub at the bridge of his nose. He then presses the fingertips into his forehead and temple there on that same side, trying to massage away the terrible compulsion that lures him.

He looks up then, eyes again blinking, his aspect more focused as he glances around, clearly trying to find something. He then stops, staring into a distance ahead and somewhat to his right. He sees something there, aglow, and it holds more luminance than would seem necessary for being a lit place at night here in the city.

His feet begin moving again, and he knows, without comprehending it in any normal way, that he is headed there. He gives little thought to what he may find, what he may do once there. He does not even think on why he is even out and about this night. He is moved, as though he were some marionette on ectoplasmic strings connected to his very nerves, tugging at him with an undeniable insistence.

The path he takes curves toward the right, going down a lengthy, gentle slope. There are still others out on foot, some vehicles passing by on the street. The traffic even increases, the businesses more numerous here, and then with just as much lack of notice, he is heading back up, having turned a sharp right, and is away from the density. He plods on, head down, hands stuffed in the front pockets of his zipped hoodie, his tall, almost skeletal form laboring with a slow, ceaseless determination to get where he is going.

He turns another corner and looks up, eyes squinting. The fog has grown here, but his destination beams with a bright aura, a corona of light that acts like a harbinger even as it draws him in. The place is large, but he cannot make out all the details what with the intensifying mist and the illumination. He must just go to it, then he will better see. He cannot

DANCE OF THE BUTTERFLY

avoid its hypnotizing enchantment. He even hears it, like a gentle buzz, a welcoming hum, such is its potency. *Why is it so well-lit*, he wonders.

He tucks his head back down, continuing his inexorable march.

*****

The place is large, comprised of more than one building on the expansive grounds, though the main structure quite obviously houses the vast majority of activities and operations, various sections and rooms, different floors, for their own specific functions. This front portion, though gated and guarded, is quite elegant, meant for the reception of guests, clients, and thus is it appointed as such.

The foyer is possessed of state-of-the-art detectors and scanners, though they are all hidden. It would not do to force such important visitors through a crass form of disrespect. The entryway and first room, vast as it is, shows to largely be composed of a rich brown wood that is so dark as to appear black in the soothing lighting, the colors of the antique-seeming décor mostly darker blues, blacks, shades of white and gray, though shocks of crimson are throughout, adding a deliberate punctuation and tone to the effect.

There are posh, leather seats here, even a lengthy couch, but few of such offerings are partaken. Most of the guests are dressed in elegant finery, some of the women even also brought along willingly to partake of the evening's offering, though others, especially those who show clad in nearly nothing, may not entirely be present of their full freedom. Even those, though, show some degree of cultivation in their visage, even if a deeper examination of the made-up eyes might reveal bleaker depths.

There is a grand staircase here, its wide progress leading in a generous curve to the second floor, dark wooden steps partially covered in a richly red material, the contrast evident enough, even as the edges almost bleed together. Hosts, servants, guests, even guards hold place in this 'receiving' room, engaged in various modes of drink, conversation, luxuriating to different levels of the basting preheat, but for those who wish to press further, the way is open.

The second level leads into an even larger, more impressive room, openings in it showing their way back to the first floor and up to the third, giving this chamber a very spacious feel. The vast exposure that leads down shows an encased topiary, winding walkways suggesting pathways through the enclosure, giving up smaller areas that reveal exotic and rare animals held to limited range within the transplanted garden.

The main space of this floor, exposed and open as it is, proves to be further grounds for entertainment, illegal gambling tables that would rival the finest of casinos, an open space in the back of fluctuating, colored lighting for dancing, and rising up a few, broad steps to a sub-section that gives up the main bar, the large, square station offering approach from three of its sides, the rear taller and possessed of various artwork in the same opulent vein as the rest of the more public areas – bold paintings as though from some bacchanalia, statues of thickly segmented zmey, the dragons' three heads coiling out in eager tumescence, some of their mouths open, ready at any moment to expel their burgeoning fire.

A smattering of patrons stands about the bar, drinks held, some single pours or mixtures contained in eloquently simple-seeming, yet fine, stout glasses, others of a more mixological flair displayed in somewhat ostentatious vessels. A few of the drinkers appear inclined to not set down their glass until the contents are completely consumed.

The third story shows a broad balcony going all the way about the interior of the spacious quarters, allowing those upon it to peer down at all the goings-on, if they are so inclined. There are also walkways and doors leading to other delights on this, the topmost level for general public entertainment, and yet just as one may not access the topiary from the first floor foyer, one may not gain access to all of the second and third floors through this entertainment avenue.

Another door, one more closely guarded and for only those select clients who have prior qualified, leads to a further area that opens to a darker, sumptuous chamber. There are more places to sit, and another bar from which to request beverages, as well as waitresses in addition to the bartender. This room, though, is not yet in full swing, for the night is yet young, and the large, black stage at the rear is presently lit by one downward lamp, inviting limited sight and perhaps even fantastical speculation. In time, the raised section will be better illuminated and

DANCE OF THE BUTTERFLY

used to display the various slaves available for more permanent procurement.

The guests are of an eclectic mix, not merely hailing from the predominate places that make up the majority of origins in this already cosmopolitan city. They do all share a few commonalities, though, wealth seeming to be foremost amongst those sparse similarities, mayhap a liberal view on some morality also being another. One person in particular has a rather interesting take on ethics, and though it might appear fluid to some, it is actually quite rigid in its own right.

"William C. Webb," says the rather attractive lady in the very form-fitting black dress, "Ah, here you are," as she finds the name on her list, offering the man an increase in pleasantry of her already quite warm smile.

"I had rather thought I was right here," the impeccably dressed man says, giving a charming little smirk and rise of his groomed eyebrows to the woman.

She gives him a reasonable chuckle, noting that the man is indeed handsome, but well-dressed, attractive people are certainly not in short supply at this soiree. She proffers a very elegant, yet small and unobtrusive pin which he allows her to attach to the front of his jacket just near the boutonniere. He knows it is a tracking device as much as something to identify him.

"Do enjoy your evening, Mr. Webb," she bids.

"Ah, it's Professor," he speaks in a very cultured Transatlantic accent, "of Anthropology, if you must know, from Princeton," and he offers her a very tempting smile.

"Of course, Professor," she says, lowering her chin a bit, giving a subtly coquettish view of her eyes beneath her luxurious lashes.

"I do expect to find some rather interesting observation for study," he adds, letting that smirking curl touch his lips as he moves inward, his hazel eyes casting about in a seeming casual study that belies much more focus than the charming rogue persona he affected for the receptionist.

As if this were not enough of a hint at his secret nature, the edged weapon he carries within his bespoke Anderson & Sheppard tuxedo jacket does not set off the sensors in place here at the foyer, and thus the falsely assumed Professor Webb enters the compound unimpeded.

Members of faculty from prestigious universities are not the only ones to enter the grounds this evening under false pretense; however their credentials may have been obtained, and the darkly-garbed figure pauses in the rear approach, still outside the main building but having gained entry beyond the surrounding wall. This person would surely set off the sensors, what with the weapons and other items bristling upon the form, notably the back-sheathed katana, but the front entrance will not be used. Two guards had been narrowly avoided, the intent to penetrate as deeply inside without giving any alert to presence. The normal methods of subduing would surely eventually lead to a noted absence at regular posts or duties, and this mission will take more time than most.

Two outlying buildings stand within the compound's barriers – a security station, and a larger, less protected one that acts as covering for vehicle storage and maintenance. The former had been avoided, but as the infiltrator had pressed in, the other had been visited, a small explosive device left attached to one of the slumbering trucks, near the fuel tank. This is the second such item to be placed, the first hanging silently against a rear portion of the property's heavy fence, waiting for its signal.

Slow, careful steps are taken, lights and cameras avoided, as the patient route is followed to gain a way inside the main building. A notice of sound, and the figure presses back against a nearby crate, the short, diminutive size working in their favor to hide them from the lone, armed sentry who wanders by. An earpiece is noted as well as some body armor, a holstered stunner, and the strapped Skorpion held at the ready. Defenses have assuredly been stepped-up.

Movement is not resumed until the steps of the guard are no longer heard, the figure coming out of the shadow of the large crate, peering in the direction both that the sentry has gone as well as from whence they came. It looks clear, and the soft reports of the jika-tabi can be heard as the figure moves quickly to cover some open ground, getting into the shadow of the tall main building. A glance is spared upwards, the roof four stories high, a difficult obstacle to approach from that angle. It is known, though, that there is a loading dock none too far away, and that is the main plan of ingress, making the way through the more day-to-day

DANCE OF THE BUTTERFLY

business-oriented locations that will likely prove less occupied at this time during the gathering.

The loading area may be less used, but it is not entirely empty of activity. The vigilante watches from a distance as the delivery truck is vacated of its contents. This is a smaller vehicle, though still decently enough sized, but no tractor-trailer. The boxes being unloaded are not very large, manually carried by the workers under the somewhat watchful protection of two armed guards. It is soon apparent the cargo is being moved off toward the left, further in. This may well prove a better way inside than using a locked door that could possess an alarm or other sort of sensor.

A slow, careful approach is made, continuing to make use of the shadows and darkness out here, coming in from a wide angle so as to avoid the broad scope of the truck's headlights. There is a wood railing going along the edge of the raised area, and as men are occupied with moving more of the boxes and crates out of the deeper recesses of the truck's compartment, the figure slowly ascends, moving over and dropping near soundlessly on the inside, creeping back and away into further darkness, which conveniently happens to be heading closer to the door.

A crouching position is gained, hands holding the strapped and suppressed G36C, one about the fore grip, the other near the trigger, eyes watching closely. It does not appear that these guards are wearing armor, and the workers are dressed in coveralls. Still, no confrontation at all is the desired outcome.

The men pass close to the shrouded person, completely unaware of the presence, their focus on completing their labor. Noises are heard from inside, eyes of the infiltrator on the two guards who exchange quiet words, hardly taking note of their surroundings. One flares up a cigarette just as the workers return. It seems the unloading is done, as more talk is traded, these louder, mentions of inventory, checks, and then two of the workers get into the cab of the truck, starting it up and driving it off. The others pull out cigarettes of their own or grab bottles of water; time for a break, and in the noise and distraction, the vigilante slips inside through the door.

This room is much better lit, but a quick scan reveals it to be a staging area. There is noise, though, of approaching footsteps from further within. The intruder scans about quickly, noting another door, but even if it is unlocked, it would be foolish to rush through it, so instead, a hiding place is found.

Three more people enter, none of them armed. One is a woman, and she is smartly dressed, and she looks around, eyes gliding over the stacked boxes in search of something else. She walks quickly, and opens the door leading outside, apparently wanting the other workers in here as she quite demandingly summons them. Once they are inside, she gives out quick, terse orders to the quartet, as it appears the recently unloaded goods are needed for the ensuing party.

The intruder watches as the workers are corralled to their duty by the insistent woman, her hands dancing through the air as though carrying an invisible whip to aid her. Movement is not resumed until the sounds of their feet have retreated to silence, and then slow, quiet steps are taken to the other door, the fiberscope used to check the opposing side, which turns out to be a somewhat lit hallway with several doors, the passageway leading off into various other directions. The tube is retrieved, the door checked, unlocked, and the figure presses in further.

Meanwhile, the soiree continues to slowly grow in numbers. Even if everyone on the guest list shows, it will not be that large a party, such is its exclusive nature, but the turnout will still be greater than the usual types of entertainments hosted here.

"What brings a Professor of Anthropology to something like this?" the woman asks, bringing up her martini glass after using her other hand to subtly indicate the area.

Her eyes stay on him as she drinks, her companion of the evening off talking within a small group of other men.

"Why, I am here to observe," the so-named Professor Webb replies, smiling quite charmingly at the attractive woman, a gesture she proves inclined to return.

"Really now?" she almost purrs, dark red lips pressing together. "Are you trying to tell me you are here in a 'professional' capacity?"

DANCE OF THE BUTTERFLY

"Ah, well, 'academic' might be a better way to put it," he fine-tunes, "An event such as this affords some very interesting opportunities for observation and study."

She somewhat smirks at him, though the distance between them is only lessened by a slight movement on her part, "If you publish a paper about this evening, then I suspect you'd be making many powerful enemies."

"Oh, I am not a journalist," he retorts, "Merely a humble scholar, very interested in humanity and its culture and behavior."

"Humble ...," she continues that eloquent smirk.

"Do permit me some theatrics, hmm?" He perks up his eyebrows, and she grins, then he carries on, his own held glass ignored, "I am not here to judge or expose. I am a student of morality and ethics, and I find this sort of thing quite fascinating."

"This sort of *thing*?" she pushes.

"Why, yes," he turns back to her from having been looking out over the gathering and its people, "Societies make rules in order to function as a society, but really, those laws are more meant for the masses. Those possessed of a certain Will, especially the ability to turn that to proper action, well, laws may not apply as much to them."

She presses those lovely lips of hers together into another smirk, and it slowly grows until she lets a short, low chuckle emerge.

"I hardly think the authorities would agree."

"Of course they would not. They are an institution put in place to protect those who cannot protect themselves. As human society has aged, fear, necessity, even pragmatism has somewhat given way to self-righteousness. Eventually, as maturation continues, such shackles shall be discarded."

"Hmmm," she muses, quite non-committal, but still, not ending the conversation or moving away; instead, she has another lingering sip of her cocktail.

He finally decides to have a taste of his own, sipping of the rich, amber liquid, eyes staying on hers throughout. He swallows, giving a very light lick of his lips.

"Something on this scale does not happen without some knowledge on the part of said *authorities*," he continues, "If the rules of society are not enforced, and that society does not breakdown, then there is no issue."

"So, we're above the law?"

"Outside it," he amends, giving a tiny smirk of his own, "Until we are not."

"Ahhh, well, that seems to make your position rather convenient," she gives a playful jibe.

"Not at all," he responds, "Societies are somewhat self-regulating, seeking a balance from their own motive force to counter entropy. Once you do enough potential damage, you will be discovered, stopped, and punished. It's all an elaborate game, really."

"Well, I will agree with you on that," she says, watching him closely as he takes another drink. "Those are lovely cufflinks," she says, noting the jewelry, "What stone is that?"

"Ah," he smiles, turning his hand to give better access, "It is merely lapis."

"Is it?" She takes hold of his cuff, "It doesn't seem like any I have ever seen."

"Well, even as I say 'merely', I suppose that is again my being theatrical. This is actually a very rare form, quite dark in coloration, polished and treated in a special way."

"It's beautiful," she comments, slowly moving his wrist as well as her own angle of observation, "It almost looks like it's glowing."

"Yes, well," he says, gently pulling his arm in, so he may look at the stone, "That is all part of the process."

"Oh, I must know it," she says.

"I am sorry, my dear, but ... family secret," he says, gaining a very subtle pout from her in response, and even as inviting as it is. "I have enjoyed this conversation, but I am afraid I am here with some duties, and I must tend to those now."

As the handsome professor heeds to this call, the vigilante continues to explore other areas of the expansive building. It is large, the hallways complicated, leading off hither and thither. A passing moment is spared in contemplation as to who might know all the avenues, or if they are perhaps made convoluted on purpose. What matters, though, will be finding the way out, and exits may be created. It doesn't take too long,

DANCE OF THE BUTTERFLY

though, to find someone who is not a guard, and the half-naked girl in this room stands with a look of utter despair on her heavily made-up features. Beneath the cosmetics and negligée, she cannot be more than fifteen years old.

The obvious natural beauty she holds shows through even beneath the dress and depression. She does not even look over as the person moves closer to her. The intruder walks in slowly, moving to in front of the girl, and those eyes finally focus, looking over the other, noting the weapons, the clothing. She does not respond in any other way except to move her eyes up to those of the masked figure. Those orbs are glassy, and fresh tears dribble out. Upon this closer examination, fifteen may even be too old an assumption.

"It's going to be alright," comes a whisper, making some meager attempt at comfort, for the young girl shows nothing but a disturbing despair in her appearance.

Indecision attacks. The intent tonight is to deliver a hopefully crippling blow to the crime ring, not to escape with one unfortunate young lady. The plan is suddenly brought into question, suffering doubt beneath the wave of negativity felt emanating from the poor girl. A forced blink and shake of the head breaks this spell, and a hand is dared to be set on the doll-like youth's shoulder. A moment passes, determined, sympathetic eyes looking into those that seem little more than glass, and the vigilante heads out to scout more of the immediate vicinity.

Other, small rooms dotted throughout here prove to be of similar purpose, each holding a single, made-up person, not all even female, making them ready to be auctioned off to the highest bidder. It is time.

A button is pressed, the trigger activated, and a distant sound is heard. Chaos does not ensue, of course, and it is quite probable that few, if any, at the soiree have awareness of the explosion. The compound's security, though, will be buzzing into action, convening on that breach in the rear boundary. A few short moments later, and the second charge goes off, this one causing a much louder report, which is not long followed by others. This has been the vehicle pool, and the initial detonation resulted in more, no doubt as the fire has spread beyond the first truck. This one must have caused some interruption to the gathering, and if not, the third device then exploding much closer, taking out a portion of the main building's wall, definitely garners more immediate reaction.

Doors open, voices raised in alarm, demanding questions, people told to stay where it is safe, armed guards rushing about. The figure remains in the shadows, watching, waiting, until the hallways are again clear, the chaotic-sounding cacophony rising in the distance. None of the people that have appeared in the wide passageway are those who were lately planned to be sold, thus belying the fear and conditioning on those very persons. The intruder has counted on this, and now rushes through the avenue, opening doors, calling out in that loud, forceful voice.

"Get out! Into the hallway! Everyone! Fire! We have a fire!"

It takes longer than one might expect from a general crowd, but eventually the would-be slaves emerge, some rushing with evidence of fright, other peeking out, afraid to break the rules even under these obviously alarming circumstances. Eventually, though, all but one make it.

"Get out! Get to the exits!" the voice commands, trying to keep them moving and not focusing on who is issuing the orders, hoping they even know where the exit is. "Down the hall! Go!"

And once the direction is issued, the vigilante runs to that one room, seeing that the young girl has not budged an inch from where she stands. Her body trembles, wracked with a greater outflow of tears. She must be crippled with fright, confusion. The figure moves in, extending a helping hand to the left shoulder.

Once the physical contact is made, the girl turns sharply, and she now shows an aspect of rage, her eyes seeming to glow red, teeth bared, arms brought up, fingers curled and tensed into dangerous claws. She lunges at her rescuer, those hands pressing in, doing no damage to the intended, but causing deep rips and bloody tears to the girl's own fingertips. Thus gripped, she brings her face quickly to the neck, trying to use her teeth to rip out the figure's throat.

A quick bringing in and out-thrust of arms shoves the small girl away. She stumbles back but does not fall, regaining her balance, and then emitting a startling snarl which turns into an all-out scream, the girl rushes back in with another wild attack.

DANCE OF THE BUTTERFLY

The vigilante holds up both arms, hands shown, palms outward, "Calm do-," is tried, but before the statement may be completed, the enraged girl is on the figure.

The girl's arms are grabbed, held, her head moving about, beast-like, teeth pushed out in promise to use her mouth.

"Calm down," the vigilante tries again, though it is evident the girl has no intention of doing so, seeming beyond reason or hearing, so the other moves about, putting her in an armlock, again speaking in a soothing, though insistent tone, "Calm down."

The girl continues to froth and writhe, uncaring of causing her own joints to dislocate, so the figure slackens the hold. The vigilante then carefully and firmly presses her to the ground, struggling to maintain control without harming the girl, then reaches for a zip-tie.

"What's going on?"

Looking up, another woman has entered the room, another obviously who was meant to be sold, though she is older, probably eighteen or nineteen. She sees the black-suited figure atop the rage-filled, struggling young girl.

"What are you doing to Darla?"

"She attacked me," the masked person grunts out, still holding Darla, and though the bind is now applied, the girl continues to snarl and try to bite like a rabid animal.

"What's wrong with her?" the other asks, stepping cautiously into the room.

The vigilante continues pressing enough weight onto the girl to keep her somewhat under control, just looking at the other as though it is evident enough that an answer is not forthcoming.

"She's not …," the other begins, kneeling down, holding out a hand.

"Careful," comes the barely voiced caution.

The other's eyes go to the masked figure then back down, and she rests on her knees, laying a gentle hand on the girl's head. Darla snaps at her, teeth clacking together audibly, and the other jerks her hand back, then resumes the petting at the girl's shoulder.

"She's not like this," she says, trying to soothe with her touch, "She's usually so quiet, withdrawn. Some of us worried that she'd kill herself if given the chance," she explains, then coos, "Shhhh, Darla, shhhh. It's Monique. Shhhhh."

And it appears to work as the young girl calms, the struggles ceasing to such an eerie extent as if they never happened in the first place. Instead, her body becomes wracked with sobs, and the vigilante gets off her.

"Darla, honey, what happened?" Monique asks, trying to embrace the girl as best she can under the awkward circumstances.

The darkly-suited figure looks about, listening, noting now that there are greater and more obvious sounds of alarm, chaos. They need to get out of here. The knife is slipped quickly out of its sheath, and though Monique gives a worried glance, the blade is used to cut through the zip-tie. Darla seems unaffected, bringing her arms around, using her hands to get up, though she stays mostly seated on the floor.

"You have to get out of here," emits the voice from behind the balaklava.

"We-," Darla begins, but her stress stops her, her breath heaving, sobs still emerging, her make-up all but ruined now, giving her face a creepy aspect, "We can't leave them down there. You have to save them."

The figure looks from Darla to Monique, obviously curious, and she sees a comprehension spread over the older girl along with growing fright.

"What?" grates out the vigilante.

"She means the basement. The underground level."

Tense, narrowed eyes piercing out from within the dark face-paint make an obvious bid for more information.

"I don't want to go down there," Monique says, her fright evident, and the two girls clutch each other, Darla still crying.

"You two *get out*."

Monique nods, "Come on, baby," she says to Darla, and they help the young girl to her feet.

The vigilante heads over first, checking the hallway. It is empty, but those sounds of fear, chaos, emergency still emerge quite noticeably from nearby parts of the compound. A hand is waved at them, a finger pointed in the direction of an exit, an obvious command. They move

DANCE OF THE BUTTERFLY

past, Monique still holding onto the younger girl, leading her, but she pauses, glancing at their liberator.

"You have to go down there and save them," she pleads, "No one deserves to be left in that terrible place."

*****

The compound is being evacuated, though it will take some time. Security is also trying to keep apprised of who all is leaving, especially that there are many in here being held against their will. They also know they are under attack. They have not confirmed it is the "pest", but most everyone assumes it is.

The opening at the back barrier has been contained, but the fire that has spread from the vehicle shed is proving more an issue. The fire department will arrive soon, and the situation must be sufficiently contained before they and other public servants show up on the scene.

Guests are pouring out of the front, some finding their own cars, not wanting to wait for the interrupted valet service, and getting away from there as quickly as they are able. A call goes over the security channel to lock the gates. A retort is given, asking won't this cause more trouble, and after a pause, the order is given again, more emphatically.

The closure comes much too late to have impeded the meandering entrance of someone who is decidedly not on the guest list, someone who looks to have little concern for the fire and explosions and chaos. Those are just noise and lights to add to other noise and lights, all of it somewhat blurring together into the bright, undeniable compulsion that has drawn him here.

The sickly-seeming young man wanders in, the confusion creating the perfect camouflage to keep him from being halted by any guards. He pauses amidst the people and movement, shouts and other noises, raising his head further, his eyelids still heavy despite his direction of focus, almost as though he absorbs his surroundings. And there, he senses it, coming from below, a great concentration. He moves on.

Getting to the lowest level may be done via a secure freight elevator, which happens to be on lockdown now with the current situation. One may also access it via other ways – two being more straight forward, one of those a staircase, though it is not generally used by guests, the others more hidden. Once in the basement, one may encounter guards, depending on what may be going on, though it is not entirely unusual to find none. The work that goes on down here is grisly, the main room going down rather deep below the tall ceiling. The small surgery happened upon that one night is naught but a dribble compared to the massive undertaking here. And this room is not just used for harvesting of organs from relatively healthy specimens who may meet an untimely demise, it is now used to dispose of anyone who meets their end, sometimes even causing that end. It has become a concentration of pain, suffering, leaked vitality, and such may charge into its own power, shining like a beacon to those sensitive to such things.

And now the vigilante is trying to find the way here.

The trigger of the G36C is squeezed, a few rounds fired off, and the body armor of the guard proves ironic, for the subsonic rounds will not penetrate it, but it makes for a larger target, now allowing for the generally avoided body shots. The guard is stunned by the hits, allowing the figure to rush in, keeping low, sweeping the legs, then moving quickly to an armlock and the zip-ties.

"Help! Help!" the guard calls out, coughing, struggling, obviously angered, and he is left there.

The intruder moves more openly now, less cautious, heading toward the calamity, though still preferring to avoid most of that commotion, checking in rooms, hoping to find a staircase leading down. Mostly empty quarters are found, some showing a clutter that may indicate the rapidity with which the chamber was vacated. Peering into one, and though it looks empty, there is an insistent thudding coming from behind a closed door within.

The figure rushes in, peering around, barrel of the compact assault rifle pointed until the room is cleared. The door is locked, but a quick glance shows a latching mechanism higher up on the portal and once released, it is swung open. Two pairs of wide eyes greet each other, and then the vigilante moves quickly, removing the black rubber gag from the prisoner.

"Why are *you* here?" Therese sputters as the leather bonds at her wrists and ankles are cut through, "I didn't call you this time. It's a trap."

DANCE OF THE BUTTERFLY

The rescuer is back up, peering outside the closet to be sure no one has shown up, looking around for any signs of said trap, then just looks at the hacker. After a short moment, a small shrug is given, then a point of a gloved hand toward the door, eyes giving an obvious inquiry as to their departure.

"Shit!" Therese exclaims, and it sums the entire situation as well as provide some motivation, for she gets to her feet, ready to follow her rescuer a second time.

They are almost to the door when the vigilante tenses, halting their movement, and then the sounds of rapidly moving feet gets to Therese's ears. Before anything else may be done, a figure appears in the doorway- one of the many workers employed here, not a guard. This does not mean he is unarmed, though, as he brandishes a large cooking knife, one with a dark sheen of blood on the blade to match the stains peppered throughout his person, and with the red glare of anger in his eyes and a yell unleashed from his mouth, he lunges at the pair.

"Get back!" comes out the forcefully delivered command, and Therese needs no further encouragement as the crusader moves toward the attacker, hands going up to catch the man's wrist as he strikes downward, the knife in reverse grip.

He snarls, trying to break free, but the momentum is kept up, the other moving around and behind, keeping a hold of that wrist, turning and moving the arm up. The attacker lunges out with an ineffectual, instinctive slash of his left hand, his body also turning in the direction pulled from his held arm, but the vigilante pushes in, thwarting that direction and providing a counter-force to the continued up-thrust of the weapon-wielding hand. A yelp comes out within the growls of uncontrolled anger, but he doesn't release the weapon, instead managing some chaotic movement of his wrist, still trying to cut with the blade. The arm is pushed up more, and a louder cry of pain arises as the joint is dislocated, and finally, the knife falls to the carpet.

Therese watches with rapt attention as the vigilante releases the attacker, but though one arm has been rendered useless, the man still evinces rage, swiping out with his clawed, left hand, moving in quickly toward his intended prey. This rapid attack is met with an even speedier counter, movement a blur as several strikes lash out and soon the man is on the ground, slumped against the wall, eyes blinking in a daze, all that rage gone.

A hand is gestured sharply at the hacker, then the figure turns, moving out, and she grabs the knife on the way out of the room.

"What the hell is going on?" Therese asks, once they have regained the hallway.

The masked person does not give an answer, but the sounds of general alarm are easily noticed. Therese follows as best she can, feeling an almost overwhelming sense of disorientation. She wonders how her savior knows the area so well, because she feels like she is being carried on the curving and careening track of a roller coaster. She feels a sudden rush of nausea.

"H-hold on," she bids, her voice clipped, and she pauses, holding her stomach.

The vigilante turns, looking her over, noticing the knife. She gently takes it from the hacker's hand, who does not resist. She then waits, watching, letting the girl have a short breather, keeping her eyes out for any other people. Therese swallows, tension evident in her jaw and neck, then she blinks a few times, deeply, then rises back up to her full height, ready to continue. She certainly has never been in stressful situations exactly like this, but she wonders about the 'spell'. It seems more frailty than she'd expect of herself. Perhaps she's dehydrated.

They prove able to avoid any more encounters, finally locating a window on the expansive front portion of the main building, and peering out, they can see people off to the left, milling about, waiting, wondering what all is going on. The vigilante quickly cranks open the window, then motions Therese through. Once out on that tended grass, the hacker looks back.

"Aren't you coming?" she asks.

The masked head moves in an obvious negative.

"Then I'm staying with-," Therese begins, making like she will go back through the window, but the other steps up, blocking the way, holding out a hand, palm forward.

The head is moved again, this time more emphatically, another 'no', then the hand points in a quick jerk toward where the party-goers are waiting to get out.

DANCE OF THE BUTTERFLY

"But I …," the hacker tries, but just exhales a loud sigh, "Fine, and hey," the black-garbed figure halts in closing the window, eyes on the girl, "Thanks, again. I … uh … I'll try not to get in trouble again, okay?"

And now she gets a single nod from her rescuer before the window is closed and relocked.

Therese turns her eyes to the crowd, noting that most of it looks to be made up of very well-dressed people. She also sees the guards, and though some of them are also done up for the occasion, they do stand out, especially as some of them are openly displaying their firearms. She doesn't know if heading there is a good idea, though she moves tentatively toward the mass, her heavy boots crunching on the cultivated grass. It's possible a guard might notice her, especially as she does stand out from this lot. She glances around, seeing the thick, tall brick wall that goes out in both directions. She doesn't think she can scale that wall. The gate is closed, but surely it will be opened to let these people go. She wonders if emergency services are on their way. If she could get a hold of a smart phone or tablet …

She pauses in her musings, still walking slowly toward the group, as she sees a familiar face. There, standing on the outskirts of the crowd, smoking a cigarette, is one Agent Gaspare Duilio of Interpol. He is calmly scanning his surroundings, and the motion of his head indicates his eyes will be on her shortly. She freezes in place, not sure what to do. If she turns and bolts, he will obviously see her. She wonders if the lack of light where she stands is enough to keep him from noticing her, or at least recognizing her. She'll wait. If he sees her, he'll react, and there is enough space for her to run, if-

And then the screams arise, and Duilio turns sharply to look toward the crowd as people rush to get away from something. He flings his cigarette aside and heads toward it, as do some of the guards, and as the flood parts, there is a scene of violence and blood.

One of the guests lies on the ground, in a growing pool of the red liquid, another guest atop him. The larger man above is savagely stabbing into the prone body of the other, holding a torn piece of metal, having been drafted as an improvised weapon. Each stab into the left side of the victim's torso produces more spurts of fresh fluid, the attacker painted with it, giving him even more of a horrific, demented look than his own expressions and actions already convey.

"He's killing my husband!" a nearby woman screams, her own shrieks part of those making up the cacophony, though if the lack of resistance on the part of her spouse indicates anything, he may already be dead.

The guards point their weapons, nearing the terrible happening.

"Get out of the way!" Duilio commands, and the other party-goers and workers do just that, clearing more area around the attack.

"Do something! Do something!" the woman, rushes over to Duilio, her heels clicking on the pavement.

The guards look to the inspector, and Duilio spares a short moment of assessment, then, "Stop him."

Gunshots blast out, causing more screams and dispersal of the crowd. The attacker is quickly removed from atop his victim, crumbling away and to the ground, flopping to his back as the firing ceases, his breath coming out ragged and wet.

The inspector walks over, looking over the two forms, one quite dead, the other mortally wounded. The woman scuttles over then, going down to her bloody husband, wrapping her arms about his head, raising him up a bit as she cradles him, sobbing, still bidding for help. Just then, sirens are heard in the distance. Duilio glances at the guards.

"Get that gate open," he orders.

"But we were told-," one of them begins.

"I don't care what you were told," the Interpol man calmly says, turning to more fully face the sentry, "The authorities are on their way, hmm?" He perks his eyebrows, holding up a hand to indicate the inevitable arrival, "It will look very bad for that gate to be closed. It will keep them out, and it will seem you were preventing the guests from leaving.

"And," he continues, stepping closer, speaking with more menace, though he still holds on to the cultured, smooth tone, "*I* cannot be found here. Do you understand? Do you want to end this evening in a holding cell ... or worse, hmm?"

Another brief moment passes before the guard turns to his colleagues, "Let's get that gate open."

DANCE OF THE BUTTERFLY

Back inside the main building, some sounds still emerging in the distance of people in the throes of stress, he stands still, looking at the eviscerated corpse. He is in the kitchen, and some items had been left on, such is there a lingering haze of smoke in the decently-sized space. Is that a sound of bubbling, breathing? Is it his own respiration?

He stands so still that one might think him devoid of animation, save he is standing, and his eyes are open, fixed on that body. Is it male, female? One might find it difficult to tell, as it has been lain open so viciously, the innards gleaming out in an abstract wetness, a dark mess. Clearly, though, the blood was not drained from this one, as that vitae shows itself splattered about, only adding to the gruesome display.

He just stares, wondering if he can still see life there, wondering if he might glimpse something meaningful within the mess, the torn organs, shredded muscle. Can he see the future there? He can certainly *feel* something, and he slowly, slowly moves his head, craning it about on his thin neck. And there, almost like iridescent tracks, he senses a trail. Then, as if once noticed, it grows in power, pulling to him, compelling him. Forgetting the fresh corpse, he turns and plods off in that direction.

The masked intruder, though, is finding the trail less obvious, still working to find a way to the lower level. And then a loud report booms through the area, though still muffled. Another explosion, one that has come from a depth. This charge had not been set by the intruder, and it proves as good a lead as any, so the figure turns and sets off in that direction.

And finally, there it is, a doorway opened to reveal a staircase winding up … and down. A general peer is given, one hand still on the doorknob. It seems quiet, clear. A shout booms out, a horripilating scream, obviously a woman, and the vigilante pauses in heading down, moving back to the hallway, peering off in the direction from which the sound emerges. The alarming noises continue, someone obviously being attacked, harmed. The vigilante takes to a jog, deciding to investigate, even as the cries are cut-off, but the jika-tabi do not stop moving until the large figure walks in view from around the bend, turning to face the infiltrator.

291

The man is tall, well-fleshed, close to two meters, likely around six foot four or five, upwards of ninety kilos, and the blood on him implies he has just ended the life, or at least done some serious damage to whomsoever had been lately screaming. His eyes bore into the much smaller form of the other person in the hallway, his breath coming in great waves, audible through his nostrils, even as his top lip is curled up, revealing his teeth. His tense hands show blood on them, traveling up to forearms, more across his broad chest and shoulders, some even on his face, about his mouth. His eyes gleam with a red of rage, but that must surely be the light. He also looks not at all concerned as the vigilante brings up the H&K, pointing the barrel at the sizeable target.

The breathing becomes more intense, more rapid and noisy, as whatever anger that fuels the large man has apparently not been satiated. The other begins to take slow, careful steps backwards, assault rifle held unerringly on the threat, laser sight wavering only slightly over the man's mass as the retreat is begun. The large man emits what may only be described as a snarl which peels into a scream as he takes to his own feet, sprinting with a sudden burst of speed toward the dark-suited person, hands showing clawed fingers as the burly arms pump with motion.

The gun fires, the suppressor coughing out three bullets, all hitting the man's powerful legs. He falters but does not fall, emitting a louder yell, and the vigilante turns, also sprinting for the doorway that leads to the stairs. Quickly through, the portal slammed shut, a short inspection given, time dwindling before the enraged man will cover the distance outside, and the lock is a simple one, the mechanism turned, engaging the bolt.

The stairs leading down are now taken, ground covered rapidly as the loud noises are heard from the man as he bangs against the door, trying to break through, his frustration evident in his shouts and grunts. The door ought to hold, but then, those bullets should have taken the man down. Something is not right. Why did the young girl attack? Why the man with the butcher's knife? Surely some anxiety is expected in this sort of situation, but most people would be rushing to get out, not searching about for victims due to some uncontrollable bloodlust. Something is most definitely not right.

DANCE OF THE BUTTERFLY

The noises from above have stopped by the time the fleeing figure reaches the door at the bottom of the stairwell. It seems the man is not so lost to his passion that he has failed to discern he is incapable of just bashing his way through the door. Maybe he has gone looking for a tool to aid him. Maybe he's just given up and is off in search of other potential victims.

The door to the basement is unlocked, even possessed of a small, vertical window offset from center, more toward the knob. A peek inside shows nothing but a small room, empty of people, and the vigilante heads in.

There is a credenza against one wall, two small, potted plants atop it. There is a set of double doors, and a wide stair case leading even further down, lasting for a short time before coming to a landing and disappearing with a ninety degree turn left.

The room needs checking first, and a slow entry, gun barrel pointing the way, reveals what looks like a place for information of both physical and digital types. There are filing cabinets, computers, some chairs, the cabinets showing drawers for paper files as well as others holding what are obviously storage devices for electronic records. This room is likely a treasure trove, but time is not a luxury right now. Some thought is given to nabbing some of the smaller items, but a glance through a window here halts that train.

The masked figure looks out, noting how large and expansive this lowest level is, marveling at the architectural acumen displayed in the design and layout of this main building. The basement is no small area for storage and possible hiding from bad weather, but it appears almost as broad-reaching as the entire building itself, going further down, making the ceiling very tall, a walkway going around a portion of the room further away, giving passage to the central region via other, less obvious methods.

Off in the distance, further down, seems the site of the explosion heard earlier, as equipment of what looks a medical nature is strewn about, metal torn, bent, less stalwart materials and items obliterated, and a hole shows in the ground, the force erupting from beneath. It is difficult to tell from this distance, but there even shows a sheen, a liquid of some kind collected there, perhaps a burst water line mingling with oils.

Then movement is spied, off across the expanse, up on the walkway. The vigilante crouches, offering less visibility upon their form, peering, but the distance makes it difficult to determine details. There is obvious motion, and then a flash is seen as though from a firearm, accompanied by a telltale pop.

The vigilante turns, rushing out of the room to get a better view of what may be going on out there. The short flight of stairs is taken with speed, agility, turning to see another few stairs heading down and opening into this portion of the large chamber. The sounds are louder now, obviously someone engaged in combat. Careful steps are now taken, looking up, moving closer. There is another staircase around and to the right, and that would allow access to the walkway. There show also other doorways, some closed, some not, and then the low breathing is heard, almost shallow enough to have been entirely eclipsed by the noises from above, and the large man from earlier springs forth from the darkness of an open room, swiping at the darkly-suited figure.

The vigilante dodges back, fast enough to avoid most of the hit, but the attacker's left hand finds the assault rifle, striking with such force that the holds on the strap break, the weapon scattering away, sliding along the ground and coming to a halt too far to be of use as the offense is pressed by the enraged man. There is still the Glock, but if the way he shrugged off the bullets of the H&K is any indicator, another weapon may be of better choice, and jumping back from continued swipes of the man's large, clawed hands, the vigilante sidesteps, pulling forth the katana.

A short moment is spared as the red-seeming eyes of the man travel over the gleaming, polished blade, and he shouts out a cry, offended by this challenge to his lust, and he attacks. The distance between them is now very small, a mere few paces, one that may be consumed faster than most people may register and react, but the masked figure is well-trained. Legs muscles are flexed, movement happening in the blink of an eye, using the short, slender shape as an advantage, dodging from further attacks as well as moving aside from the bull rush. The large man

DANCE OF THE BUTTERFLY

evinces his own speed, turning, just as the blade arcs out, shearing through his neck, nearly decapitating him.

The vigilante dances further away to try to avoid the jettison of blood as the man's head flops back, spewing forth more of his vitae as the body crumbles. Then the katana is re-sheathed after a quick, sharp movement to shake off the blood, the G36C collected, held in gloved hands, as the sounds from above have increased as that fight has continued, now at the top of the very stairs nearby.

Another man is up there, and though he is somewhat tall, he is not like the giant so recently dispatched. His form is lean, his dress dark, combat-oriented, though not as military or even utilitarian as that worn by the vigilante. He holds what looks like a stick or rod in one hand and a pistol in the other, and the things attacking him do not look entirely human.

They hold human shape, but just as with so much going on in this place, they are behaving more like animals, and just as they enter a greater degree of light, their heads show a grayness of flesh that cannot be normal, as well as a lack of hair that reveals ridges and boney protrusions along with tapered ears angling back from red eyes. They are also bereft of clothing, their squat, powerful bodies possessed of noticeable muscle, and as if this were not odd enough, they lack any identifiable genitals.

The masked figure stands there, somewhat frozen in place by the oddity of it all, brain having trouble accepting what is seen. The other man shows unaffected by such a paralysis, moving with a grace and fluidity of martial expertise, using the polished wooden cane to block a strike from lethal claws, then pointing the custom-modified Walther P99 and firing off two rounds into the beast's chest, causing an eruption of some black fluid that could be blood. The creature howls, stumbling back, only for the aim to be adjusted, and a bullet fired through the forehead, causing an eruption from the back of the head, the thing collapsing.

The gun's slide is now held open, the magazine empty. A button is pressed with a casual familiarity, even as the second beast lunges, and the top of the gun shifts smoothly back in place, the hand moving to slip it into the shoulder holster as feet move to avoid the thing's attack. Then the cane is held in both hands, pulling apart, and a thin, almost rapier-like blade is revealed. Much less easily seen are the complex sigils etched into the bottom of the blade, but the observant, though somewhat stunned, eyes of the vigilante catch a shocking blink of outré color about that sleek metal as the thrust is made, the point rupturing out the rear of the monster's neck, then being twisted and pulled back out. The beast gags, falling to its knees, fluid, like ichor, pouring from its wound and coughing mouth, and it crumbles, facedown.

A flick of the wrist causes most of the fresh liquid to be flung free, and the blade is slid back into the cane with a firm snick. The man then turns, looking down at the darkly-garbed figure, a subtle, almost calm expression on his face.

"I saw what you did," he says, gesturing to the dead form of the large man, "Very nicely done."

There is no response, just a stare, immobility evincing continued shock.

"You are the vigilante, I take it?" he walks down the steps, getting nearer, eyebrows perked up to accentuate the question, but there is yet no voice emerging from behind the mask. "I realize this all must be very difficult, and I would be happy to …," and then that voice halts.

He steps closer, peering, his own blue eyes narrowing as he looks intently into the sparkling, more hypnotic blue shading of the other pair staring back at him.

"Lilja?" Skot asks, his voice turning into a breath of disbelief at the end of the spoken word.

One hand moves from the firearm, pulling away the concealing parts of the balaklava to indeed reveal the face of the curator.

"Skot!?" she retorts, "What are *you* doing here?"

"I could ask you the same," he replies, shock taking both their features.

She blinks, lips parting, but she does not speak. Then she blinks again, shaking her head.

"What were those *things* you were fighting?" she finally plucks a question from the many that buzz around in her head.

DANCE OF THE BUTTERFLY

"Ah, yes," he looks slightly sheepish, glancing toward the bodies, then back to her, eyes fixed, his face now serious as he utters a single word, "Demons."

"What?" she finally manages, having to force the word out from within her continued, shaking head.

"It seems we both have some things to explain to each other, but now may not be the time," he says, "What I am doing here is trying to stop *that*."

She looks over in the direction he points, indicating further in the deeper recesses of the room, the area from whence the explosion has occurred.

"I …" She peers over, blinking more, her lips working as she again tries to formulate something to say, "I don't see anything. Stop what?"

"I'll show you," he says, tucking his cane under his arm and reloading his pistol with his last magazine, slipping the empty one to the other side of his shoulder holster, next to its equally empty sibling, "That's a … very nice rifle, by the way," he comments, looking at the G36C with a bit of a raised eyebrow.

"Thanks," she somewhat mutters.

"Alright, then," he says, "Shall we?"

She gives a single nod, following as he moves to get around the multi-leveled flooring and debris so as to get to the further, deeper area he earlier indicated. They barely make it five paces before they both stop, hearing the approach of running feet. They share a glance, then both pairs of eyes look toward the incoming noise. They separate a small distance, aiming their weapons.

A young man rushes into the area, panic evident on his thin, skeletal features. Though his feet prove very determined, his eyes are open, unblinking, almost as though not seeing this world, but then they latch onto the pair, and he comes to a stop, breath heavy.

"The killer! The killer!" Ernst cries out, pointing back in the direction from whence he came, moving to put the others between himself and anyone who may be coming on his trail.

"Just calm down," Lilja tries, having lowered the barrel of her assault rifle.

"What are you talking about?" Skot asks, his handgun also now pointing downward, "What killer?"

"The serial killer! The one who has been stalking the city!" Ernst all but shouts, his body trembling, "Behind me, coming," he adds, trying to indicate with a shaky hand, and he moves again to try to get further away, and as he turns to glance deeper into the large room, he stops, going rigid.

"What-?" Lilija notices, moving closer, peering at him.

Skot does the same, looking at those locked open eyes, the statue-like aspect that has suddenly claimed the ill-looking man, and he looks in the direction those pale orbs stare, then back.

"You see it?" he asks, his voice barely above a whisper.

Lilja's brow wrinkles with confusion, curiosity, and she also looks in that same direction. She sees the same blasted, trashed condition from the explosion, the pooled, thick, dark liquid. She presumes they must be talking of something else.

"You can see it," Skot concludes, as no further words emerge from the transfixed young man, Ernst's already sickly pallor appearing to pale further.

"See what?" Lilja asks, her voice also pitched low, taking the cue from Skot's tone even though she is not sure what is going on.

"The gateway," he says, then he looks at her, holding up a fist, hoping to remind her of their prior conversation, and then he relaxes his fingers, spreading them, space now there, "It has been opened, and it is opening further."

"What gateway?" she persists, "Where?"

Before he may answer, an eruption of noise takes their attention. It comes from the direction Ernst has arrived. Skot glances back at him, but the young man still seems lost in what he now sees, whatever fear he felt at running from the city's serial murderer now gone.

"Will he be alright?" Lilja whispers out the question, eyes darting from Skot to Ernst then back in the direction of the growing ruckus.

"I have my suspicions," he answers, and she looks at him, that furrowing again found on her forehead, wondering what he means with this odd response.

DANCE OF THE BUTTERFLY

He gently takes the unfocused young man by the arm, then looks again at her, "Come on," he says, motioning his head now toward the noise, and though she is still filled with questions, she hefts her rifle and follows.

The racket is coming now from an adjacent room, and they make themselves ready at the doorway. Lilja checks the handle, finding that it is unlocked, then she glances up at Skot.

"I'll go first," she says, and he nods, one hand still guiding the other man, and he decides to gently move him aside, placing him against the wall as a method of safekeeping, then he nods again to her, and she slowly opens the door.

Whatever is inside causing such a turmoil does not seem to care one whit for them. They move in, immediately noticing that the chamber looms larger than they had anticipated, and even with everything else going on, she still manages to register some awe at the make-up of the compound, especially this underground level. For the first time, she wonders if it has been here longer, the more modern structures erected above it, even as additions and reinforcements may have been made down here. Time for such thoughts later, though, as she and Skot again spread out, weapons leveled at the far corner, where the darkness is thickest, where violent movement shows along with the continued noise.

She then sees flashes of color, just like that she thought she saw glimmer about Skot's sword before he thrust it through that thing's neck. These flashes are smaller, though broader, and they are indeed there, coming out quite frequently in the contrasting darkness, a sort of dark magenta flaring up.

A figure then spills into the light, and she blinks to wide eyes, the aim of her barrel not faltering, though her grip lessens. She sees a man in what had once been a very nice Anderson & Sheppard tuxedo, its current state showing dishevelment, stains, tears, and she has seen this man before. He does not yet notice them, though, instead springing to his feet, taking a fighting stance, and she spies a very curious weapon in his right hand. It appears to be a rather wicked-looking dagger made of black glass, and though she is no expert in such, she presumes it is obsidian. It is somewhat broad at its base, wider than the fist which clutches about the handle, tapering in jagged, lethal aspect to its point. He lunges back into the darkness.

The sounds of fighting resume, and she spares a look at Skot, her eyes more curious whereas his are watchful. She prepares to ask him a whispered question when another sound emerges from within the turmoil of the nearby fight, a noise that sounds like the curdling growl and cry of a beast. Her legs tense as she lowers, bringing the G36C to a more pronounced aim, the laser site's beam penetrating the darkness but not showing her what she might hit were she to pull the trigger. The green beam from Skot's Walther also unerringly points in the direction of the combat, and she wonders if he is able to see better in that darkness. They both then turn on their tactical lights, and though this presents more, the confusion of the combat has not much abated.

She spies another of those monsters, the ones Skot has told her are "demons", though she has not accepted this yet on any real level. She is still in crisis mode, and to her, whatever those things are, they are an obvious threat.

This one, though, looks different than the two she saw dispatched earlier, its large hands bearing of the lethal length of claws. The eyes are long, shaped like upturning ovals that move to and aside the brow, and they are reflective, an uninterrupted deep red, as though the eyes are perhaps behind a jeweled shield. It's mouth is a puckering pinch of flesh stretched over the tapering lower jaw, and she has a moment to wonder how such a thing emitted those noises, if it even did at all, and then that maw is opened, the ashen flesh parting to reveal a toothless orifice deep within which she thinks she glimpses the sheen of small tentacle lengths splaying out and waving, whether on the current of that roar or causing it, she does not know, but the entire scene again grips her mind with a threat of paralytic insanity.

It attacks with an inhuman quickness, but the man proves ready, dancing aside with his own evidence of martial prowess, swinging his hand and causing another wound to open on the beast. With this slash, she again sees the flaring rise of color about the deeply dark obsidian blade. She knows she is not seeing things. Another strike is made, the man moving very fast, and the rising color becomes like a tracer, accentuating his speedy, arcing movements.

DANCE OF THE BUTTERFLY

It is not the only glimpse of color, though, and she peers over to see Skot taking careful aim. She looks back, trying to find where the green laser points within that chaos of movement and color and low lighting. She cannot tell which he intends to shoot, and just then, the combatants part, and the Walther pops out a single round. It is another hit to the forehead, and the monster's head jerks back. It does not fall, though, instead turning to focus its haunting eyes on the shooter, a low growl emerging. That dark fluid leaks from the entry of the wound, the moment stretching before the thing wavers, head lulling to its left, and then it falls.

"Skothiam Felcraft," the other man says, giving a slight bow of his head, "I did not know you were in town."

"Denman," Skot looks over, and though he does not return his pistol to the holster, he angles it downward with no intent of a target.

"And the lovely librarian, Ms. Perhonen. I assuredly did not expect to see you here," he says, somewhat trying to arrange his clothes to something more presentable or at least comfortable, as he walks nearer to them, eyes moving from one to the other. "I suppose I should not be surprised to see you two in league with one another."

She says nothing, and after a short time, he looks back at Skot.

"I should give your family more credit," he carries on, "Here I thought you Felcrafts were completely ignorant of the goings-on in this city, but *you* are here, the Head. No wonder I did not know."

"The gateway," Skot says, and the other nods.

"Yes, *that* one," he says, gesturing back to the now dead monster that had been lately terrorizing the city as its serial killer, "was a mere scout, but it has been here for a while."

Skot nods, "The energies have been building."

Denman gives his own nod, "Well, since you're here, will you do the honors?"

"I will," another nod is given, "Lilja and yourself can fend off any other attacks while I seal the breach."

"Wait, what?" she finally gives voice, moving to him, though she keeps a wary eye on the other, "I thought you said you two were enemies. You trust him?"

301

"We *are* enemies," Denman affirms, still keeping to that very casual, conversational tone.

"He won't kill me," Skot says, "There are too few of us."

"Too few of ... what?" she blinks.

"Hunters," Denman says, and she shoots her eyes to him, "Demon hunters, to be precise."

She looks back at Skot, the obvious questions upon questions warring there.

"I'll explain it all afterwards, but we really need to close that gateway before more get through."

They move back out into the larger room, Skot leading the way, the other two following. Lilja keeps an eye on Denman, not willing to trust him. He seems fairly intent on helping, but then his attention is caught by the other person there as Skot goes back to gather the still enthralled young man.

"Ah, so you've found Ernst," Denman remarks.

Skot shoots him a rather unpleasant look, and Lilja watches closely.

"I should have known," he utters, "He'll be leaving with me."

"As you like," Denman far too easily concedes, giving another little bow of his head.

The two engage in a very short battle of wills, eyes drilling into one another. Skot still looks perturbed whereas Denman continues to wear that underlying visage of his arrogant charm. The moment passes quickly, though, as Skot turns, continuing his way further in.

"What is this?" Lilja asks, breaking the silence that has held sway for a while as they have neared ground zero.

"It's the gateway," Denman says, then, "Ahh, she doesn't see it."

"Not that," she somewhat snaps, putting on a bit of a scowl, "The liquid on the ground. I thought it was oil or some other fluid that had leaked from the explosion, but it ….," her voice trails off.

Denman joins her in looking at Skot, a smirk taking his lips as he waits.

"It's blood," Skot finally answers.

"Blood?" she repeats, eyes widening, her feet halting in their nearing approach.

DANCE OF THE BUTTERFLY

"Yes, the final sacrifice, it seems," Denman decides to join the talk again, "All of the negative energy has culminated here," he gestures, "forming the eye of the storm, as it were, though I can assure you, the focal points of these are not calm."

She just gives him a look, then slips her eyes to Skot. He nods once, giving the verification she craves.

"They did this on purpose?" she asks, incredulous.

"Not hardly," Denman scoffs.

"The negative energies created by their actions caused this," Skot elaborates, "but they did not know what they were doing. This happens sometimes, a gateway spontaneously opening because of the coming together of many different stimuli. It's not just the bloodletting, but the things they have done, and those energies come back here. The location of this city also plays a part, as well as-."

"Do you think *now* is the time for a lecture?" the Professor of Philosophy interjects, "Maybe after we're done here, hmm?"

And just then Ernst returns to animation, crying out, shocking them all.

"No! No! They're coming!" he yells, pointing toward the site of the explosion, "We're too late!" and he turns, running away.

He proves a harbinger, for just then, a bubbling emerges at the center of the area, dark illumination coming from beneath it, and then a rumbling as of an earthquake. It is not enough to upset their balance, but it is felt, and then, as though these things are but precursors, another explosion occurs, a jettison of fluid and earth rising up from the boiling. This shockwave does thrust them back, hands and arms held up to protect faces, and then it appears.

"I see it now," Lilja declares, voice a whisper, her eyes held wide, and she does.

It is yet another thing that her mind thinks ought not exist, and she blinks rapidly, sucking in a breath, then she closes her mouth, pulling in another through her nostrils. She sees what looks like a fissure in the very air, a roiling tear of dark colors, black, blues, purples, and reds. She grits her teeth together, jaw tensed as her eyes look upon it, drawn in, trying to plumb its depths as it hangs there, the barriers moving, writhing in an obscene way.

"Lilja ... Lilja!"

She blinks, lips parting as a breath is expelled, then she stutters over an inhale, eyes darting to Skot. He has placed a hand on her right shoulder, and she did not even register it.

"It's the gateway. I have to close it now. *Now*. Do you understand?"

She nods.

"If anyone, or anything, tries to stop me, I need you to take it out. Okay?"

She nods again.

"They may come from the compound or from the gateway. They want it to stay open. They will come if they can. I need you to defend me, alright?"

"Alright," she nods again.

"If the bullets in your gun do not stop them, use your sword."

She takes a moment to understand this, but then she nods again.

"I think she gets it, Skothiam. You had better hurry."

He looks over at Denman, and the ubiquitous arrogance of his demeanor has dimmed to such an extent as to be nigh invisible. Skot gives Lilja one last look, a squeeze of her shoulder, then he moves closer to the chaotic-seeming fissure.

He again pulls the sword from the cane, though there show no visible enemies upon whom he might use it. He begins speaking in a language that sounds somewhat like Latin, but even to her less than fluent ear, she can tell it is not the dead language of the Roman Empire. He holds the sword more like a totem than a weapon, and she sees it shine with that eldritch glow, noticing that it seems to emanate from the sigils carved in the base of the blade. He continues speaking, perhaps casting some spell, his eyes intent on the gateway even as they grow further lost to this world.

She watches the area, hoping to glimpse any attacks that may come. She ought to feel a heightened tension with what she has learned. Will the bullets not stop them? The ones in Skot's Walther seemed to work. Does he customize them somehow? Are these things really demons from Hell? But instead she remains reasonably calm, alert, eyes continuing to take in the scene, ears tuned for any approaching noise.

DANCE OF THE BUTTERFLY

Then her eyes move toward the gateway, again locking on that unnatural phenomenon. The edges blur and fuzz like the blind spot of a migraine, but the inside of that fissure still shows a thick movement as of lava. But then she thinks she glimpses something more substantial in there, some hint of an alien landscape, something born from nightmare? She cannot be sure, and she feels that encroaching confusion and disorientation she saw and even somewhat felt earlier this evening.

Denman looks over from his own position, and he sees that look in Lilja's eyes. He's seen it before, and he knows the effects of the opening are claiming her mind. He doesn't say anything. If she lacks the fortitude to survive it, then so be it. Thus is the crucible of life. He knows that humans create rules, expectations, even words to try to contain and control existence. It is a case of a practical framework growing thick with the vines of fear, being cultivated by a defense mechanism that leaves one limited. He moves his eyes away even as she draws deeper in to the influence, keeping his own senses attuned for a threat to himself or Skot's efforts.

"Lilja?"

She blinks, once, very deep, then followed by a few more, rapid, eyelashes fluttering, then she looks up to again see Skot there at her side, some time obviously passed, another consoling hand placed on her shoulder.

"Be careful not to be distracted by what is coming out of that gate," he cautions.

"What?"

"It emits energy as well as being a passage. It has already seeped into this entire area, filling it like a gas leak."

"It is poisonous?" she asks, looking concerned.

"Not exactly, but it can render you somewhat disabled, defenseless, and enough exposure to people with the lacking mental defenses can contribute to insanity or other effects."

She wonders at the curiousness of this comment and what it implies, but at least she now feels back to more herself.

"I'm fine," she nods once, and he returns that with a warm smile of his own.

"Skothiam?" Denman calls over, and the two look in his direction, seeing that he faces away toward one of the many avenues into this area. "They are coming. Perhaps you ought to get back to work?"

He gives her one more look, that gentle curve still on his lips, then he goes back to where he had been before, resuming the chant, the words spoken with low volume, yet with firm enunciation.

She eventually hears the sounds of running feet coming from the direction she initially arrived at this lowest level. She turns, focusing on the opening that leads to that stairwell, pointing the barrel of her rifle, finger at the ready near the trigger. She hears the labored, frightened breathing of Ernst who has inadvertently gotten closer to that hallway in his attempt to distance himself from the gateway. She tries to get his attention, using very clear signals with her left hand that he ought to move away. He either doesn't see or will not comply, for he stays there, cowering, crippled by fear.

Then the figure emerges, sprinting down the stairs, and it is a human woman. She does not look like a party-goer or one of the many girls offered as product. Lilja assumes she is probably one of any number of other females employed here in a different capacity. Her clothing does not mark her as a likely waitress or cook, but her aspect is similar to others she has seen tonight - one of naked rage. Still, she falters at pulling the trigger even as the woman stops, red-rimmed eyes looking about with quick jerks of her head, teeth bared, her own breath short, ragged, and she sets her sight on the nearest prey, emitting a loud yell and rushing for Ernst.

"Shoot her!" calls out Denman's voice, and he rushes toward the attacking woman, his melee weapon at the ready.

She squeezes the trigger, bullets flying out of the suppressed barrel with a clicking cough, and though one misses, the other two hit the woman in her legs. She cries out, stumbling, but ready to get back up. Lilja takes better aim but then moves the barrel aside quickly as Denman reaches the scene, moving in behind the woman and dragging his blade over her throat then backing away. The woman falls onto her hands, her blood pouring out in time with the pulsing of her excited heart until she falls into that sticky puddle.

DANCE OF THE BUTTERFLY

"What is your problem?" Denman demands, walking toward Lilja, anger drawn over his face.

Lilja does not respond with a similar emotion, instead showing somewhat calm, if not a bit confused.

"That was a woman, not one of those things," she counters.

"Demons," he presses, though he stops before getting too close to her, "Those *things* are demons. You had better get that through your head. They are not going to provide the luxury of waiting for you to accept that before they kill you. Do you understand?"

"But she looks like a regular woman," she says, gesturing with one hand toward the corpse.

Denman pulls in a breath through his nose, all the world like an evaluating professor trying to decide on the spot whether to continue with a difficult student.

"They are able to influence people, even *possess* them," he explains, "And with that gateway spewing out their energies, expect more. They won't all look like monsters, so I hope you have it in you to take a life. We don't have time for *exorcisms*," he all but spits, going back to another vantage for his own guard duty, sparing a glance at Ernst as he does.

She thinks back on the young girl she tried to save, the man with the butcher knife, and especially that large guard that Skot commended her for dispatching. Were they being influenced, possessed? If so, she recalls the young girl coming around from it. She doesn't know what all is going on, but she'll be damned if she takes advice from someone like Denman Malkuth.

More noises then arise, this time it is obvious it is more than one person. She casts a glance to Ernst, and he has managed to crawl and scuttle to a better hiding place. He even registers her notice this time, and he points a shaky finger toward another opening. She trains her barrel on it. She also then hears more noise from the walkway, but a quick glance to her left shows that Denman has responded, and he readies himself for this approach.

Three more people run forth from the open doorway, and though they all appear human, two men and one woman, they bear the same vicious behavior as the others. They do not go after Ernst, though not for failing to see him but because they lock their notice on the gateway and Skot. With but this short pause, they resume their sprint, rushing toward the caster.

She fires, quickly, her barrel moving to track the targets. One goes down, then the second. She is more careful, for the third passes along the line that leads to Denman, and she does not want to miss and hit the professor. Then she fires again, knowing her magazine is low, and the third falls. She then ejects it, slipping in a fresh one and shoving the empty into that same pouch. She runs over to the fallen people just as more of those bestial noises arise from above, and two of the more obvious creatures lope to the stairway intent on coming down, moving also with the use of their hands.

She checks the three people she has hit. Two of them appear to have been broken of the spell of influence, writhing out in pain now, confusion. She does what she can for the one man, as he has taken a hit in his lower left torso. She also zip-ties them both, just to be safe. The third man, though, the one who made it closest to Skot, is still snarling and spitting, consumed by his rage, trying to drag himself, leaving thick trails of blood from his shot-up legs.

She rushes up and uses the stunner on him. It doesn't have much effect, but it does give the man reason to turn and try to get a hold of her, his clawed hands flying out. She backs off, then dodges in, trying the stunner again, and he cringes with pain, but he still does not collapse, so she takes him in a choke hold. This subdues him sufficiently, and she gets the zip-ties on him.

"You're wasting your time."

She looks up to see Denman cleaning off his obsidian blade, two dark bulks of the now dead beasts in a bloody disarray.

"I am not going to kill them if I have any other option."

He smirks, a forced exhale through his nose, "You really are more suited for him, you know."

"What?" she wrinkles her brow as Denman gestures toward Skot.

"A pity," he continues, "You do seem somewhat useful. With proper training, you'd make a fine hunter."

She racks the slide on the G36C, chambering a round, stepping closer to him, looking up into his face, not intimidated by him in the

DANCE OF THE BUTTERFLY

least. He just continues to give her that smirk, so she turns and goes back to her task.

"Please," ekes out a voice, and she looks down at the woman she shot and bound, "I need help. Why am I tied up? I'm hurt. Please help me."

"Everything will be alright," she says, "We're getting the situation under control. Help will be here soon."

She looks up to see Denman watching her, his eyes full of condescension. She finds herself thinking less and less of him, despite that he shares some secret knowledge with Skot. That will have to wait, though, as the sounds of more figures approaching arises.

"How is that gateway coming along, Skothiam?" Denman calls back, eyes toward the encroaching noise.

She glances at Skot when there is no answer forthcoming. He is deep within whatever state he has achieved to attempt to seal the fissure. She thinks she sees an outpouring of something like colored mist going from his sword and blending into the menacing hues of the opening, but she cannot be sure. She feels another tremor beneath their feet, and her eyes widen somewhat. She takes a sure stance, hoping the ground does not erupt beneath her, leveling her gun in the direction from which she expects more attacks.

Two more of the monsters run in from the darkness of an open doorway, and she spares a tangential thought to wondering if they generally move in pairs before she pulls the trigger, unleashing a torrent of bullets. Hits strike all over them, their bodies jerking with it, that black blood, if it is blood, spewing forth. They are resilient, though, and it takes nearly the full magazine to down them.

Then more footsteps arise on the walkway, and she and Denman look up to see other humans. She recognizes one of them, the man in a very nice tuxedo, though the bow tie hangs loose. He is flanked by several others, all of them carrying submachine guns. The boss, for that is obviously what he is, stands at the railing, looking down over the grisly scene.

"What have you done to my home!?" Gnegon shouts, his face tense, red, and his head shakes, his right hand coming up, curled into a fist.

"What have you done to *me*!?" he adds, clearly on the edge of bursting. "*Kill them!*" he orders.

Both of them take quick cover as the guns are aimed and a shower of bullets lashes down at them. She thinks of Skot, looking over, and he still stands there, absorbed in his activity. At least he has not been shot, but he seems entirely uncaring, if not unaware, of the firing squad there on higher ground, trying to do them all in. She hides now behind some debris, what looks like a medical cabinet of some sort, or was, along with other indications of similar use, takes careful aim, knowing she has few bullets left, peering through the ACOG, and squeezes off one round which hits one of the gunman. He drops.

The others are clearly having difficulty seeing her. She is small, dressed in black, and her gun makes insignificant noise compared to the barrage from them. Her red hair is exposed, but despite its vibrant color, it is tied up tightly. Several of the shooters stop, changing magazines, others looking about, and of course, they see Skot, and they take aim.

No, she thinks, urgency consuming her, moving her barrel, firing, adjusting rapidly and smoothly, firing again, and those two drop. She is now out, so she drops the rifle, pulling out her sidearm, aiming with both hands on the pistol and firing quickly. She wants them to see, to hear; she wants to draw their attention to her, see her as the threat. She wonders what Denman is doing, probably hiding quite well, but then she realizes her presumption, noticing that he has gone over to another staircase and is balancing speed and stealth to sneak up on them in order to dispatch them with his dagger. He reaches one who is about to resume firing, stabbing the obsidian blade through the neck, before the next explosion occurs.

A flash of colors, a surge of light from the gateway, then a greater rumbling is felt beneath them. All of this happening very fast, and then an eruption comes from a nearby room, then again as the door is blown, wood and material flying outward. Another monster emerges, and this one is larger and more horrible than the others, making them seem mere mutations of nature compared to its hideous shape.

The thing appears to be about three and a half meters long, hirsute, the thick, black hair shiny and bearing of some of the earth through which it has dug. It moves about like a giant worm, rising up, and it

DANCE OF THE BUTTERFLY

shows to have two large hands midway through its body, the digits long, bony, possessed of rugose flesh, the nails at the tips also long, tapering to thick points. These are attached at the wrist, more like flippers, and they curl out threateningly. If this were not enough, the top of it is possessed of a multitude of faces, each also showing the same wrinkled, pale flesh, empty and dark sockets where eyes ought to be, if such a thing were akin to known biology at all, nearly non-existent noses more like open nostrils, and small mouths, gaping, emitting a choir of alien sounds that threaten to bore through ones ears and directly into the mind.

She stares, her lips parted, breath caught up. The monster flings itself at the stairs, crashing through the wooden structure with ease, toppling Gnegon, his men, and Denman. Bullets are fired wantonly by those still possessed of life or consciousness, screams emitting from some, mute shock from others. She sees that some of those shots hit the creature, but they are merely absorbed by the pelt, seeming to have no effect at all on the thing.

It lunges again, taking up one of the men in its hands, bending him in two with little effort, breaking him at his lower spine, gore exploding and pouring from the victim, then casting the pieces aside. One of the remaining mobsters has gone still and silent from shock, sitting there where he has fallen, no longer firing, eyes locked on the unnatural beast. Denman peels up from the shadows, the blade of his weapon dragged over the man's neck. She sees this, anger taking her, her face tensing, and she rises from her hiding place, firing the rest of her pistol's ammunition futilely at the monster. She ejects the magazine, ignoring it as it clatters to the ground, obviously taken up in the intensity of the situation, sliding her last in place, chambering the first round, then continuing to steadily walk closer, firing and firing and firing into the loathsome beast.

It seems hardly concerned, as though it is enduring blunted bee stings, turning instead to the person closer, the one who has pulled forth a .50 caliber Desert Eagle and fired these much larger bullets into it, hitting two of its more than a dozen faces. Those mouths cry out in unison, pain and anger, and it springs forth again, moving its serpentine body with preternatural speed.

Gnegon screams as he is crumbled beneath its weight, the monster rolling and writhing over the man, sounds of shattering bones coming forth like the snaps of wet wood, the crime boss' resistant yells turning from his own anger to the unmistakable cries of someone enduring mortal pain. Lilja stands there, horrified, watching, as the thing positions itself better over the man, those many mouths latching onto him, feeding, the large, skeletal-seeming hands working over the form sickeningly, caressing and pumping the body to better force out the vitae.

"Dear gods," she whispers.

Then she spies more movement, a flash of color, and the beast cries out, jerking spasmodically, and she sees that Denman is pressing the close attack. She holsters her spent sidearm, jerking free her katana and rushes in to help.

As the thing turns to retaliate against Denman, she comes in from behind, slicing out and cutting deeply into it. She was not sure what to expect, but the beast's flesh yields readily enough to the keen edge, the blade passing through with more than half its length, and a dense spray of ichor erupts, some of it splashing onto her. It yowls again, its mouths causing a storm of sound that proves nearly paralytic, and it turns to face this new attack. Judging from the jerks of its body, Denman continues to apply wounds, but she is taken by the haunting look of those empty eyes staring at her. She still moves though, turning her wrists so the blade again faces the beast, and she pulls her arms back for better force, slicing across and upwards, cutting through several of those horrible, mask-like visages.

It screams more, agony now, unsure which to attack, lashing out with both ends. She and Denman move away with practiced ease, slashing and stabbing, causing more of that odiferous fluid to blast forth from within, as though the thing may be comprised of not bone, muscle or organs, merely this gelatinous substance. They continue to engage it with a savage ferocity, and eventually it lies prone, collapsing on itself, those eyes managing to look blank now, the mouths slack, the lengthy fingers dangling, useless.

"Not bad," he says to her, and the compliment is uttered seeming without any begrudging.

DANCE OF THE BUTTERFLY

She looks at him, her eyes beaming out with a brilliance, her form quite covered in that slime, as is he. It would be comical, but she finds little humorous about the arrogant man or their situation. She then looks over.

"Skot!?" she calls out, for he has ceased his machinations, now down on his knees, head hanging; she rushes over, taking him in her stained arms, seeing that his eyes are half-open, "Skot? *Skot*!? Are you alright?"

"He's just drained, from closing the gateway," Denman says, gesturing, and she looks over to see that indeed the fissure is gone.

"I'll be alright," a weak voice manages, and she looks back to see Skot giving her a thin smile, but that expression falters as he looks her over, "You ... are you alright?"

"Yes," she smiles, laughing lightly, giving him a deep hug.

"Good, good," he manages, hugging her back, albeit much more weakly, then, as he picks up his head, "Where is Denman?"

"So, you've proved your usefulness," the Professor of Philosophy says, looking down at Ernst.

Throughout the final conflict, the young man had moved from hiding place to hiding place, finally stopping in a locale that has not proven very adequate but did give him some distance from the goings-on. He also has again lapsed into a somewhat catatonic state, eyes drooped, a sheen of drying drool on his mouth and chin. He does not seem to register the presence of the other.

"Hmmm?" Denman continues, looking over the poor youth, "Have you finally broken? Was this too much for you? Perhaps so," he answers his own question, his hand tightening on the handle of his weapon, "I could easily put you out of your misery," he says, readying to take a step closer.

"Stop."

He turns, seeing Lilja coming up to him, the blade still in her hand.

"What?" he retorts, that smirk going to his lips.

"I said *stop*," she repeats, then she brings the tip of the katana up to very near his neck.

He blinks, eyes going wider, though he still keeps much of his aplomb.

"That's enough killing," she says, looking very serious.

"Is that so?" he chides, unworried of the lethal promise so close to his throat.

"Yes, it is," and this solid reassurance comes from Skot, who walks up to the pair, giving a piercing look to Denman, "As I said earlier, he is coming with me," he refers to Ernst.

The other quickly assesses his situation, then, "Fine. I'll leave you Felcrafts to clean up this mess then."

Skot sets his eyes on him, letting the moment linger just a touch, then, "Get out."

Denman backs away, slowly, then when sufficiently distant, he turns, heading away from the room.

Skot then looks at Lilja, his eyes changed to something much more caring.

"I am sure you have many questions, but I need to make some phone calls. This area needs to be secured and cleaned."

"You are also drained," she points out.

"Yes, that is true," he agrees, giving her a gentle smile, but it drops when she does not return it, "I want to explain everything to you. I just need some time."

"I think I need some, too," she says.

He nods, just looking at her, and he is very relieved that she does not look away.

"May I call on you soon?" he asks.

She finally speaks, "Okay."

DANCE OF THE BUTTERFLY

EPILOGUE

She sits in front of her monitor, looking over more of the same sort of information she has been perusing now for some hours. She sips of her coffee, eyes having some difficulty continuing to focus. She looks down when she hears the noise, smiling at Dali.

"Miau," she replies, their usual conversation, but then she peers more steadily at him, "So, you could see them all this time, huh?" she asks, and he looks up from rubbing against her leg to give another meow.

Reading about cats being able to sense otherworldly entities and being able to travel between worlds, sometimes even acting as guardians or gatekeepers, had been nothing new to her. Still, she'd never been so brazenly shown the existence of such things. She pulls in a deep breath, exhaling loudly though her mouth.

She starts lightly as Dali springs up into her lap, then rolls her eyes, giving another exhale, her lips curled into a warm smile. She immediately goes to petting the large cat, and his purring resonates loudly. She reaches for the mug with her free hand, taking a slow, contemplative taste.

This research has not been terribly extensive, for how could such a thing as she has now witnessed still be secret if real information of it were so readily available? The effort is more an exercise in trying to focus her thoughts, otherwise they'd be running about in such a chaos she'd have little hope of making anything fruitful of them.

She does not feel betrayed, the shock of the revelation having cleaned such thoughts and feelings away quite well. She also cannot lose sight of the fact that she has kept her own secrets. There are demons, they are quite real, and Skot hunts them, even uses something that she cannot help but think of as magick to fight them and close off their access to this world. She is the vigilante. She goes out some nights dressed like an urban ninja and engages very dangerous criminals in violent situations. They both have kept secrets, and now, they will decide how much to share and explain to one another.

After a time, there is a knock on the door. She gently pats Dali's rear, encouraging him to move as she stands, padding slowly over on socked feet. She's been in pajamas since she woke, just giving her face a fresh scrub and a good brushing of her hair. She knows who it is at the door, or at least, she is expecting him. A peek through the peephole proves that it is indeed him, and she opens the door.

"Hello, Lilja," Skot greets, smiling warmly, though she can sense something of the anxiety behind it.

He is dressed relatively casual himself, though she suspects many people may not see it that way. He wears a light coat against the coming chill in the air, and he holds a bouquet of a half dozen white and red variegated tulips.

"For you," he announces, noticing her gaze, proffering them.

A curl traces over her lips as she receives them, "Thank you," then turns, letting him inside, "They're beautiful," she adds, heading into the kitchen to give the stems a trim before settling them into a thin vase, adding water.

He follows her inside, closing her door, then turning to see the cat standing there, looking up at him. A meow is given.

"Hello, Dali," he greets, smiling pleasantly, and the feline meows again, moving in to press at his lower legs; he bends to give a brief pet, then goes into the kitchen with Lilja.

He merely watches, trying to gauge something of her, observing how she handles the flowers, her deft fingers moving over the delicate stems. So much has changed recently, and yet, he hopes some things have stayed the same. He understands what stress may do, but it need not always cause things to break.

"Would you like some coffee?" she offers, glancing over at him as she finishes the arrangement.

"No, thank you. Might I have some water, instead?" he tries on more of a smile.

"Sure," she replies, somewhat returning the expression.

DANCE OF THE BUTTERFLY

She fetches a large glass from the cupboard, turning the tap to cold, waiting a moment then filling the glass from the faucet, handing it to him.

"Thank you," he raises the glass, drinking down some of the cool, clean liquid.

"Want to sit?" she invites, gesturing to the couch, and he nods, so they both move over, taking places on the couch, turning to face one another, not touching but not as far apart as the couch would permit.

"Shall I just begin with some explanations, or did you have specific questions?" he finally speaks into the growing silence, noticing that any semblance of warmth or affection that may have seemed ready to grow upon her has now gone.

"Tell me about the demons," she says, bringing her mug up from where it is held in her lap by both hands, taking a sip, eyes not drifting from him.

He nods, "Alright," then taking another drink of his water, pulling in a breath, preparing himself.

"Demons and devils exist," he says.

"Devils?" she interjects.

He nods, "Yes, devils, or what we perceive as very rare, very powerful entities that seem to live in the same realm, acting in some leadership capacity."

"Are they like fallen angels?"

"Some think so."

"Some think so?" she queries, confusion appearing on her features.

He pulls in another breath.

"Lilja, I will do my best to explain this to you," he begins again, his hands now free of the glass, moving them a bit toward her, turning them out in bid to take her hands, but she does not move to engage it, "We have many records in my family, going back for generations. Some things we feel confident that we know as *real*, but some things are still inference, some more like legend or myth.'

"We know there is at least one other plane of existence out there, and that it is possible for gateways to form between it and our own. They can use those gateways in various ways, dependent on several factors.

We know that the ... *occupants* of that realm are not very pleasant, and they harbor ill will toward us if not outright malevolence."

"Can we go through the gates to their world?" she asks.

"No," he answers, "And we don't understand why. It's been tried, and there is even a legend of a Hunter doing so a long time ago."

"But I saw the opening," she remarks, "It looked like I could have gone through."

He nods, slowly, "Yes, it does, so perhaps I should say that it seems possible we can use the gates, but not one of us, *ever*, has come back."

She takes a moment to ponder this, then, "So, *are* they demons?" she asks, her tone somewhat flat, demanding.

"That is a common belief, and for convenience, that is the word we use, but we do not have enough information, at least in my opinion, to be sure. We refer to them as demons, and we refer to their world as the Infernal.

"But this seems to also assume a belief in certain Judo-Christian concepts, namely that of God, Heaven, Angels, Hell, etc."

"There are no angels?" she asks.

"We don't know," he admits, "There are many who believe that there are. We have allegory to support it, but the information we have is not as substantial or verifiable as what we have on the demons and their home."

"Then how do you know they are demons and devils?"

"As I said, we're not completely sure, but," he pulls in a breath, "we have to call them something, so we call them that. And there is an obvious distinction between two broad types, if you will, of creatures that dwell there, so we call the less populous and much more powerful ones 'devils' and the others are 'demons'. It seems somewhat obvious to us that the devils have a different make-up, which leads to thinking they may also have a different origin."

"Was that .. one at the end ... the thing with all the faces, was that a devil?"

"Oh, no," he says, "That was a demon, though more powerful than the others. Devils rarely can get to our world so directly. They have to use influence, minions, as it were. And they are *significantly* more powerful."

DANCE OF THE BUTTERFLY

He pauses, looking at her, giving her a moment to say anything or react, if she is so inclined. She has another sip of her coffee, returning his gaze, then she nods.

"Okay?"

"We're rather thankful that the devils are unable to as easily reach this plane," he resumes, giving her a somewhat hesitant look, moving his hands together, fingers interlacing, "You see, they seem bent on conquering this world, and their inability to get here freely and en masse is all that stops that."

"Aren't you helping to stop that?" she asks, and it is not exactly what he expected, and he is relieved to hear such a practical response.

"Well, yes, we are," he says, smiling lightly.

"And the Malkuths, too?"

"Ah, yes, as a matter of fact," he says, his appearance subtly changing at mention of that name, "We *are* rivals, but we do share some similar goals. It is largely in our methods that we differ so strongly."

"How so?" she presses.

"Well, both our families have been around a long time. We might even share common ancestry if you go back far enough and interpret the extant records in a particular way, but, well," he pauses, collecting his thoughts, "We, the Felcrafts, we want to do this to protect humanity, to *serve* humanity, and I do not say this to be trite. We strongly feel that what we do, we do for the survival and betterment of humankind.

"The Malkuths …," he continues, looking at her, noticing that her beautiful eyes do not falter from him as he speaks, "They feel that the best way to protect humankind is to rule it. They engage in activities that we find disagreeable, morally speaking, and they actively, though subtly, work to someday actually *control* all of humanity. It sounds silly, almost like some cartoonish villainy, but they do consider themselves better than others, and they look upon the rest of society as if cattle, or some such, over which they should lord and protect."

She narrows her eyes, "I noticed that Denman showed an obvious lack of respect for life."

He nods, "Yes. The needs of the many outweigh those of the few, that sort of thing, which they have distorted into thinking that if someone stands in their way, the best option is often to just kill them. They use this perversion of pragmatism to justify their methods while their end goal is nothing short of self-superiority."

She looks away, obviously displeased with this, then she returns her eyes to him, "Denman said he thought I'd fit better with you than him. Now I see why."

A brief blink of tension passes over him, then he merely nods.

"I'll give you another example," he resumes, "Do you remember the poor, young man we found down there - Ernst?"

She nods.

"He possesses a sensitivity to the Demonic, the Infernal," Skot explains, "As best we can tell, it's genetic. Some people have it, most do not."

"Do you?" she throws in.

He meets her eyes for a moment, the nods, "I do, yes, most Hunters do, to some extent or another. Ernst is one that could have become a Hunter."

"Could have?"

"Well, I suppose he still could, but, as I am sure you can now attest, learning of the Infernal, of this 'secret' world, but not having anyone to help explain it to you, well that can be quite damaging. And Ernst is *very* sensitive. We're going to help him as best we can."

She nods, "So, he is like one of the 'force sensitives' from Star Wars?"

Skot slightly raises his eyebrows, looking at her.

"Sorry," she murmurs, humorlessly, "Please continue."

"That may not be an entirely improper similarity," he gives her, "Ernst is able to see, hear, sense things that most people cannot. The Infernal requires a certain amount of ... *power* to be able to fully manifest and interact with our world. Those who are sensitive enough are able to detect the lesser presences and influences, but they cannot manipulate it.'

"The Malkuths were using him as a sensor, as an advance warning system, so to speak."

She blinks, forehead furrowing.

"They somehow found him, and they made sure we did not, and they use these people, moving them to areas they suspect may be spots of

DANCE OF THE BUTTERFLY

demonic activity. Then they observe the person, secretly, and if they find a pocket of the Infernal, then they swoop in to take it out."

"The person doesn't know they are being used this way?"

"No."

She takes a moment to think on this, then, "Why did Denman threaten Ernst at the end?"

He takes another moment to collect his thoughts before answering, "This sort of exposure can be detrimental to one's mental and physical health. Too much of it tends to render someone into a state that may be seen as no longer useful, so Denman intended to kill him."

Her brow wrinkles again, her lips turning down, anger mixed with some shock. When she looks back, she sees his eyes on her.

"And you don't do this?"

"No," he says, "and if we find people being used this way, like Ernst, we do what we can to get them away from the Malkuths and help them, even if it just means keeping them protected and in psychiatric care."

She nods slowly, ponderously, then comments, almost as an aside, "That's just terrible," then she looks again at him, "Not you helping, but what they do. How they use people, or just kill them. It's so callous."

"I agree."

"Well, he didn't seem like he wanted to fight you to keep you from taking Ernst," she points out.

"No," he affirms, "Denman is very good in combat, well, more conventional-seeming combat, as you saw how well he used his dagger," and she nods, "But he is not as adept at … other forms of combat as I am, and I had you there," he ends, smiling at her.

She returns the smile briefly, then, "What 'other' forms of combat?"

He holds her eyes for a moment, figuring this question was coming, then he speaks, very serious, "Magick."

She just nods, as though this were not as huge a revelation as he figured it might be. He just looks at her, and she eventually tilts her head as she notices the study.

"What?"

"I don't think you appreciate how well you did down there," he comments.

"What do you mean?"

He reaches over for his glass, taking a few generous swallows before setting it back and looking at her.

"This city is rife with demonic influence, or it was. It's dissipating now, but there was quite a lot, especially closer to the site of the gateway. Did you feel it? Like a confusion or disorientation?"

She ponders, then nods, "I did. That was from the gateway?"

"Well, it was from their world, but it was passing through the gateway, yes.'

"And not just that," he says, giving her another close look, "But the Demons, they are not always able to manifest themselves in a such a physical way, but the energies, even themselves, they can influence people to varying degrees, depending on the potency and the person. You saw those people that were filled with a murderous rage, some of those even being possessed."

She nods.

"Once imbued with that, they can be somewhat resistant to normal methods of combat. It doesn't mean it doesn't hurt the host, but the animating power will sometimes keep going until the body is rendered unable to continue."

She nods, remembering that quite well.

"And if they are able to come forth in a more tangible form, as you saw, they can be highly resistant, if not outright immune, to more conventional methods of combat."

"Like my bullets."

"Yes," he replies, though she had not been asking a question.

"Not like yours."

"Well, no, mine have been customized to be more effective."

She nods, taking this in with the same sort of casualness as much of the conversation in general.

"But you were able to quite thoroughly dispatch them with your sword," he says.

She nods.

"And that should not have been so easy," he concludes his prior statement.

DANCE OF THE BUTTERFLY

"Easy?" she asks, some confusion showing, ready to object to just how simple it may have been.

"Yes, easy," he continues, "Denman and I were using charged weapons and our own ... uhm, *supernatural* abilities," he adds, giving her a look, almost as something of an apology for his choice of words.

She just nods, "Yes, I noticed that. The colors."

"Yes," he also nods, but then he pauses, eyes fixed on her, "You ... were not."

"I ...," she starts, then stops, looking away, one hand gone up, fingertips almost touching her bottom lip as she thinks, then she looks back, "Should I not have been able to hurt them?"

"It's not really an exact science, but I would have thought that you would not have been able to have such a powerful effect on them without more effort."

"Oh," she says, blinking briefly, "Hmmmm," looking away again, drifting in her thoughts until she looks back, "Well, what does that mean?"

"I'm not exactly sure, but you seem to harbor great potential within you."

She smiles a touch at that.

"Though I suppose with your other ... pursuits, I should not be surprised, hmmm?" he raises his eyebrows.

"Oh, uhm ...," she starts, looking a tad sheepish, one of her trademark blushes threatening her, "Yes ... that."

"Yes," he nods, a subtle curl to his lips, "*That*."

"I guess I owe you an explanation now, huh?"

"Lilja?" he says, and she looks fully at him, and he scoots closer, taking her hands in his own, which she does not prevent, merely tucking her coffee mug closer so it will not spill, before allowing her hands into his. "I did not tell you what I did to indebt you to me. It is my trust in you, and my desire is that you'd keep it secret. I have faith in you, and I am prepared to commit even further to you. I am curious about your own hidden life, so to speak, but I want you to tell me only if you *want* to tell me, okay?"

She nods, letting a warmer smile touch her lips.

"I trust you," she says to him, then gathers her thoughts, looking more serious, "Well, uhm," she tries again, then pulls in a deep breath, looking him in the eyes, "Sometimes, I disguise myself and go out and beat up criminals."

They look at each other for a moment, the air somewhat weighty yet still silent.

"It sounds kind of silly when I say it out loud like that," she murmurs.

"Yes, well, I am a demon hunter who wields magick," he says, giving her a playful smirk, but then he looks serious again, "And there is nothing silly about what you do. It is highly risky, yes, but not silly in the least."

"You don't …," she speaks after more of a lengthening silence between them, "You aren't upset with me for it? I don't want it to bother you."

He looks at her, then he takes in a breath, letting forth a mostly quiet exhale, "It's very risky, as I said, so that part worries me, but I am not upset. It would also be very hypocritical of me. The things you face are not quite as dangerous as those I do."

Just then, the cat springs up onto the couch, causing them to separate. Lilja quickly snatches up her coffee mug, holding it up and away.

"Dali," she scolds, but the large feline meows, standing up straight, looking at both quite proudly, demanding attention.

Skot chuckles, reaching over to pet him.

"Hmph," she comments, "You don't have a Dali living with you," she smirks.

He scritches behind the ears, smiling warmly, "I bet Dali would love the Felcraft manor," he says, then he slips his eyes to her, just looking.

It takes her a moment, but she finally blinks, eyes snapping to his.

"Are you … asking me to ..?"

"Would you think about it, at least?" he pitches, voice calm, the inviting smile still on his lips.

A moment coalesces between them, quiet save for the gentle, contented purring of the cat. They just look into each other's eyes. He sees some growing tension there on her, some hints, even, of fright. And

DANCE OF THE BUTTERFLY

then, like a knot releasing, she resolves to her general appearance of openness, a light curl to her lovely lips.

"Okay. I'll think about it."

ABOUT THE AUTHOR

Born in Houston, Texas into the temporary care of a bevy of nuns before being delivered to his adopted parents, Scott discovered creative writing at a very young age when asked to write a newspaper from another planet. This exercise awakened a seeming endless drive, and now, many short stories, poems, plays, and novels (both finished and unfinished) later, his first book, *Dance of the Butterfly*, is being published.

The seeds for this tale began with dreams, as many often do, before being fine-tuned with a whimsical notion and the very serious input of a dear friend. Before long, the story took on life of its own and has now become the first book in a planned series.

Having lived his whole life in the same state, Scott attended the University of Texas at Austin, achieving a degree in philosophy before returning to the Houston area to be closer to family and friends. During this time, he wrote more and even branched out into directing and performance art, though creative writing remains his love.

Please follow me for updates and information regarding new books at:

Scott's website/blog – www.scottcarruba.wordpress.com/
Scott's Facebook - www.facebook.com/AuthorScottCarruba/
Scott's Twitter – www.twitter.com/scott_carruba
Scott's Tumblr – www.scottcarruba.tumblr.com/

CHECK OUT THE OMP WEBSITE FOR
A COMPLETE LIST OF OUR TITLES

WWW.OPTIMUSMAXIMUSPUBLISHING.COM

BOOKS ARE AVAILABLE IN BOTH PRINT
AND ELECTRONIC FORMATS

The Optimus Maximus Publishing Shield Logo, the character of OPTIMA, and the name Optimus Maximus Publishing are registered trademarks of Optimus Maximus Publishing LLC. The OPTIMA character is also the intellectual property of Jeffrey Kosh Graphics.

RICKY FLEET
HELLSPAWN
SERIES

10.35 AM, September 14th 2015. Portsmouth, England.

A global particle physics experiment releases a pulse of unknown energy with catastrophic results. The sanctity of the grave has been sundered and a million graveyards expel their tenants from eternal slumber.

The world is unaware of the impending apocalypse, Governments crumble and armies are scattered to the wind under the onslaught of the dead.

Kurt Taylor, a self-employed plumber, witnesses the start of the horrifying outbreak. Desperate to reach his family before they fall victim to the ever growing horde of shambling corruption, he flees the scene.

In a society with few guns, how can people hope to survive the endless waves of zombies that seek to consume every living thing? With ingenuity, planning and everyday materials, the group forge their way and strike back at the Hellspawn legions.

Rescues are mounted, but not all survivors are benevolent, the evil that is in all men has been given free rein in this new, dead world. With both the living and dead to contend with, the Taylor family's battle for survival is just beginning.

Book 1 in the Hellspawn series.

Kurt Taylor and his family have battled the living and the dead and now find themselves on the run, their home reduced to ashes. With unimaginable horror lying in wait around every corner, the onset of winter and the plunging temperatures only add more danger to their precarious existence. They decide to forge ahead and try to reach the protection of others who have hopefully survived the zombie apocalypse. If this fails, their only choice would be to try and reach an impregnable fortress, a sanctuary that has stood for a thousand years.

Standing between them and salvation are the villages and cities of the damned, a path that will test their spirit and resilience unlike anything they have faced before. More companions are rescued from the jaws of death and join them in their perilous journey. Mysterious attacks befall the group and it becomes clear the dead aren't the only things that lurk in the darkness.

Tempers fray and personalities clash. The group starts to fracture and Kurt is forced to commit acts that cause him to question his own morality. Can they survive the horror of their new existence? Will they want to?

The Hellspawn saga continues.

BALLYMOOR, IRELAND, 1891

Patrick Conroy, a young American student of medicine in Dublin, decides to take a break from the hustle and bustle of the big city and spend a month in the quietude of the wild and beautiful Glencree valley, County Wicklow. However, surrounded by local legends and myths, he is soon dragged into an ancient mystery that has haunted the village of Ballymoor for centuries. Set on the background of the tumultuous years preceding the War of Independence, and colored by Irish folklore, the Haunter of the Moor is a ghost story written in the style of Victorian Gothic novels.

To Fight Evil with Evil

England, 1392.
As the Black Death quickly spreads through the kingdom, the little hamlet of Blythe's Hollow suffers under the yoke of a sadistic Lord. Desperate, the villagers decide to seek out the magical help of a local witch, causing the wrath of the Church. Torture and murder befall on those accused of being in league with the Devil, adding more sorrow to the beset folk of Blythe's Hollow. Yet, one man will rise against the tyranny; a man willing to learn Black Magick to fight back.

Made in the USA
Middletown, DE
05 March 2017